The Knight
of a
1000 eyes

```
     o
   <|>
   (  )
```

a Tai Chi Long Form

by

Michael Lyons

HiT MoteL Press
www.hitmotel.com

Library of Congress Cataloging in publication Data

Lyons, Michael
        The Knight of a 1000 eyes
I. Title

ISBN: 0-9655842-2-4

Published by HiT MoteL Press

Designed by Michael Lyons

To my teachers

. . .the hexagram was the exponent of the moment. . .
— Carl Jung

Fixed Frame

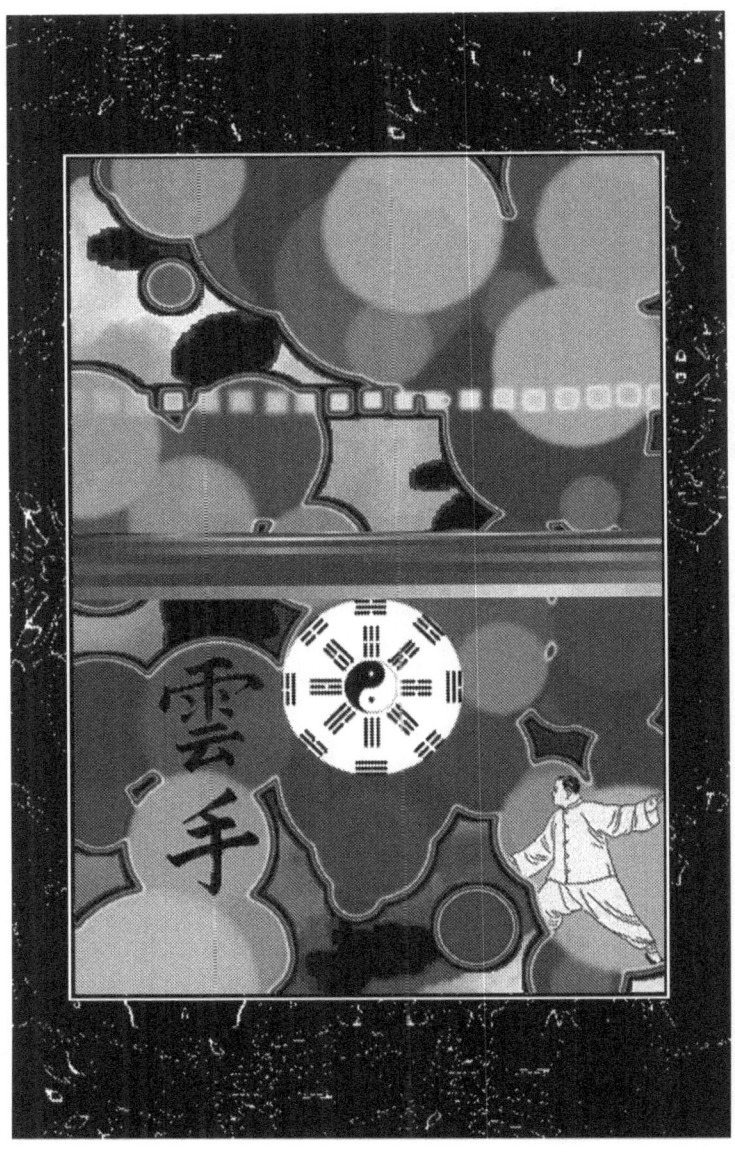

A Pot Rustler Interdiction Program

By the end of August, the patch growing in the abandoned farmyard, behind the little house on the prairie outside of Austin, was in full flower. Gregory and I worried about pot rustlers. Greg kept talking to me about Rip-off, the person, as in: "Walker, we've got to do something about Rip-off. We've got to set some kind of booby trap for Rip-off."

For Greg, Rip-off was some kind of heinous tobacco-spitting redneck white devil like those mountain retards in the movie *Deliverance*.

"The Rip-off might have a gun," he said, his eyes buggin' out. "You never know what they might do to you out here. There's nobody around." He got a panic stricken look on his face. "We've got to get something that is a strong deterrent."

"Well, what have you got in mind?"

"Well, I don't know. But it's got to be something strong. And quick."

"Well, we can't kill him. Do you want to try and capture him?"

"I guess so. It's not like we can tell the law that he was out here ripping off our pot patch."

Looking a little pained I asked. "What would we do to him if we caught him?"

We looked at each other aghast. We hadn't thought of that. "We'll have to catch him first," Greg said.

"We could make a trap," he mused out loud. "We could make one like in Viet Nam, —a hole with sharpened sticks in the bottom of it, pointing up, like spears —pongee sticks. The hole would be covered with grass, so that Rip-off would fall in and become impaled on the sticks."

Talk like this from my partner made me paranoid.

Gregory started buying back issues of *Soldier of Fortune* magazine from the Half-Price Book Store on Lavaca Street, not far from the capitol buildings. *High Times* magazine didn't mention what to do about pot rustlers; *S. o. F.* did.

"This issue shows how to make booby traps," Greg said, pointing to a *Soldier of Fortune* cover. The cover showed the face of a soldier with black grease smeared under his eyes. The soldier in camouflage fatigues was peering out from behind bushes with the baleful stare of a war hardened survivalist. Across the cover it read "My First 1,000 Yard Kill."

"Look at this," he said, slapping the magazine with the back of his hand. "They show how to make a pit with ponjee sticks."

I was *really* freaked out when Gregory showed me a booby trap he had actually gone ahead and built. "It's called 'A Poor Man's Land Mine', he said cackling to himself. "I built it in my shop."

It was a little wooden box with a circular hole drilled through the center of one side. A nail had been driven through the other side exactly opposite the center of the hole.

"You set a shotgun shell into the hole," he began.

He set the shotgun shell into the box pointing up so that the firing ring of the shotgun shell just rested on the nail.

"Now you bury this box in the ground," he said.

"The business end points up," he continued "This part you cover with a board." He bent over and covered the up-pointed shotgun shell with a board.

He held the board above the box. "If you step on the board," he said, "it pushes the shell into the nail and ka-blooie—it explodes.

"God damn!" I said aghast.

"Since there is no rifle barrel to channel the shot," he said, "it goes off in all directions." He shook his head in dismay and admiration at the device.

"Man that could really tear up somebody's leg," I said.

"Yea! That's the idea!" Greg said. "Teach them sons-a-bitches not to come 'round here. Ever."

He saw my wide-eyed look of disbelief. "But it's not fatal," he quickly, added, making a mollifying gesture with his hand. "But it would definitely make it necessary for Rip-off and those in his tribe to get out of here in a hot-footed hurry!"

At this he started doing a kind of a hot-footed dance, like a one-legged man, dancing a jig. He cackled and twirled around: "They'd have to go immediately to a hospital."

I shook my head. "Gruesome business."

I talked my partner out of any of this, and we settled for stringing the grapefruit juice cans around the perimeter so that anyone moving through there would make a lot of noise. We also made a rule that one of us had to be out in the patch on sentry duty every night. Gregory started bringing his Dobermans out.

Gregory brought to field-duty the same kind of methodical zeal he brought to building. He set up an army-surplus cot under a camouflaged mosquito net in the shade of the old oak tree. He wore camouflaged fatigues and a redneck bill-cap with ACE lettered across its front. Gregory had the great Texas savvy of managing to avoid the heat by not working at the wrong time of the day. Yet he always seemed to be busy puttering, tweaking, polishing his binoculars, sharpening a knife. He was so methodical. He built a balance beam scale that was super accurate. We checked it against scales in grocery stores. He built hiding holes for the various kinds of mushrooms, peyote, speed and acid showing up at the farm. Some of these hidey holes were elaborate affairs with hidden drawers and false bottoms. I worried about him. Texas is a hot and hissing place. Gregory had a really red neck and seemed to have high blood pressure for one so young.

I started doing Tai Chi out in the patch as part of my anti-pot-rustler maintenance program. It made me feel totally competent and able to handle anything to be out there with my dog by my side, keeping my watch under the stars. It was scary being out there all alone, but for the first time in my life I had hope. It looked like I was about to walk into a bright future with money and I did not want to see it ripped off. Walker, I said to myself, you're gonna be a free man walking down a Paris boulevard when this is all over.

I wanted to be out there and be so quiet that I could make the wind my ally. I enjoyed being in a state of hyper aware-ness —due to a mixture of fear, marijuana and adrenaline, thrilling through my body, surging through the night air in every pull-back, push, dodge and parry. I did have some compunction about violating the sanctity of the Tai Chi head space by doing it stoned. I could see the lineage of Taoist saints shaking their heads in dismay at this infidel, who had been taught by a white Presbyterian minister in Berkeley.

The struggle for control that occurs in learning Tai Chi is between the mind, trying to maintain the supremacy of thinking in continuing its hegemony over the body, and the body, trying to communicate through that mind some of the vast powerful storehouse of knowledge it has inherited from evolution. I think that this story is told over and over again, every time the Tai Chi player does the Long Form: the attention relaxes in layers, or what might be called frames of experience. The fixed frame where one is awkward paying attention to the outer detail as he shifts from the ordinary world to the quieter, more meditative world of Tai Chi. Then to the lively frame, where one has the moves and can explore doing them faster or slower, with flow or with suddenness. And if one is lucky, the changing frame where for whole moments, one sees himself from outside as an archtypal pattern, a reflection of Form emerging here now.

The "plot" of this story is the concatenation of the moves; it proceeds like science in an approach that alternates theory with experiment. Sometimes the experiment is done to investigate the theory, and sometimes it leads to a new one.

I have pulled together some thoughts on doing Tai Chi; unfortunately the beginning student needs to wax philo-sophical. Chi is such a big change of paradigm and I, of course, had to take this to unbelievable lengths. I had a few books I had picked up in San Francisco and Berkeley. But I soon began to feel overwhelmed by the plethora of detail. I began looking for a more basic set of generative principals. Thinking that there was something about the way the ideograms for the Tai Chi moves are built out of basic set of strokes that would also lend insight, I started figuring out how to make some Chinese ideograms using the typewriter. I also thought to build myself a kind of mnemonic theatre, in order to remember the moves. I wanted it to be a kind of generative mnemonic theatre and for the craven images to be placed on the "walls," I began to investigate the hexagrams. I also got into Laban Notation and actually started to make these kind of space/time/weight diagrams. I even made these little Tai Chi figures out of characters on the typewriter to help me focus on the Form. I also evolved a weird kind of grammar, that the line was like the foot advancing and moving around, in which levels of movement were brack-eted and broken out. It became that Tai Chi was somehow "writing" me!

1   Commencement of Tai Chi, Long Form

I'd start doing tai chi as usual by doing the warm up:

knee circles, wrist circles, waist circles

It's very hot.

I'm by the side of the house in the shade of a tree.

The towering oak tree at the edge of the patch rose high above the tall weeds and thick surrounding bush. It was a welcome shade. There was a well worn path from the back of the house out to the well. You couldn's see the hidden path to the beautiful marijuana garden where the luscious full-grown pot plants were so dense it looked like a full Christmas-tree sales lot.

I don't have to feel self-conscious
because there's nobody around.
But my internal voice of self-criticism
speaks to me in a condescending way:
"When they were handing out balance,
        grace,
                poise and coordination,
you must have been in bed,
because you didn't get much."

I'm always in my head,
feel no connectivity below the waist. . .

2 Self 2, the criticizing Voice in your head

I asked myself: "What is this voice?" But I know it too well. It is the subversive shadow voice that goes against your first self, who knows how to be.

I was never into team sports, didn't do well in the camaraderie of athletes, or the authoritarian condescending regard of coaches.

For a long time, when I'd start to do Tai Chi, the voice would start to come up beside me: "What," it says, "do you think you're doing."

I was so sensitive about my lineage, because I took a couple of basic lessons from a white guy in Berkeley, and the rest I had to try and learn from books.

I'd say: "Trying to get the inner chi going."

Then defensive — superior: "re-ching out for the inner efficiency, efficient-chi."

The voice of criticism says, "You've learned it all wrong. You are just perpetuating error."

And I get defensive.

So often I have wanted to be a part of a group, to go out onto the tennis court with a group of Asians doing tai chi and just merge into their flow. But I was always too intimidated to do that.

Then the voice would start to bring up the endless admonishments, "That god damned bow stance, you are doing, it's the worst I've ever seen."

"Where should your feet be pointing."

"The forward foot should be in the direction you are going and the back foot at 45 degrees."

I'd have to write out elaborate directions step by step from the book and go through them to learn the moves.
Tai Chi walk
Knee follows foot,
hips follows knee,
body follows hips.
Torso follows body.
stand erect
shift body weight back onto right foot
allow the arms to rotate around the waist

as though they were rotating on a ball
left arm rising right sinking
lift left leg and foot with bent knee several inches
above ground while balancing on right foot
extend left leg forward and place foot on ground, heel first,
several inches ahead and to left of right foot
shift body weight to left foot while at the same time
warding off — bringing left forearm high
and pushing down with right hand
rock back onto right foot, turning out left foot
shift body weight to left foot
while at the same time embracing the moon
lift right leg and foot with bent knee several inches
above ground while balancing on left foot
extend right leg forward and place foot on ground, heel first,
several inches ahead and to right of left foot
shift body weight to right foot while at the same time
warding off bringing right forearm high
and pushing down with left hand
rock back onto left foot, shift body weight to left foot
while at the same time pulling down and turning left
rock forward onto right foot, shift body weight to right foot
while sweeping hands, right arm rising and turning right
shift body weight to right foot
while at the same time embracing the moon
continue sequentially left, right, left right until process
becomes automatic

you get this feeling in the repetitive motion
of springing back to the way you were at the start,
into the mind of the body the way you have always been,
your spine springs stockingly, like tall grass,
and the image of the whooper stepping stiltly occurs,
you are the catcher in the rye parting the grass
the way the wind riffles through it
and you could move that way for hours,
lost in this time-destroying rhythm
on a watch that was a compass with no points.

I concluded this self-critical voice is counter-productive, so I decided to make up my own teacher and my own lineage. I would let the Form be my teacher. When I was in the Form, or trying to find my way into the Form, I gave myself the name Yum Chi. It was a friend, Neal Paris, who gave me the idea for the name Yum Chi. I must have been trying to talk to him at some point about the experience of Chi. And one day he started teasing me about it. We were in the 7-11 store, and I must have been making moon-eyes at the lovely Asian girl who worked behind the counter there and Neal started teasing me because he knew I was sweet on this little dark-haired beauty. She looked more like she was from Vietnam or one of them places. And Neal kept saying, "He love you." And rolling his eyes over toward me.

"He Yum Chi," he'd say, poking his pointing finger at me with glee. "He love you. Him Yum Chi." Putting the heavy accent on the yummmm.

"Cut it out Neal," I said, embarrassed. "You're going to embarrass the salesgirl."

"Him yummmmm chi," he continued rolling his eyes.

She just smiled sweetly.

So later I make up this name for myself: Yum Chi.

Yum Chi, of the Phlung Hi! School of Chinese Butt-Kicking.

And Yum Chi had a symbolic name, written ¥, like those Chinese do —long hand. ¥um Chi –the love being.

```
¥ , ¥um
   \ | /
   - | -   Chi
   / | \


        \ | /
  ¥    - | -
        / | \
  ¥um   Chi


        ¥     ¥um
   \  |  /
   - | -    Chi
   /  |  \
```

¥ it is an abstraction of the body

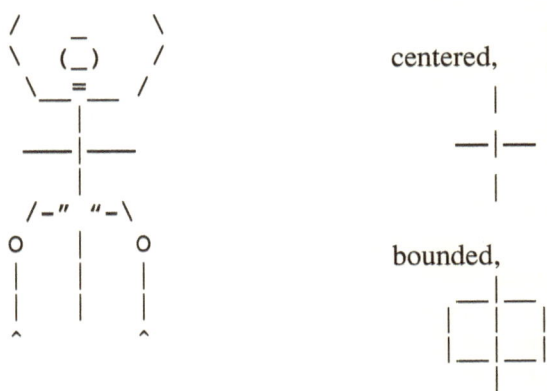

centered,

bounded,

as in trying to defend the center, (the center being a continuous connection between the self and the Self) and a kind of vehicle for getting into

```
          _____
      ¥  |  \ | /  |
         |  —|—   |
         |  / | \  |
          ———  ———
```

¥um   Chi

```
      \ | /
      —¥—
      / | \
```

These are the notes I kept on some topics to perhaps be presented in a manual or pamphlet from the Phlung Hi School of Tai Chi.

The Form would become my master now, Master Yum Chi.

When first getting into the Form, one warmed up in the
Ward off
Roll back
Push
Pull

A back and forth rhythm gets going.
                — momentum waves —
when you are doing the Form. A little fast
                swashing of momentum back and forth,
        and you are feeling the ebb and flow of momentum and
inertia reciprocating.
        It starts with the movement
                and carries out to the fingertips,
        then ebbs when pulling back. You feel the momentum
pass through the center point of the body and you are
bobbing on a wave.   Momentum moving now
        as I try to be the unwobbling pivot.

        Am I moving it?   centered,
        Or is it moving me. |
            Ward off   —|—
            Roll back |
            Push   bounded,
            Pull   _|_
                                  | | |
        momentum moving |_|_|_|
        DRIVE! |
        it down through the heel of the foot!
        I'd be out on the farm getting high on momentum
        nothing to do but repeat
                    Ward off
                    Roll back
                    Push
                    Pull
        and turn my head up a little in the sun,
            —low rent —
                — crop coming in —
                        —no heavy commitments—

. . . the Form is a vehicle to get into
and you *can* get into it, and it gets into you.

It has mirrors
pointing in at all
angles
    showing you
who you were,

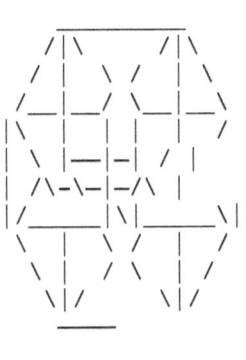

who you could be.

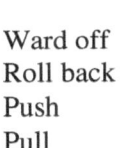

Ward off
Roll back
Push
Pull
    Move so slow
and gently so as not to even disturb the air.

Inside the Form you are checking out your balance,
    the balance across the spine Left and Right; Up and
Down
    rotational.

Ward off
Roll back
Push
Pull

as you move along in this vehicle,
— enjoying the ride —
surfing on the linear and angular momentum
around various symmetry axes of the body:
"Walker. . ."
— a thought arises —
it is somehow calling you from far off
and yet near. You turn. It is no one.
It is inside you.
It is your mind but you don't recognize it.
. . . or it might be your body.
. . ."Hey Walker why don't you get busy and drag out
your old physics books and look up the differential equations of motion for torque and momentum and stuff."

All this Tai Chi is too good for me, I think. I must stop
and get all cramped up and study and get the names of these
things.

For this really is quite marvelous.
The body is out here doing this,
solving differential equations of motion,
and you could be visualizing the equations while you
were doing it!
That would be a singularly pristine experience.
Wouldn't it?

I stop and sit down telling myself I need a rest.

It's the beginning of a new partnership
and you are not sure who is in this partnership.
You could suspect that it is the mind trying to keep the
body from feeling, for if that ever happened the mind would
loose control,
or it could be the mind is maybe listening to this body,
seeing it again for the first time after a million times,
and trying to learn from it.

And you think you might start an essay
*Soma-semiotics: the Pragmatics, Semantics and Syntac-
tics of What the Body Knows*

And you think, yes, how exciting.
But then you realize how terrible.
The mind has tricked the body once again.
Chi is like momentum, you are moving it, channeling it
forcing it along strong but conducting; then, putting a kind
of restful light touch at the end of a move.

Ward off
Roll back
Push
Pull
I am a thought in the natural mind moving at the speed
of thought in the world of will and idea.

Being present will
    protect me from evil.

Ward off
Roll back
Push
Pull

    roll back is complementary, theses are the two
compliments,
    draw back the bow
    bending the bow

    bring the power in, from without, move the power down,
sweep the power past, dodge, become invisible,

    not only are you blocking you are moving physical
power around,
        Ward off
        Roll back
        Push
        Pull

        gold is growing on these trees
        gold flowing down like honey, dripping
from these branches reaching their twig-tip fingers to the sun

        Ward off
        Roll back
        Push
        Pull
The universe is a green dragon,
We are swimming in a sea of green,
    a green fire,
an inverse fire fanned by the breath of animals.

        objects move along
            the shortest path in curved space
                –geodesics,
            light moves along it too.

5   A chop wood and haul water day

Here is the humble student of Tai Chi, way out alone on the redneck Texas plains beginning his study of this ancient way of being.

Here is the shuffling, chop-wood and haul-water guy, trying to learn Tai Chi from a book. He is actually out there with his book, actually turning it AROUND with the cover toward himself and standing *behind* the book, as if he were just someone in the back of the class. He feels ridiculous trying to look over the top of the book at the picture of the guy doing Tai Chi. Strange, whacked-out, weird, way to be learning Tai Chi, — from a book, Master. Trying to follow as though observing from the back of the class! Most hideous —insane, trying to learn Tai Chi from a book. How was I ever going to come close to the mastery I sought and personified in the model of Yum Chi.

The Form is my master now. Yum Chi's mind was . . .

In the beginning you are completely overwhelmed with imagery and energy and with the particulars of trying to do it right. Quite a workout for the old memory. I'd have to memorize the written directions, and repeat them over and over like a mantra. It would be like some kind of awful concatenation of indications, an incantation of indications.

Enter into conflict with opponent.

If B punches at your head with right fist uppercut, you — A, use left hand to lift B's right hand up higher by lifting him at his right elbow. (Helping him going in the direction he is already going.) At the same time, step forward inside with right leg. Then execute Step Forward and Punch with right fist, using the forward thrust of your stepping forward to increase the power of your punch. Turn your hips into him as well, getting that torque from rotation to add to punch.

Wow, I was learning the martial art AND science.

And for a time, that did quiet the negative inner voice.

But soon my shadow would be back and I'd be putting myself down with: "That god damned bow stance, you are doing, it's the worst I've ever seen. Where should you feet be pointing. The forward foot should be in the direction you are going and the back foot at 45 degrees."

Luckily in life, the Tao, the thing you want to pursue or love, or the enlightenment you are trying to open yourself up to, has its inducement to give out; enough to keep you on the path. Sometimes in the forest I'd really feel alive and apart of it all. Here's the great ancient sage walking through the forest. Slow down man you've got to enter forest time. Flashing in and out of feeling self. feeling Yum Chi, wearing impossibly faded, washed-a-thousand-times pants to blend in with the earthen color of the forest floor, and beige flannel shirt to diffuse with the trees. Yum Chi moving like a shadow. Being careful. Watch out for the rock, man. Don't trip over that rock. Yum Chi walking through the reeds. Pay attention to the snap, crackle and pop, man, don't want to give yourself away. Just be a silent observer. Yum Chi on a creep and crawl.

Beautiful early morning August light slanted just right, illuminating branches and patches of land. Yum Chi notices a dragon fly. It just drifts in on a beautiful, complex, differential curve — complete and utter control over roll, pitch and yaw. It lowers itself onto some habitat, and clings there silent, still. Its diaphanous wings are splayed like a church window. I will watch it. Yum Chi watches for a few moments.

I get impatient and start to continue. At the movement of my feet, the dragon-fly leaps up and S curves off a little distance. Oh. Sorry, little brother. Didn't mean to disturb.

Yum Chi shifts back into his position of watching. Maybe little brother has something to teach me here. Sure enough, the dragon fly reverses the S curve and zips back into his position. I stared at it for a while — a good long while — and began to notice how my mind wanders in and out of attention and my gaze becomes soft and out of focus and as soon as I take my eyes off the dragonfly I have to look around, and I have trouble finding it again. It blends in so well with the background! It becomes invisible.

I get impatient and shift my weight again, disturbing the dragon fly and it flies off.

Sad that he has interrupted this little scene Yum Chi changes his stance and shifts his position slightly, finding a comfortable stance, than enables him to becomes still for a longer time. And soon the dragon fly comes back in and takes up *his* position again. Sorry to disturb you Yum Chi says to himself. The dragon fly has a lesson to teach. What is your lesson little brother? I am going to teach you about camouflage. Is that it? Yes. And about time. Slow down! Stop and stay a while. Pay attention to your breathing if you have to have something to occupy your mind. I am inviting you in to the kingdom. I am inviting you into the time of the forest. Wow, thank you master I will go there with you.

I stand still and watch the dragon fly who now has taken on almost mystical proportions. It is as though when my attention opens to admit including me in being a part of what is going on in the forest, the dragon fly is communicating with me: You must learn to move at *our* time, you must learn to hang out and relax. Now I will give you the lesson of camouflage. I am so still that the attention wanders and forgets where I am and I become invisible.

My god I think, being in Yum Chi mind: there must be myriad life-forms that I do not see, all around me doing this stillness. I will just be very still and quiet and see what I can see. My mind has wandered and I have to search and search for the dragonfly to see if it has gone away, and with great difficulty I finally find the spot as the dragon fly comes back into focus. I thought about how this focus seems to separate out the dragon fly from the background. The content from the context. Focusing deeper on the object of his gaze, Yum Chi notices that the dragon fly is the same color as the background it is against, and that its body seems to be encased in a transparent sheath. Or, that at the boundary where the dragon fly leaves off and the habitat begins, there seems to be this very complex thing going on, where one is distinguished from another. Wow, the endless fractal diffusion of order and pattern at a boundary. Oh, oh, I'm drifting into abstraction, master, and you have disappeared. Yum Chi focuses his eyes and moves them around the terrain looking for where the dragon fly was, and after a bit brings the diaphanous being from another world into focus again.

Astounding, there is some kind of lesson here. If I could just open myself up enough to receive it.

The dragon fly invites you in, to show you. As if to say,

stay here, quiet a while. You are in our time now. Be still and
I will show you the secret of camouflage. How to blend in.
Keep looking at me, relax, sense . . . sense your breathing. If
you take your eyes off me for a moment I will dissolve into
the landscape and become invisible.

What is this dragonfly trying to teach me here? Something about holding your course, staying steadfast, being on
center, doing what you are supposed to be doing. Doing your
thing. Do not be so quick to judge, to dismiss, get bored, to
blame. These are forces moving your self off of alignment
with the Self, that cause your self to become dissociated from
your Self. Calm down, pay attention to your breathing. Find
your center and try to hold on to it, that's the big game here.
Don't just look at the content, look at the compliment of the
content, the context. Look at the relationship and the dynamic of the relationship. This is nothing less than the
mentality of the ancient man, the hunter standing by a trap,
or a fishing hole. This silence and patience can bring you
into the larger consciousness of nature. Don't just following
the thinking mind which requires endless concatenations of
separating distinctions. The Cartesian paradigm is a big one
to overthrow, but if you can, you will be opening the doors to
paradise. Your mind is just like this forest —no, it is not *just*
like it, it *is* part of it. Don't let your mind separate you from
it. Blend in, merge, keep aligned with your Self while all
this buzzing confusion is going on around you. Camouflage
to blend, stop thinking and let the heart and the body be in it.
Then you can feel the florescence of love, like soft colors
and fibrous longings reaching out into it, emerging from the
heart.

7 Word as Object

One gets very particular in the physical, right off,
(
into the main channel >
into momentum, divergence , curl @
o call me warrior   o
/   \
o   o call me priest   o
\
change \ my name to the
' | >
<   wind or 'sky being'
Find me floating
(shuddering push) >
< (pull back)
(

shift weight /
(
, -exhale while pushing hands forward -,
(
, both heels are in firm contact ,
with ground
) End weight shift
) End breath in
) End balance
o   o
)   \   /   \
o
, o   _   \
')
/ <   ' | >
< \

Then one might relax into a stretch with Single Whip

```
        O
   >-/|\ -,
      /
     /\
    |  \
  _^   _^
S t r e t ch
```

my anatomy out

in *Single Whip*
turning west,

```
        O
      '-(
      /<
```

making my shadow sharp
as an ideogram.

```
        O
      '|'
      > <
```

The force becomes
the letter of the law;

```
      O_,
      )-'
      > <
```

the ideogram

was a surfer

```
      ,O
     _`)   .
      /<
```

balancing

```
    ,  O
     `)-'
    /  >
```

down the face
of a wave.

9 Mnemonics

While I was in the Form I would be telling myself a little story. It was a concatenation of mnemonics, thought-forms, poetic sensations, and cross references, to help me remember the Form.

Mnemonic 1: The Mnemonic Theatre — I knew that I was defending the self from all directions in turn and turn about.

```
                    N
                    12
           11                1

        10              O         2
                       /|\
     W  9            ,/ ,/        3   E
                       /\
         8            |  \        4
                     _^   _^
           7                5

                    6
                    S
```

Mnemonic 2: Images — like carrying a large ball to remind yourself that all movements are circular, to remind you of the ambiguity of the hand forms, (could be punch, block or grab), to remind you of the great circulation of being, circulating around and moving on the wind.

Mnemonic 3: Chi — Look for the chi, relax and let the chi flow through you.

I start to dissolve into the landscape. . .

Yum Chi steps of the porch. I must step off the back
porch and walk to the garden. There is a Yum Chi footstep,
Yum Chi, and there is another one. I must get to the Tai Chi
tree. And now I am walking into the background hiss of
summer and it is moving all around me within and without
me. I am walking in the Form. I am in the Form, Master,
and when I am in the form it means that my self and my Self
are getting aligned.
It means that you are starting to find a place where you
can stand and push off from — a place where you can drop
off all the resistance and indecision and get connected, get
attuned. You have to be willing to sacrifice your fear, you
have to slow way down and become give equal attention to
the text AND the context.
The wind starts to fill the inner ear with empty space,
and chi takes over the balance mechanism there. "I" draw
empty spaces in the air, through which to draw the chi
through
the chi moves the subtle body
across the isoc ines of this multidimensional space:
I am solving partial differential equations of many
variables with my body in real time.
"This is the strangest most mystical science
ever on the earth.
The body is my instrument,
and I am bowing it, and playing it like a violin
sad rapturous violin, climbing and moving and shifting
in a landscape of my own design.
It is dance but a dance to natural music,
like leaves in the autumn wind
like the float of a black bird spying down
like the charging up of atmosphere before a storm
--compression.

You start off humble
and become the dragon.

This motion in a circle moving around and around
presenting a defense in 4 directions

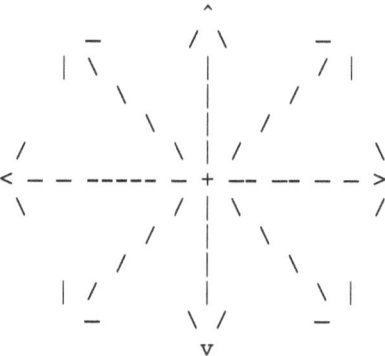

everything is produced from the ground,

or the center

```
        |
      —+—
      ___|___ grounded
  _ |  _ centered
  | | _ |
  |_|_|
        |
```

—that is the outside, what you see.

This is an ancient science, a holistic science that includes
the perceiver; a science known through a kind of imagery
programming
    combined with
    a motion process in which you had to visualize your next
move or even a *few* moves ahead.
    . . . turning tai chi ball
    with just your breath . . .

Chi starts at the fingers for me.
I first felt it in my hands or rather between my hands.
I got a very strong, clear confirmation of it when I got a
acupuncture. The needle precipitates a needles and pins
sensation in a limb. (Well, duh.) But still it is a kind of
inflorescence.

I start to dissolve into the landscape. . .
It sometimes is just a racing horopter
the sun at sea
the horizon
the long view along a lake
or of a strand along the sea shore.

It is a landscape in which you can push energy,
and pull it back in, isometrically.

The path will lead down from the clouds to ground . . .
 and some floor sweeps . . .

There is a Fair Lady Who Works at Shuttles,
a Tiger and Monkeys.
Or whatever you want to call this ancient forms play,
to make it new.

There are tricky little moves at the end of big sweeping
ones;
 the universe is a green dragon and we are part of its body
 (moving)

The path you follow in Tai Chi is a trail through craggy
peaks in which you start low and go high
 a typical floating world landscape
 and you will find yourself moving
 in quick motion
 and sometimes relaxed.

There! A white crane in a marsh,
 — a sea
 of yellow flowered reeds

the white bird spreads its wings.
*White Stork Spreads Wing*s

—stepping wearily,
setting each foot down
 logically, lightly,

You find yourself a bird in a Chinese emperor's garden. Beyond, the emperor's pool sparkles in the starlight.

For a moment you remembered a prior life of being a shy concubine raising her hand, to shield her blushing face from the lusty eye of the emperor, spreading out her fan with a flick of her slender white wrists.

Then I would return to the moment and hearing the cicada chatter soundscape on the farm, meandering and shape shifting its way, spiraling, infinite, supreme —Lift hands.

I began to feel invincible to step so lively, to be grace in slow flight. Fan out, pull back—push—sending out my signals like lighting in the four directions, and pulling back the response from the many sentries that were my minions out there on the outposts of perception.

In the form you could reach out
and with the concussion of your push
warp the space you were in.

If the universe is a green dragon, then the soundscape was a picture of the universe, circling, swirling in all directions, moving through. And then, to suddenly pull away from your head,

to swiftly change your motion and direction,
to be pulling back.

I practiced very slow,
      very quiet,
         over and over for hours, as steady
            as the ocean
    coming in and going out,
        swirling and washing up,
bouncing back like the sea—turning,
        turning
            always turning. . .

11 Chi as grace

I was surprised to find that both the Catholic Church
concept of Grace and the Taoist concept of Chi have quite a
lot of similarities. They both have the concept of an original
quantity of grace and chi given at birth. The Catholics loose
this with Original Sin and have the sacrament of Baptism
and other sacraments to restore this. They both have the idea
that grace is something you can store. In Tai Chi and Taoism
chi is built up with meditation and received through openness.

It would be so nice if the beginner could be given an
infusion of chi right off, — an existence proof. Then you can
use it as a kind of feedback, to help you get the sense of
being present and open and aligned

I first start to feel the Chi
    in the middle finger
    or in the hand,
or between the hands in Post.
At first it is just a subtle sense
of the presence of the other hand.
I started to feel the chi
in my middle finger . . . It . . .
    wagged
        on its own.
Eventually, you want to be able to feel it in the hip joint,
—that universal joint,
which goes forward and backward,
and side to the side, and torques around.
Eventually, you want to feel It move
in and flow
through all your joints and hinges,
up in your back, and shoulders and arms.
And eventually you want to feel It doing tai chi.

Repetitive motion.
Trying to bring up the chi, you can feel it in the hands
but want to feel it everywhere

It is a kind of object oriented self-programming,
a kind of Elysian mystery induction.

Differential Equations
The Form . . . Yum Chi, the form

present mind
Preeeee-sent MIND!!

Look for the sloshing mode, of momentum waves in the
Form. The body becomes a vehicle for the Form.
The Form comes to inhabit the body.
In the form the vehicle does not need the thinking mind
to tell it what to do next.

Moment(um) waves - sloshing mode.
Momentum is felt as a slow motion
wave, floating through the body.
As an arm moves to the right,
a wave of momentum
slowly spreads through it,
until reaching the fingertips.

Ward off
Roll back
Push
Pull

This wave slowly bounces back through the center of the
body and perhaps into the opposite leg, which steps out next.

Mind gets suspicious of this groovy behavior and sends
Walker off
trying to figure out what is Momentum?

Well you call up the wave equation, where the oscillation
in space is related to the oscillation in time.

$$\frac{d(\mathbf{p})}{dt} = \frac{d(\mathbf{p})}{dx}$$

You've got linear momentum and angular momentum.
Linear momentum is $\mathbf{p}$, a vector
with components (roots) in the 3 dimensions . . .

Wait a minute! Come back . . .
Present mind!
I try to recall . . . The function of the martial artist, is
probing weakness,

to be a true martial artist,
you are detached and you are probing weaknesses
deficiencies in preparation or understanding.
If the guy is there menacing in a big hard stance,
you can go low and trip him.

But I can't. I'm off thinking about Enlightenment East
and West. How calculus is the completely general method
for studying Change. The methods it uses to study and
model motion are identical to the structures that model
aspects of economics, traffic flow, finance, electricity,
hydrodynamics, baseball, war, the weather and other topics.
It is a momentous experience,
it is Western enlightenment
started by watching
         a ball   roll
             down hill.

DE   Differential equations.
Feel it.
$\mathbf{p} = m\,\mathbf{v} = md(\mathbf{x})/dt$
Say it:
Momentum is mass moving, in space, with velocity.

$$\frac{d(\mathbf{p})}{dt} = \frac{d(m\,v)}{dt} = \frac{md^2(\mathbf{x})}{d^2t} = \text{Force}$$

Make the statement:
Force brings the change of momentum;
change of momentum brings the Force.

And torquing around and from the hips, I recall that
angular momentum is a cross product of a distance of all the
parts and the momentum of the parts from the center.
$\mathbf{l} = \mathbf{r} \times \mathbf{p}$
Wow! The cross product is a matrix of all the parts
spinning around their axes . . .
I am undergoing mathesis mind-expansion while
experiencing and controlling physical forces through grace
and consideration!
Logos and Eros in struggle,
truly this is the word made flesh.

13 Push Hands Solo

Stepping off the porch I sometimes feel myself slip into this Yum Chi character. He is just this simple man, a farmer, a laborer. The discipline of Tai Chi was starting to become a bigger influence on my life. I'd find myself as Yum Chi going about the work day, reaching for something on a shelf, scooting across a car seat. I'd find myself as Yum Chi as he starts to slow time down and to explore his movements for their own sake, to analyzes them for differential tension.

One I liked in particular was Reeling Silk which I tried to experience by hanging a towel and punching it with different speeds.

Another, I called Reeling Water. When I was pulling those green five-gallon pickle buckets full of water up from the 25 foot deep well — pulling about 200 of them for each watering — I used it as a good opportunity to practice Reeling Water. I spread my feet just far enough to give myself a good base yet give the longest possible reach up to the top of the chain, almost all the way up to the pulley, so I can get lift the bucket the maximum amount with each stroke. In my pull I would dive backward, arching with all my weight, trusting that the chain will hold, and letting grace help me.

Another: I dug a hole and jumped out of it just by using my stomach. Yum Chi wants to be able to do back springs off of a horizontal surface like they do in the kung-fu movies.

For me to do Push Hands by myself I had to hang a pickle bucket of dirt from a tree. In my push and receive, I knew I had good alignment when I could feel the bucket pushing all the way back against my back heel.

Also, I hung a sand bags to exert constant pressure on my structure. When I pushed the bag I tried to observe that the angle it moved to was also the same as my angle off the vertical. I tried to feel the resulting force (Fx+Fy) point to my back foot.

I could stand in Ward-off and have the weight apply pressure to my forearm. I could then absorb this pressure through my arm, and eventually through torso, thigh, knee, shin, ankle into the opposite foot and into the ground. Then, keeping this connection, I'd relax (or drop or extend) my shoulder. Again, making sure all the while to be aware of the path to ground, then relax, or round (the opposite of arch), my back a little. It got so I could relaxed and yet still be applying a force to the pressure on my arm. The idea is to resist more force with less muscles. It felt good to connect with the ground in a resilient, non-rigid way. I learned this grounded feeling and tried to find this connection in the other movements of the form.

I am under the towering oak tree at the edge of the patch with no clouds above in the night sky, the stars soar and wheel like energy shapes. The moon is nearly full. I can make out the tall weeds and thick bush surrounding the patch. Off in the distance, a tree line at the fence told of the creek there. I can move the trees with my hands. Beyond were the just the shadows of hills. The freedom garden was growing even though locusts have been noshing on it severely, in what must have been the best earth there ever was. It was like devil's food cake came up beautiful on the shovel.

I got it that the well is about halfway between the barn and the house. The old people had centered the whole farm around the well. It went deep, deep down into a cistern that collected rainwater, maybe 8,000 gallons under there. We had no telling. We thought that since the water was a brown tea, dead things had fallen in there: that gave it an almost magical potency. Because all the plants we put it on did grow well. We had some beautiful plants, one gigantic tree we called the Texas Twister, from an ancient seed stock that had come down to us from ganja farmers in India, by way of a traveler who had nipped a bud off a bush outside his hotel window.

The whole place back there was over grown, had been colonized with grasses, and was thick with fallen leaves suspended amid the towering prairie grass and weeds ebbing and flowing in the wind.

14 Sky being

When doing Tai Chi outside,
to quiet yourself
listen for the birds.
Be on a kind of
bird watching expedition.
Raise the gaze
and look for the amazing
    Sky-Beings.

Yes! Make Grasp Bird's Tail
an inviting roost for a Sky-being.
We keep coming around to the movements:
Grasp Bird's Tail
Stork Spreads Wings,
Golden Cock Stands on One Leg

Maybe Tai Chi is partly a bird-watching expedition:
walking around with feet in the mud,
in the forest growing from the fertile earth,
watching up into the brawny boughs
looking among the trees with strangeness
as they are writhing and spiraling and reaching up their
limbs — arching and dancing so gently in the breeze,
combing the wind
like a weir,
to catch the Sky-beings
in their upturned twig-tips there.

Yes, to let the head loft on high
to be suspended in a sling from the sky
and to fly with the birds . . .

We are privileged to live among
the creatures of the sky
who sometimes glide down
like a sigh to sidle by our side.

It was the wind that drew them
out

shaped them:
smooth to slide
    soft, sleek
slicing
through the thin air.
Yes we are out looking for birds — creatures of the wind.
What a long journey! it has been for them.
Do you know they evolved
from dinosaurs?
Great soaring sky beings!
Shaped by the winds of evolution.
Form is natures's answer
to the problem of Flow Control;
it had the birds drop off all that cumbersome dinosaur
mass
    in time;
they got light as . . . well, birds!
    in their feathers,
and moved into the atmosphere
to soar on the winds . . .

In Yang style Tai Chi,
Grasp Bird's Tail
is repeated the most number of times.
I want to hold a soft bird
beating like a heart in my hands or at least
to provide little fuzz-lined nest like they're used to.

Oh, great Sky-being,
I love how you draw me out cf my grasping visual
intense space
    into your audio localization sound space
    through the call of your birds;
    as sometimes I track their sound first,
    from hearing their chattering
    and endless commenting about the day

How I've missed your call to the day
when I'm indoors
or just too pre-occupied

to be present.
On rainy days they hide out
and are mostly silent. Where do
they go? Under leaves and eaves?

I liked to do tai chi out in the woods.
Amid the high speed coffee-klatch of
birds endlessly keeping up social relations,
as talkative as teenagers,
as though they didn't have a worry in the world.
Then the attention moves, returns once again
from the hearing space back to the visual space,
to see them jumping behind leaves, in the bushes
flickering like energy or fire climbing
on the heavy muscular tree limbs of the forest.
Then all of a sudden they
    take off!
with an explosion
    of startling wings.

Reaching for light, for flight —
they have left behind the heaviness,
as I let my spirit soar with them here now
at this moment
in the horizon of the world.

15 Base Frequency

Bow-who Hoooo

Wow Wwwoo-oh Oahaa

The Base Frequency at the
  bottom of life

Big bowed base
taut string taut as a tautology

Through the purple brown earth
— ground —
the big base booms.

Upon the dark
wind
there is a rising and falling
in sympathetic vibration.

In the brown
ground
the bow stops.

The sound,
the fundamental frequency
of which all things are harmonics
sets up standing waves in the surface of things.

There is a surface around all things
there is a bubble around all things.

It holds the universe together
it is light on one side
dark on the other.

16 Sound Cadas for Solo Form

By now I have at least learned by rote memorization most of the first 19 moves in the form laid out by one of the grand masters in the lineage. Each form is a form to get into the Form. One is trying to conduct Chi down into his being from the Form, and have it circulating through the joints.

I'm moving in the slowest possible way, like, well not quite as slow as a Wilson play, like *Einstein on the Beach*, but as if somehow in a dream. The ancients created the forms by watching young trees sway in the breeze, resiliant and sensitive to force. I'm a tree on that beach; I am in a swirl of confusion about remembering the forms, their names, the mnemonics, how the moves should be done, and to add to that confusion, I have devised breathing sounds to be done along with it. Yum Chi! Breathing sounds that go with the action, like a sound tract to a movie, and further add to my confusion, to bring about an almost rhapsodic state of synesthesia. The sounds mimic the air moving by, the waves crashing on the beach. The sounds and breathing are done slowly letting the breath go out or come in as if you were an ocean wave breaking through a tunnel or cave. Unvoiced>

Brush Knee Twist Step

```
o_,      o      o,     o_,     o,      o_
) ,     ( | \   ) ,     ) '    ) '     ) - '
>\      / >     >\     / >     >\     / >
```

Out: *shhhhheeee aaaaaah ddchshhHHH*

while doing a long easy exhale

  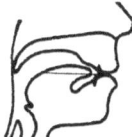

Twist Step

```
o,       o       o
/ 0 '   , = (    / 0 )
/ >      >\      < \
```

in: *sheeee oooowwww—oooohhh ah—kooch*

in a long easy inhale through lips shaping a cave.

The tongue is moving in the mouth, like how a wave of the ocean breaks in a cave or blowhole. Like I, in my body am a tongue anchored to the earth articulating with my body. I want to talk, I want to be said. I want to turn myself into the tongue that speaks this language of forms. The object is to slow the breathing down so that the movements, in synch with the breathing, are part of the same mental physical landscape. Synchronize the rhythm of your breath with the rise and fall of the efforts of your actions.

```
o_,    o     o,    o_,    o,    o_,
),     (|\   ),    )'     )'    )-'
>\     / >   >\    / >    >\    / >
```

Out: *shhhhheeee aaaaaah ddchshhHHH*

I am walking into an ocean of sound, making the soundscape all around me. Sounds: she shhh part of crash --a wave crash) opening to the unvoiced open vowel e; ah, relaxing voices or unvoice sigh; whah (as in wall without the l); ou (as in couger) unvoiced; 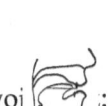 dsss, voiced d followed by unvoiced sibilant s or voi ; gzch voiced labial alvilar plosive, 00 bilabial unvoiced (makes almost a whisting)

```
o,     o     o_    o     o_,    o     o,
/0'    ,=(   ),'   /0)   ),     (|\   ),
/ >    >\    >\    < \    >\     / >   >\
```

in: *ou------/+ -\she shhheeee ahhhhh ou ------/+ -*

Like waves breaking around some caves (shaped by the rsing + and falling -) or turbulent vortex of cross currents, cutting a hole in the wall of time. On the inhale it comes in.

```
o,     o     o_    o     o_,    o     o,
/0'    ,=(   ),'   /0)   ),     (|\   ),
/ >    >\    >\    < \    >\     / >   >\
```

Out: *shhhhheeee aaaaaah ddchshhHHH*

Making sound on the breath amplifies the transcendental feeling to the point of distraction. I used the human breathing tunnel to make voiced and unvoiced labiodental fricatives to make sounds like waves breaking on some far distant shore. I am in the form, Yum Chi, in the Form. Pushing, Pooshshshshinging Pwooooshwoosshinging

Single Whip

```
   o      o     o_,    ,o     , o     , o ,    , o
 '-(     ' | '  )-'    _`)    `)-'    `)-     `)-'
 /<     > <   > <    /<     / >     < \     / >
```

in: *ooshshshshinging* out: *Pwooooshwoosshinging*

Going through the motions Yum Chi, through the motions into the Form. Slow down man feel the breeze caused by your own body moving, sense the mass of the things around you, what else could one want? It's beautiful.

Apparent Closure

```
   o_,    (o)     _o_      o       o        o
 )-'      |     ' | '    (x)     ' | '     [ | ]
 / >    / >    [ ]     ( )     [ ]       [ ]
```

in: *shhhhheeee aaaaaah ddchshhHHH*

Now some voiced sound coming out of the guttural chase and thud of the ocean breezes. Think of the great Kerouac by the shore, taking dictation from the ancient sea.

Moving from the tunnel inside a great holy humming cathedral hive full of chanting monks and I join them with a great aughsuuuummmmmmaaaahhhhhh on the exhale
Trying to get caught up, in the great circulation of Chi, trying to catch the motion and be carried along with it like a surfer on a wave. I know this Great Circulation will not wait. I must meet if halfway; it has grace to give out. If I can just get into the Form and stay in the Form, Yum Chi. The Form is floating toward WHAT Yum Chi, I don't know, and I am floating in it.
I am so blissed out, man, I can't stand it. This is so different from other act. So authentic.

Brush Knee Twist Step

```
   o ,     o      o,      o       o_      o_,      o ,
 )<      )=,    /0'     ,=(     ),'     ),      )<
 >\     >\    / >     >\     >\     }>      >\
```

Out: *shhhhheeee aaaaaah ddchshhHHH*

easy push — roll back — separate —press

Twist, wring, that's what it basically amounts to, think
of all the possible kinds of holds and gabs and situations
you can get into and work out several ways of getting out

```
o,      o     o_      o     o_,     o     o,
/0'    ,=(    ),'    /0)    ),     (|\    ),
/ >    >\     >\     < \    >\     / >    >\
```
Out: *shhhhheeee aaaaaah ddchshhHHH*

always breaking the incoming down into its situation.

And I am doing low trips and swipes across the ground
of the planes.

Play guitar
```
.o;     o     o     (o)     o      o      o ,
'|    '|>   '-|-'    |    '-|'    ,|)    )<
< \    < \   < \    < \    < '    / >    < \
```
Out: *shhhhheeee aaaaaah ddchshhHHH*

It wasn't until much later that I realized in a way I was
performing the rites laid down in ancient books on Feng
Shui. But instead of reciting the name of the gods, chanting
prayers and making prostrations before the altar I was
making rhapsodic sound and falling into a moving trance.

The purpose of the dance was to importune the gods to
manifest their magical powers and compassion for the
benefit of mankind. Feeling my joints and muscles was
gods enough.

I began taking the Tai Chi out into the world, and
looked for the movements in everyday life. I began to enjoy
just doing the movements of ordinary work with grace and
relaxation. I'd look at myself and how I was using my body
to relate to space, time, weight, and flow.

Apparent Closure
```
o_,    (o)     _o_      o      o      o
)-'     |     '|'    (x)    '|'    [|]
/ >    / >    [ ]    ( )    [ ]    [ ]
```
Out: *shhhhheeee aaaaaah ddchshhHHH*

the snake creeps down,
sssssssss

Sound Cadas for Solo Form

The sounds and breathing are done slowly letting the breath go out or come in as if you were an ocean wave breaking through a tunnel or cave. The object is to slow the breathing down so that the movements in synch with the breathing are part of the same mental physical landscape. Synchronize the rhythm of your breath with the rise and fall of the efforts of your actions.The analogy is the joints of the body are articulation points like the tongue in the mouth.

With the sound cadas, I came to the end of the first phase in learning Tai Chi. The 3 phases to cultivating Chi are 1) rote memorization to deal with the overwhelming on-slaught of detail in to remembering the steps, 2) the emergence of chi and grace in the movement and fighting of everyday life, through analysis of space time and force, exploring the Chi in the joints for its own joy and 3) stepping into an ancient world of energies and archetypes whose landscape is the I Ching.

1. Commencement of Tai Chi Ch'uan ↑ ⊗

2. Grasp Bird's Tail Right ↑ ⊗ →

3. Grasp Bird's Tail Left ↑

4. Ward Off Slanting Upward →↘

5. Sit Back & Pull et ← ↑ →

6. Press Forward o →

7. Push Forward o→

8. Single Whip e← → ↗↖ ←

9. Raise Hands and Step Up ↖ ↘↗↑ ↖

10. Stork Cools Its Wings ↙←e

11. Brush Knee Left e←

12. Play the Fiddle e←

13. Brush Knee Left e←

14. Brush Knee Right e←

15. Brush Knee Left e←

16. Play the Fiddle e←

17. Brush Knee Left e←

18. Step Up, Chop, Block & Punch ↑←↖←

19. Apparent Close Up ↑→ ⊗

in	*ou*———————————————————————
out	*ou*———————————————————————
in	*ou*———————————————————————
out	*ou*———————————————————————
in	*OO*———————————————————————
out	*shhhh*—————————————————————
in	*shhhh*—————————————————————
out	*shhhh*——————————————*whah*—————————
in	*shhhh*—————————————————————
out	*whah*————————————>*shhh*—————————
in	*shhhh*—————————————
out	*whah*—————————__–>*shhh*—————————>*tsss*————
in	*tsss*———————————————————————
out	*ehhh*————————— >*ee*——————————>*dsss*—————————>*gzch*——
in	*ehhh*—— >*ee*————————>*dsss*—————————>*gzch*—————
out	*ehhh*—— >*ee*————————>*dsss*—————————>*gzch*—————
in	*rest in*—————————————————
out	*t shhh*————*t shhh*——————————*ss shhh*—————————*zzgzch*–
in	*ssss*———————————————————————
out	*gzch*—————————————————
in	*shhh*————————————————————
out	*whah*————————————>*shhh*—————————>*ssss*——
in	*shhhh*—————————————————————
out	*shhhh*—————————————————————
in	*shhhh*——————————————*whah*—————————
out	*shhhh*—————————————————————
in	*whah*————————————>*shhh*—————————
out	*ou*———————————————————————
in	*ou*———————————————————————
out	*ou*———————————————————————
in	*ou*———————————————————————
out	*OO*———————————————————————
in	*whah*————————————>*shhh*—————————
out	*shhhh*—————————————
in	*whah*—————————__–>*shhh*—————————>*tsss*————
out	*tsss*———————————————————————
in	*ehhh*————————— >*ee*——————————>*dsss*—————————>*gzch*——
out	*ou*———————————————————————
	shhhh————————————————————
	shhhh——————————————*whah*—————————

Sounds: ou (as in couger, unvoiced), shhh (as in the sh part of crash --a wave crash) whah (as in wall without the l), dsss (voiced d followed by unvoiced sibilant s), gzch (voiced plosive), OO (bilabial unvoiced, makes almost a whisting)

17 The Prettiest Word in the English Language

Ocean . . .
has got to be the prettiest word in the English language,

O-shun   like a wave crashing on the shore
O ceeee-aaannn.   O she aaaun
O shun.
What did Lao Tsu say about the water?
Be as water,   evapora-tion   condensa-tion
               precipita-tion   collec-tion

We come from the O-shun
where the water is in collection.
The water cycle makes it rain
evaporation makes it rain
condensation makes it rain
precipitation makes it rain
water running down a hill,
water running down

We could come to know how to feel a part of the cyclic
of water: collection, condensation, precipitation, evaporation
— one of the oldest cycles, billions of years old—the reason
everything on earth is here and alive.

Water keeps cycling round and round
through and through.

Throw water on the window pane
and watch it trickle DOWN like rain.
Precipitation-shun

Water seeks to be the antidote to your excesses?
Shun.
Be as lotion, lubricating the flow all round you.
Be in motion from a place that is authentic.
Watch. Do you want to be where your notion takes you?
Attention. Stay vigilant lest erosion wear your attention.
Move smoothly, but be ready for explosion.

All these shun words, do you suppose they have, at their mimological heart, this basic effort to fly apart? To shun each other, for the molecules to shun each other like in evaporation where the molecules get heated and separate and rise into amelioration, or condensation where the water molecules do the opposite?

I wonder if the ancient Taoist could see this basic expansion and contraction in the hydrological cycle this — pulsating:

evaporation   — molecules getting energy and flying apart

condensation — molecules loosing energy and adhering to something

precipitation   — molecules of water stuck together in falling drops

collection   — molecules of water collecting together in bigger drops.

We have one flying apart and 3 types of adhering and collecting.

   ‾‾‾‾‾   —   —   ‾‾‾‾‾   —   —

   ‾‾‾‾‾   ‾‾‾‾‾   —   —   —   —

evaporation   condensation   precipitation   collection

Do you worry about the future?
It is an endless cycle,
(Sung to a rap rhythm):
Evapora-shun
Do you want to know what to do with your life?
Condensa-shun
Do you want to know how to begin a new venture?
Collect--shun
Do you want to clear away misconceptions?
Condensa-shun
Do you want to know how to be thorough?
Precipitation-shun
Do you want to create order?
Collect—shun
Throw water on the window pane
and watch it trickle down like rain.

As he moved around
the place, he'd notice
the movement . . .
in everyday life.

CHI

Scooting into
the car to reach across
and get something out
of the opposite seat
was like a Snake Creeps Down.

Reaching down to
place a doorstop
in a door
    was Needle at
        Sea Bottom

reaches down to tie shoe:
    Snake Creeps Down

gently kicks
    a drawer closed:
Turn and Kick with Heel

    Single Whip: trying to keep one catastrophe from
happening while
    another . . .
— reach to a shelf in the cupboard
and pluck something off,
while reaching over
to get / put away
      something in a
        drawer.

The Story of the Form
seemed to be about
getting the knife,
slicing the melon and

serving parts of it.

High Pat on Horse
— stepping
down steep hill.

Lady
Hangs up
Wash
on Lines

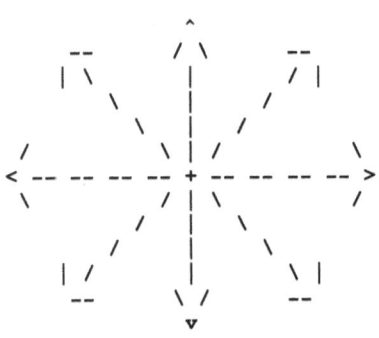

Reached in and
grabbed a
handful
of grains:
—> Step Forward
and
Punch.

0

315   45

270   90

225   135

180

Open the door
and going in and
out of the Room
(hut)

That allows you to
turn around and
go the other way
into the Room

Also might sit
down on a bar stool

Sit Down on Bar Stool

Door is
low to the
hut (Room) they
go in and
out of.

CHI

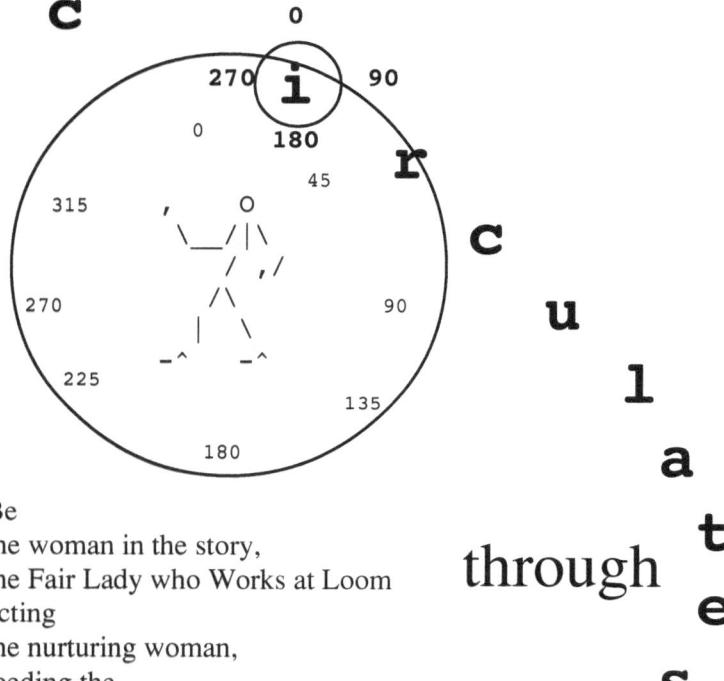

Be
the woman in the story,
the Fair Lady who Works at Loom   through
acting
the nurturing woman,
feeding the
kids and people

Doing the wash —
Reach and Box Ears
is her putting up or
taking clothes
down.

Then she might
feed the
chickens . . .
might mimic the
rooster . . .
might relate to the
monkeys and animals around
    her.

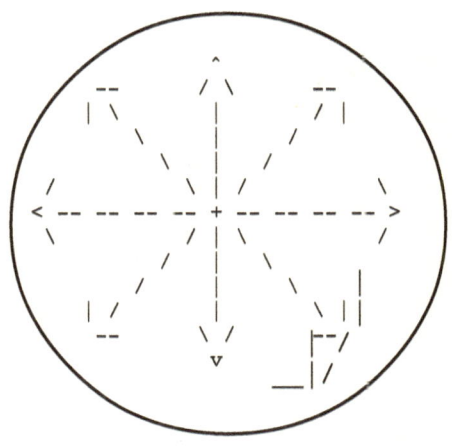

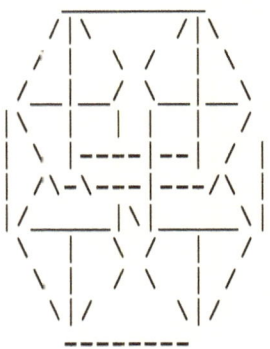

Walks through
door and
(brushing the door open)
reaches across
himself, to flip
on a light switch.

Pulls the door
open — out to him,
and reaches across
to the light switch inside
on his right.

Reaches back and
    slides open
        the mirror
            cabinet . . .
Reaches in
    gets something out . . .

CHI

c

0

270 **i** 90

180

r

c

u

l

a

t

e

s

```
       /|\       /|\
      / | \     / | \
     /  |  \   /  |  \
    |\  |  /| |\  |  /|
    | \ | / | | \ | / |
    |  \|/  | |  \|/  |
    |---|----|---|----|
    |/\-|-\--|---|----\|
    |   |  \ | | /|    |
    |   |   \|N|/ |    |
     \  |   /| |\ |   /
      \ |  / | | \|  /
       \| /  | |  \ /
        \|/       \|/
       --------
```

^/‾\‾/‾\‾\‾/‾\‾/‾\‾through‾/‾\‾/‾\‾/‾\‾

me

Fixed Frame

19 Apparent Closure,

Standing in meditation, until I start to feel the Chi running in my hands, a tingly sensation that I am trying to grow and have flow or at least not disrupt. It is a game of mechanical alignment with gravity feedback to let you know when the alignment is good. And Chi feedback to let you know when your circulation is unimpeded.

I like to move around and feel at ease and explore various energy feeling states. So much mitigates against feeling at ease.

I like the sense of being, just plain dumb animal being. I like to know about being in the universe and to know I know. Ontology and epistemology 101. I have my own self to watch.

Someday I'd like to write and study the *Vectors Fields of Tai Chi*. It would be a book looking at both the vectors of force and balance and also the fields, the auras, the fields of psychic energy, the gravitational and electromagnetic fields you can relax into and get information from. It is hard for me to just drop all that being in your head and just be. One day you start to know the first 19.

1. Commencement of Tai Chi Ch'uan
2. Grasp Bird's Tail Right
3. Grasp Bird's Tail Left
4. Ward Off Slanting Upward
5. Sit Back & Pull
6. Press Forward
7 Push Forward
8. Single Whip
9. Raise Hands and Step Up
10 Stork Cools Its Wings
11. Brush Knee Left
12 Play the Fiddle
13. Brush Knee Left
14. Brush Knee Right
15. Brush Knee Left
16. Play the Fiddle
17. Brush Knee Left
18. Step Up, Chop, Block & Punch
19. Apparent Close Up

Got to take it more easily, maybe it is more about slowing down and letting IT find you. Being ready for it when you see it. Being open to it. *Yeah.*

Lively Frame

In the Carry Tiger to Mountain move, the Form asks
you to greatly expand the range (while standing on one leg!)
Sarting from facing North, turn all the way around,
more than 180° to the right past South
to facing South West.

It is the first turn
to face along the diagonal
— a big turn.

Carry Tiger to Mountain is a turn
followed by a kick!

```
                              N
                   --      / \      --
                  | \     \   0   /   / |
                   \         \ | /       \
W < --270-( -- + -- )-90 --->E
                   /         / | \       /
                  | /     /  180  \   \ |
                   --      \ /      --
                              v
                              S
```

The Form asks you to really expand
   the reach of your leg.
It is also like you grab and drag someone around.
                        Who? — the Tiger?
After the big turn, and you have stepped down, (your
torso is facing SE) you raise right hand in a block along the
SW diagonal, turning wrist out. Then swing that raised hand
back to chop down in front of you as though to catch a kick
in the groin, facing now the SE diagonal. Then you keep
that right hand low, and bring the left hand up as you turn
back to the SW diagonal, sweeping everything in front of
you, in a double block. Then, from that spring loaded
position (turned hard into the SW) you throw a right cross
punch into the East, making sure your feet stay firmly
planted, and being sure to rotate your waist and hips into it
from SW to SE, unloading like a wound-up spring.

Inside this reach space, the player,
         —within a solid angle described by degrees of
pitch, degrees of yaw, combined with roll motion —
         is drawing shapes with his hands,
      which are both blocking AND punching AND in fact
doing neither, but just being free to do something.

Is there a literary significance in Carry Tiger to Mountain? If you can't bring the mountain to the tiger,
      carry tiger to mountain?

As I make a move,
the rules of the Form ask questions:
"Are you thinking about mindfulness in Tai Chi, and the
value of suddenness in breaking through mindfulness. The
idea of a shock?"

I think about when I was walking down the street the
other day,
and I noticed my teeth bounced up and down when I
walk, unless I had tension in my jaw or clamped my teeth.
I wonder if there is some way to walk
    and step
    such that the shockwave from the step
        is dampened in the joints
            before they get coupled to the jaw.
Maybe I need to get better shock absorbers in my
ankles?
I wonder,
"Is that a physical property of joints?
or does the suddenness
cut through mindfulness
    (concentration, focus)
by invoking
    a tensing up and
        a fight or flight response."

The Form asks . . . and sends the mind in search
or invokes the mind's resistance.,
"What about that term mindfulness. Does that have a
particular meaning for you?"
At first I objected to it,
as being loaded with Buddhist connotations.
But now I'm trying to understand it in a Tai Chi context.
I tried "attention" or "focus," but
mindfulness seems to be a lot more all-encompassing.

"Mindfulness," I answer, "seems to be
about relaxing, but at the same time
really focusing the mind
into the hand or just the fingers.
The fingers in a pluck say, they are hard and dangerous

and cannot be pulled apart slowly.
But when attacked suddenly,
things are pulled apart easily."
The mindfulness of the focus was broken by the shock
of suddenness.

I started reading more trying to pick up some of the
Chinese words for the qualities in Tai Chi I was trying to
explore.

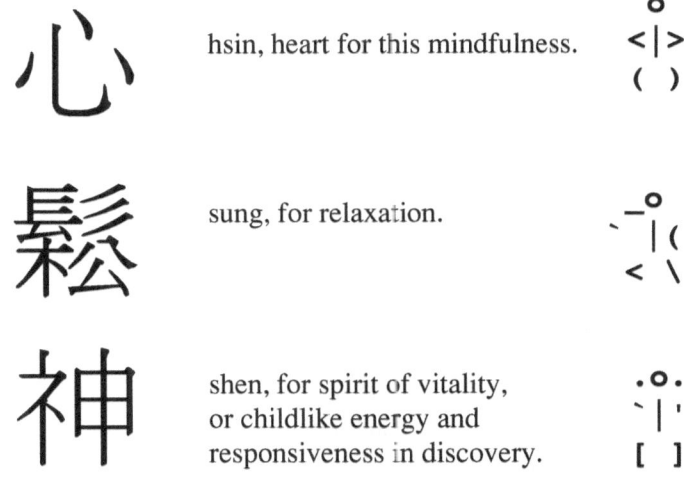

心丶   hsin, heart for this mindfulness.

鬆   sung, for relaxation.

神   shen, for spirit of vitality,
or childlike energy and
responsiveness in discovery.

The Form asks and I answer yes.
And know it, he, she! will release
an expansion of ease, which I hope
may quickly bloom into
the fluorescence of grace.

Wow, these are all big questions about the haptic device,
— the light assault vehicle.
Yes! I am the Tiger, the light assault vehicle, or at least I
aspire to be.
And the mountain I am trying to carry the Tiger to, is the
perennial philosophy of the Tao.
And one way I will get there is by deconstructing a path,
through going beyond language, and following the ideo-
grammatic language of pointers into the inchoate.

Around every being,
enclosing each individual,
    is the bubble.
Surrounding every person, place or thing
    it begins to exist.

At the interface of every encounter,
    is the merging of two bubbles.
One can breach his bubble by,
    getting close.
Then the bubbles can merge,
    go down and can even join!
But, you have to be careful!
The bubble can burst
    with the crush of continual presences,
and coping with the expectations and reactions of others.

We think it's our manners,
— the way we relate. Our customs
            ARE
                    these bubbles.
But it's more than that.

In my mass society,
    the bubble is violated every microsecond.
"What are you doing?" constantly asks media, schools,
business, the economy. "Every moment must be accounted
for."
"Your uniqueness, your intelligence,
your sensitivity, your perceptions
are of no use in the mass situation."
Oh . . . *really.*

But what do you care. Right?
You all have your bubble,
your houses, your trust funds, your family,
your education,
and it is bigger and better than mine.

The bubble is floating on the stream of time,
it's been kicked up by the turbulence of a kind of
moving water,
and I am wading out into it,
stepping from the shadows of experience
into the flow of fate.
I am playing lightly with my weight,
negotiating the undertow.

Into the river then I go;
something is calling me:
sound falling —like rain — out of the air.

The motion in stillness;
the stillness in motion.
Will I ever come to know it?
They say it circulates and splits apart with a laugh.

The ground is moving,
the bubbling springs well up and carry my feet.
Into little rivulets, that grow into rills
running down hills,
        into brooks that riffle over boulders
            into creeks that stream through valleys
                into rivers that flow through canyons

I step catlike over the smooth stones
at the river's edge
listening for admonitions in the tumble.
I wade in.
My feet are parting the waters of
the undertow
flowing past
        causing turbulence giving off
more bubbles,
        to the channel, the lifeblood, of
rivers.

I relax the spine and sink into a seated down sensation
and let myself be carried along by the flow.

Down, down,
        the river,
                to the sea.

Dragons poke their head up out of the water.
Beasts raise their heads and pose
        looking out at us with baleful eyes
                from behind bushes
                        as if we were meat.
We are.
We are waterborne babies drifting away from home,
flung out into the Euphrates of space,
denying our serpentine fathers, along the Nile,
coming to the delta zone of the new Amazon.

I sacrifice my fear on the altar of ego
and am admitted to the channels that flow
from the source of my becoming.
Slowly coming to know
its expanding and contracting surface,
I marvel as the bubble floats
down the river,
        out to the ocean — an ocean of existence
                and non-existence.

I am playing going down
down,
down beneath
the up and down,
into an emptiness
from which we all come,
that moves through us,
yet that we can't see
unless it moves against something,
like the wind blowing tree branches.

I love to watch the chaos of flowing water,
        for it is like listening to the deity speak to us in the
language of forms
        with well-defined shapes
                vortices, circulations, tight runs, mixing, isovalues.

We are flowing in it and it is flowing through us,
and we can play happily in it or we can drown.
It is gas. We are the engine.
It is the ecology. We are a life-form.
It is the dance. We are the movements in the dance.

Around every presence
    it begins to exist
—a bubble.
Slowly, we come to know its existence,
    because we have come to know the emptiness beneath
the surface.
YES! it is the Emptiness,
in which a stream of entropy flows.
Entropy is the stream,
and time the water, flowing (mainly)
in the stream's direction.
Entropy obliterates existence, yet it creates order
because order creates more entropy!
Thus, in Emptiness prior to existence,
entropy comes —existence thrives
and creates more existence!

The face of emptiness is like a mirror.
Emptiness is no dead thing!
It is as fierce as a mother cat.
It's alive and pushing behind what's happening in the
world.
    It is not to be feared, for we have already sacrificed our
fear on the alter of our ego.

    It is the slurry of life and it is listening to everything we
say,
    — all our secrets —
        and caring for us,
                every moment of our breathing.

    You want to talk to her, for she is your mother.
She's *this* ocean keeping you afloat. None other.

22 but what has all this to do with Chinese butt kicking

Martial arts teaches that you are going to have to deal
with violence. It is a violent world and instead of having
others to take care of you, and take care of the violence, and
absorb the karma of being violent, you have to take care of
your own self. You have to engage in violence, you have to
study violence, you have to participate in violence for
yourself.

A fight description:
they're gonna have to grapple,
trying to do damage by a thrust
of fist
or knife.
Or a throw.
You must instantly go into a relaxed thing,
—best chances of not getting hurt.

You want to step aside from the force
and let it go past,
then, kick hell out of opponent.

There you have it —a fight:
—an aggressor and a defender,
turning round and round each other
the forces of survival brought up close and physical.

The Knight of 1000 eyes,
looking at the surface tensor to avoid the vector
    looks
          with his shoulders
          and chest,
he analyzes from myriad points of view.

Watch the opponent's upper & lower body
        left & right side of body.
Is a foot coming off or onto the floor?
Like a chess player moving in
for mechanical advantage,
you need to have the cadas second nature,
—in place — from much practice.

Everything comes down to being grounded.

```
 __|__      Look at the center line,                |
|  |  |     is he asymmetric?                       |
|__|__|     —be able                              __|__
   |        to push him off balance.                |
```

Will you have to use a simultaneous block-punch?
like in wing chung,
or is their time to be sequential.
If there is time, then worry about it later.

```
        |
   /   _   \
   \  (_)  /
    \__=__/
       |
 ------|------
       |
 /-"  "-\
 o   |   o
 |   |   |
 ^   |   ^
```

Worry about force first.
                (weight)
    Look for strong or weak tension
    touch and grip.
Fighting could be occurring in an alley, against a wall,
or in the park against a background of trees.
    Watch feet, hands or other parts of the body.
        Are they going to touch — collide?
        What objects?
        The floor. The wall?

And space second.
Separate and look at each other's patterns,
        directions of levels,

of steps,
        changes of front,
        hand moves.
    Do they favor one side?
    Take a while to draw them out,
    Check out their repetoir of moves,

If his style is just to run at you flailing away,
the only thing you can do is back away,
Step Back and Repulse monkey,
try to grab one of his flailing arms.

Now. Time.
If it is not to be quick,

59

then a question of aerobic stamina comes in.
Quick and slow in gesture and step...
all this is supposing you've got your aerobic capacity up
and he
doesn't have a gun.

Think of it as a crazed insect attacking you;
flip flop get him away.

The fast way to stop him
would be hit the head with enough impulse
— (that's force delivered very quickly in time),
so as to jar the brain for a moment,
and cause a black-out to occur.
Another way would be to amplify the force of your
opponent so that he could get that kind of damage to his
head using his own force amplified with yours.

You are trying to balance chance,
do least work.

What IF he runs at you.
Lower weight onto away leg and get out of his way,
jump aside
and slip around him,
and maybe try to hit him in his body as he goes by.
Fearing that might make him mad,
what if he grabs you with his strong hands?
You have to twist your hands into this thumb and get his
whole hand pointing away from his body, because that
makes the thumb part of the hand hold the weakest.
To get release from a strong man's grasp,
it is necessary to be strong.

Of course if he gets you in a bear hug,
bring your knee up into his groin
to protect your own,
and damage him;
or bash your head into Redneck's big ugly face.
The head of Ripoff the Redneck is probably so big and
bony

you'd break your hand hitting it anyway.
But you might do well to bash it with your own head.

The other thing is to try for the throat,
a slash or open hand to crush the windpipe
might give him pause.
Don't forget to go loose, to relax.
Whatever you do,
don't let it get you down,
because then it can get on top of you with its weight,
    it will then proceed to stomp
        and kick you,

       . . . o happy day.
Then all you can do is try to roll away from his
trammpeling feet.

Remember to go low in your lunges.
Step forward parry and punch.
See if you can get a good one into his bread basket
or if you can slip out from under his grasp to the side
and get off the side snap kick
to stove in some of his rib cage.
There.
That oughta really slow him down
if he's got a piece of rib
puncturing his lungs with every breath.

I kept on working in this way,
imagining this big headed redneck from hell
coming at me,
with all kinds of attacks
and me doing my blocks and counterstrikes
against this realistic opponent.

I had not been in that many fights in my life.
It certainly had been a long time since grade school and
highschool.

Now, what if this guy can jump
    way up in the air

like those supernatural fighters in Kung Fu movies.
When he goes high,
you go low:
Snake Creeps down.
(Be careful this huge hulking brute of an insect
doesn't land on your trip leg.)

Don't get winded, and don't let them knock the wind out
of you, because then they'll really pound you, give your
head a whipping and tie you up and you'll be at their tender
mercy.

These were the thoughts running through my head,
while I fought the brute
coming through the manifold of my imagination
—trying to make the cadas realistic.

If he gets you by the throat,
try to knock his hands away
by coming up with both hands like a wedge.
Do a double block knocking is hands away.
If that don't work,
come in from the outside and drive a knuckle into each ear,
Step forward and box ears.
And if that don't work, lay your thumbs into his eyes.

I did my Tai Chi, much much faster then it is ever done.
I began to think Tai Chi was not that good as a self
defense thing.
It was probably intended as more of a kind of graduate
school of movement study and philosophy.

It is amazing
how much the body knows
about the space/time manifold.

make your move up under the swipe,

23 Bug

I stepped on a bug and that crushed it a little bit.
It crunched before I could get my foot up.
I felt bad, but not too bad.
I picked it up and one of its antennae fell off.
I was bummed.
I thought about how O. Wilson said,
there is more life in a handful of dirt on this earth
than anywhere else in the universe.
And I felt grateful.
And I felt the abundance.

24 Step Back and Repulse Monkey

I loved that move.
I would get so much fear and adrenaline going.
You were stepping back

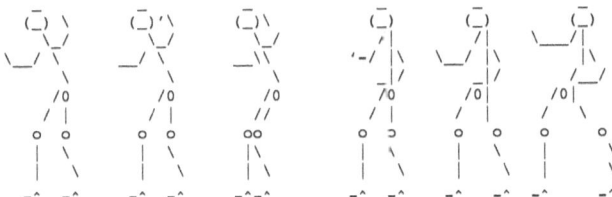

and at the same time reaching out, grabbing your opponent by the wrist and wrenching him hard off balance
carrying his forward momentum further toward you while at
the same time, using your grip to pull yourself toward him
and smash the heel of your palm into his face.

The move aroused a wily awareness and maneuverability
tinged with fear and blood lust.

Next I'd be admonishing myself with: "This is not right,
this is not the peaceful warrior that Tai Chi is supposed to
make you be."

I'd look again into the form for a move to quiet myself
down.

to forget.   to long for.   to remember.
to lose   and   to find again.
thinking, grasping   — it cannot be grasped.
it cannot be apprehended.   it can only be experienced.
it is your own nature,
it is doing you.

Walker Underwood. Here
you are on this land,
in a modern century,
speaking of the ancient Tao
with your self. To get into that
truth and to grapple with that
other, to help them get to
that truth.

That point of view . . .
how can you get that
TAO point of view?
It was here before you
and it will be here when you are gone.
You are not that important
and yet you are all that is.

We are storks standing — spreading our wings.
We are tigers carrying ourselves into the mountain
by forces we know not
and we
throw out our arms,
and we
throw out our legs,
like it was us doing it.
But really we are trying to shift point of view.
I is another,
who has mistaken my experience for the nature of things.

May I bring my darkness to the fire,
bring my doubt to the alter too and sacrifice it.
Don't let it burn up my energy.

26 Dog Bite Enlightenment

On my walk perambulating the reservoir a dog nipped me.

I am shocked by the meanness and anger and rage it brought up in me. Way out of proportion to the event.

I was ready to kick the dog and pound-out the dog owner.

Of course, I didn't.

But as I walked off I felt this tremendous anger propelling me over the fields. My back was straight, I was in a kind of awful grace, my hands were loose at my sides, I was ready to fight! I was in a rage.

I have to say I liked the sense of grace and power. Haven't felt that for a long time.

This anger is some kind of gift.

When I got back home I kept imagining fight scenarios. For hours.

I began to wonder what gives here. I thought to sit with it in meditation. I could see the source(s) of the anger which I won't go into here, (my mother, the castrating culture etc.) I was taking righteous umbrage to avoid other painful feelings. I was trying to be Buddhist and get above it.

I say righteous because here is this individual walking two poodles on long leashes and he knows their behavior. The exchange went like this. I'm walking by, kind of spaced, minding my own business. As I go by this gay old boy with his two poodles, one of them turns — I thought, to sniff my leg. The dog nips through the pant leg, his tooth touching my skin! I got instinctive, whirled and kicked at the dog in self-defense. Unfortunately I missed.

"Don't you kick my dog!" he said getting arch.

"He tried to bite me."

"He didn't!"

"Yes he did!"

"He only wanted to take a little nip out of your pants."

"*WELL?*"

"Oh . . ." The haughty arrogant poofter walks off. I was outraged! He knows this dog does this to people and yet he doesn't reign him in when he passes people on the path. This has got to be corrected.

I threaten: "Next time I see you out here, that dog will be flying!"

And he retorts: "And you'll be talking to the police."

He walks of and I stood there glaring at him.

I am practically possessed with a demonic energy. It is frightening, I am just barely able to keep it under control. After a while meditating though, I think it would be nice to be able to have this anger in some safe way. To contain this anger. And from there contain other emotions.

I wonder if there is some kind of sparring, or hitting the bag that could help one have this anger in a safe way. I'm not saying I would like to do Tai Chi this way all the time, I really like the peaceful graceful flowing meditation of yang style Tai Chi. Maybe there is more of this anger edge in Chen Style?

Anyway this must be what martial art is about. To be able to access this grace through containing the emotion of anger (as opposed to avoiding or denying it all the time). To be able to contain and have strong energetic emotions, to wrap your body around this fountain of feeling the way a singer wraps a song around a column of air being steadily pushed out by the bellows of the lungs. Yes, that would be a martial art indeed.

I blessed the dog, a messenger. Though I was ready to kill the messenger. I hope I got the message.

27 Slantingly Flying

Or Diagonal Flying, is another move like Carry Tiger, where you take a great stepping to the side and thrust your hand up into opponent's armpit, while holding his wrist and bend him back over your extended knee.

In Carlos Casteneda, Don Juan teaches Carlos to fly in his dreams. He does this by having Carlos hold his hands out in front of him while he is lying down and drifting off to sleep. Right out in front of him. Then in his dreams Carlos was to look at his hands. Carlos is to try and maintain the focus on the hands across the threshold into dreams. This lead to much more control over his dream travel.

At certain times in my life I have had days on end of dreams about flying. I could hover and float out over the city. After a while I began to have some control over it and I couldn't wait to go to bed at night and fly in my dreams. I could rise and go down at will. It was lucid dreaming though I didn't have that name for it. How I have longed for that feeling from my childhood again in my life. I did not have control over dream travel but I began to try and practice it out at the farm, at least keeping a dream diary.

***

Wed Aug. 22, 1976

Last night I awoke in the most marvelous dream. I was doing push-hands with what, I don't know, call it an entity.

In the dream I was being pushy and aggressive and trying to feel my power in a contest of push hands with, I don't have any picture of it — it just seems to be associated with light and warmth. But when the entity, an ally, received my push, it returned it. I immediately sensed that it had such exquisite balance that it could always absorb any aggression down through it. And when it returned my push it sent a warm energy passing through me. It was the Healing Touch. It began as a trickle of warmth which became like a tickle, that sends humorous waves of well-being passing down through me.

I awoke eyes shining in the full moon. I was astounded by how the Somatic Intelligence could, in the passing of seconds, construct a dream in which the sense of physical resistance at the wrists, the point of contact in push hands, could be felt by the sleeper. Moreover, that with no more than a flick of the wrist, it could demonstrate a sense of balance and rootedness that went down into the bottom of nowhere, and with that convey enlightenment, and grace and a sense of generosity that was so profound that it was beyond the merely human manifestations of these attributes but reflected a universal generosity.

I knew that ultimately this is who one is shadowboxing with in Tai Chi. I didn't know what it was — projection? A personification conjured up by the Somatic Intelligence? I knew it was a gift, this entity — I'll call it the Automorph since it is axiomatic that all characters in my dream are me and the entity was me in a dream coming back at me (see the story of deriving this name later). And I was overcome with humility and gratitude at this gift from the Somatic Intelligence and I realized it has so much to teach us.

* * *

I started to write an essay to reflect on some of the struggles I have been going through to learn Tai Chi. It seemed to me that the main struggle was the fight between my mind and my feelings. I wanted to get a picture of a search and a struggle, a fight between the mind's attempt to maintain hegemony over the body. I wanted to at least get a frame of reference on what the Somatic Intelligence so easily and instantaneously gave a resolution to.

In my attempts to write the essay I had started off asking the question: What on earth is the Form anyway? To find the answer, I looked back to the beginning. I recalled my introduction to the term "Form" was with the personification, "The Form asks." As in, the Form asks that you: balance on one leg here; or, the Form asks that you: test this balance while on one leg by turning 180 degrees toward the corner. So Tai Chi is a dialog with the Form —whatever that is. I called my essay *Dancing with the Form.*

Then in my essay I examined some of the metaphors we used to speak about the Form. There is 1) the Language metaphor —I was moving from the block alphabet approach to where you start to join the block letters together into whole words. I mentioned other metaphors: 2) the martial arts application of each of the forms, 3) the visual metaphors

—buoyancy, etc., and 4) concepts from physics. I recalled how I learned Brush Knee from visualizing the wonderful thing that it is: turning to go with the energy of a force coming at you and *not* confronting it head on —but helping it along. A very central concept to Tai Chi.

These attempts began to seem kind of academic, and I thought to do something more artistic, more concrete — celebratory. To write something in which one got a sense of steps in a path, as if there was a parallel between the distinctions being made in the mind, and distinctions being made in a space. As if you were following the logic of some persuasive argument through a path of images and associations. The writing evolved another title: "*On the Tour Jete with the Form*". It was a goof on Seruat's painting *On the Grande Jeté* where people are forever relaxed in a diffusion of pointilist light. They had entered the perennial philosophy of their birthright. I imagined myself at home with those people in the great French painting but transposed — to here on the ramshakled farm in the Texas prairie. (Instead of the lake beside which people are walking in the painting, I had the stock-tank, which — about half-acre in size and all set about with mesquite trees hanging down, was quite an ideal landscape in itself.) The writing was based on the unconscious pun: jete — the path leading out into the lake, and the leap in ballet. That set me on a path. Here is a bit of it:

***

To someone seeing Tai Chi for the first time, the players might appear to pantomime the pulling and pushing of an invisible vehicle, a vehicle with several round wheels and dials that must be turned.

The wheels and dials turn and roll forward and rock back as real as the trees dancing with the breeze coming across the little lake. The structure might remind you of some kind of a cross between a unicycle and a windmill and a gyroscope. And though some people may find this odd, when you look a little closer you see that it is empty. It is a vehicle you can get into, to sometimes experience a wonderful emptiness, that at times contains absolute nothingness. These are beautiful moments, when you can ever-so-briefly drop distinctions and abandon yourself to the flow.

The whole Form pushes and pulls silently along a path that is small in space but goes *way* into time. And where does this time bound path take us? you ask. Let us follow it as it turns, this way and that. You encounter someone (let us say an entity who represents the spirit of Tai Chi, perhaps the Fair Lady Who Works at Shuttles, herself) who turns to you and asks: "What do you mean by these movements— these movements that your are making to follow me into this landscape where the standing waves on the lake dissipate energy from the wind, and the trees keep everything feeling with that oxygenated aliveness."

And seeing that she was a person of quality and sympathy, I tell her about how my mind has uprooted my body, how it drives my body around — feet never grounded — by imposing the logos over the intuitive to assert its hegemony. I tell her that am trying to come to know the somatic intelligence at the base of mind. I say this all the while admiring women with their low slung center of gravity thinking they would be more suited to doing Tai Chi then men with their upper torso bulk and indomitable ego pushing their body around. And she replies, "The trees are part of our lungs."

* * *

Well anyway it was clever and went on like that. But didn't have much substance. I found myself asking questions like: Why aren't the movements pushed to maximum extension to elongate the muscles and enhance expressiveness like ballet? Or, Why wasn't it more hard edged and martial? Or aerobic? I was not yet able to grasp the intention of motion originating from the center of mass.

This path of questioning led back in time to the originators of Tai Chi, as I thought to try to read their original intentions from the "text" of the Form. I tried to get into the mindset of the originators back in a time when the dew of consciousness was still wet on the dawning world and they designed the Form to celebrate and observe the turning and turning of seasons and wind and water and these thrusty little stick-figure humans translating linear motion into circular by going around the pulleys of the joints. I was hoping to find some invariant that gets transmitted across time in the Form. I imagined it to be an experimental study of their physics, seemingly based on a primal energy called

Chi, which was able to project itself into both the physical and psychological world.

I realized that what I was going back to find was something I had lost, my original childhood attention, the simple joy of playing the gravity game, something that is closer to childhood. It is the physics of relationship. I was going back to soak in the waters of relationship, to uncloud the brow, to be here and now in the flow, let it go. Focus not on the object but the space between. The emptiness.

Chi was starting to be more and more real. Chi, bioenergy, morphogenetic field energy, flows within and without every person, animal, tree and flower. Recognize it. It is the gift of creation. It is always near, we just need to step out of time for a moment to receive it. What is the nature of Chi? It is the nature of Chi to be continually recombining the world. Chi's joyful movements are the stuff that dreams are made of and this is what the ancients sought to classify and manipulate in Tai Chi.

I ran into the problem of what to call this alternative psychology. The term Somatic Intelligence came after being stumped for a while. I thought to access the terms Kundalini which comes from a mythology and religion that Joseph Campbell calls "the most accomplished aesthetic psychology on earth." (I think Taoists would say that the Kundalini is a manifestation of Chi.) Or the term Tan-Tien from Tai Chi, which on a physical level I think means the center or mass or the centroid. I felt uncomfortable and embarrassed for my culture that we had to import these terms and did not appear to have these concepts in our own make up.

I began to think about the mute inarticulate body intelligence that was based on pure mechanics. The Tan-Tien or the center of mass seemed like a kind of generalized focus point – the center of the body mind. I seriously perturbed my peace by inventing an analogy between the eye and the Tan-Tien. Just as the eye gathers separate points of light energy reflecting from objects in space and focuses them into a unified visual image in the mind, the Tan-Tien — situated at the core of the body — coordinates discrete spiraling chi energy given off by emergent possibilities coming from farther afield than the local space into unified coherent actualities. Yes . . . I walked around thinking about that one for a while. I was feeling a lot- and felt the body as the support for all endeavors as well as life, and that the Form is a technique to release the thinking mind and experience the totality of yourself. It is a short step from Body Mind to Somatic Intelligence.

* * *

Note: The term Automorph came after a search among Greek and Latin roots for something to convey the ability of Chi to react and shift shape among physical and psychological realms.

I thought of the ontomorph, based on the ontonaught, an astronaut of being; as opposed to an oneronaught —the dream traveler.

I looked at phantomorph, ideomorph, pantamorph, phenomorph, and pheromorph. These had roots in: phantasm — the wraith-like apparition; pantheism —seeing deity in all things; phenomenon — the thing as it makes itself known in the mind; pheromones — the smoke-like circumperambulations of smell driftings and signaling.

Remembering it is the nature of chi to be constantly morphing and projecting into other types of energy I thought of intromophics and kinemorphic. But with a psychological component. Mythomorph? — which is not a kind of lispy baby talk. What about euchariomorph? the tendency of everything to get changed into food.

I thought about the earth mother —the geomater — and geomorph, pertaining to, resembling the earth and its surface forms —geology. In geology we have metamorphic or heteromorphic rocks which combined with other elements and the idomorphic rocks which are self-contained. But that sounded idiotic. What about another word for this coherency in the crystallization process in a molten flow? This was automorphic. Changing into the self same is automorphic. Yes! The automorphic rocks are the gemstone, whose structure coheres even as they emerge and crystallize out of molten flows. Self generating. *That's* what I wanted.

My mind was active on these problems when I had the dream.

Something there is out there that is to man as man is to dream. Something that wants to go out of itself and come through and be known.

28 Me and Lao Tsu

I was finding that I was at times entering a world, that
was not timeless exactly but large. The ecology. The chaos
of life with its attractors and coherence and alignments. Yet
it was a Jungian world that spoke a telepathic language of
images. It was the context against which the content formed
a meaningful gestalt. Call it the Tao, the Form, the unconscious; I called it the synchronic.

The Tao, the union of opposites. My mind turned to Lao
Tsu and the Tao Te Ching. I had read it once in a big coffee
table edition with photographs, and remembered being
struck by how the antinomies were set up. However, in the
end, I became disenchanted with the work because I thought
Lao Tsu was manipulating this texture of opposites for a
confounding effect. But then, that summer on the farm when
I took it up again, I had to admit it was pretty modern, like
an abstract painting. I thought of it as "grinding on the
opposites".

I began taking lines out of the Tao Te Ching, and saying
them while doing movements. In particular vigorous boxing
movements, as if driving opposites to left and right.

— *driving a right in low uppercut to body*

    the crooked shall be made straight

— *driving a left uppercut to the body*

    the rough places

— *driving another right*

    shall be made smooth

— *a right*
    the pools

— *a left*
    . . . filled.

I began looking for the passages in the Tao Te Ching where there is this grinding of opposites toward the Mean. I wanted to have some great sing-songy rhythmic poem theater piece that I could recite while doing Tai Chi in lieu of making just the sounds, a theatre that would induce some kind of great trance-like state of being, a theatre in which I could somehow move from the rhythmic motion in time to a more timeless states --the synchronic. I got going on the Tao Te Ching, weaving lines from the great work into my theatre piece.

— *a little fish tail move with hand*

Actor: The empty is filled.

— *show a crotchety old man straightening up*

Actor: The old is renewed

— *he spreads his hands out*

Actor: Sustainer of all things.

The Great Tao flows everywhere.

```
     O          ,  O        ,  O  ,
   ' | '        ` ) - '      ` ) -
   >   <        /   >        <   \
```

It may go left

```
     O          O          O _ ,
   ' - (      ' | '        ) - '
   / <        >   <        >   <
```

or right.

```
     O          ,  O  ,        O
   ' | '        ` ) -       ' - (
   >   <        <   \       / <
```

All things depend on it for life, and it does not turn away from them.

I began quite a study of the Tao Te Ching. I found several translations of it in the UT library, and even bought

two editions at the Half-Price Book Store on Lavaca St. I
would have several translated versions of the Tao Te Ching
open at once and read across picking out the best one.

I thought to go through the Tao and find out if there
were some parallels to what I was seeing. I thought if I
were to start out writing the Tao Te Ching, the beginning
would be something like this:

> 1.
> The universe is fractal.
> And the binary tree
> is the archetype of the fractal.
>
> The old guys didn't have fractals
> so they called them "dragons"
> mythical beasts that go
> back to the dawn of creation.
>
> The universe is a chaos
> that settles down around attractors

—that ought to be somewhere in the Tao.

> It is a synchronistic universe,
> in which causality is the most often perceived
> connecting principle

—a special case.
Where does it say that in the Tao?

As I read the same passage across several translations
at once, they seemed to take on different characters. I
noticed some seemed scholarly and very awkward. Some
translations, written by the Confucianists, seemed embarrassed by the romantic nature of Lao Tsu's openness. I did
not find any translations that really got across the primary
experience or gave a sense of the looseness and gestural
openness and trusting innocence I thought was there. Maybe
someday I'd get to do that.

I did come up with a neat phrase myself: "quiescent
plenitude", which really did happen to me, and I could feel
the Old Man smiling at me in it. Lao Tsu says the space
between heaven and earth is a box with heaven for a lid and

earth for a floor. The medium between heaven and earth is a quiescent plenitude which can't be felt (by one within the box) and the more it moves, the more prolific it is. I really did slow down and feel the support of a kind of fluid I was floating in. I thought of Lao Tsu as Tesla and the space between heaven and earth is a capacitor with heaven for one plate and ground for the other.

14.
tao coming in to you through the world

moon up in the clear blue day
contrails arching
across the sky
indicate the curved
        orb of atmosphere
cirrus clouds high in the cold blue
The man in the Tao

Do you not see your self
in the branching trees
—your lungs and your nervous system —
they have been in this world much longer than
you have.
    These are representations of the Self.

Notice the Tao in a blade of grass
bending itself in the wind.

Do you not see your self
in the flowers?
—the flame of color struggling to burn bright
in celebration of the great sun —
you have these jewels of the body,
eyes ears taste touch
flowers in the light.
in the sound vibrations
in the molecular sea of disassociation
is the gentle winds and hard thud of pressure

29 stillness in motion (key concept)

Sometimes, for a brief moment when I was doing Tai Chi I'd get a feeling like it was not actually me doing the Form. It's like someone else has entered your body and is doing the Form along with you, causing your limbs to move in arcs like a hose suddenly filling with water and whipping around. This surging of fluid in the limbs causes them to move in the correct way automatically. Perhaps someone is inside of you? I don't know, or perhaps it is just the Chi flowing perfectly that causes your body to move automatically. I need to research this area more.

Standing in a relaxed Horse pose,
motionless, eyes closed,
hands slightly curled
at my side,
the way they like to be
when walking:
there was still some internal shifting,
as I went through various checks and balances
of vertical alignment
with each part
of the body
balanced
over lower part.

I start getting into the Tai Chi set,
easing out into that long slow walk
through the mnemonic theatre of Taoism,
where you are constantly making excursions from center
into insubstantiality
and nothingness,
and finding purchase
in your own ground.
Where your body is shifting
from center to stepping-out,
— again and again —
and from stepping-out, or twisting
back to
center.

It's like the idea of key-center in music.
The journey — away from, and then
back to the established ground —
is what adds tension and
resolution to the piece.

But my mind is still a riot of the day's affairs,
it keeps going in and out.
I was feeling sorry for myself.
The moves were starting to become
a stale repetition of the same old ritual.
Where was the FORM that had so bravely
instructed me before.
Everything was taking SO long....
I don't have 15 years to become a Tai Chi master.
It's not going to be my job in life.
I'm looking for my *enlightenment* here . . .
I want to feel:
what — as the pinnacle of creation on this planet —
I'm SUPPOSED
to be here to feel.
Where is that great divine pulse
driving everything?
I know intellectually that god is an endless sphere
whose center is everywhere
and whose circumference is nowhere,
and I'm down with that.
Hey, where else is the universe going
to be centered
except in you. That's
what you were created for. To experience
the source.
Well,
I'm *W A I T I N G*.

(Some days I get into such a pique of spiritual materialism.)

I try to calm myself down
with the circular breathing:
taking the breath

down into the expanding pelvis,
circling it back to the coccyx,
up the spine and over the top of the brain
and melting back down the forehead
and around
again.

I was looking for a strange whirling vortex
to begin to move me upon the surface of my breath,
in consonance
with the pulsing of my heart.
But it didn't. And
I began to wonder, WHY can't I be moved
by anything
anymore?

What moves me?

Then as if in a trance
my arms
LIFTED UP
ever so slowly
a few inches, a few more, a foot, 2 feet!
I stood there
held by an outside force.

I waited to see if
it would move
my foot.
And lo and behold, when my weight
is completely off one foot
and completely on the other foot,
(when I was completely balanced on one foot)
the other foot slowly rose up!
There was MOVEMENT!
And I stepped forward into a ward-off position
and found myself back in the center of my vehicle again.
SOMEHOW
I had gotten out of the way
and *had been moved* from

ward-off left to
ward-off right.

So That's! what we are
trying to achieve.
IT was still trying to learn
and teach me
to listen
through the body.

We are like the magnetic needle
of an early pa-kua compass
floating in a clear bowl of water
on a mirror table;
reflecting the motion
of clouds going by
in a blue
SKY.

Oh Vehicle,
moving in a field of golden gravity,
giver of everything between heaven and earth
— I enter you and give myself over,
so that you
may enter me.

I was starting to have lots of questions, and found the books I was getting my hands on confusing. Especially their use of the concept of Energy. I figured out yin and yang were probably potential and kinetic energy.

One night I saw Yum Chi in my dreams. He was a kindly, older, humble, Chinese gentleman. I saw him sweeping the sidewalk in front of his house in an unknown city. He just smiled at me.

The Form, began to more formally intimate the teaching. I'd be walking on the path out to the garden and hear sentences to write. Or I'd awaken from a dream, reading something in a book. I started trying to get it down as best I could in the note pad by the bed. More and more I'd wake up in the mornings and find that Yum Chi was suggesting things to me. I thought I'd better write it down, perform a service for the old guy. Maybe it's just myself telling me things or perhaps it could actually be a guide or some angel telling me things.

The Introduction came in little parts over a long time as other parts were written and more was known about the book. The Introduction revealed many of the concepts of the users guide. I broke it out into manual style. It was like a perfect book that answered my questions.

Somatic Intelligence

**A manual
for answering the questions
generated by the western
mind surrendering to the
wisdom of the body**

by
Sifu Yum Chi
with Walker Underwood

Purpose

The purpose of this course is to teach you how to play Tai Chi for the pleasure of exploring body movement in space for its own intrinsic and spiritual reward. Or for dance, martial art and theatre.

Introduction

This book is a journal of my experiences learning Tai Chi. It does not teach you Tai Chi step by step, with pictures and description of body part positions. It assumes you have already gone through that long period of ritual learning in which you progressively challenge your balance. This book is to answer the many questions that are inspired by the Form as someone starts to know it, and wants to deepen their experience of it.

Disciplines

We will be using many disciplines, from physics and biomechanics to eastern religion. We will explore the philosophy of movment of Rudoph Laban, inventor of a dance notation. In order to get a frame of reference in which to integrate the profound influences of somatic practice, we will explore concepts in Taoist energetics. Our goal is to get you set up to do improvisational Tai Chi. You will learn what to move, how to move it, and why we are moving it. The course is organized around the what, how and why.

Visualizations

From time to time in this manual we will have shorter or longer visualizations. There is a beautiful poetic in the visualizations that Tai Chi uses to help you organize your body attention. For example: "Gecko feet." You see how they can run up a sliding glass door and adhere there by using little suction cups on their feet. Tai Chi asks you to plant your feet in a way that you are in a sense gripping the ground. In organizing yourself to do that, you must make sure that you are not cantilevered and easily tipped, but that your weight is evenly settled into the feet. Use visualization to organize many body parts under a simple control. As in "hanging a weight from the tailbone." That aids you in bringing your weight into the center of the support area.

As you begin to find yourself, in this everyday world, maybe lofting some sheets onto the bed or making a low slide across the car seat, and realize how you've been blessed with all kinds of kinetic highs (Chi experiences) you will long to be more and more in these moments of grace. Just remember to do things with ease. Do things with a lightness in your heart and it will be reflected in the lightness of the way you move and touch the world. Don't be trapped in always trying to achieve the idea of great perfection and being driven by its associated guilt from constantly having to compare against it. We get this report card syndrome from our religion: that grace is like a bank statement that we must check our balance against. A bank account with energy running out. How dreary and heavy. Heaviness of heart makes you sink. Lightness lets you soar. Keep doing Tai Chi out in the world, in easy push, in roll back, in separate, in press and you'll find that sometimes you will be stepping into the moment, the current now moment of existence.

Parallel Times

When you set out to do the Tai Chi Long Form the process of relaxing into yourself moves through three distinct phases or frames. The Fixed Frame, the Lively Frame and the Changing Frame. These stages of progressive relaxation and atunement can be thought of as roughly corresponding to the 3 sections of Tai Chi. They are also the stages of a players growth over this lifetime. I think of Tai Chi and the Tao as reflecting this self-similarity across parallel time scales.

Basic Principles

But you might wonder: There must be some easier way to remember all these moves! Some kind of abstract hierarchy that organized them. On the most basic level just watch what the body does, think about how it moves, the twisting body to evade, the gripping and wringing body to hold on. When you start to be able to mentally visualize going through the moves, to actually stand outside yourself and watch a simulation of yourself, then you will have entered the 2nd phase of your Tai Chi development, the Lively Phase. You can think of all the possible kinds of holds and grabs and situations you can get into and work out several ways of getting out — always breaking the incoming down into its situation. But at the beginning it does seem ridiculous that you have to learn all this *material,* down to the angle of motion and the proportion of the weight for each move. Surely there must be some easier way. Some way to abstract the information into a few basic principles.

And indeed there is: The 8 gates. The ancient system of the 8 gates is an organization principle (index) that cuts through the plethora of moves in Tai Chi.

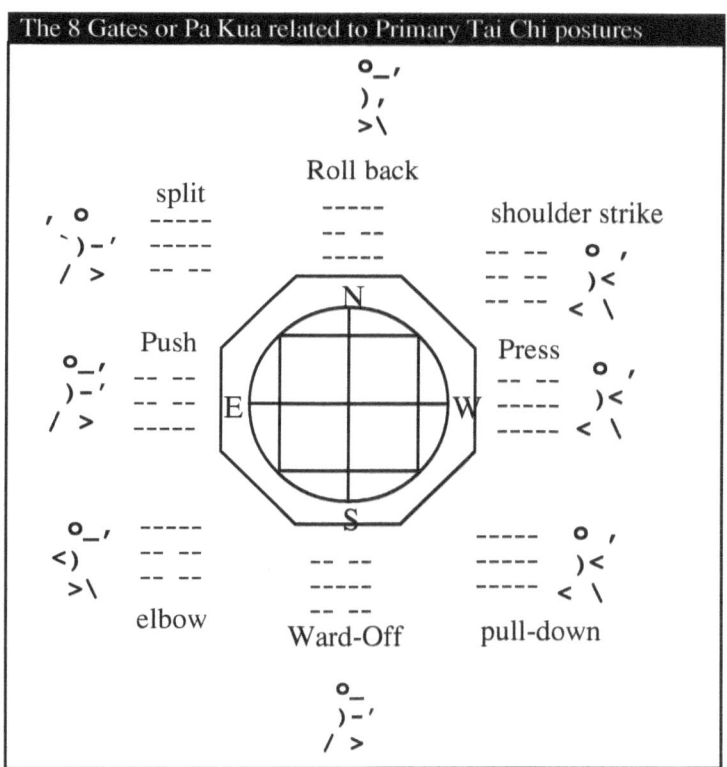

The 8 Gates or Pa Kua related to Primary Tai Chi postures

Probably more has been written about the topic of the 8 gates, and variations on the trigrams and the hexagrams than any other subject. A good introduction is the little book by Da Liu, titled *Tai Chi Ch'uan and I Ching — A Choreography of Body and Mind.* He relates the movements in Tai Chi to trigrams and the hexagrams of the I Ching. For the

beginner this work will appear arbitrary and almost axiomatic. This may be because the writers, having a deep lifetime
experience with the I Ching, not to mention being able to
read the names of the hexagrams in Chinese, are very used to
the elegance it brings to their world. On the other hand, it
may be they have a complete lack of feeling on the subject.
But in any case, these associations of energies and the
archetypes they coalesce into, are expressed in the hierarchical trigrams of the I Ching and they are displayed on a grid
of quadrants of the cardinal and ordinal directions. The
Circle in the Square.

Suffice it to say that these 8 movements are supposed to
be the basic moves of Tai Chi and are sufficient to span the
space, i.e. upon them the other moves are embellishments.

Deconstructing Tai Chi Forms to find Basic Principles

With the 8 Kua, we begin deconstruction — of what you
had learned as a kind of ritualistic placement and stance —
to see the stance's "meaning" in the sense of being used in a
martial arts situation.

Start by looking in Tai Chi for the basic movements:

[push, press] would be the compress, where you placed
your weight into the other, or compressed and folded into
yourself, the way a cat kind of goes limp . . .

[Roll back, ...] would be neutralization, where you
removed any way for opponent to get hold on you

They had these special Chinese words: p'eng (wardoff)
lu (rollback) chi (press) and an (push) on the ordinal, and

Attract to emptiness and discharge; Attach (chan, lien,
t'ien, sui) split, shoulder without losing the attachment on
the diagonal.

You might think, Yes! Apply the system over and over.
Break it down. There are stances and hand movements.

Stances. There were some 4 stances from which one was
either leaving or going to in the main sequence:

1. a bow or horse,

2. the cat, —one weighted foot, usually a transition or a
prep to kick

3. the dragon, strong pushing with back leg extended
like a tail

4. push, not so long as the dragon, set up for a punch

Plus the kicks. And the Hands
And you just linearly go through and exercise all the joints of the body from a standing perspective.

For example, Hands. Starting in Post.

Stretch out to the bow; flex the bow. Which is the arch made as if you were hugging a big tree. Turn the hand over in an up and down direction.

Language of Effort

In order to help you look at yourself and how you are using your body to relate to space, time, weight, and flow we'll discover Laban and his language of effort.

For example, the act of getting up out of a chair: the effort was light and strong muscle tension against weight and is flexible and direct in space. In the first movement of getting up, we plant the legs and scrunch up the stomach, maybe brace the arms on a chair arm, we are bent and twisted, getting ready to unwind (strong and flexible) going into, then the second movement though it is direct in time it, stretches out in space.

It can be a quick jump up or a sustained and stately rise.

The flow of the whole moment can be fluent or bound. The fluent effort cannot be easily arrested, while the bound can be stopped at any moment. That fluency is what we are trying to achieve in practical Tai Chi. Later we will get more specific about Intertia and Force in uniform motion.

It is quite an awakening to become aware of your movements that way. Studying Laban will help your Tai Chi practice move from the Fixed Phase into its second phase — the Lively Phase.

The Secret of the Kua

It takes quite a long time before you learn the true meaning of the mandala of kua. I'll take you through the explorations of the Lively Phase in the next several chapters, but here I'll sum up the simple results. It is about the joints. The 8 kua are the 8 joints associated with the major muscle groups. The Feet, the Legs, the Knees, the Hips, the Back, the Shoulders, the Elbows and the Hands. The particular basic moves are designed to exercise these joints.

In playing Tai Chi, especially outside in the forest — think of yourself as a kind of Virtual Instrument. With your body, you and your attention can play a kind of music of awareness: watching, noticing —especially out of peripheral vision — what the light is doing to the objects around you. Notice too, what articulating (miming) this awareness in your motion does to them — the trees and the leaves and the projection of your own shadow. Notice the way objects manipulate themselves to be in the way of light and how objects — to hide and reveal other objects — turn spaces of awareness on and off. It is a kind of dance in which the whole body is the instrument. In order to play the "music", you have to *be* the music. The Music of Awareness.

The "music" is the moment to moment feeling of existence, the presence of place. Music composed in the moment and played inside the head from sounds heard on the fly.

Visualization: (Body as stringed instrument)

The arms swinging out are the violins
the bowing and movements of the legs
are the deep tones of the basses.
The breath resonating with the movement
of the air (buoyed up on an ocean
of atmosphere and gravity) is the voice.
It helps you listening to *the* Voice . . . calling.
Together they embody
the power of your own body.

And I saw my next series of moves
as a Kandinsky composition,
wild, strange lines and crazy curves
being sketched in front of me
and the spaces being shaped
had the most soft and endearing colors,
that made you want to protect and love them —
colors like maple leaves, and cranberries,
the multifoliate rose with the most fragile bleed
of color blending at its edge where it ends.
And where the edges left off, there was dissolve
movement into other living systems.

The Form as Virtual Instrument

I wanted to create a machine, a vehicle to get into, a kind of mnemonic theatre, a philosophical mandala, a simulation of metaphysical experience. All these attributions are summed up in the *pa kua*, which is a kind of geomancy compass in *feng shui* from long ago, (so much has been written about it). It is a grid or scale that you could throw down on the ground, or in the space you are in and in that way, you created a sensitized ritual performance space.

Consider the motion of the body and hands in Tai Chi and imagine using them to play a kind of virtual Theramin. Things give off vibrations. Things are in circuits with each other and you change the circuit by your presence. Like the way you change inductance and capacitance. There might be a sociology circuit, . . .

The Tai Chi ball is capacitor (mainly there for you to learn about moving the legs and hips first to get to the alignment).

The hands are velocity wands — like virtual batons — used as they are with a regular theramin, where you have two antennas coming out of a box: one antenna going up and the other going sideways. There you use your left hand and right hand to control volume and frequency of sounds coming out the speaker. Effectively when you move your hand near the antenna, your mass changes the inductance of the antennas; then the voltages on a capacitor somewhere change the frequency of an oscillator, or the volume envelope of the sound. Here you want to move in a way such that the hands don't move until the body does. You are playing gravity, making sure you are balanced under the hands. You return a great sensitivity to the hands, the hands were for listening.

People relax when watching you, as they see you relax.

Think of the ball that you are holding and shaping as you do Tai Chi as being moved closer to, and pulled away from, various objects in the space. And *that*, gets reflected in some way that was admissible and has meaning to the player.

The Tai Chi Keyboard

The player moves in the 10 directions as we watch him create, conjecture and conjure in this Taoist theatre.

When the Taoist goes into a space —the glade or a

room, he sets out a mental *pa kua*, which could point in any direction one can move. Usually it points to the business end of the situation, to the incoming, to the direction of something you want to look at: wind, sun, audience, opponent. You are the instrument, or the world is the instrument and the *pa kua* is the scale, the notation . . .

You can think of it as playing a big piano by dancing on a big keyboard like Tom Hanks did in the movie "Big." Except you don't have to run a really long distance to play large intervals, because in our Virtual Instrument the "notes" are laid out in an octagon of three interlocking rows of trigrams that bring the full *pa kua* scale within close range.

The 8 Gates or Pa Kua related to Primary Tai Chi postures

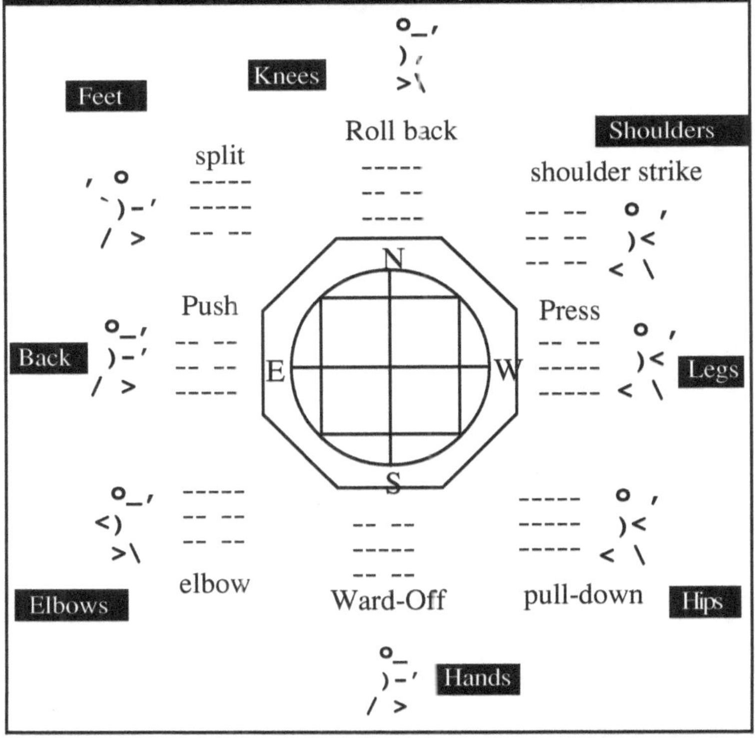

Feet | Knees | Roll back | Shoulders

split — shoulder strike

Back — Push — Press — Legs

Elbows — elbow — Ward-Off — pull-down — Hips

Hands

Authentic Movement

The aim of this Music as Awareness approach to Tai Chi is to develop a whole-body art form that was theatrical, spiritual, musical and useful: theatrical, in the sense of an actor liberated from being controlled by his emotions; spiritual, in a Taoist, deep-ecology, real, physical sense as opposed to church; musical, in the sense of tuning and listening to the world; and useful in the sense of being practical for work and defending yourself with martial arts.

It is a discipline that both limits the number of influences — thus shielding from the anxiety of influence — and that stimulates the composer, performer and spectator in you and in the theatre in which you dwell. This might only be something you do for yourself or just in front of a mirror or in front of an audience. This California-Zen Aesthetic circa mid-1970s delivers you from the received opinions of the status quo, but at the same time liberates you with confidence so that you could, in the real now moment of existence, get into a 'true' dialogue between movement, the free energy of place and performance. By performance I refer not only to the actions of the Tai Chi player / Taoist actor, but to the very nature of the visual, sensory, performance space, and the various modes of 'theatricality' which might occur within the space. It was the total art work. Imagined a text written large off the page into space with images being created by the body and the voice doing incantations. The idea is that one would speak about things and energies and mime handling them. Music is a superior art to poetry alone, because of its inherent connection to motion in the world, and this has to get described in the abstract language of notation. A language in which the words are objects, sounds, — motions.

Let yourself think of the objects in the space as Spirit Tokens, (or maybe Ghosts, in the sense of psychological constructs — blocks, paranoias, obsessions, addictions — are entities) that stood between you and really feeling the world through your personality. Envision the world as an arrangement of custom-designed 'Controllers' and 'Virtual Instruments' that were augmented by Proximity Sensors. Ultimately the world **is** a skrim over "light". Seeking the light is the most basic motivation of living things. We *are* light, assault vehicles.

Learning Tai Chi becomes mastering the movements required to play this "Instrument" fluidly.

Psychological and Physical approach

We need to know how to approach Tai Chi from both the physical standpoint and the psychological.

Physical Approach

From the physical standpoint let's examine alignment, floating, folding.

From the physical standpoint, we'll go through a check list for standing. Pay particular attention to the shoulders, examine hand position and how to tuck the tail bone under in a sitting sensation.

We are looking at the basis for the 8 basic configurations of the body —the gates, the *kua*.

Feet, Floating, alignment

In the opening move of Tai Chi Chuan, called Raise Hands, the forearms and hands are raised vertical (by sinking the elbows) and the hands are allowed to be — floating through the wrist joint — on the forearm. Ideally one can get this same feeling of floating balance for the whole body — through alignment. The shoulders and hips are in alignment and the torso is floating on the hips. The hips are floating on the legs and feet. This is all achieved through alignment in which there is a minimum cantilever in the forward, backward sideward directions. Weight is evenly distributed on the sole (that is the whole) of the feet. Furthermore, one is to maintain this alignment throughout the forms. In particular, during the rotation of the body about the central axis of the spine. This is achieved by maintaining the shoulders in alignment with the hips.

Refinements

The seated-down sensation also implies: the shoulders relaxing, the hands hanging, the waist and buttocks loosening, even the gut hanging out. Feeling good after a good meal.

Hang the head from a sky hook on high elongating the neck. Nothing cantilevered. Then stop thinking about it. Like when you are walking — that relaxed.

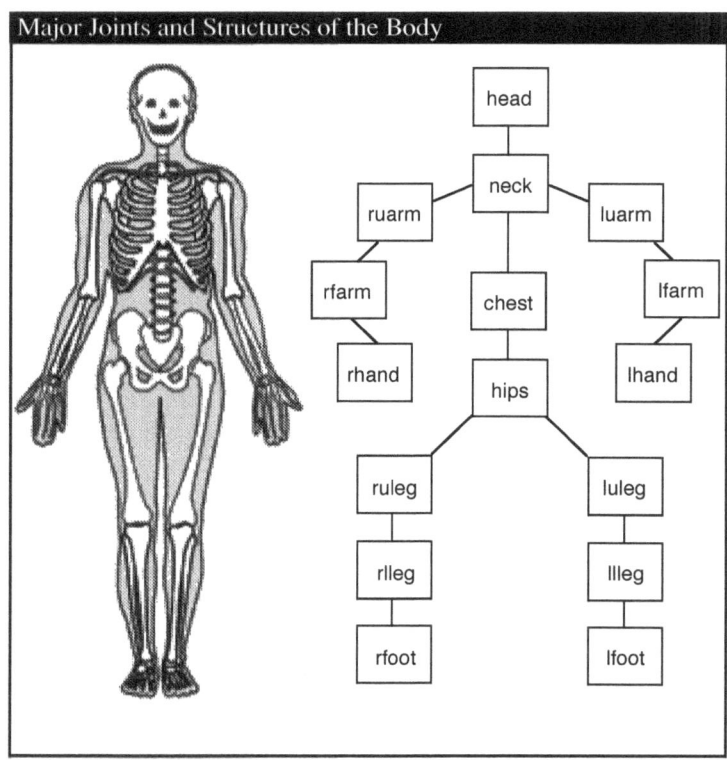

What does it feel like to finally get connected? Try several standing positions. Think of your self in a seated down position.

Sink your Chi after each movement. You want to always be coming back to this basic state. Each move should transition through this sinking relaxation state on its way to the next move.

Psychological Approach

There are many psychological approaches to Tai Chi. We will mention here briefly several:
1. the idea of shadowboxing with your Reactive, unsupportive Self
2. developing your sense of visualizing the body
3. the placement of attention
4. becoming sensitive to the Now

Tai Chi is a form of moving meditation and any progress in meditation is helpful with your Tai Chi.

Inner selves
There are at least 2. Self 1 is anything that gets in the way of your playing well. Self 1 is the criticizing voice in your head talking to you while you play and giving you instructions. It may say things like "that sounded terrible", or "curve your fingers", "relax", etc. Self 2 is the self that already knows how to play. Self 2 is often hampered by Self 1's chattering.

There are many ways to do Tai Chi. You can act, and imbue your Tai Chi playing with physical and dramatic attributes. Is it going to be hard-edged, and getting off anger? Is it going to be soft-edged and feeling, exploring? Is it going to be done in a small closed framed or a large stretched out frame? Are you going to be like a priest in a metaphysical continuum reaching up and communing with the energies and generosities of nature. Or are you going to be kind of punked-out and doing the moves in a desultory manner. Are you in a ballet, doing it with expressive energy? Are you the old man and the sea holding back the tides of time? Are you a smoothie.

Visualization.
You need to know that the next move is from any point. You need to be able to go over the whole form mentally. In the Lively Phase, the journeyman phase, you start bringing the Tai Chi internal, so that you can feel — just from your imagination — the kinetic sensations of doing Tai Chi.

34 The Human Body Inertia Tensor

A number of choices comes up as you get into the Form. You may go it fast and hard-edged, or slow and soft-edged; it may be an outer set, or an inner set. There are so many ways. You can exaggerate and pretend you are stretched out like putty. Or perhaps you just want to throw off the tyranny of the day's disappointments and breathe; and follow your feet. All the moves have a beginning middle end. A getting ready, a wind-up and a delivery —be that delivery in the reverse direction, in escape. You have a set grammar for each move and you see there are repeats — after all there are only four basic stances, bow, cat, horse, empty.

Martial art is a language in dialog. What are the hands doing? Left hand is throwing a block, and the right hand is curved to slip back around and get a wrist lock to possibly grapple. You have seen the character of a move and sensed the statement made through the body with more or less authority. The statements can create poetry in motion. To develop this language metaphor, we introduce the matrix which collects together an expression for all the limb segments — rather their masses and the resultant inertia — that must be overcome to have them change position. This matrix, in field theory, is a tensor.

Chen Wei-Ming (1929 Shanghai) was speaking about the inertia tensor of the human body when he wrote:

"Seeking suppleness enables you to separate your body into pieces. If an opponent pushes against your forearm, your elbow doesn't move; if against your elbow it moves, but not your shoulder; if against your shoulder, it moves but not your body; if against your body it moves but not your waist; if against your waist it moves but not your leg. This process leaves you as stable as a mountain. When you discharge your opponent, then it is from the feet through the legs to the waist, body, shoulders, elbows, and hands —all connected as one unit, discharging energy like an arrow toward its target. If you cannot relax, your whole body becomes one piece and, even though it is strong, a strong person will be able to push your one piece and cause you to be unstable. Thus the use of suppleness is crucial. With it you can be one unit attacking and fragmented parts defending—able to be

relaxed and hard, agile stepping forward and back, and substantial and insubstantial as needed. With these abilities you will then have all cf the Tai chi function."
— trs: Pang Jeng Lo, Smith (1985 Berkeley)

To translate that lovely descriptive statement of how the body is articulated across folding joints into a more general one, we will use the concept of the matrix —the inertial tensor matrix of the human body. The human inertia tensor **I** expresses the cross-coupling of joints.

$$
\mathbf{I} = \begin{pmatrix}
I_{11} & I_{12} & I_{13} & . & \\
I_{21} & I_{22} & I_{23} & . & \\
I_{31} & I_{32} & I_{33} & & \\
. & . & . & & \\
. & . & . & & I_{nn}
\end{pmatrix}
$$

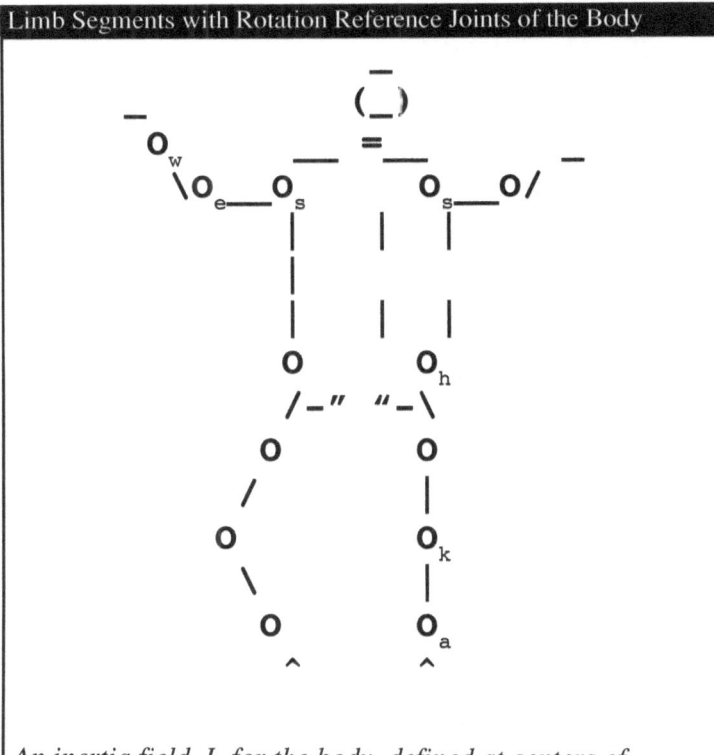

Limb Segments with Rotation Reference Joints of the Body

An inertia field, I_{ij} for the body, defined at centers of rotation O_i for each of the primary body segements.

If all the joints were mutually independent, it would be a state of supreme looseness. That is to say, if the Matrix were a positive-definite matrix with only elements down the diagonal, and no cross coupling, it would indicate coupling factors among joints do not exist. These cross-couplings are tensions and rigidities, sometimes even fused muscles.

It is the responsibility of the Tai Chi player to get the cross-coupling and lumped inertial moments (which are unstreamlined mass) as small as possible to insure well lubricated movements of the joints.

This is a kind of tuning. It is of the most important work of Tai Chi to relax these couplings to reduce the mechanical noise, and this tuning lets one feel reality a lot more.

The Kua in a Field Analogy

You've seen how a wind hits water and spreads out quickly in ripples. The surface of the water is a tensor.

An example: if your shoulder is being pushed back, the hip must rotate accordingly and your kua will open like a door. To clarify, the kua is a hinge that connects the opposite side of the body to the part being pushed. When you push a sphere it reacts instantly proportional to the push, rotating the push past coming around with a push its own. Around the outside of the sphere are 'great circles'— geodesics (the shortest line in a curved space) that you could use by opening and closing the kua, to let this kind of electromagnetic or tensor-force energy be redistributed to ground through the easiest methods possible.

For example, outside when you see lightning, know that lightning is seeking the easiest path to ground with respect to its surroundings. When you get into a fight, you need to get into this dynamic cage, the manifold that is shifting in time. The cage you have around you, is for directing and lining-up the integration with the earth making a path for the lightning to ground. This tensor is the manifold, the space, the cage, in which there are many potential vectors.

```
      /  \./  \/\_
   _{!\_ _e_   )  e/!\  ──    o   |‾‾‾‾|
  /  /\_/!\._e_/  //  /  ─ ─  \_/|\  |____|
 (  (__{(@)e\__e.//_/__  ──    /__/   ‾‾‾‾
 \__/{/(_)\_e  )\\ \\-  ──  /\     |‾|__
   (  (__)_)_/  )\ \>  ──  |  \   |\|  ‾
    \_/     \_/\/\/  ─ ─ -^   -^   /  \___
      \_,-'
```

The Head is the Root

The Beginner starts with an inverse kinematics approach to learning Tai Chi. That is, he gets an image of the static postures to be obtained and goes about arranging himself to fit into the posture. The motion is: to move through some transition and settle into some final look at the end. This is called inverse kinematics because the balance and organizing principle is from the outer limbs and extremities toward the center.

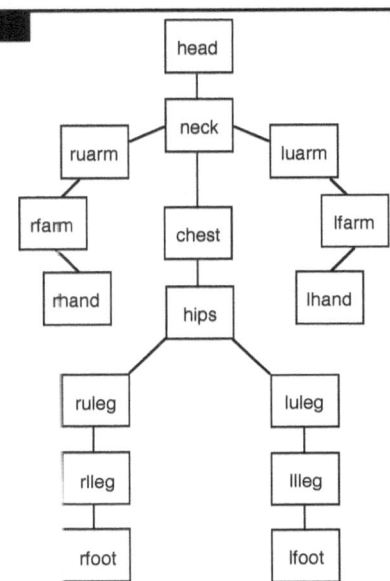

The Hips are the Root

The next phase in learning Tai Chi is to shift the attention and focus to the center, and have that *center* inform the disposition of the limbs and extremities. This is done by associating a fluid called Chi logically with lower torso region of the body, and allowing this fluid — emerging from this center — to be the end-effector of the disposition of extremities. It is like water suddenly turned on and making a hose whip around. In real-time interaction, one maintains the Chi within the supporting polygon for static balance. In the Lively Phase you have to loosen up the pelvis and the hip as a mechanism for motion balancing, and *sourcing* all motion.

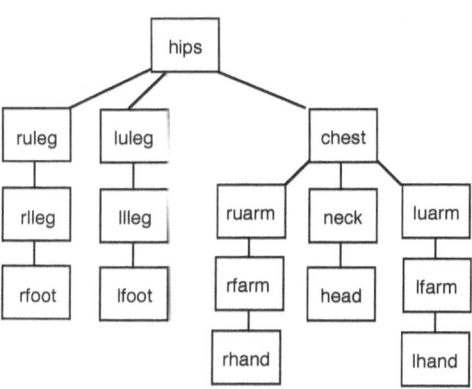

Wave Hands Like Clouds

Wave Hands Like Clouds

It was a relief to get to this move in the form,
it was as if a vortex @

@ the whirl-swirl
vortex
moving mandala

came along and dragged me aloft into the sky

```
   o        o        o_,      ,o     , o     , o ,    , o
 '-(     ' | '     )-'    _`)    `)-'    `)-    `)-'
 /<       > <      > <      /<      / >      < \      / >
```

and I became this huge wind quickly shifting around
touching the wall of the perimeter of my charge.

```
   o        o        o_,      ,o     , o     , o ,    , o
 '-(     ' | '     )-'    _`)    `)-'    `)-    `)-'
 /<       > <      > <      /<      / >      < \      / >
```

I could dissolve myself in the vaporous mist of clouds
    my arms became shreds of fog moving through the trees,
back and forth across my all-seeing eyes looking in all
directions.

```
 ;o.          o           o        (o)
 | '        `| ,    `  -(-'          (
 < \        < \        < \         < \
```

Ideograms
Yun shou (prounced: yoon show)
Cloud hands

Wave Hands Like Clouds
Gathering Clouds

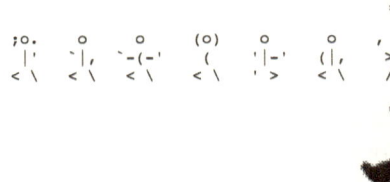

Above:
clouds gathering,
hanging from sky,
falling drops, rain

Mid: Vapors rising
up to heaven.
(Cloud Speaking)

Bottom: hand

Wave hands like clouds

37 blocks and grabs in wave hands like clouds

I began to notice the
blocks and grabs and
etc. in wave hands like
clouds. It was a great
grappling thing.

Here are 16 kinds of hand
movement forms:
push,
support,
carry,
thrust,
block,
parry,
interception,
smash,
grasp,
twist,
hook,
punch,
seal,
closure,
dodge
and stretch

all to be used in a flexible manner
in attack and defense,
in preemptive strikes and in
dissolving the opponent's force.

Much to my shock and dismay
I managed to get a slipped disc.
It taught me a lot about the spine.
We are
RETICULARIANS
Each vertebra is cushioned by
a disc
— in between —
to act as a shock absorber.
The disc is soft on the outside,
but contains a liquid substance inside of it.
The discs allow the joints to move
smoothly.
If the disc tears and the inner substance
flow out,
you have
what is called
a ruptured disc.
It is like an IT's IT ice cream cookie sandwich
in which the ice cream has oozed
out
of the slipped disc.
Then
it passes out stress
to all the support,
it gets mixed up with the signals
going up and down the spine,
and propagates itself all over the body
in sympathetic vibration.
Repeated incorrect bending or lifting can cause a
slipped disc.

After hobbling around for a week,
I decided the slipped disc was a gift too.
It showed me
I was still way out of touch
with what this was about.
I need to learn how

to get my base
set so that it is
always under me.
Not cantilevered.
Lack of MINDFULNESS
will always get you
in the L5.
All the
lower back
vectors
focus on
that joint.

Feeling the skeleton beneath,
you start to dialog with gravity.

Feel the joints,
especially the knees
as pumps to move gravity along,
move the Force along.

Maybe the joints really are
beautiful crystal jewels
in the clockworks of the body,
like transducers
—pizo-electric transducers—
that convert mechanical energy
to electrical
and electrical to mechanical.

Must always keep the alignment.

We are QUATERNIONS
— numbers —
in a partly-real and partly-imaginary space
(we are evolved reticularians)
and our body is a vector space
with everything going
through the *tan tien*
the center of mass.

squat down
The natural way

squat down.
feet slightly wider than shoulder width apart.
toes out,
hands out slightly above your knees
(for counter balance)
breath deep filling your chest.
This forces your back into a straight line
from neck to tailbone.
Don't want a rounded back when squatting.

Looking straight ahead,
raise your hands out straight in front of you.
as you
lower yourself another 10 inches
Keeping your weight on your heels
and your feet flat on the floor.
Center of mass is
over support
and under load.

Squat down!
Thou art but a monkey pooping in the woods.
Adopt a relaxed, FULL SQUAT POSTURE
and the anal canal STRAIGHTENS.
Squat Down
when dropping a load
use the Asian / French / Italian /Turkish / Mexican toilet
SQUAT DOWN.
The current toilet seat is a comparatively new invention,
contra natura,
developed in the Industrial revolution
of Victorian England by the Queen's plumber Mr. Crapp
who thought it was more 'dignified'
to sit on a 'throne'
than the way the natives did.

SQUAT DOWN
when lifting a load.
Improper lifting causes most back injuries.
Correct lifting procedures:
Stand close to the load with feet wide apart.
Squat down,
bending at the hips and knees.
As you grip the load, arch your lower back inward
by pulling your shoulders back
and sticking your chest out.
Be sure to keep the load close to your body.
When you set the load down,
    squat down,
bending at the hips and knees,
keeping your lower back arched in.

Squat Down
when lifting a load
or "dropping a load".
Pull down thy vanity,
become human.

Squat down.
Feel this world
passing through the body . . .

It was the rain. . .
I was standing under an awning in front of a bank.
Yes. I think it was a bank or a real estate office
and it was raining,
and the rain was coming down
and it struck me, it was gravity
that made the rain fall down.
I realized that I can get under an awning
and shield myself from the rain;
there is no shielding from gravity.
I was standing there
watching the moving throng of people hustling by
and for a moment
I slipped into one of those reveries
you get into when you are sidetracked by rain
and have to wait.
Have you ever noticed that?
How time kind of
stops in the rain.
(What if time IS like a river? And it flows
around things and there can be turbulence and
circulating static points in the flow.)
And I kind of slipped
into this movie.
It was supposed to be called
I walk among them but am not of them

Movie
    This film follows a man's lonely wanderings on a rainy
night in a modern city. We hear his thoughts in Voice-over
as he begins to feel intimations of alien transcendence, as he
thinks about his physical evolution, and feels a kind of
connection to other civilizations in space.

Scene: *Looking up into rain. Light illuminating falling drops
from below. Streets lights, shop window lights, reflections of
moving car windows. Background of bright rain-slick
reflections off moving streetcars. People moving past. Shop
windows streaked with dissolving neon signs. There is*

*heaviness of the city in the background. We hear traffic and
the conversations of moving people walking by.*

Scene: *Short Asian people, with bags, trudging along the
sidewalk. We see our tall character in the background
behind them under a big corner awning in what appears to
be a bank. He is quite out of place. We hear his thoughts in
voice-over.*

Voice over:
    Gravity draws the rain down to earth,

Scene: *He begins experimenting with his balance, teetering
back and forth on his toes and heels for a moment, then
settling down.*

Voice over:
    Man has always recognized its force:
        . . . fear of falling; . . . up and down.

Scene: *Ball falls to ground in slow motion*

Voice over:
    It moves the earth around the sun.

Scene: *Deep space animation of the moon orbiting the earth.*

Voice over:
    Gravity is the feeling of reality.
    The simplest assault on gravity is made by the tree,
    by the column, the strut, the member.

Scene: *Skyscraper building implodes in slow motion*

Voice over:
    What is it when they implode those buildings?
    They just know . . how to . . . cut the supports and
    the building falls under its own weight.
(*pause*)
    Yes Gravity THAT's what the Old Man must
    have been trying to describe with the concept of the Tao.

The Tao is gravity: all paths . . . must get their purchase
. . . to continue . . . on the way . . . by upsetting and finding
balance.

You can't see it but it permeates all things. Every object
in the universe . . . is attracted . . . to every other object . . .
dependent on how large their mass is, . . . big planet or a
little person. . . . It is our destiny. . . . And the force of . . .
attraction falls of . . . as the square of the separation—the
distance between them.

Tai Chi means separation.

It is the martial art that teaches people how to find . . .
their center . . . and knowing this . . . how to separate the
opponent . . . from his center . . . so that they fall.
(*pause*)

I started feeling the fragility and elegance of human
bipedal motion, feeling a kind of kinship to the people
dashing around under awnings in the rain.

Scene: *Slow motion parade of humanity carrying bags.
Zoom in on the action of the knee. Zoom in on the backs like
yokes carrying weight.*

Voice-over:

We are in possession of all the tools . . .
We evolved from simple machines . . .
What about me? How do I walk?
Here on the ground. . .
I walk by using my feet as levers. . .
The bones are levers! (*excited, discovering, insightful*)
And joints . . . which act as pivot points or fulcrums!
And muscles apply force!
to the lever bones at specific points.

Scene: *Actor begins pacing, (walking the boards).*

Voice-over:

I began doing this performance on the street corner
under the bank awning, in the rain, in front of GOD and
everybody. I decided, *what the hell*. Nobody knows me in
this town, and I was just feeling so alien and I just started
talking out loud, to no one in particular.

Actor:
  The Knee is a pulley!
  . . . to. . . to. . . to redirect

(tracing the motion of force as he lifts his knee)
  the line of action of a force
  exerted by a muscle.
  So is of course the butt!

Actor: (*Sticks his butt out and winks at the "audience")*
  From the vertical to the horizontal.
    Through many redirections
    . . . where the load to be moved is,
    where the fulcrum is and
    where the force is.
    This Force is the Effort!

Voice-over: *(fastidious, righteous like he is some kind of
tour guide for aliens and illustrating the movements)*
  The way we walk . . . Gravity produces a force which
always pulls the man down, toward the earth. In order to
move, the bipedal primate must make two forces. One, in the
upright direction away from the earth with his reticulated
spine and the other with its feet and legs in the direction of
desired motion.
  The force on the bottom of the ball of the foot is the
foot acting like a lever. Yes, the ball of the foot is the
fulcrum for moving the man! . . . Then the knee is a pulley!
(illustrate with movement) . . . that lifts the leg off the
ground,
    (Isn't it amazing that evolution would just figure this
out from pure mechanistic forces?) But then, what else?

  The foot lever lifts the body by a pulley motion around
the heel. The leg is pulled up by a pulley motion around the
knee. The body is leaned forward by a pulley around the
butt. To walk fall forward and we let a leg fly out and under
to catch ourselves from falling. *(illustrate with movement)*

Scene: *Actor says the following while performing pure,
exaggerated, almost gawky movement.*

Actor: *(thrusting a leg out to start walking)*
    then we thrust the whole body forward
        so that it is falling
        ratchet the leg out front get it
        under the body to catch it
        from falling.
(bending low and reaching a leg way out)
    Gravity is our Friend!
    Reach out with your foot and feel the
    gravity as you fall into it.

Voice over:

I don't know. For some reason I was really feeling a lot. The idea of being able to say what the Tao was, that the Tao was Gravity was freaking me out with the magnitude of the implication.

Gravity is the secret operating in the heart of every star, making possible the reactions of nuclear and electromagnetic force. It controls energy as well as matter; time slows down and space is warped by its pull. There is no escape from its force. The gravity game of dropping things on the floor and seeing if they fall every time is the first game we play as children. Gravity is steady and changeless. It is within all things and affects all things; it is what holds the universe together. Gravity is the resistance against which the stuff of life forms its existence. Newton and the western enlightenment showed us how it shapes all forms.

I was alert to the fragility and elegance of human bipedal motion, and feeling a kind of kinship to the people dashing around under awnings in the rain. Somehow it was all mixed up with gravity and sentient being all over the universe. And I was feeling so alien, and almost kind of relieved that at least physics was the same on other planets.

I began to imagine people in beings on other planets, -- they would have the same concept of wonder and appreciation of the complexity, and the awe, ... Bilateral symmetry, sexual reproduction. . .
(actor shivers, shakes his head)

Voice over:

I become afraid, the thought occurs to me: I'm not

supposed to know this. I become afraid I'll get some kind of permanent nausea.

Scene: *(close up, eyes wet, tears welling)*

Voice over:

After a while I began to go into a kind of meltdown. I thought I might dissolve into the blurry neon reflections of lights on rain slick streets and the glass shop windows streaked with rivulets of precipitation running down.

Scene: *(images of star-birth from orbiting telescope Galileo)*

Voice over:
other civilizations out there
I get this feeling sometimes
of walking down the street on another planet.
I could be on another planet.
But of course it would have the same laws as this one.
Oh gravity might be a little more . . .
But would the intelligent animals
and the plants be all that much different?

I look at my own self here in the window of the bank,

Hub at the center of galaxies are black holes
How does a bird use gravity to fly.
Gravity produces a force
which always pulls the birds down, toward the earth.
To fly, the bird must make a force
    with its wings
in the opposite direction,
away from the earth.
When the bird flaps its wings,
the air moves around them in such a way that
there is more force on the bottom of the wings
than on the top.
The force on the bottom of the wings pushes the bird up.

Did Leonardo know this?
Probably. Maybe not.

Maybe I know more than Leonardo.

Scene: *(tears in eyes causes scene to dissolve into the blurry neon reflections of lights in rain slick streets and the glass shop windows streaked with rivulets of precipitation running down.)*

Voice over:
Life on other planets . . . What if they are like . . . tube worms slithering around a sulfur . . . vent. Can't appreciate too much . . . of god's creation *(pause)*
They must be up-right. . . . Don't you think? Have a certain brain mass? . . . to body ratio.
(pause)
I have to deconstruct my culture input . . . to be able to feel something. . . . What would it feel like to have a character SEIZE you . . . To be seized by a character . . . As a playwright you have to let yourself be seized by a character.
(pause)
Big G is so platonic . . . on the astronomical scale making those spheres, platonic orbs, half moons.
Think of it. . . . Feel gravity and the universe holding you up . . . and loving you.
(pause)
Think of it . . . Gravity's Platonicity the way it shaped planets into beautiful spheroids (from afar) . . . its sculpturing acumen, the way it does shape work in geology . . . its biological primacy the way it got animals to align in bilateral symmetry around a central axis.
(pause)
I must learn . . . to get . . . a much . . . longer stretch . . . across the spine . . . and in the legs

But what are the issues here?
What is it about yourself that this is expressing? Invasion of the universe because of opening up?
And the fear and wanting to protect against that? And the fear of being possessed by someone not yourself?
But then what or who are you? Yourself. You don't really know. Do you?
God as gravity . . . A kind of ultimate . . . answer. How to

feel . . . I'm just a guy . . . trying to learn to feel more.
Trying to make that cosmic connection.
Weight, we are so used to it.
Gravity is the feeling of reality.

Scene: *(him looking up from under the awning, then walking in the rain)*

Actor:
Looks like it is not going to let up. *(pause)*
I better start walking to the car.

Voice over:
But what would it feel like to be seized by Yum Chi?
(pause)
That's how we'll contact them . . . Through gravity.
I know they're out there. They've got to be.
What is it? 100,000 million stars in a galaxy?
10,000 million galaxies.
And even if there is only one sun like ours in a million
stars, . . . and say among those 1-in-a-million stars there is 1
in a million planets like ours . . . far enough away not to get
burnt up . . . close enough to have liquid water . . . with a
moon for tides and a big sister planet like Jupiter to sweep
up the meteors so life can evolve, — that means . . .
(holds chin, calculates) one in a million million chance.
Counting zeroes thats 6 zeroes for each million and divided-
by, so minus exponent, thats 10^{-12}.
But that occurs across 10,000 million . . . times . . .
100,000 million possibilities. Thats $10^4 \times 10^6$, thats 10 to the
10 (adding exponents) . . . TIMES 10^5 $\times 10^6$, thats 10^{11},
times the 10^{10}, thats 10^{11+10}, thats 10^{21}, now divided by the
chances, thats 10^{-12} times 10^{21} subtracting exponents, thats
10^{21-12} thats 10^9. A 1 followed by 9 zeroes, thats a billion.
That still leaves, what? — a billion earth-like planets! A
billion planets out there with life on them. Gotta be.
We'll learn how to contact them.
We'll learn how to manipulate . . . gravity.
Just as we always . . . have and we'll send messages . . .
faster than light. Yes. . .faster than light. Somehow, somehow we've got . . . to do it.

41 Contact

Scene: *The rain stops as he walks around a corner past a children's playground. He enters the empty nighttime playground. He starts doing Tai Chi in the big circle at center court. He starts slowly talking while doing Tai Chi.*

Actor: *(saying direction name as he moves in that direction)*
    Saying things in the cadas   going out to the forward
    and saying things going out   coming back
    left and right   the reverse
(long reach toward the sky)
    We look out and let the view range across the horizon
    and there is always a place —the still point—
(here he is staring singly pointedly at one place)
        where
    the surfaces of the bubbles of expanding space intersect
    and things change direction and we implode and fill up
    and are tumbled out like stars in the milky way
    hurtling through space on the shoulders of giants
    through passages and tunnels not available to science yet
    but it is a space that can deform
    and funnel itself down to the tail of an animal
    and compact around and fold up . . .
(pause)
    as I perform the dragon kick
(stretching out his back leg, looking back at it)
    and the more we stretch out the longer we become and
the longer we become the more numerous are the stars out
there
    and we are falling through the lines falling like coming
back to the earth from a far of space trip like that movie
Planet of the Apes
    and with our hand . . . reach out . . . and recover from
the firmament
    an energy that has come down from a very long distance
the immensity of the scattered clusters and voids, thrown
like seeds unto the blackness by the Great Hurler
(pulling in)
    everything that appears to us comes through two
windows

windows so small that the dimensions seem only to just
barley exist . . . and nothing that small to measure
(pushing out)
and we get into the wind out of our Chi,
the flow of our Chi,
and it is the Chi that shows us the trail of a being going
past us,
(grabbing at somTHING's coat tails and trying to stay it)
that we just can almost see but that we can sense
and we wonder about what dimension it originated in,

Actor: *(pushing out, really exploring the push)*
all movement comes from ground through friction
all movement goes through friction from ground
all movement goes from ground through friction

and we make the sign of elongation
and we make the sign of heightening

and every gesture that we make
lets us know that we are held in the arms of gravity
it is within and without us . . .

. . . gravity ratifies
our existence . . . gives us identity
under the sky . . . and on the earth.

(really getting loose, getting into the dance of Tai Chi)
we boogie and groove and relax into the trance of
powerful movement
we dance and relax into the trance of shifting and
sliding into one stance after another
(pull back)

Actor: *(pushing out dancing, letting hands rise on their
own)*
and push with the desire to fly off this world
and fly out of our body by flying into it

these hands, *(makes a shape with them)*
these legs

(stands on each leg makes a shape with the other)
celebrating the immense distance between our soul and
the sun
(gestures long and away into the night sky)
and the soul gets this sense of infinity going out
and a kind of rapture of matter and energy going on
forever
and this dance is an attempt to levitate the soul,
to fly with the soul (the Soul Levitator)

Scene: *(Actor takes on a shrouded, phantom of the opera
aspect playing the Soul Levitator)*

Actor: *(articulating with great theatricality):*
the Soul Levitator
(pause)
if Chi energy gets itself blocked
by being spun down to a low level
it is because it has been intercepted in mid-flight
and been fixed and captured into something
Chi swells itself up like a balloon

*(he holds the ball, tries to push it down and it expands out,
oblate. play with being unable to control a bulging shape.)*

it comes though a patch of skin
(gently places hand on wrist in push)
and seeks to facilitate respiration

and what has caused us to inhibit respiration?
fear? terror? a double bind?

and we have these surfaces around ourselves
that are shaped by the arc of a moving limb
and these surfaces interact
*(here he is drawing shapes in the air with his Tai Chi
movement)*

and these shapes are all seeking to roll along the ground,
(makes motion like rolling a hoop along)
and these shapes that are like bubbles that surround us

are like a second skin around our being
and this is a world of which we are blind with our eyes,
but it is a world of extension that we can feel and touch
a world that we can be delimiting with our extremities,

Chi is like the light of this place, it passes through and reflects off
(punch and round roll off)

and we try to feel the shape of these transparent surfaces
and with our relaxed wrists and movement emanating from core
the hands are like eyes,
and the hands open to this world of feeling shapes so fluid,
delineating the curves that illuminate our path
as we tour and turn about,
perceiving the Chi through this Second Sight, and
recovering the Chi through the making of transparency.

42   Yum Chi seizes me and we enter the Tao

The Form settles down around you slowly; the player
uses whatever relaxation techniques you know, relaxing
yourself with a favorite mental imagery, or just emptying the
mind of racing thought. The point is to escape the controlling
grasping ego, letting go of anger, or horniness or anything
that drives you around and out of your own authentic consciousness. Getting back to a state of emptiness where you
can tune in. Begin washing the body down in *chi gung,* the
fingers splaying out bolts of energy probing into the body
cavities.

doing chi gung,
washing the body with energy coming out of the hands
electrical energy
leaping and crackling from the slow hands,
etheric plasma held between the fingers,
killer Kirlian aura frizzed out like
the hair standing up on a cat,
the hands are tingling, he washed down the body,

The chi begins tingling, and you must not become aware
of it, or start marveling about it, or you will have lost it
quicker than you can say 'free-flowing synchronic bio-
fluorescence'. You must just go with it when it is moving
through you on its own.
One of the striking things you learned in push hands was
not to give into the initial desire to flee, to pull back, to run
to hide, but to go into the source of danger.
Step in closer to the Form; offer yourself in sacrifice;
find the erotic in your fear.
I wanted to become my master, Yum Chi. Would he be
there to lead me, to meet me from the other side and take me
through. I felt my Other, over there. She (it?) was always
there, always concerned, always looking out for me.
I stepped closer into the Form — looking through the
kua like windows and doors into the Form, as it taught me.
Look through them, go through them into its dimensions.
The center of my mass, relaxed and I began to feel what
was almost erotic tingling at the base of my spine.

The Cauldron, in the Tan Tien. Giving off vapors of wavering heat and churning percolating up into the space. Walker passed through this delicate veil into Yum Chi for a moment. Yum Chi seizes me and we enter the Tao, (which is the Form of forms).

May this happen to you. One day you step up into the Form and it all becomes clear. What you had thought was very fast and closed now becomes open and taking place in slow motion. Each of us has a Form, a Tao, and you can step into it and through it into the Big Time of the Great Tao.

And you use the moves in the forms to reach for your Self, your self when you were younger and filled with grace and charged with energy. An earlier self, your teenage self filled with fear and awe of the opposite sex.

Reach back to an even earlier self, when you were an accomplished child filled with enthusiasm for the next thing.

Back to earlier self, a child smiling in a world of giants and the world held you in its arms and you knew it back to your infancy and the spaces wild and tame and the close love and protection of your mother's body before you even knew you had a body. Back to the darkness of the womb, when you were womb fruit undergoing the ancient recapitulation of phylogeny. Back through the ages of evolution, the parents and their parents and who among us knows any further back than that.

But no.

Walker pulled back from Yum Chi, pulled back from being in the Form. It can't be this good, this fine, he tells himself. It can't be this simple, this easy.

It is man's lot to struggle and be frustrated.

Letting layers of tension fall away I had mixed with an entity and merged — then separated. But I learned something: if you move very slow and steady you can feel this body mind, the Somatic Intelligence —what are we calling it? taking over —the Automorph. And it wants to speak to you in its own language, which is a kind of telepathy of images. Yet it seems so strange and far off because we have forgotten it so much.

Walker . . .

Relax into doing by not doing, relax relax, let it do you let it find it's way to expression through you.

On a lovely spring day in May I was hangin' at the art gallery, taking in the Georgia O'Keefe exhibit that had come to town. Being in the crush of fans at the show was being like a bunch of bees buzzing around super-sized flowers of the self. I was transfixed before giant lavenderescent peonies flopping over a large hill like they were emerging from a dream landscape. But I was really shocked and stunned by the pelvis bone, in one of her landscapes. It was in the foreground taking up most of the lower right half of the painting, bringing in the edge of the bare canvass, and behind it the landscape of buttes and arroyos in the back ground. And there was a shape —like a flash, moving in the shadows of this earth. It made me think of a line from the Tibetan Book of the Dead: "like a mirage moving across a landscape in spring-time." Note that the translator does not mean the Springtime of the year, though he does, he is trying to create[1] a new word suggesting the idea of a coiled poten- tial, a dimension like time but one containing beings with a potential to emerge into the real landscape.

In Georgia O'Keefe's painting it was like we were seeing the landscape from the standpoint of an evolutionary god, and he was thinking: 'I'd like to make me some creature that could get up and move quickly through these forests and through this landscape', and he evolved the marvelous pelvis as part of the plan.

I often think of O'Keefe as the artist who was not just "trying to emulate the emerging art of photography in her paintings" --as one critic has said, but as the supreme artist capable of painting pictures of the Source of all creation. Perhaps this Source **is** like a multidimensional space time manifold, folding and convolving in and through itself with world lines fractaling out into many dimensions. We have symbols and images of this Source within our deepest levels. She invites us to stop and meditate and ruminate and groove on these levels.

---

[1] (by the ancient process of kenning, —it is interesting to note that the author of Beowulf does this too, for sea he writes whale-road, right about at the same time as Padma Sambavda was writing the Tibetan Book of the Dead)

The foot is the root

The Yang Long Form has a lot of standing on one leg and doing kicks. I started doing a lot of the Tai Chi walk and exploring the idea of a Zero Moment Point, that instant where the foot meets the earth when stepping for example, just before one pushes off on the ball of the foot, where the acceleration stops and changes direction.

Standing on one foot balance is achieved when there are no forces but the normal (perpendicular) reaction force of the earth holding up the weight force of the body. There are no torques around the center of gravity of the foot, that is to say no moments due to incorrectly or uncompensated distribution of the body parts.

Balancing of a human in motion is not just due to having nice big feet. It results from the complicated coordination of the body parts.

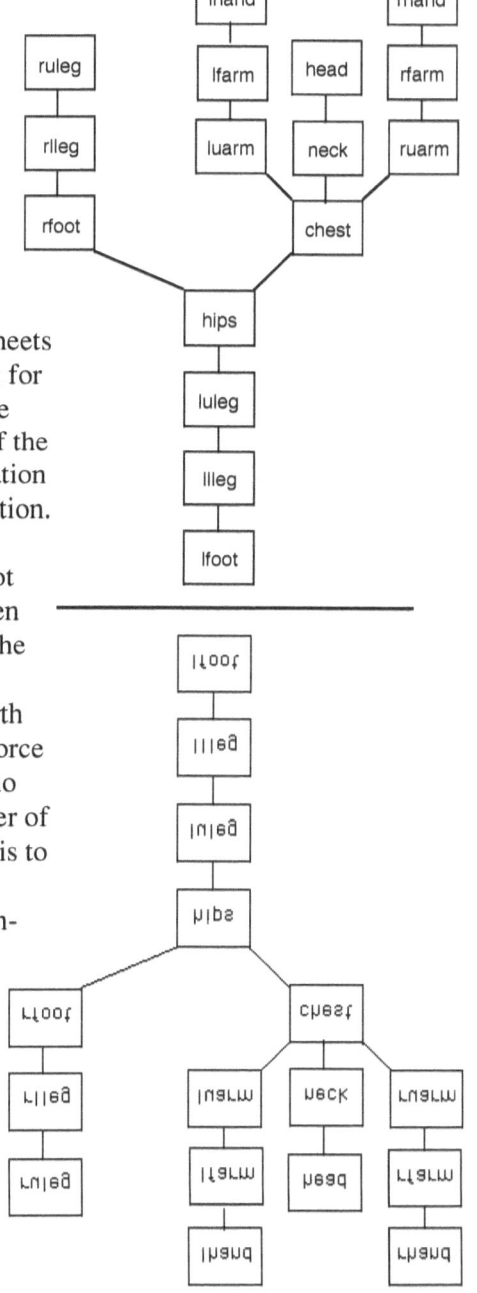

Many of the Tai Chi forms are named after animals. Animals are wonderful in the ferocity and tenacity and courage and elegance and grace they show in their own defense. Each animal, has a special adaptation strategy for which it is known. You might think about your own animal nature, and what aspects of your nature you share with an animal, and where you need to develop more. What are the Animal Forms that Tai Chi studies? The Bird, the Tiger, the Snake, The Monkey. And others in other forms. Do these forms help you access a little of their special power?

The Bird for instance. The way it hops around and is very circumspect. It's defense is rapid flight away and its offense is plucking, pecking. Nasty. Or the Snake. The way it strikes, attacking vital points and injecting poison. There is no malice in it. It just is. You need to get free to be like that, if need be. Maybe your form is the cat, the tiger clawing, ripping, — jumping in there with his big weight and clawing and ripping, or the panther, hanging back, circling, then leaping on the opponent, and tearing them up.

Or maybe you have the patience of a python for grappling, slowly wearing down the opponent by gripping, crushing, and even strangling. Ocooh what a gruesome thought. What about the gentleman monkey. With his agility and confidence. Already the primate is playing with the lesser forms. Maybe the best style is that of the deer: alertness, and fleeing. Naw, that's for prey. Be more like the Bull, charging, head butting, trampling, tossing?

If you look at your human opponent, here is the hierarchy of damage.

Martial Art Maneuvers of Increasing Damage
Graze
Low kick
Body punch
Side kick
High kick
Vitals punch
Vitals kick
Head punch
Head kick

o body of mine with the long torso
loaned to me for a while:
as a youth
I ignored you,
wrapped up in my intuitive Thinking,
—I think it was thinking, it might have been feeling —
I get them confused;
I said, "I will leave this world of pain. I will furnish my
mind. And move in."

The body knows.
It is the place where the muse lives,
that 10-year old, you
— who feels left behind.
The body forgotten
hummed along: heart beating,
—accounted for— every microsecond of every day.
Bellows working,
legs still good.
I didn't want to know.
Trapezius, where's that?
I abused it, used drugs,
Pectorals? What has that got to do
with being hunched over in your head.
The body knows shame,
it served me as a means of expression
I became a gangly youth;
and worry:
it served me as a sex object,
and a slave that I could sell on the labor market;
and deceit
(I worked painting with asbestos because the older men
said it was safe.)
And yet for years and years it carried me without protest.

But when I started studying Tai Chi,
it flowered.
I found my root sinking down
on my own two feet.

And them I bloomed!
I'm a tree
with legs!

The great flow between the earth and heaven
flows up its branches.
I turn
through the waist
and punch!
an uppercut to the air.

Body: Your are
the inheritor of millions of years of wisdom.
What an incredible gift!
The head
filled with spirits
— the abstractions of drives —
houses the Psyche in the Cortex and
the Self in the Cerebellum.
The "little brain" coordinates
the elaborate interplay of sight, sound, smell, pressure
and pain into a continuum, against a background of information about the angles and position of joints, the length and
tension of muscles, the speed of movements. . .
    just to take
      a step
          down
            stairs
I am descending stairs a step at a time
stepping into a freeze frame,
one with motion superimposed from past and future.
Movement begins in the brain
  Electrical impulses from many regions of the brain feed
into the motor areas.

The body easily
stealing — body ex-
pending, gathering, pouring,
insinuating, upon the
mesh of rhythm;
being mindful so as not to use muscles you don't need to.

The clock works
    in a tower —the spine,
the organ of vertical —
    integrating the world above
    with the world below,
        floating,
    rooted on the (level) hips,
    a plat-Form to operate From:
    legs going way down
rising all the way up
    to the stars
        (someday)
to make a step of authentic movement . . .
Sense nerves send information toward the center
—contractions
and motor nerves send impulses to the muscles,
— expansion

stress strain gauges in the joints
test for the roll pitch and yaw.
All this gets instantly transmitted
    back to
    the little carpenter bubble
in the level that keeps us held
        upright.
It is a feedback and control system.

In the flow of destiny
the foot is
flowing under the heel. To feel
with articulation
the muscles become relaxed into the wave
of authentic movement.

From the center couched
between the hips of level pelvis

learn to articulate it, let IT relax down,

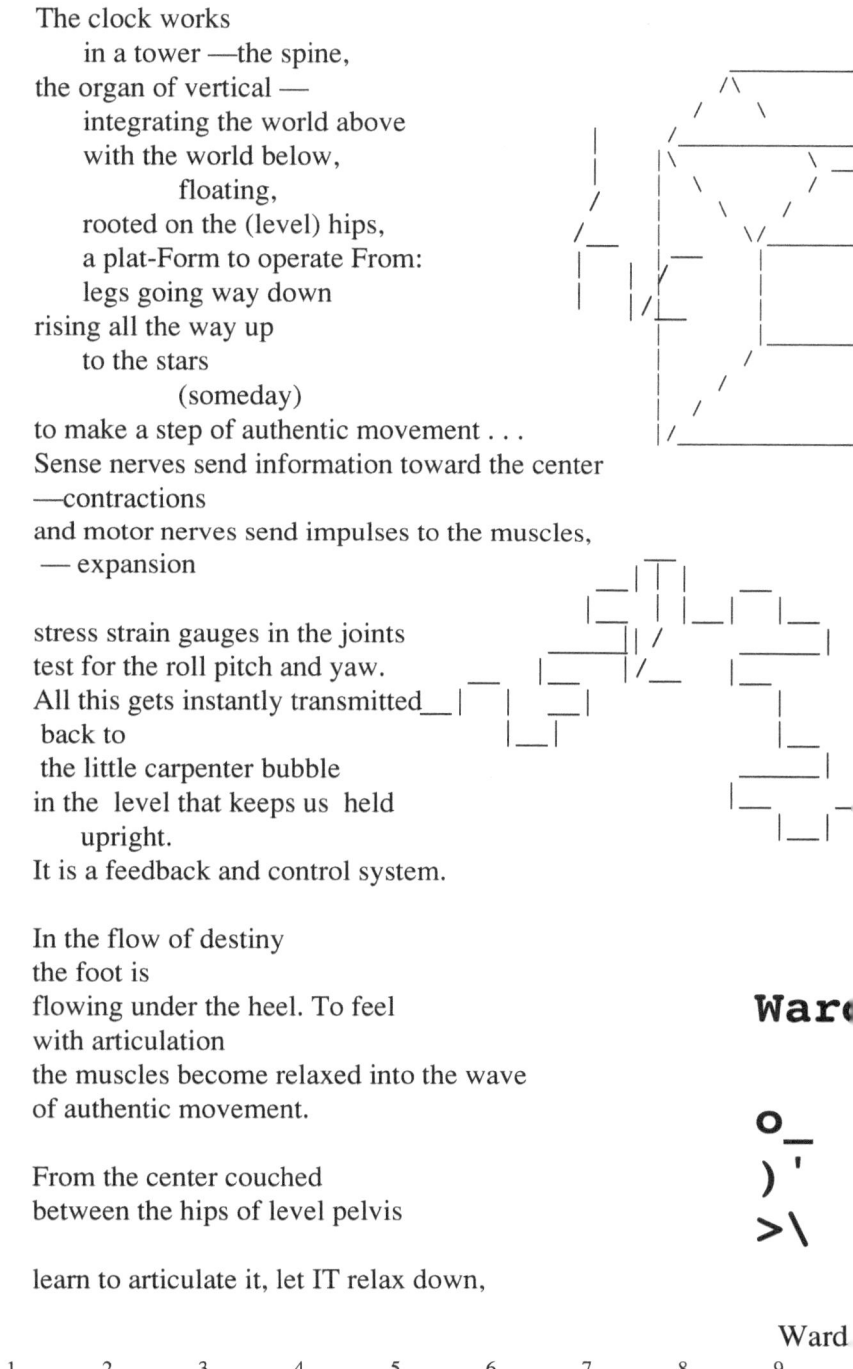

Ward

In stepping, a little spacetime window shows the trajectory of the Zero Moment Point when everything is balanced *en pointe* on the ball of the foot relative to the support area boundaries. We activate our balancing algorithm only for the parts that are cantilevered outside the support boundary. In Practice one learns where the body elements that fall outside this boundary are, and calculates the force or the counter distribution of mass to bring them back inside. This is learned in the body so that after a few iterations of Planned Balancing and Preparing Earlier, one doesn't go outside the boundary.

This is moving of the attention through little space-time windows.

space time window

f right   Ward off left

Hand Step Ward off w. L Hand Rollback Press Rollback Push

"...starts from nothing, grows possibly a little bit
feminine, then a little bit masculine, then breaks up and
has children. It's a sexy thing."- Craven Walker

the lava lamp, that eerie, undulating source of light and
enlightenment . . .
something changes density

Whether something sinks or rises
is determined by its density.
If something is more dense than the surrounding water
it will sink.
If something is less dense it will rise and float.

The "Proprietary Lava" expands with heat,
from the light at the bottom,
becomes less dense than the water,
and rises to the top.
Away from the heat, the lava cools
and becomes denser than the water
and falls.

The lava at the bottom
reheats and begins to rise all over again
continuing
in up-and-down waves.

I don't know if I was depressed, or what, but I started to
slow myself down, became downright lugubrious, started
getting into what I might call my lava lamp phase.

But that is OK. Maybe I'm coming
into myself
and this is just an argument
from my head
against giving up hegemony
to sink
into the body

think of yourself moving
in a peaceful blue mood fluid
you are the beautiful pink floating lava
transmitting waves of peace and tranquility with every
movement.

Have the Convection of your conviction
perhaps you are just something less dense than what the
earth is made of,
and you are floating and sinking on its surface.

You are here after millions of years, since the evolution
of this earth
the layer of rock under these plates acts like a seething,
bubbling, flowing liquid.
This is carried on as rotation of the hips because you
always want to keep moving.

I had hopes of someday feeling the Chi emanating from
my core
to feel it coming through from deep within myself,
to feel that deep within yourself
 you might feel with a churning motion,
kind of like your center was grasping and receiving and
pushing away.
Of course it was,
carrying Chi momentum through your trunk
from the support reaction force on the earth

It is like you are sending reaction force down into the
floor,
with your mind you are looking through the connection
with earth
and seeing a mirror image of your own self down there,
in terms of the reaction forces of parts of your body.

I start to make my movement be more like subduction
as a moved along the floor,
that is thinking of my feet as being beneath the floor.

The interior of the earth to the surface where it is cooler.

These motions of the material under the earth's surface
in turn cause the plates to move. The plates
The eight areas of our bodies
foot, knee, hip, waist, back, shoulder, elbow, and hands.
Drift so slowly
that we wouldn't think of this process as shaping our
martial art
being abstractions of several potential blocks, attacks,
locks shift holds

Within the *tan tien*
an empty rice field at the center of mass
where the Chi grows, the one from our original birth,
and the one dissolving and moving back and forth with
the outside world

a kind of oil that roiled and seethed,
parting and closing ceaselessly

Chi as a concept, a placeholder, an abstraction that we
use to speak about and try to glimpse through
a shining world beyond.

Whenever I can slip into Tai Chi, I can slip into this
world.
Feel your skin and body shift shape
and melt into the warm glycerin

see the bubbles floated into beyond.
Rising and falling with hypnotic grace.

Feel the earth as it is alive, it loves you and you are its
dream as it carries on
asleep and gently breathing.

the voice was low and soft and sweet,
like the wind makes, mellowly blowing across
wooden flute chimes, hanging in the tree, —aleatory,
opening to channel a song emerging from the wind,
as though the flute were trying to remember when . . .
— its own reedy origins in the marsh by the lake.
You too, it is breathing
you too.
The "words" of the song
were the movements
that seemed to flow together
and twine around each other.
There were unions of opposites,
separations of polarities,
in a language where verbs shifted speed
and only slowed down to nouns
for an instant at the end of something,
then started up again.
The player comes to see,
more clearly reading the form,
interpreting the world underneath the "words";
the song itself is used to *hear*,
a form already there
that you could catch and ride perhaps.
As if something were playing you too, rising and falling,
in and out, blowing air into your lungs with every breath.
It is.
If you "listen" you can "hear" it:
something strong and wild and fearful,
that you must know.
It is your anger, your energy, your survival.
That is what you are trying to touch in the movements,
in the dangerous dimension of the song,
streaming past you and down into the profound.
You want to make your singing reach people,
play with them like a force
— though you might slip, scramble, want to be running
toward or away from something.
And your eyes . . .

They are not grasping the world
but letting it swim in.
Being careful of what the eyes show to the world,
watch for changes in your opponents eyes
that betray his intention.
And you can let that dictate
the measure and counter measure
in your song.

There is much to see in the mandala of the other's eyes:
if the eyes are dim,
they tell about the lack of inner strength.
The un-resolved step: reliance on rigidity for support.
How well has the martial artist prepared
his central command.

Look at his shoulders with your peripheral vision.
Look at the immediate threat with your central vision.
Give yourself time to look at the way he sings his song.
Learn to harmonize with him.

I think this too is the meaning of the *kua* mandala.
Take a fierce pleasure in this fight.
Be springy and eager with anticipation.
Yet at the end of a movement
allow yourself a silent sigh,
to let out the breath of relief.

This deep song has many breathings.
When you roll-back
be like the tongue getting ready for the next articulation
in the song.

Let your self be like a shadow cast in light.
Let your figure shimmer and spread out into your space
like moonlight on the lake.

Let the song change,
becoming softer and more plaintive.
Feel your longing. Let others feel it too.

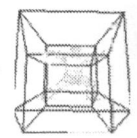

After practicing Tai Chi for a while, you realize that you are using way to much effort. This starts in the way most people hold themselves up with their muscles, rather than letting their skeleton do it through alignment. This suggests how the body becomes a repository of rigidities. Many men, for example, are still holding the body in a rebellious pose —a holdover from your disaffected, gangly youth. They are still living in the '60s! Be aware of it; shift attention; allow your skeleton to hold you up; don't make your muscles do the job. This is why the muscles are always too tense. It is due to using them as armor. When doing Tai Chi just relax, and feel what it is like to just have the skeleton doing the moving. Let the skeleton hold you up and let the muscles relax; this is a very simple idea, requiring awareness to put into practice.

Without getting into the psychology of why the body is locked into defense postures, or constructing "interesting" theories of why the brain insists on maintaining its hegemony over the body, let us instead, explore further this extensive analogy between music and Tai Chi.

Notation for the Instrument Body

I wanted to be able to feel and speak about concepts like harmony, improvisation in an interval, phrasing, punctuation. . . I had in mind the analogy that the body was an instrument to be played. I wondered what the keyboard would be, what the input device would be. What were the points of articulation. And what would the necessary kind of notation. I needed this language because I'm trying to figure out and describe my movement pattern.

To speak the language of articulated movement

The physical keyboard would be the basic 8 joints, the *kua*. One or another of them are found in every move.

I looked up the components of effort in Laban, and found that he had quite a lot to say about it. We can interpret the 8 joints, the *kua,* with Laban — especially the orientation in space and the understanding on weight.

I set out on a three-step program:

1. Find the basic movements.

2. Realize what they are in terms of locomotor and space exploration.

3. Start associating 3-group words into actions and watch if the forms don't fall out.

We are looking at a stage of words into actions, we want to get the equivalent of a Tai Chi keyboard. We ask where do the forms come from? Thus, in 2 we are getting a general description which we think will eventually lead to a kind of notation description. Way in the back of my mind was a kind of relationship between the Kua, the trigrams, and this language of motion-energy-effect. A kind of matrix or hexagram.

Here's an introductory summary of what we will look more closely at in the next few pages.

Components of Effort	
Speed	
Fast	Quick; sudden, explosive; anaerobic; muscles tight
Slow	Careful; drawn out; sustained; aerobic; muscles relaxed
Force	
Strong	Strong; intense; heavy; muscles tight or tense
Light	Easy; weak; buoyant; slight; muscles loosened up
Flow	
Bound	Controlled; jerky; robotic; restricted; muscles tight
Free	Smooth; fluid; continuous; muscles move easily

The purpose of doing Tai Chi is to embody the Tao.

Chi is a multidimensional energy / force that animates human activity. Laban was the great analyst of human activity. One dimension of Chi is organizational. Intelligence. You start to do Tai Chi much better when you shift the root from the head to the hips in the hierarchy of body organization.

51 Tai Chi and Laban: Effortshape Grid

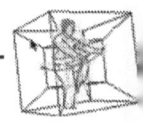

Laban was the poet/scientist of human movement. He developed a notation capable of articulating dance and probably most human endeavors. In addition to his notation of human movement he developed a representation to study human effort. He partitioned the space of all human effort into a Space/Time/Weight diagram. Weight (w) (or Force) was on the vertical axis; time (t) was along the horizontal axis; space (s) was in the plane behind weight and time.

Dimensions of Effort

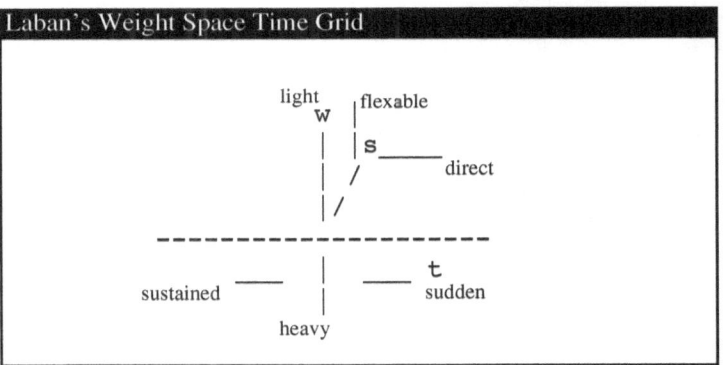

He assigned the verticle weight axis to have attributes of light to heavy; the horizontal time axis as spanning from sustained to sudden; and motion in space to be somewhere between the attributres of being flexible to being direct.

Dimensions of Effort as opposites symbolized as Grid elements					
(time)		(force)		(space)	
slow	quick	light	strong	flexable	direct
				openess	focussed

Elements of a Notation for the Instrument Body

Then he could look at ways of combining these fundamental opposing (binary) attributes taking one attribute from each dimension to find the different types of effort.

From this Laban could describe the effort that went into most gestures. For example: **wringing** would be a sustained, heavy flexible maneuver, whereas **flicking** would be a light sudden flexible gesture. He could abstract out a notation for these efforts:

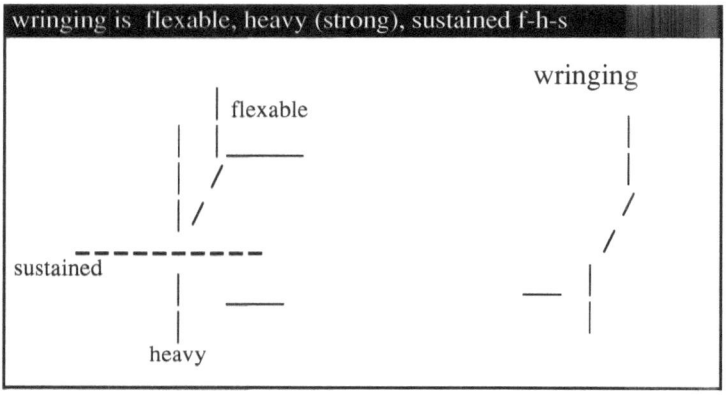

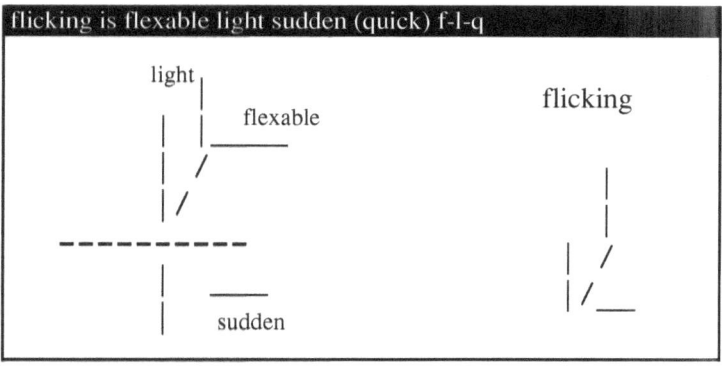

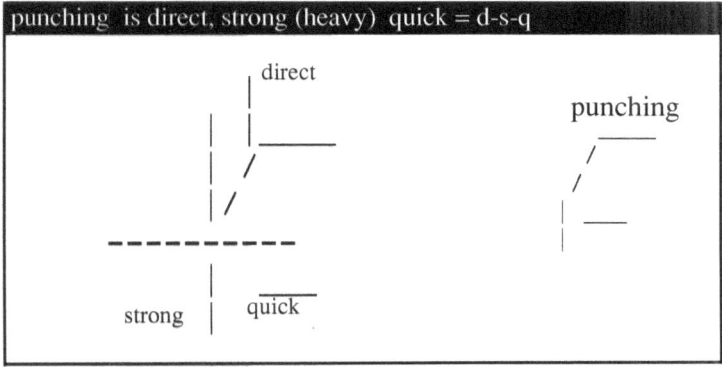

Mixing the hard-edged and the soft-defused

```
                                        light   |flexable
   floating    fighting                    w    |
       |                                    |    | s____
       |            ___                     |    | /      direct
     | / ->        /                        | / /
    _|/           /___                      |/
                  |            -------------------------
                  |                      ___  |    ___  t
                              sustained      |         sudden
                                          heavy
```

changing the force in floating from light to heavy and
changing the space in fighting from focused to across

```
   wringing    slashing
       |            |
       |            |
      / ->         /
    _ /           /_
      |            |
      |            |
```
changing time in floating from sustained to quick to get flick
changing the force in fighting from strong to light to get dab

```
   flick       dab
      |            ___
      |          | /
    | / ->       |/__
    |/__
```

```
   glide          pressing
           ___            ___
      | / ->         /
    _|/           _/
                    |
                    |
```
changing space in floating from difuse to focused gets glide
changing time in fighting from quick to sustained gets press

The combination space of a trinary

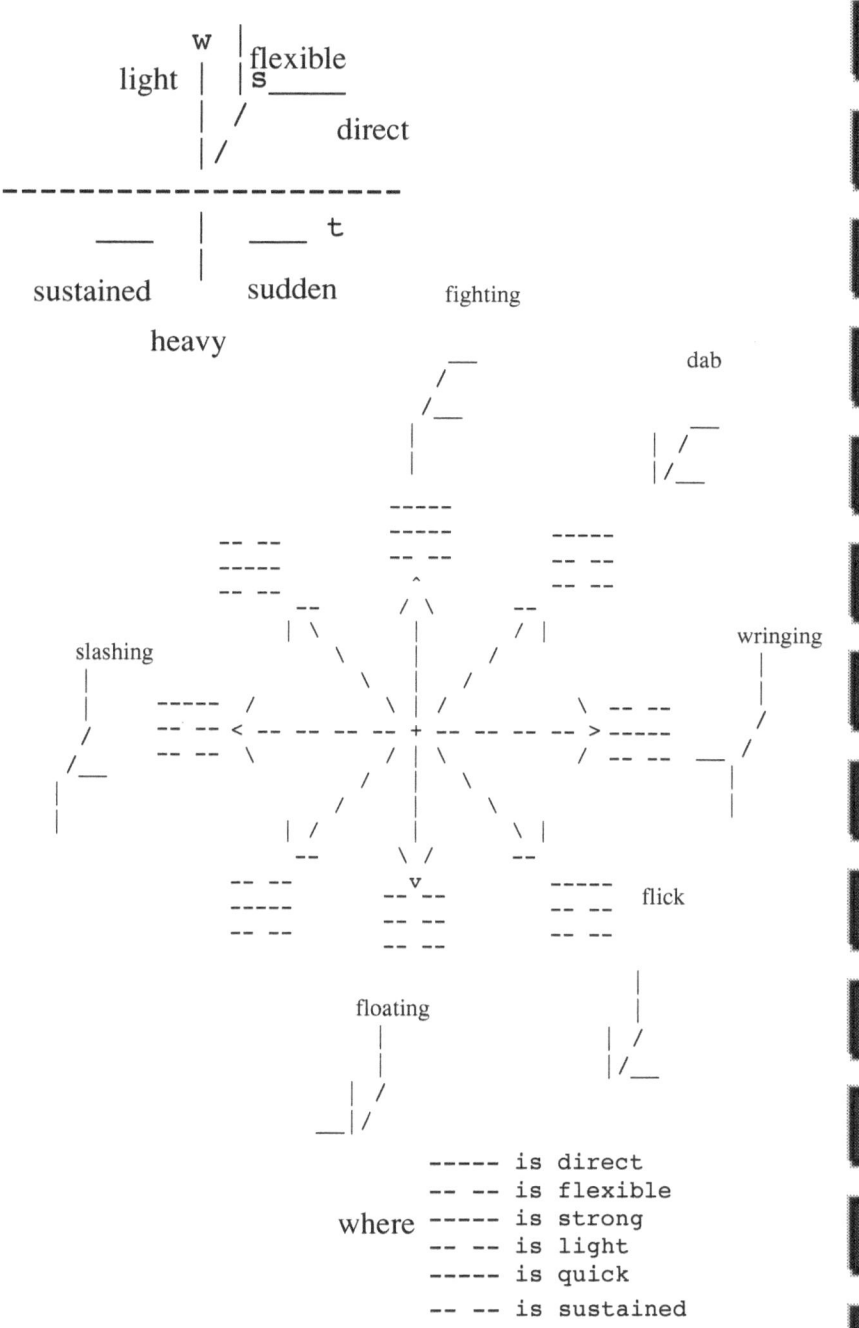

where
```
----- is direct
-- -- is flexible
----- is strong
-- -- is light
----- is quick
-- -- is sustained
```

A Trinary hierarchy of movement falls out

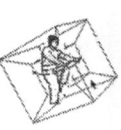

```
floating          |    weight is light      - -
               | /     time is sustained    - -
             __|/      space is flexable    - -

                 __
               /       force is strong      ---
fighting      /__      time is quick        ---
              |        space is focused     ---
              |

wringing          |
                  |    force is strong      ---
                 /     time is sustained    - -
              __/      space is flexable    - -
                |
                |

slashing        |
                |      force is strong      ---
               /       time is quick        ---
             /__       space is flexable    - -
             |
             |

flick          |       force is light       - -
               |       time is quick        ---
            | /        space is flexable    - -
            |/__

                __     force is light       - -
dab         | /        time is quick        ---
            |/__       space is focused     ---

               /       force is strong      ---
            __/        time is sustained    - -
pressing,     |        space is focused     ---
pulling       |

                  __   weight is light      - -
               | /     time is sustained    - -
wave         __|/      space is focused     ---
```

It happened when I was running from a cop
it was a cold clear night in January
in the suburbs of San Antonio where I grew up.
I must have been 13 or 14;
I was out past curfew,
—way out, in the night —
maybe walking to see if Irene was at her window.
All the little sub-division people
were sleeping or bathed in the glow of TV.
Then sudenly a cop's car whips around the corner,
and we see his high beams shoot up and down me
as he bounces over the ramp into the driveway
next to where I was.
Like a scared animal I took off.
Hear the cop — jumping out of his car, shouting:
"Hey! You there! Stop!"
But I'm gone, through a doorway of fear —
into a dimension of grace. When I reached the
fence into the citizen's back yard I seem to float,
as I place one foot lightly
right on the top rail
of a 6ft cyclone fence.
And just for an instant, sense myself poised there
— like a ballet dancer on point.
In his bright searchlight —sweeping,
projecting a huge shadow image of me
and the chainlinke fence onto the houses,
Weight and Space didn't matter.
I was flying over a fence as if it wasn't even
there.
I was on the m o o n!
I was *made* of moon,
smooth and
round and
luminescent and
untouchable.
I continued across the back yard
and steped over a second fence.
Then highstepping down the alley,
vanished into the night.

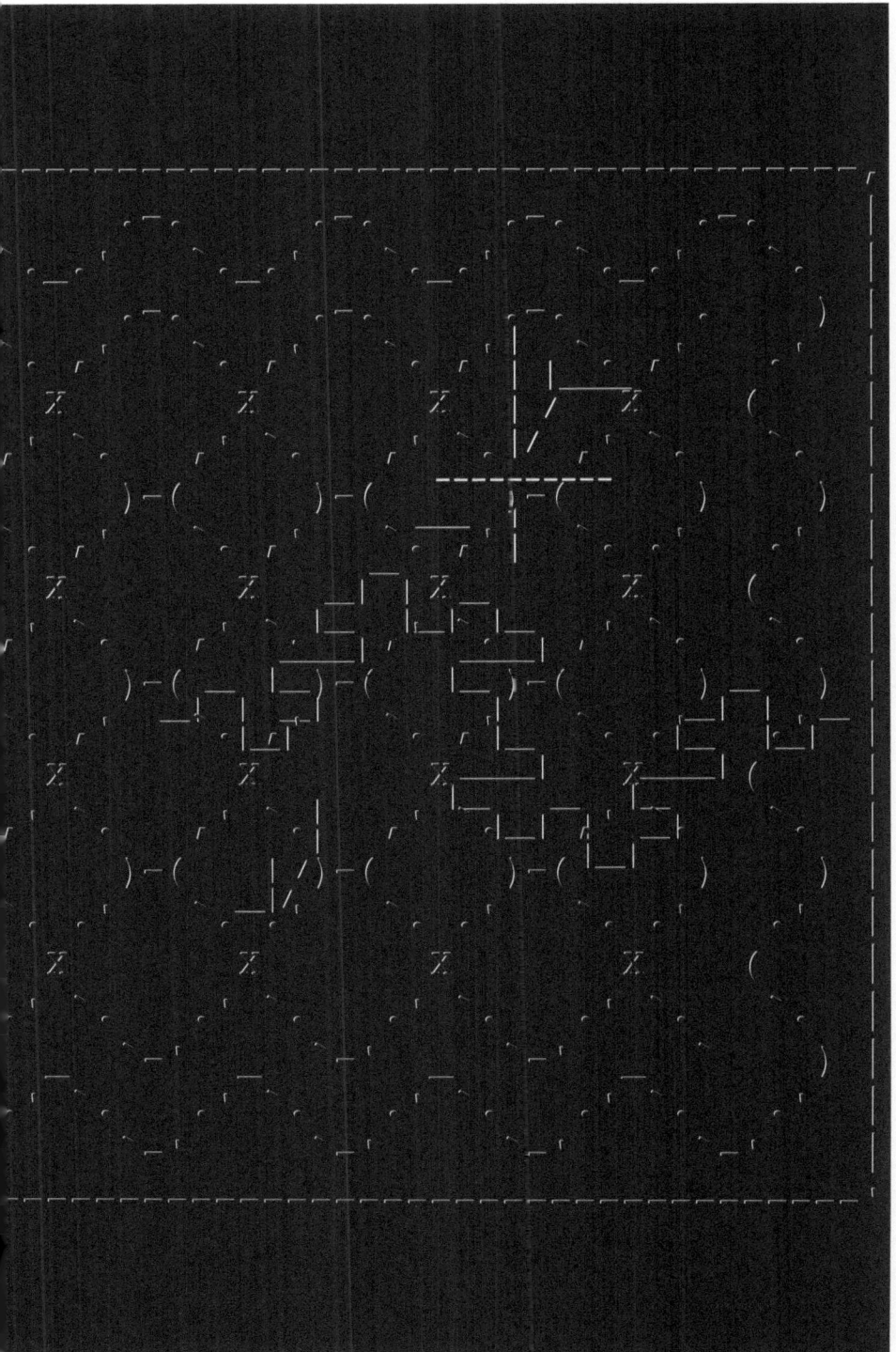

139

53 Knight's Walk and the Cadas of Energy Splitting

I felt the Form had assigned me the task of looking at the energy shape of each movement. I felt a need to maybe get past mnemonic poetical name into a more physical name. I started calling them by other names, looking at specific combination of several of these 8 elements of movement to see what was observable in every action, what was the most easily discernible fact.

the quick:
    direct — a strong punch
    a flexible and strong slash
    a direct and light dab
    a flexible and light flick

the sustained:
    a direct and strong press
    a flexible and strong wring
    a direct and light glide
    a flexible and light float

Certain movements can be considered modifications of the basic actions
    Modifications of punch are shove, thrust, poke
    Modifications of slash are beat, throw, whip
    Modifications of dab are pat, tap, shake
    Modifications of flick are flip, flap, jerk
    Modifications of wring are pull, pluck, stretch
    Modifications of glide are smooth, smear, smudge
    Modifications of float are strew, stir, stroke

A person lifting a heavy sack on his shoulder starts with a kind of slash movement down to pick it up, then a wring-ing movement to hoist it up onto the shoulder.

The point is to look at the energy shape the hands are sculpting in the air. And I set about to describe the energy shape for each Tai Chi move. I wanted to abstract this detail out of the form.

As a purely formal exercise I arranged the opposing
effortshapes around a circle of opposites.

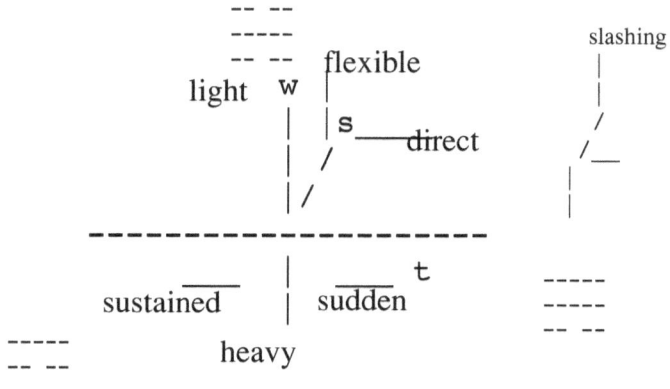

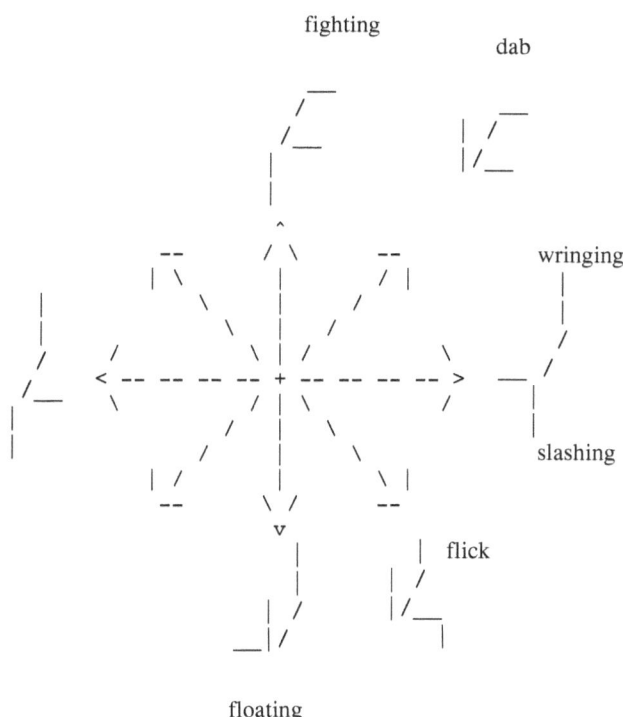

fighting

dab

wringing

slashing

flick

floating

I started to imagine these effort-shapes as "corners" of a higher-dimensional model, a coordinate system in 4-space.

I thought of it as the Knight Walk in chess. Move the knight in his hook move through every point in the board without going through the same square again.

Knight's Walk on the Plane

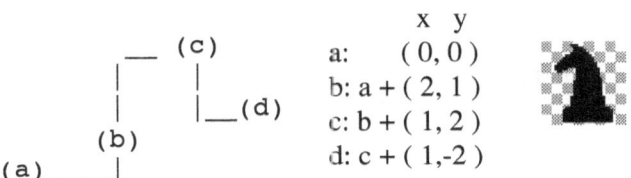

x y
a: (0, 0)
b: a + (2, 1)
c: b + (1, 2)
d: c + (1,-2)

Every location may be reached from the previous one by moving two units (+/-) in one coordinate direction and one unit perpendicular. There are 8 reachable locations by this step, except from a corner or an edge. Lattice points are chosen such that the first point is at the origin.

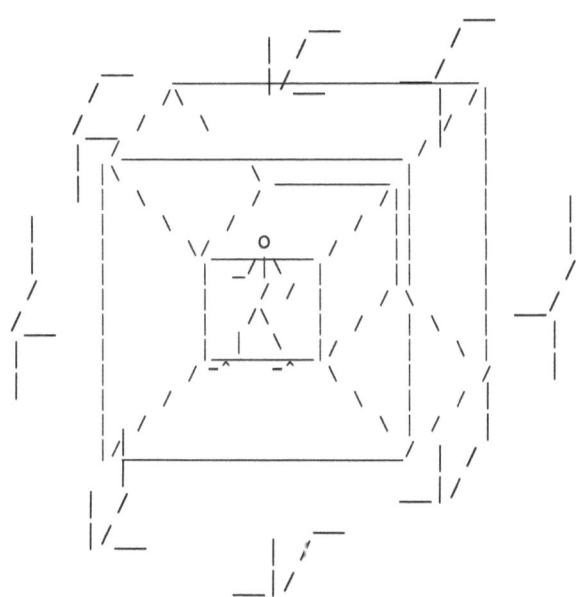

The tesseract unfolds into action!

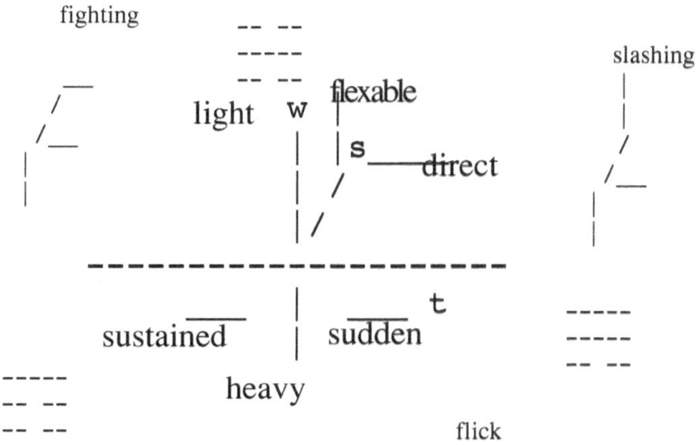

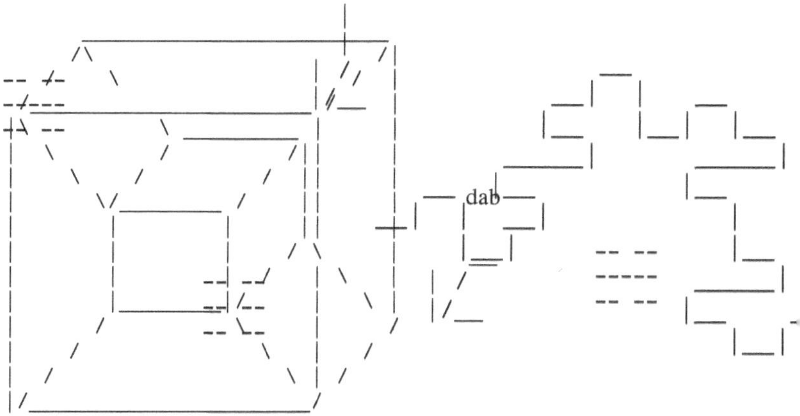

fighting

light w flexable

slashing

s —direct

sustained | sudden t

heavy

flick

dab

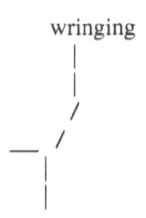

wringing

I wanted to transpose these effort-shapes into a more formalistic system. And I noticed there were gaps in the distribution around the mandala.

The combination of three elements of space time and weight for each effort-shape suggest trigram.

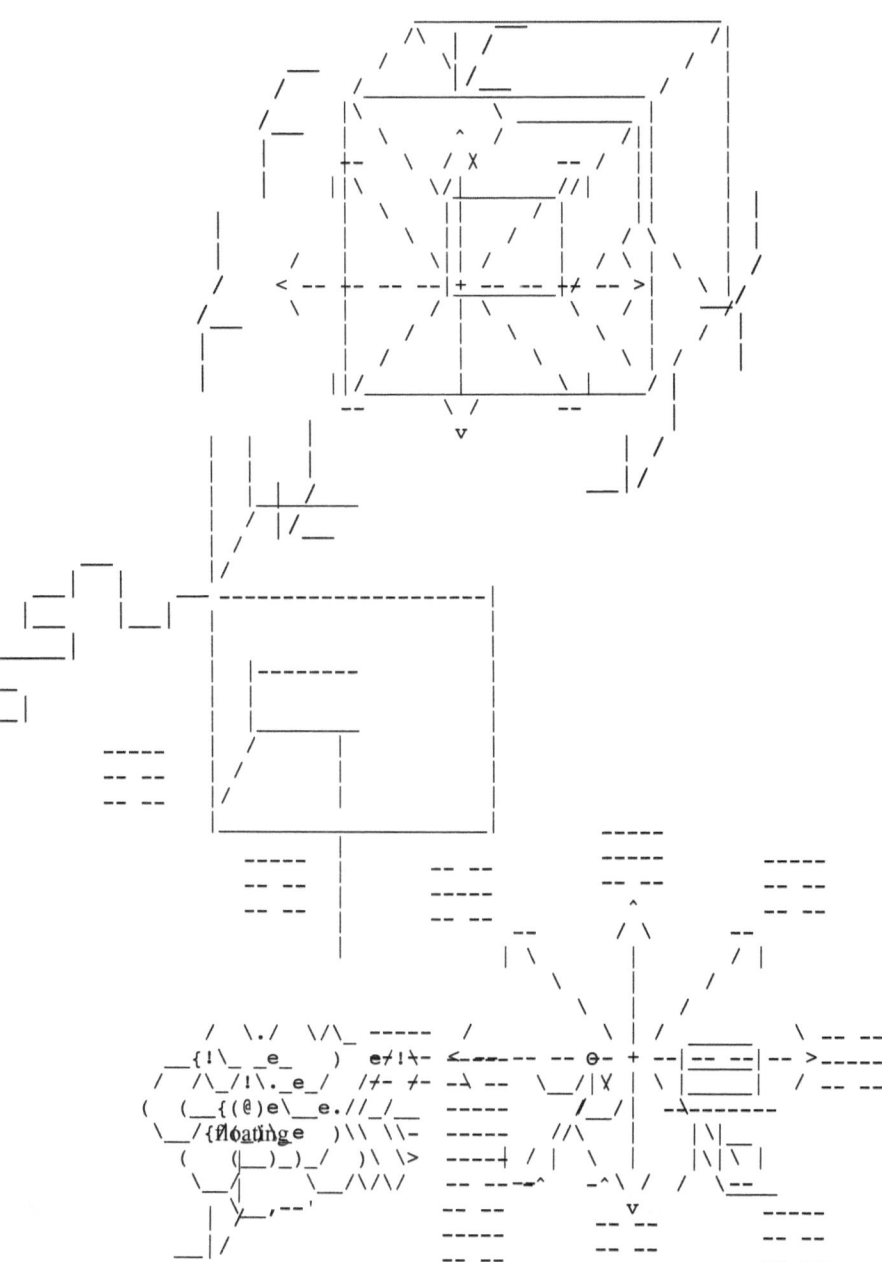

floating

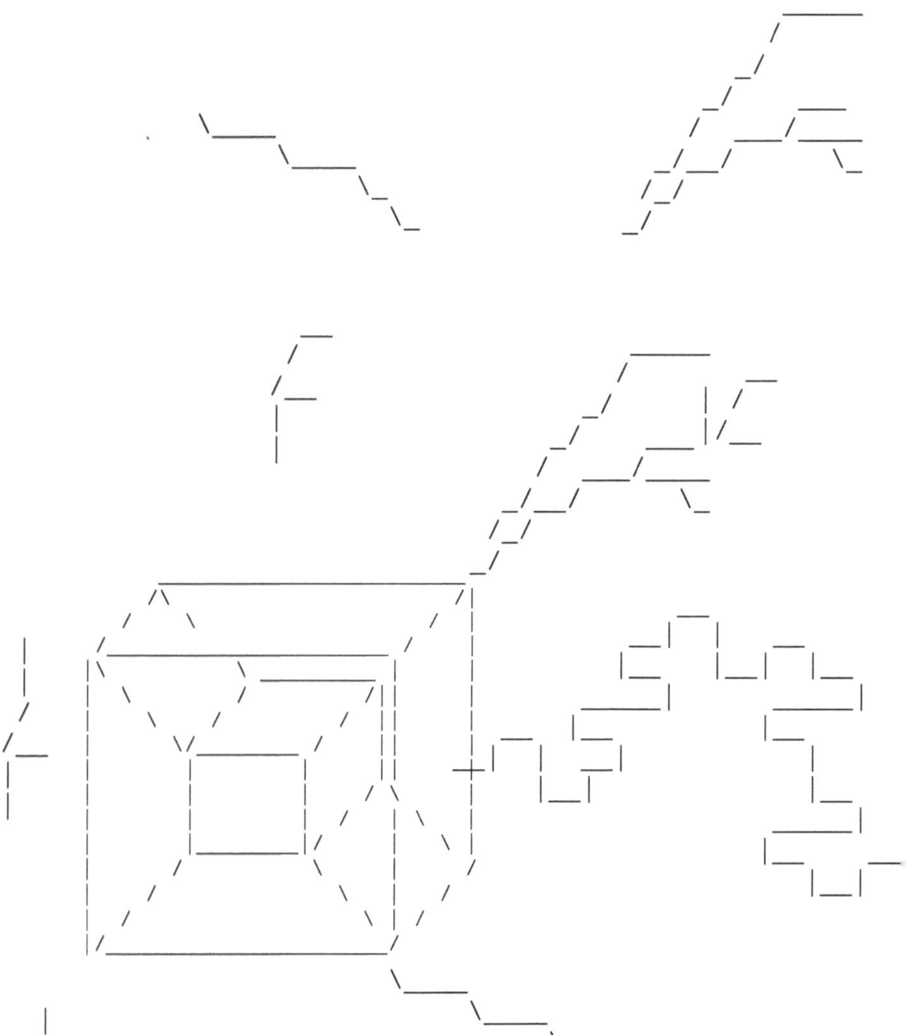

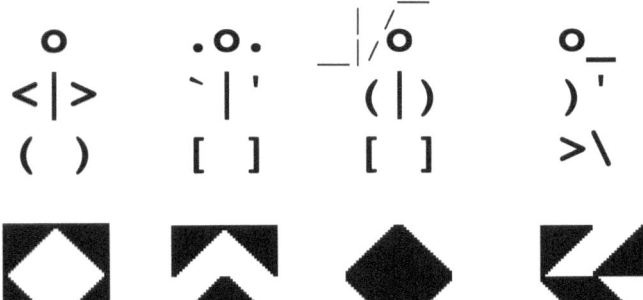

Start form   **Ward**

Step out Raise Hands Lower Hands Sun House Sphere   Ward o

```
    o          .o.        _|,o         o_
  <|>         `|'         (|)         )'
  ( )         [ ]         [ ]         >\
```

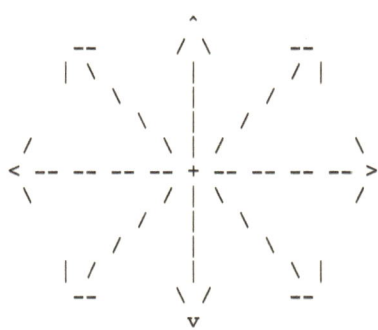

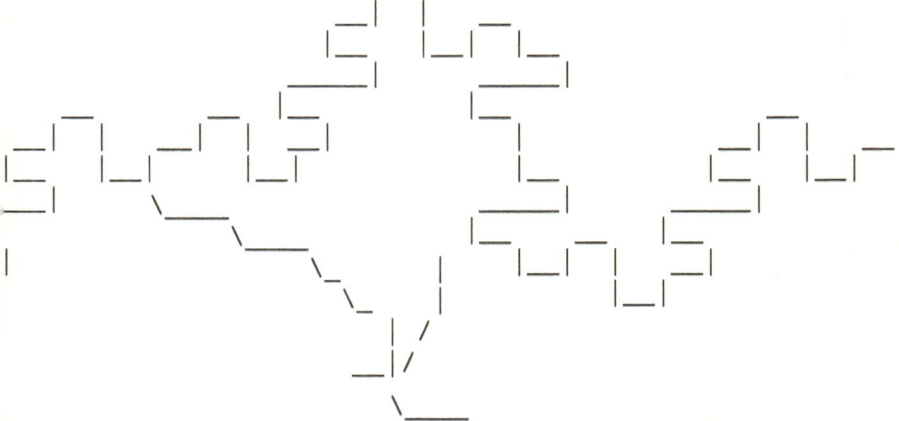

f right   Ward off left

Hand Step Ward off w. L Hand Rollback Press Rollback Push

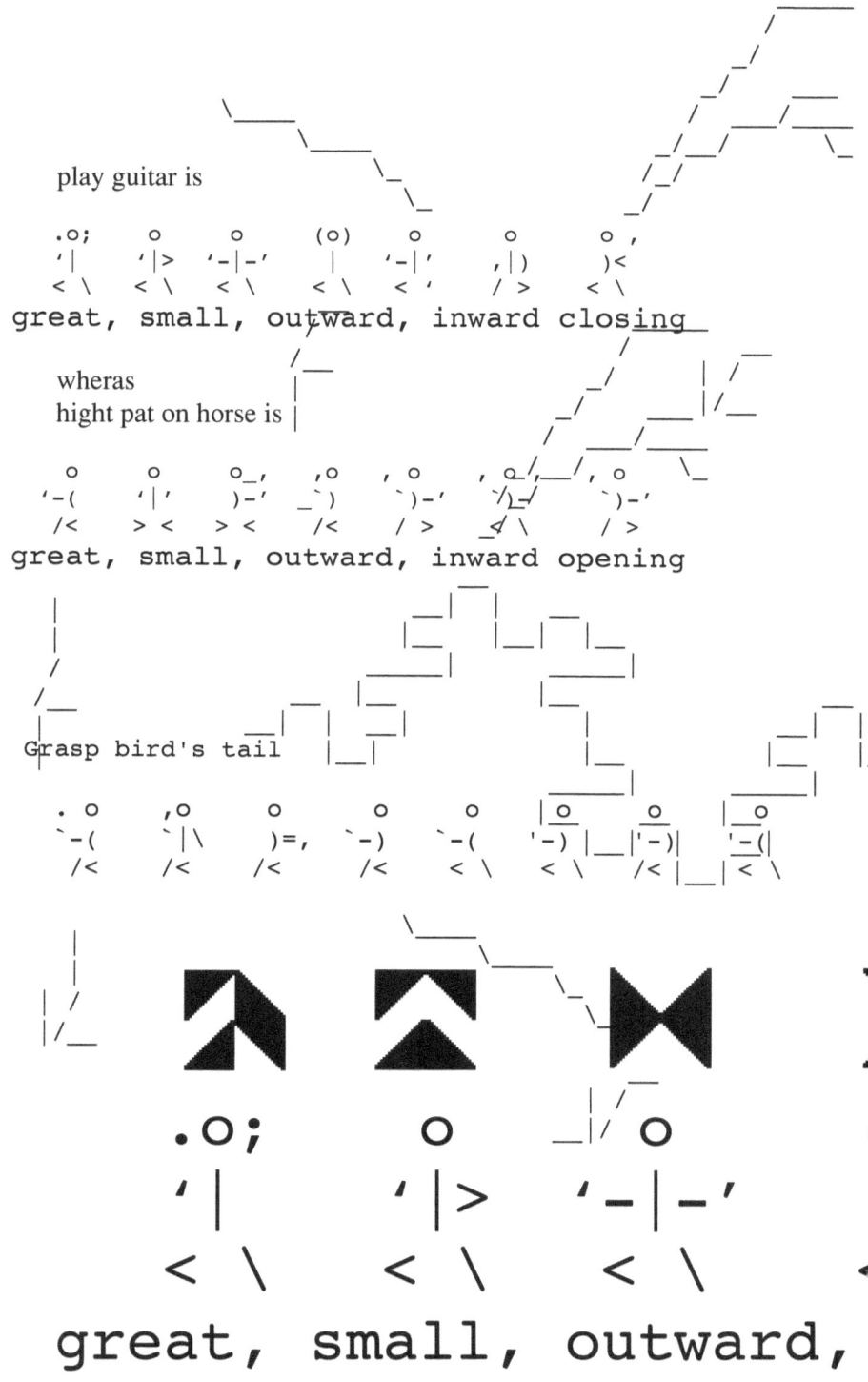

play guitar is

```
.o;      o      o      (o)     o       o       o ,
'|      '|>    '-|-'    |     '-|'    ,|)     )<
< \     < \    < \     < \    < '     / >    < \
```
great, small, outward, inward clos*ing*

wheras
hight pat on horse is

```
  o      o      o_,    ,o    , o     , o/_/, o
'-(     '|'    )-'    _`)    `)-'    '/)_/    `)-'
/<      > <    > <    /<     / >     _/ \     / >
```
great, small, outward, inward opening

Grasp bird's tail

```
  . o    ,o      o       o      o    | o     o    | o
`-(     `|\    )=,     `-)    `-(    '-)|  |'-)|  '-(|
/<      /<     /<      /<     < \    < \  /< |__|< \
```

```
.o;          o       _|/ o
'|         '|>      '-|-'
< \        < \      < \
```
great, small, outward,
```
```

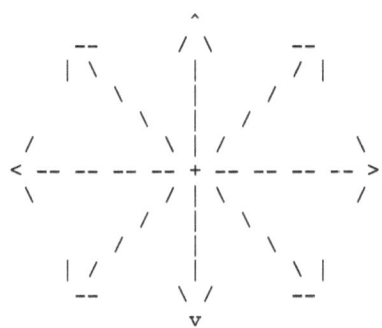

Single Whip
Lift hands

```
Single Whip
```

```
     o        o        o_,     ,o      , o     , o ,    , o
   '-(      '|'      )-'    _`)    `)-'   `)-    `)-'
   /<      > <     > <    /<     / >    < \     / >
```

Out: *shhhhheeee aaaaaah ddchshnHHH*

great, small, outward, inward - divided

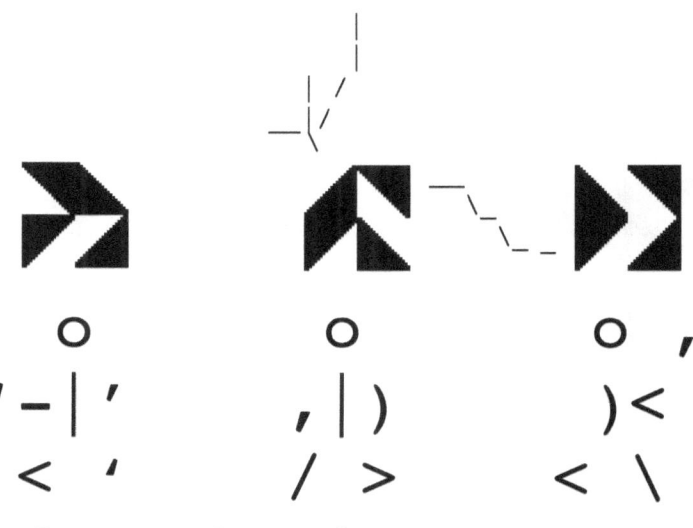

```
       o         o         o ,
   '-|'      ,|)      )<
   < '      / >      < \
```

ward – closing

```
        _
      _| |  _
     |_| |_| |_ _
       |_|  |_| |_
     _| |  |_|     |
    _|_|_  |_        |
   |_|_|      |_
    \_ \        |_      _ _
      \_\_       |_    |_| | |_
         \_    |_|_ _   |_| |_| |_
           \_  |_|_| |_   |_|     \_
             \_     |_|_|
                      |_|
```

Brush Knee Twist Step

```
  o ,    o     o,    o     o_    o_,    o ,
  )<    )=,   /0'  ,=(    ),'   ),    )<
  >\    >\    / >   >\    >\    }>    >\
```

left, right, outward, inward releasing

```
        |
        |
      | /
      |/__


      _|/‾
```

Shoulder strike
Stork spreads wings
Brush knee and twist step
```
```

```
                                                                    |
                                                                    |
                                                                  | |/
                                                                 _|/
                                                                  __
                                                                 /
Ward off & Grasp Bird's Tail (1)                                /__
                                                                 |
       o ,    ,_o      o_      o      o ,     o,      o          |
       )<    ,-(     <)  '   ,|'    )-'     / '    ,=(          |
      < \      >\    / >   < \     >\      >\       >\          |
                                                                |
                                                               /
  _____                                                        __/
 /___                                                         _|
 \_         o       o      o       o        o                 |
           )-'     )-'    (-'     )-'      )-'                 |
           >\     / >     >\     / >      / >                  |
                                                               |
                                                               |
                                                              /
                                                            /__
               Deflect downard, Parry and punch             |
               Rollback                                      |
               Press, Cross hands, Close                     |
 _                                                           |
 \_                                                          |
                                                           | /
                                                           |/__
    \_____
      \_____  \_     __                                    | /
               \_ __|/ /                                   |/_
                                                            __
                                                           /
                                                         _/
                                                         |
 Apparent Closure                                        |

      o_,     (o)     _o_      o      o       o           |  __
      )-'      |      '|'    (x)    '|'     [|]          | /
     / >      / >    [ ]    ( )    [ ]     [ ]           |/
     left,   right,  outward,  inward   receiving      _|'
```

Here is the student of Tai Chi in his big yellow kitchen chopping up endive and scallions to put in huge wooden mixing bowl to toss healthy salad-day dinner. Scallions is part of a new anti-tick program, the idea being to eat lots of nasty scallions so that it is exuded in sweat through the pours, drives the critters away by exotranspiration of onion sweat. While chopping, he nips a little nail of index finger. The student of Tai Chi pauses to inquire about the move that went awry. He goes over his thought process, and realized his mind was not present in current time — it had fugued-out into a future time-frame.

The student of Tai Chi realizes that even though the movement was correct, the differential equation of motion of knife-fall had been intersected by a different time series. The time series upon which the differential equation of knife motion was based, had been intersected and diverted by another revery-imbued time sequence.

The student of Tai Chi admonishes himself: Try to move objects along their geodesics, the path of least resistance. He practices the move over and over, until it is like reeling silk with relaxed smoothness. Let the objects settle into their angle of repose.

You may begin to see the time-line or the geodesic path of objects in 4-space. You may experience the objects as alive when their path goes into a spiral or corkscrew and they rail out of sorts, go awry, run amuck, crash and break and come to the end of their integrity.

The student of Tai Chi catches his mind taking over and further admonishes himself: Be careful of falling into a kind of spiritual materialism, with all this thinking and processing going on. It is a terrible kind of nominalism appealing very seductively to your type of Intuitive pattern recognizing personality, eternally questing for the significance of things. But really, to find the way of least action, you have to do the analysis and break down of the movement only once. You are looking for Chi, wanting to get a situation where Chi can emerge — that is to say, setting up nodes and filters with a specific orientation to capture the Chi as it flows through, like thermals drifting in, on the gradient breeze.

Once you start to understand the relationship between your energy, your attention, your intention, and your actions in any given event, and how these arise through your neurophysiology from the matrix of the world, then you can relax and watch IT do itself. You can conduct yourself like a transistor, a small amount of energy at the base, used to move a large amount of energy from stance to torso.

That's what Chi might be, just the signal — a kind of meta-communication moving with, and controllable around, physical energy.

You need to look for what is obstructing the flow, what is causing bends, tight angles, constrictions. It is all about expansion and contractions.

You can bring this experimental study into several, if not all, types of binary or dichotomous systems and feel the neurology beneath the psychology moving, organizing. You will find that you can move —you can ride on, you can surf on — the flow of analogy. You can move beyond the obstacle path of your weaknesses and the peculiarities and vagaries of your attention span.

Tai Chi is the whole, the mixture of Yin and Yang. You will integrate the negative, harness it to do the positive.

The discipline of Tai Chi brings you into present time.

You can take the yin with the yang, the negative with the positive, the fire with the water, the position with the momentum, the velocity with the acceleration, the content with the context, the wave with the particle, the expansion with the contraction, the active with the passive, the flowing-out with the flowing-in, the past with the future, the diachronic with the synchronic, the precedents with the antecedents, the sign with the signal.

55 Second Apparent Closure

Keep doing the first move, Preparation for Tai Chi. It tells us that Tai Chi is an extension of Chi Kung.

Here is a Vision about the Senses falling down into the Will; about learning to relax the spine. It uses an image, a thermodynamic metaphor of melting at the base of the spine. We are going to ask you in your breathing, when you move energy from the *tan tien* (center of gravity) to the spine, to feel heat coming toward the back of the spine, making that whole area relax.

Visualization: (Senses falling down into the Will)

Feeling the support beneath your feet,
you open your eyes and instead of looking out
with a concentrated grasping,
look with out purpose.
Just let the scene flow in,
let it come through the eyes and just
fall
over the edge of a waterfall.
See yourself standing, floating just above
the top of a waterfall
just watching the water fall down
into the pool below.
That pool is your Tan Tien,
and there is a sense that you are falling
along with your senses, falling in a stream,
going down with the breath,
into the center of mass between your hips.

It is a small, beautiful, waterfall cascading into a rock pool where the water is crystal clear. It is a hot pool down there, waves of warmth are shimmering on the surface of it. And there is a hint of vapor rising out of the pool, for it is warmer there, than the air.
It is a hot springs at the bottom of the waterfall,
and the falling senses heat things up even more
— helping you to know the froth and mist and turbulence and chaos of the Tao.
Ground zero.
The center of the body mind.

Stepping into the pool
feel the warm water washing over your feet
and ankles,
and then your legs
and waist
as you go a little deeper.
It is gravity converted to heat.
The earth is alive; pantheism is afoot.
Gravity is the attention of the earth, pulling in
your feelings, perceptions, intuitions —your
attention down though you.
Meet this warmth coming from below
with the senses falling through you from above,
generating warmth
spreading out from your center.
Feel your heart becoming warm as it opens up
like a flower to the morning sun.

You will be moving shapes
like the blob in the old hippie lava lamp.
The energy can travel
through your body to your back
or into your mind or maybe to an internal organ.

See and feel the shape of healing energy
radiating into the part of your body that needs
it most. Feel the love and energy of the
universe settling down into you, healing you,
enveloping you,
falling down through your senses
into ground.
Gradually the heat that is flowing into that area
begins to expand and spread out until eventually
your whole body is glowing, healing,
tuned into, the universal energy:
—efflorescence! The Old Guys talked about
sometimes this happening on a cellular level.
though they wouldn't have used those words.
Keep doing Preparation for Tai Chi Form,
sitting a little each time,
rising and falling like a cork on the surface of
this pool.
Just this little motion,
brings the spine and hips into alignment over
the legs

and the torso supported in line on top of that.
Then just let this all sink and fall down
into your self.
The Senses moving down into the Seat of Will,
are turning into relaxation and warmth.
Or is it the seat of Being?
You have every right to be here in this space
even though you share it with others,
as they must share it with you. It is
the Center of Mass,
the center of mechanical motion.
Move the Tai Chi ball like you were
carrying your own child
a precious cargo.

You will be wanting to come back to this
relaxed state at the end of every move.
In the beginning you don't go on until you have
reached this relaxed state at the end of every
move. This place is always available for you.
It is the ground from which all movement
springs.

Crystal — > joints   also light from Tan Tien
Now you direct
the beam with your mind
to any part of your body
that may need healing.

Standing at the water's edge you look back to
the waterfall and the bubbles and give thanks to
nature for the healing that has taken place.
Once again the mist appears in front of you and
wraps you up like a cocoon.
Feeling safe and warm, be like the mist as it
begins floating up toward the mountain top, as you
bring your awareness back to your breathing.
Floating higher and higher, begin to wiggle your
toes and fingers. Let your head roll from left
to right. Nearing the top, move your arms and
legs. Have a good stretch. There is no hurry.
In your own time slowly open your eyes and
change awareness when you feel ready.
Remember the image of melting at the base of
the spine

Changing Frame

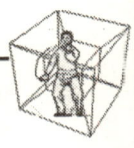

The second Carry Tiger to Mountain begins the third section, after the second Apparent Closure. Now you know you're into the home stretch. It is the same move as number 20 but by now you see a lot more in it. The Form is asking deeper and more technical questions.

As always, the Form is challenging you to keep the line of center within the area supporting the reach of this rather extended footprint. Carry Tiger to Mountain asks you to investigate any wobble when making the big turn around to the corner. This is done by paying particular attention to the hips, opening up that joint for added degrees of freedom. The constant gyroscopic self-monitoring which is an extension from static balance to dynamic balance and accompanies the beginner's motion has, with practice, begun to subside. The Form asks you to explore your balance more rigorously. Why do you wobble? Why do you oscillate back and forth, trying to find balance. Is it a question of static balance — optimizing the static *structure* somehow? Or is it a problem in *dynamic* balancing — do you need to greatly increase your damping ability?

Static and Dynamic Balancing

The goal of being dynamically balanced in Tai Chi means that the center of mass, CM, (the center of all the moving parts), remains un-accelerated regardless of the player's movements. This is best accomplished when the center of mass coincides with its support center. This most sought-after accomplishment in Tai Chi eliminates the need for gravity compensation. You might have seen how static balance is accomplished on car wheels by placing the tire hub on a point beam, and affixing compensating weights around the wheel rim. Dynamic balancing maintains some kind of correction function — a vector, pulling the system back into balance — and seeks to optimize and minimize this function. Which is the long way of saying: adjusting the limbs on the fly to keep balance on the move. This is done mainly by pre-planning the moves. Eventually this pre-planning becomes second nature and is no longer conscious or required.

The Form settles down, relaxes around the player.

In upright bipedal static balance, the center of mass is within the area of support delineated by separation and spread of the feet. (The area of support is a weighted cross-section of the volume of the person, projected onto the ground beneath the person). The CM is not extended beyond the boundary of this area such that it is cantilevered in some way. Ideally the CM of the person is on the *center line*, a line perpendicular through the centroid of the support area.

In a dynamic balance, all the moments of inertia from the connected, distributed limb masses remain zero, as the center of mass of the person moves. And this center of mass follows a curve that is perpendicular to a curve moving within the plane of the support area. Simply put, dynamic balance is where the moving parts are instantaneously counter-balanced in such a way that the net forces (due to torque from cantilever arms) remain zero regardless of the body's movements and the CM coincides with its support center. If you do Tai Chi slowly with attention to individual muscles, your focus can advance from exploring the 10 principal degrees of freedom in the horizontal and vertical plane, eventually beginning to know something of the 250 degrees of freedom associated with the available reach of human joints. Yes, a big lifetime project.

Noise

Control originating from the center of the body resulting from balance that has been more naturally positioned in best comfort, is of great benefit. If you are unbalanced you will perceive extra weight along an axis. The Tai Chi player monitors small changes in inertia through stress strain gauges in the joints. The player ideally treats these as noise, — that is unnecessary muscle tension and tries to minimize them. The noise of muscle tension has the effect of unevenly distributed inertial mass, and causes rigid coupling through the joints to the center of mass, leaving the body vulnerable to being easily unbalanced by a force on the periphery.

Mathematically (and here I had to dig out my old linear algebra book and pour over diagonalization and symmetry adapting and orthogonalizing matrices), dynamics balancing refers to two properties of its multi-body dynamics. One, the inertial tensor of the human body is almost diagonal, which means that linear accelerations create no coupling torques; angular accelerations create no forces. Two, it also means that the inertial tensor is uniform, it does not vary in large proportions throughout the workspace (ellipsoid of inertia).

Moreover, from a metaphysical point of view, this noise gets in the way of reception, of tuning into a deeper sense of presence and participation in being.

Accurate position sensing

Through selective application of attention and muscle tension, the player seeks to redirect force by the application of controlling smart force. This contact force is at an angle anywhere within the workspace defined by the ellipsoid of inertia of the limbs involved (made up of the available reaches corresponding to degrees of freedom.)

Uniform motion

The dynamic balancing function we mentioned can help insure the desired uniform motion. The idea of uniform motion is to maintain an isometric tension such that one is not so fully committed to the motion of the moment, that is, the inertia of one's moving should not take a lot of force to halt or turn or change. A uniform response everywhere inside the workspace (ellipsoid of inertia), characterized by a ratio of output inertia to the output force required to change, should not vary by a factor larger than 1:2. From this criterion one sets up the motion.

Power Conservation

It is a criterion of Tai Chi to keep the ratio of the output inertia less than half of the output force. That makes it easier for you to start and stop movements, to change, to become uncommitted to directions if blocked or anticipated. One does the Form with the idea of keeping the response uniform. Keep the response proportional to the threat, be a gentleman and in control of the situation. Have and bring a lot more to the situation than is called for by building up the strength of the body, so that using only a portion of the strength results in a net increase of the application of strength.

Sensitive Hands

The Tai Chi players's hands are trained for sensitivity, for "listening" through "sticking" --maintaining direct contact. The act of grappling in Tai Chi looks for rigid connections to the center of mass of the opponent. Or for easily collapsible linkages leading to rigid connections to the center of mass. As a haptic device the human hand is unsurpassed. Outside of the brain it has a higher neuronal density than anywhere else in the body. Perhaps you've seen the homunculus map, showing the body parts scaled to size according to the number of neural connection to the brain. The thumb and the lips are the most sensitive haptic devices.

The training of sensitive hands is part of the ancient Chinese art of "bone setting" or chiropractic. These people can use their sense of touch to find kinks and blockages in people and animals. Some can heal directly with their touch. Much has been written by naturopathic healers, especially in America.

It is said that experienced Push Hands players are able to communicate directly, mind to mind with the sensitivity of their touch and it is supposed to feel quite exquisite and intimate. Some of the old Taoist healers and Buddhist monks are actually charged with the responsibility of "karma-mechanics" the ability to affect the alignment of the world. But that does beyond the scope of this manual.

Shock

High frequency response due to optimized structural design combined with very small amounts of damping. A target small-motion bandwidth of 100 Hz along or around all axis is targeted in the sense that a strong output response is available to that frequency.

Can one speak about an overall frequency response? There are oscillations or small motions along or around an axis, Indeed is there a way you can amplify these oscillations in a helpful way?

Think about mindfulness in Tai Chi, and the value of suddenness is breaking through mindfulness. The idea of a shock.

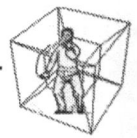

Master you r ego, master your body movements in Tai Chi, and the inner player will come to the flow. You need to move around underneath the teaching of Tai Chi, to get better at it. You need to visit it every day.

Avoid Spiritual Materialism

The trick is to prevent the conscious mind from sabotaging your efforts. This sabotaging is what might be called spiritual materialism — the idea that spiritual growth is something you can schedule and produce. If we can keep our mind from sabotage then we'll be able to hang-in and let it take us where we need to go. Here are the things we do to sabotage ourselves: We exaggerate our weaknesses, our strengths and how much or how little we know. And we distort who we are and where we are in our journey of learning Tai Chi. Self sabotage causes us to move away from learning a form before it is mastered, to go through the motions instead of really practicing, so the material we've practiced comes out strained and awkward in performance, or doesn't come out at all. And then when you try harder you play worse.

On the other hand, remember to have fun. Remember the times when you played and there were absolutely no consequences. At those times it really flowed.

Do not let your Somatic Intelligence be bullied by the unreasoning pressure of the ego saying, "Come on! You should have already gotten this stuff and improved." Unreasonable pressure destroys the natural growth of progress in dance, and causes us to skim the surface rather than dig in.

While the ego does this the Chi that wants to manifest itself is blocked and lost.

This is why we don't let the Chi fly with love and inspiration all the time. Our egos prevent us from focusing on the process of practicing and improving.

The Music of Tai Chi

What is the inner music of Tai Chi? The rhythm to which it flows? It is the breath. You might start doing it to the yogi breath: in 6, hold 4, out 4, or something like that.

Try to breath out on the going away from the body and try to breath in on the coming toward the body. You will also need to take rests.

Make a Taoist Space

Let us walk into this space, a process space to learn how to improvise Tai Chi moves, connected, quiet, yet attentive.

You are the instrument and you are going to experience this instrument being played by an entity beyond yourself but within yourself. Relax every part of your body, keep your posture straight. Imagine that your arms are being raised by someone else and watch as your fingers effortlessly touch the world, seemingly of their own accord.

Carry the space into the movement. Say to yourself, you are only going to be doing a couple of moves from the Form. Get around the space playing only a few brief cada motions at a time. Using brief portions of the Form, feel your stance and your legs, feel the motion driven from your center of mass percolate up to hands. Let it be gentle and familiar to you. Watch your hands play on their own, driven from below. This step is an information gathering step, it gives you the clearest indication of what you need to do later.

The Form is your teacher Now

The form is your teacher now, doing the form effort-lessly in the space you have established. Always do Tai Chi effortlessly.

How much do you play? As slow as it needs to be while you are in the effort space.

Here are some fragments of qualities relating to music.

rhythmic	motion in time, expansion — contraction
harmonic	cross -coupling spacetime, the chord, the tightly coordinated knit flowing of body
melodic	motion in space, the content, that is to say the letter, the blocks of the form, the out ward form, the nameable move

rhythmic	rolling along, translation movement in space
harmonic	tuning, resonating, reacting, listening
melodic	emotional content, segment, connected speech

your Tailbone is your rudder
 The phrase "Tuck Under" . . .
means to tip-up your hip girdle
so that it is parallel to the floor.
The pelvis is level.
The stomach, back, and core muscles are engaged in
helping maintain alignment.
 You get a sense of dropping your tail bone —your keel
board, your navigator, into the waters.
 You're in a sail boat, setting keel to breakers.
Floating from the waist,
the hip girdle is your boat; your Tailbone is your rudder.
You are floating, perhaps on ice — gliding,
or walking — on water.
 You shift the weight,
 —rather, change the support —
to go to the left, turn rudder to left
to go to the right, turn rudder right.
Sailing on a sea of grace,
your figurehead is your face,
—your sail is your broad chest,
let it billow out on the breath,
stretching to the four points:
shoulders and hips,
toes and finger tips.
You want to let them sail in the direction of Force
on this gravity ocean.
All kinetic motion
is a tack at an angle to navigate gravity,
which is always pushing against you.
You are in a kind of vehicle:
to operate it, relax into awareness.

It's as if you have this line, this sailboard
going down from your center of mass,
(a spot between your navel and your spine)
dipping into your center of gravity,
which is the center of the area of support for your body.
Move that Center of mass first,

just ahead of shifting your weight.
(The body is doing this unconsciously anyway.)
Think of the dinosaur and his ballast tail, or the cat, who
can twitch her tail in flight to chang direction;
your Tailbone as your rudder
Our brachiating ancestors had a prehensile tail. (That
must have been nice.)
With better bipedal balance it got abstracted
became a little fused bone sheath.
Now it is not used except in pregnancy.
Tickle, tingle little vestigial fused bone sheath
kind of a penis,
which way does your tail bone point tonight?
Tail as metonymy: Get your tail over here!
Mercury has moved its tail into your fortune house.

I'm floating in a blue sea, beside some Aegian isle
a snorkeler drifting above it all, beneath a blue sky.
We come to that moment in a trip when you realize
what you set out on the voyage to find.
And the sea rolls in.
I was by myself floating in a warm blue realm,
Going further and further from the shore
dazzled by the light filtering down through me,
shimmering down into the depths.
I was drawn further and further out.
There wasn't anything near.
I'm floating there in the sea's amniotic fluid
that supported me once. As it does now.
I'm trying see it as a field, to feel it, to float
        in it   and   above it.
Be able to know how its currents are superposed:
bark of politics, hand of economy,
job as opportunity to know yourself in group,
love as a mirror to feel yourself.
All the joys and sorrows that come
are made from waves reverberating off distant boundaries
and I'm trying to stay above it.
Blue baby born on the internal tide,
blue blood, gills before — oxygen to lungs
We all recapitulate phylogeny.

I began to feel that the Automorph was watching me. That it was teaching me, as he teaches all of us, to adapt. The Automorph taught this through the Form — for the Form is a gentle and considerate playing field of stylized ritualistic simulation. The Automorph teaches us to adapt through the Somatic Intelligence, whom I call Yum Chi.

For I, Walker Underwood, was starting to play at being Yum Chi more. It was a way of taking on mastery. And Yum Chi was great company to have around the farm, this focus, this entity, this Friend, this character, this Alter-ego, this Ulterior motive to drift into. Yes. I, Yum Chi, 27 — itinerant share-cropper, by now was developing a personality that was made up of Charley Chan, Caine (the Wanderer guy on Kung Fu), Bruce Lee, a beatnik, and an ancient Chinese sage.

At any moment in the day I might pretend to be, silent long-suffering Caine, student of the Tao, wearing his loose fitting peasant clothes and great floppy hat, having false memories of life in the Shaolin Temple. How was it in that first mystical, eastern Western? Caine had tatoos on his arms, from lifting the boiling pot — how was it? — the dragon on the left and the tiger on the right? I find myself in, maybe, the famous grasshopper scene:

Master Po: Close your eyes. What do you hear?

Young Caine: I hear the breeze, and some birds. . .

Master Po: Do you hear the Grasshopper which is at your feet?

Young Caine: Old man, how is it that you hear these things.

Master Po: Young man, how is it that you do not?

Or, I might do a Bruce Lee, punctuating the solitude of his day by pulling a hard edged stance. And letting out the loud   Yeeeeeyaaa   audibly snapping the block and giving off sound effects like they do in those Kung Fu movies.

Or as a beatnik, I might start spouting haiku.

BEATNIK: in standing meditation   o   o   o ,
              somewhere i am   '_|'   ,|)   )<
              not there   < '   / >   < \

And at other times I might be part ancient Chinese sage.

I started to drift into the I Ching at this point of turbulence in my life, and I started to make a study of the I Ching.
I began to keep a little notebook. I was struck by the poetry
in the lines of the I Ching. That's what led me in. I just loved
those disarmingly cryptic lines dripping with meaning and
portent. Using the Coin Toss method, I'd sample the synchronistic vortex and look up the lines in the I Ching just to
see what I got.
I might get the hexagram.
    lake/sister Rhythm diminishes

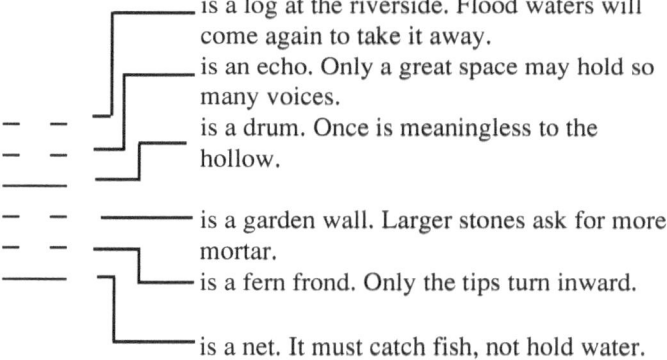

                  is a log at the riverside. Flood waters will
                  come again to take it away.
                  is an echo. Only a great space may hold so
                  many voices.
                  is a drum. Once is meaningless to the
                  hollow.

                  is a garden wall. Larger stones ask for more
                  mortar.
                  is a fern frond. Only the tips turn inward.

                  is a net. It must catch fish, not hold water.

But I did not like the authoritative and overly-assuming
way the poetry was presented; nor the arbitrary randomness
of the way the hexagrams were generated.
In a way it was like reading your astrology in the paper
or like believing in God. One was more likely to believe in
providence if the system is accurate with predictions and
when He (She? it?) provides.
I felt that I had to do something to get at what I thought
was the original sense of the I Ching. The problem is that the
original text was probably an image in the unconscious of a
man, a symbol, things seen in a state of heightened awareness by a diviner. And his interpretation has been commented upon and commented upon down through the ages
and appended to the Oracles as the 10 Wings, one in particu-
larly the Great Treatise, and this translated so that nowadays

the answer is made up of interpretation layered over interpretation, layered over even more interpretation.

I had to somehow go back from the words, which have been handed down to us through the past three millennia. I wanted to get at some kind of transcendental haruspication. It was an attempt to capture the spirit of the Oracle as it was before the written Chinese language became a representation of spoken language. I decided to have this body act out the ideograms in a kind of talking chanting mime theatre. I saw myself as an Old Man with coin in palm of hand. Blowing on it, bouncing it around inside cupped hands. Getting the lines, calling them out. Saying what they are: yang yang yin yin yin yang. Then saying the name of the hexagram. I wanted to be like this Old Sage that had them all memorized. Then starting to say what I remembered for each line, and making things up with what I felt. The amphictionic theatre.

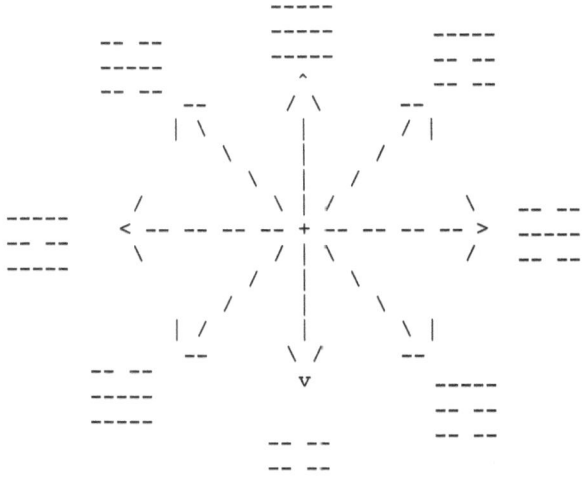

Pa kua diagram made on a typwriter

I got this idea to try and memorize the oracle that had been given me for a particular day. And to take it out into this day, and see if correspondences would arise. And sometimes at night I would even dance the oracle. It was an attempt to duplicate the feats of the ancient Greek oracle in the amphictionic theatre and I would speak the lines over and over again while getting into a looping rhythmic chi gung set. For the broken line I drew in, for the solid line I pushed out.

At any moment in the day I might be Charley Chan trudging along, spaced-out, through my day making pithy little statements I'd gleaned from the I Ching, like: "Aah so. The roof is — — Yin. What holds nothing, shields best."

I built a little theatre piece based on a hexagram.

Scene: *The Actor twists and turns as if floating in a river across the stage*

Actor:
A log at the riverside is Yin. Flood waters will come again to take it away.

Scene: *Spreads arms and hands out exploring cavernous space*

Actor:
Yin is an echo. Only a great space may hold so many voices.

Actor: (*Stomps foot, steps back and listens for an echo*)
Yang is a drum. Once is meaningless to the hollow.

Actor: (*lifting a heavy stone into a wall*)
A garden wall is Yin. Larger stones ask for more mortar.

Scene: *Single whip*

Actor:
A fern frond is Yin. Only the tips turn inward.

Scene: *He casts his arms out like casting a fisherman's net, leaves lingering sense of net in space*

Actor:
A net is Yang. It must catch fish, not hold water.

60 The Impetus for Deconstructing Synchronicity

I had Da Liu's book *Tai Chi Chuan and I Ching — A Choreography of Body and Mind*. I thought to "perform" the section where he draws parallels between the Tai Chi forms and trigrams and hexagrams of the I Ching. I imagined it would take place in a theatre somewhere. I set the scene where the hexagrams were scrims over the spot and projected over the actor, or on the wall beside the actor. I started pairing down the lines for the actor to speak.

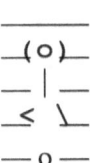

But I was struck by how apparently arbitrary the reasoning was for assigning a hexagram or trigram to a Tai Chi form. I thought I was on to the right stuff but he assumes too much. Right away, in the second movement, Grasp Bird's Tail he starts talking about "9 in the 2nd place" and that the 2nd place was the abdomen. That perplexed me. The 2nd place was the abdomen? Why not the knee. If the hexagram was the layers of a standing man, it should go 1 —> 6 , feet —> head. The 2nd place should be the knees, or even the ankles.

So my next thought was that what he meant here was the trigram. The trigram of the human was legs, torso, mind. Wasn't it? But maybe it was feet—legs—stomach, heart and head. Then the 2nd place would be heart. So anyway all these systems have a couple of things in common: a simple system has a huge amount of approximation to detail; it is about increasing resolution, about closer and closer approximation to the real. We are always dealing with imperfect information, and using whatever gestalt we can to enhance it.

I had to understand it on a deeper level or it wasn't going to work at all. Since I was my own teacher, I was trying to "interpret" the forms, to find out what the old masters who had invented them meant, what they intended. I was coming out of, or trying to awaken from a sleep or a prison, trying to awaken from being a prisoner of mind. The world I wanted to tune into was a much larger world of being. It was so foreign to be able to be in my feelings, that whenever it happened, it was like suddenly awakening to a much larger world. A world that was not dominated by the cause and effect of the mind, but a world that contained cause and effect and probabilities and possibilities, and non- or a-causal connections. Jung had thought about this and had called it synchronicity.

I needed to understand synchronicity, which Jung, Pauli and others saw as a superset that contained causality. It seemed to be like the way semiotics contained logic. The great C.S. Peirce, an American philosopher, was the pioneer of this. And yet here in the I Ching, a well-formed body of work going way back 3,000 years into ancient China, was a great sign-system exploring the oracular. Had anyone worked out a theory of the semiotics of the I Ching? I'm not Chinese, nor do I read Chinese. But I know from Worf and Ezra Pound how language influences thinking. The *I Ching* and the *Tao Te Ching* have a huge influence on Chinese thought. The *Tao Te Ching* is the third most widely trans-lated book in the world after *The Bible* and *Don Quixote*.

My goal in this was to develop the mnemonic theatre for a play or a rite or a ritual. I thought to make my mnemonic theatre the *pa kua*. I was struck by how, in the performances of Tai Chi I had seen, that you see a lot of technical exper-tise, —great attention to the arc of movement and placement and balance; but it is rare to see someone being innovative, and being authentic in their feeling. That is to be really there and to be using it for feeling. Although I have heard that some of the great old healing masters do it this way. I was thinking of it as an amphictionic theater in which the player was a diviner in the sense of coming to consciousness.

There ought to be some way to think of a move at any moment as some element in a hierarchy based on combina-tions of lower elements.

```
 _____      _____       _____
 __  __     _____    —  — sun rising
 _____      _( o __    _____              o
 __  __     _ | _     —  — over         ( | )
 __  __     _< \_     __  __            [   ]
 _____      __  __    _____ the earth  —beginings
```

This spaced-out Laban motion study coupled with the ancient I Ching philosophy of combinatorics was acting upon my Yum Chi mind. I felt this entity Yum Chi within me, and with unmitigated chutzpa and hubris, I wondered what *his* commentary on the I Ching would be. What *was* it about the trigrams that lent themselves to this kind of hierarchical categorization system.

I was trying to understand the modern world view of probability. I wanted something that was not based upon our Indo-European linguistic tradition. Something more like the matrix algebra of Heizenburg. —the combinations, the quantum level transition matrix, the idea of number as matrix, the idea of a functor diagram as mandala.

I got this idiea that the I Ching was an ancient philosophical aesthetic system that embodied the new world view presented in physics which I was trying to reconcile with ordinary living. While in college I had run into an essay about synchronicity, coauthored by Carl Jung and Wolfgang Pauli in 1936, and it had changed the course of my life. It had inspired me greatly, enough to move from studying physics to studying psychology.

I read everything that I could get my hands on about the *I Ching*.

Spiritual Intelligence

A Modern
Commentary
on the I Ching

A Users Guide
for Coordinating the
Dichotomous Nature of Reality
into Structured
Probability Matrices
for Risk Assessment
and Authentic Action

by

Sifu Yum Chi
with Walker Underwood

Preface

I am indebted to the many, many scholars of the I Ching, especially two modern masters: C. J. Lofting and T. Smith.

Introduction

The I Ching is a representation of a simple system of living with hierarchical structures and approximations. That is, the hexagrams and the collection of observations around them is a sufficiently free system without the bias of a particular structure. It has been studied for a very long time.

The first explanations of the *I Ching* are written by various philosophers in the ten commentaries, called "wings", appended to the book. Confucius is attributed to be one of the writers. The main wing is the first one written by King Wen and his son, the Duke of Chou, called the Great Treatise. It describes how the attributes are assigned to the trigrams and hexagrams and their arrangements.

In Jung's preface interpretation of the I Ching he wrote: "the hexagram was the exponent of the moment in which it was cast —even more so that the hours of the clock or the division of the calendar could be, in as much as the hexagram was understood to be an indicator of the essential situation prevailing in the moment of its origin." I got this idea of the hexagram as a kind of probability transition matrix for extracting information from the synchronic. The image, — the object, the instrument — they use for this sampling is the *pa qua*. It is a stunning piece of intuitive technology, an amalgam: of compass, a clock (a sun dial with a golem), a calendar and an astrolabe. I pictured it in an ideogram (the hexagram is the exponent of the moment).

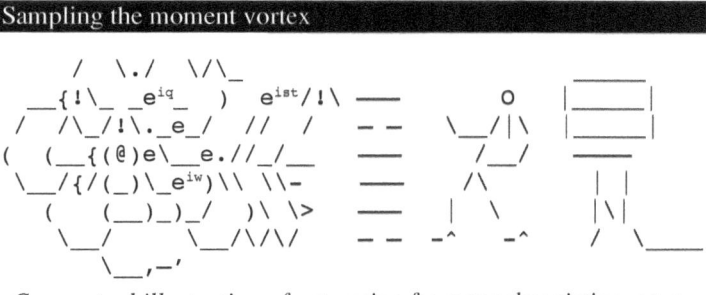

Sampling the moment vortex

Conceptual illustration of extraction from synchronistic vortex, (modeled as a cloud with complex exponential wave behavior) by hexagram, of hierarchical emergence information.

For Jung, oracular techniques were about understanding the self through communicating with the unconscious. These amphictionic movements are a method for exploring that.

The Eastern and Western Sense of Time

The group of writers who wrote the *Bible* were influenced by the western sense of time especially as it is reflected in the drama of story telling. Similarly, the group of writers that pulled together texts on oracles and process of augury and commentaries to write the *I Ching* were influenced by the eastern sense of time. They are quite different. I think the Western and Eastern sense of time reflect the way the brain organizes the world with its two hemispheres, left brain and right brain. Having evolved in a diurnal world we all have access to basically the same sense of time, but one is more "natural" than the other.

The European Christian Judaic sense of time coming from a northern clime where there are seasons, and one feels the pressure of preparing for a winter, begets an art form that reflects the pressure of time in its dramatical presentation. Whereas in the east, where it was pretty much summer all around in the hot climes, and all one had to do to eat was reach up into the nearest tree and pull down a luscious fruit kindly provided by the Source, the sense of time could be more right brain, have quality, and not be so inexorable.

Disciplines

So to mount an assault on the understanding of Synchronicity, I thought one piece of the puzzle would be to begin with what Jung called his Analytic Philosophy, which sought to be a kind of philosophy rooted in the real—in the useful. It is an understanding you come to when you get out of the ego, and come to inhabit the Self as it is manifested in time in the body now. And it requires some strange tools to get at this, for we are trying to capture the Great Formless Tao in our puny words now (which is a hopeless task but nevertheless one worth attempting).

Here are some of the background texts to prep ourselves for the voyage. Jung's and Pauli's work on Synchronicity. In general the probabilistic theory of quantum mechanics is a very good picture of what we are dealing with. Matrix mechanics, the theory of games and strategy, math of fractals, set theory, topology, Bayesian inference. At the same time we need to start opening up to dreams, and meditation. And most of all, to open up to the wisdom of the body because we are trying to understand being and how it is manifest.

I have pulled together a journal of I Ching studies from that time. It explores some of the following ideas. How the mind embedded or reflected in the I Ching is both analog and digital. How the I Ching is a combinational model of the branching fractal nature of reality, and as such it reflects the structure of our own nervous system. I trace this binary modeling paradigm in a few representations: weather, mathematics, personality theory, botany.

Later we'll look more deeply into the fractal, which is the model of branching bifurcating dichotomous reality *par excellence*.

I give this effort the ponderous title: *The Ontology and Epistemology of Onto(/)slashology and Hexotranspiration — A New Commentary on the I Ching.*

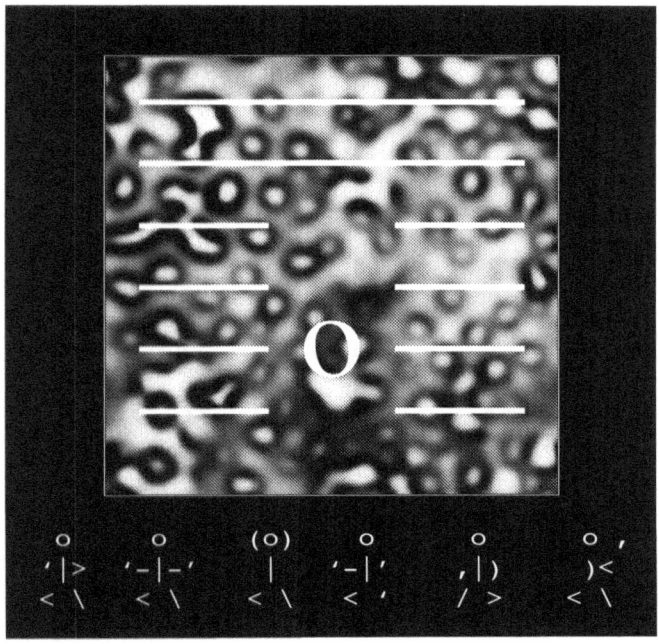

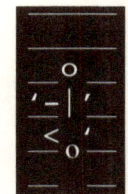

Entering the I Ching we are entering a holy and wholistic landscape of the mind. More than thinking of it as a way to get privy information about the future, I was curious about the primitive mind, with its concrete science that was so elegantly evidenced here. How did they build up the imagery of the trigrams. There has been more commentary written about the *I Ching* than any book on earth. Our two guides in this landscape are Fu Hsiu the primogenator of the trigrams, and the father and son team: King Wen and the Duke of Chou. It seemed to me that the Fu Hsiu story was about the digital mind in the I Ching, and the Wên story was about the analog mind in the I Ching. Wondering about how the trigrams got their meaning we go all the way back to Fu Hsiu and the origin of the I Ching.

The stories of the originators of the I Ching are apocryphal. One was the story of Wên who is supposed to have invented the I Ching while in prison, to while away the hours, to keep himself from going mad and to beguile his captors. The other originator of the I Ching was a wandering sage named Fu Hsiu who discovered the hexagrams in a stroke of enlightenment while boiling water in a turtle's shell on his campfire. It seemed to me that the Wên story was about the analog mind in the I Ching, and the Fu Hsiu story was about the digital mind in the I Ching.

The Digital Mind in the I Ching
Fu Hsiu and the Crack in the Cosmic Turtle Shell
Imagine yourself sitting with Fu Hsiu, a garrulous old hermit, who lives in a hut and spends all his time wandering the woods and meditating in his cold autumn camp beside the river. It is 2500 years before Christ. The Celts rule Europe. Egypt was building its pyramids as a testement to immortality. Here is Fu Hsiu alone in the primevial forest, sitting before his camp fire, warming his body and cheering his spirit. For him the forest and his world is alive with spirits. It is a world of animism. Fu Hsiu is at the cusp of a world emerging from primordial animism, a world carried through space on the back of a giant turtle, yet enamored with the number patterns of a Magic Square.

Perhaps Fu Hsiu is engaged in the unitive contemplation of the transcendental reality, dazed in meditative thought by the flickering fire. On the fire is a tortoise shell being used as a pot to boil a little water for tea.

What did this great ancient sage, wandering the countryside, think about when he fell into the reverie of fire. We might ascribe to him our quest: He is maybe thinking about how he wants to communicate with the source of existence, the OM SAT TAT, the All that Is, the one god, who some 4 billion years ago wrote a program that got stored in matter and evolved into the fabric of life. The All-that-Is, She-He wrote the program and scattered it in the primordial soup of several planets. It has been running on this planet ever since.

Fu Hsiu is maybe thinking something like: the tree is a memory and the acorn which created the tree is a "word"— a seed/word, which creates the memory of the tree. The memories are passed around. The acorn food is passed around to others so that it may survive if it is useful. Also this great caretaking entity, the Source, is constantly sampling the world. It re-members. It is constantly re-supplying the world with "beings", with new "memories", as the old ones wear out.

But then we must realize that even though these ancients were great minds, they would not be thinking at all about the same kinds of things we might think about. They would have been astounded to know that the sun was not the center of the universe, or that we evolved from bacteria. Maybe not.

Fu Hsiu might be wondering about the weather. Like all people who live outside, close to the earth, he is wondering about the weather. The other thoughts were Yum Çhi's.

How much more the average person knows and has! Fu Hsiu would have been delighted to be able to turn on a tap and get cold water suitable for drinking any time he wanted. Fu Hsiu probably believed that the world traveled through space on the back of a turtle. Turtle Island it was called. How delighted he would have been to talk to us.

When suddenly CRACK , the water had boiled away and the fire went into the shell instead of the water. And CRACK a huge pop shocks the dreaming sage into enlightenment like Newton when an apple fell on his head.

Fu Hsiu notices the cracks in the tortoise shell, some long and some short, and he realizes that because the world moved through space on the back of a cosmic tortoise and because the tortoise is a projection of the great cosmic one, which generated the illusion of motion, that interrogating the cracks is a way to interrogate the OM SAT TAT, the all that is. The crack was a crack in the world, a gate that opened up and Fu Hsiu went through that gate.

At first it is like a game of 20 questions, in which someone thinks of something and the others have to ask questions that can only be answered by yes or no to guess it. Good players have found 20 questions are all that is needed to categorize anything on this earth.

For example a child says, " I am thinking of something." (A bridge, say.)

You ask, Is it animal. No -- -- (Using a broken line -- -- for no; an unbroken line ----- for yes)

Is it vegetable. No -- --

Is it a thing. Yes -----

Is it bigger than a house. No -- -- . . .

You have got to come to the oracle with a question in your mind. Because you are part of All that IS then you influence how the tortoise shell cracks and you can communicate with the OM SAT TAT.

Well that was wonderful. To be able to walk around in the world and think about the continuous and the discrete as a way of communicating with existence. It was a wonderful feeling.

But what about asking more complicated questions. Like how will we survive the long winter? What about maybe?

With that came the idea of stacking the broken and unbroken and the idea of "emerges from."

-- -- -----	became maybe no and
----- -- --	became maybe yes
----- -----	is positively yes and
-- -- -- --	is positively no

Clearly we have the idea of refinement of the question going from bottom up, but what about going further. And so we take refinement of the question to the third level in the formation of the trigram.

I had a problem with how Hsiu introduces the third level of the trigram because here Hsiu introduces the idea of the family. I didn't get it at first that it was a natural man's relation to nature in the way truest to him. But here we have an opportunity to switch to another way of looking at it, from the digital in Hsiu to the analog in the Wên way.

The Analog Mind in the I Ching
Wen's Space/Time Transcending Window Grid
Wên is the author of most of the commentary on the I Ching, in particular the Great Treatise. Legend has it that he composed most of it around 1042 BC while languishing in prison at the hands of another king. He invented the sixty-four Hexagrams and their names. Legend has it that Wên, trying to keep himself from going mad while looking out the horizontal bars of his prison cell, began to try and dissolve the bars of his cage with his mind. Apparently he was successful, because legend has it that he so beguiled and delighted his captors with his poetic insights, that the emperor who had imprisoned him gave to Wên his own daughter's hand in marriage.

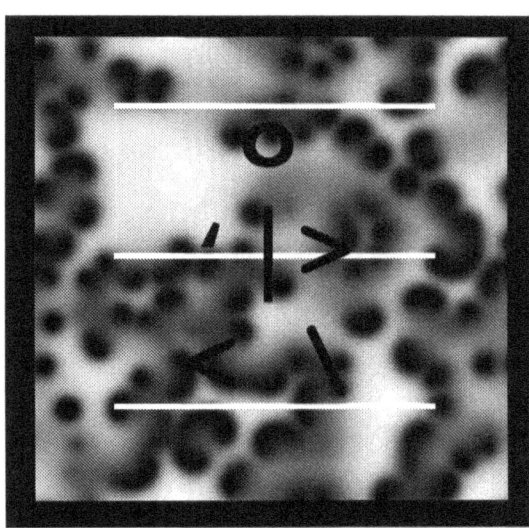

63 The Prisoner of Mind

I was attracted to the idea that the hexagram was a graphic but also a tally, a table, a collection of observations, a matrix. Upon thinking about it, I began to imagine its designers being so sensitive that they apprehended it as a representation of the mind scanning across, and up and down. It was a grid, or a filter, that one could open and close, focus. Maybe one could look at this ancient world of mind, untrained by western literacy, through a kind of venetian blind. I imagined Wên in prison looking out the bars of his window.

Scene: *Pantomime of Wen, holding bars, looking off into the distance.*

Wên:
Long periods of idleness of the prisoner makes him quite a talker.

Scene: *Wen pacing around exploring the walls of his cell with his hands, feeling for a feature.*

Wên:
A man is in a cage.
It has one window. Covered with bars.
The man spends his days looking out the one window,
at a mountain.
A mountain that is way off in the distance
at the end of a winding road.
He can see that the road winds through a forest
and past a lake.
The man spends his days in a cage, looking out
the one window
of horizontal bars,
blinds that he can not change.
The man regards the bars,—(*grabs and shakes bars*)
IRON!
The man tries to think of them as a, . . .
a seine or a weir, —a net —
in the rising and ebbing of time-flow,

something stuck up (*thrusts hands in air*)
upon which to capture what?
himself maybe, or a representation of what
is going on in the outside world?

Actor as Narrator: (*Aside directly to the audience*)
   Wên developed ways of selectively seeing and not
seeing the bars. They formed a kind of grid and he visualized
various organizations of the landscape outside this window.
He got this idea for getting an emotional cathexis around the
mountain off in the distance. Being a well-educated man,
Wen had studied the trigrams of Fu Hsiu and other spirit
token systems of oracular numismatomancy.

Scene: *Hexagrams are projected white against a black wall
behind the actor. As he speaks, he changes character into
Narrator. He points to features helping the audience
visualize. Then the actor changes back into Wen.*

Wên:
   Mountain

——— Mountain off in the distance
— — road into the distance at foot of mountain
— — road on earth over hill into distance
   Mountain Scene
He stands back and considers it.

Actor as Narrator:
   This trigram wants to be read from the bottom up. That
way you can get an almost 3D effect.
(*Addressing the Audience*)
   Another day he saw lightning from a storm,

Wên (*considering the next hexagram*):

   Chen (Thunder, Air, Electricity)
   — — lightning in the upper air
   — — striking through the middle air
   ——— coming down to the mother earth
   Thunder, Air, Electricity. Easy for lightning to strike
down between the two top yin lines. It is like the lightning

that cleaves the air, a cut.

Wên *(considering the next hexagram)*:
Kun (Ground)
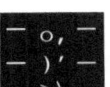 — — the Earth
— — Plains
— — Meadow

The earth absorbs, it is spongy, takes energy and
grounds it, uses it, recycles it. The Green Force that recycles
and recirculates the matter, the genetics

Scene: *Wen addresses more hexagrams as he points*

Wên *(considering each next hexagram)*:
Kan (Water River Rain Moon)
 — — clouds
———————the moon floating over a landscape
— — a river flowing in a plane

Good, you've got to start seeing the landscape behind
the hexagram.

Tui (Lake, Metal, Cave, Valley)
Read it from the bottom up and you get
— — sky
——————— lake, looking up to the high country to sky
——————— Land, earth

Wên: *(continuing)*
Lake, high country seen in the distance beyond
Land, earth.

Li (Fires, Sun, Hearth)
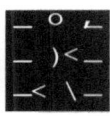 ——————— Fires, smoke rising
— — Sun off in the distance
——————— Distance. Fire, flame rising into the distance

Actor as Narrator: *(Addressing the Audience)*
To Wen, these hexagrams were like a window into a
land of not-yet-formed possibilities.

Prisoner Wên is a great talker and he began telling his stories to the guards and then eventually the Emperor — whom Wên beguiled.

Wên had made a kind of mnemonic grid based upon what he saw outside the bars of his window. These he compounded and combined to help him telling his stories. He used images —ideograms — to help everyone remember the points he wanted to make. He called them hexagrams. He saw his hexagrams as a kind of television and the beings and things moving around in his landscape were, though real, also omens. They brought with them portents and other bits of wisdom and advice which the people were eager to share.

Wên *(considering each next hexagram)*:
Sun   (Sun Tree Wind Wood)
We tend to read from the sky down. *(POINTING)*
Try reading from the Ground up.

————sky seen through tree branches
————upper branches of tree in sky
—   —lower branches of tree, earth, terrain

Here the idea of emergence — the tree cleaves the space with its trunk, but you see the background, then finally the tree itself emerges from the background.

Chen

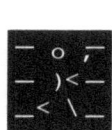
——— heaven light
——— airy expansive
——— rises.

This creativity, that is the mind moving.
So could you, upon presentation, see a gallery of landscapes?

Earth	Thundr	Water	Lake	Mount	Fire	Tree	Create
– –	– –	– –	– –	——	——	——	——
– –	– –	——	——	– –	– –	——	——
– –	——	– –	——	– –	——	– –	——

The literature on Taoism is filled with details on the performances of ritualistic walks. It seemed like the form Fair Lady Works at Shuttles, # 64 was a mini-mandala asking the player to turn and turn about into the 4 directions. It looked like other "walks" I was finding in the Taoist literature.

I began to think about taking the Images and Commentary from the I Ching readings and placing them at strategic places in a closed walk. I could do I Ching readings and say the material into the 4 corners. At the same time I could be thinking out loud and improvising on the material.

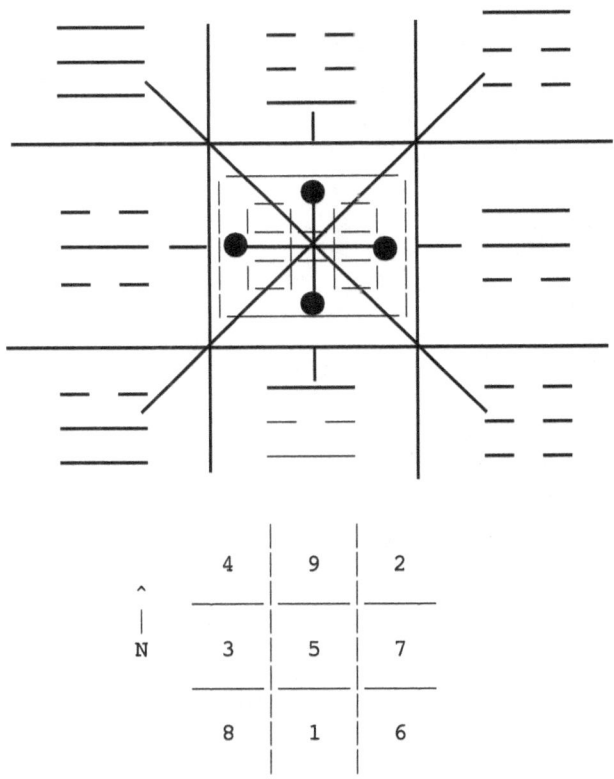

Scene: *(From above, plan of farm, the big oak tree out near the patch high above the tall weeds and thick bush surrounding the patch. There is a path from the house out back to the well near the tree.)*

Player:

We look in four directions;

The house off in the distance that you could only see the roof of,

the dirt footpath through the tall weeds zig zagged so there was no straight view into the garden.

And from there to the small marijuana forest.

The big oak tree's shadow fell over the well where I drew the water up.

When doing Fair Lady you swing out wide in the 4 directions.

I have been out here 4 seasons, seen the land go from somber brown and gray—denuded in the winter, to lush green in the spring, to a riotous green hell that eventually

dried into burnt out in the summer, to just the bare machinery of life now in the autumn.

Rising and separating
sinking and merging
—convection.
A person is like the earth whence he rises.
From afar the earth looks like a sphere, but close up
it is made up of some 20 plates,
called the lithosphere,
floating on a molten mantle.
This occasionally punches through the lithosphere as a volcano.
What if we thought of the person as an icosahedron,
and we could assign plates to the various areas.

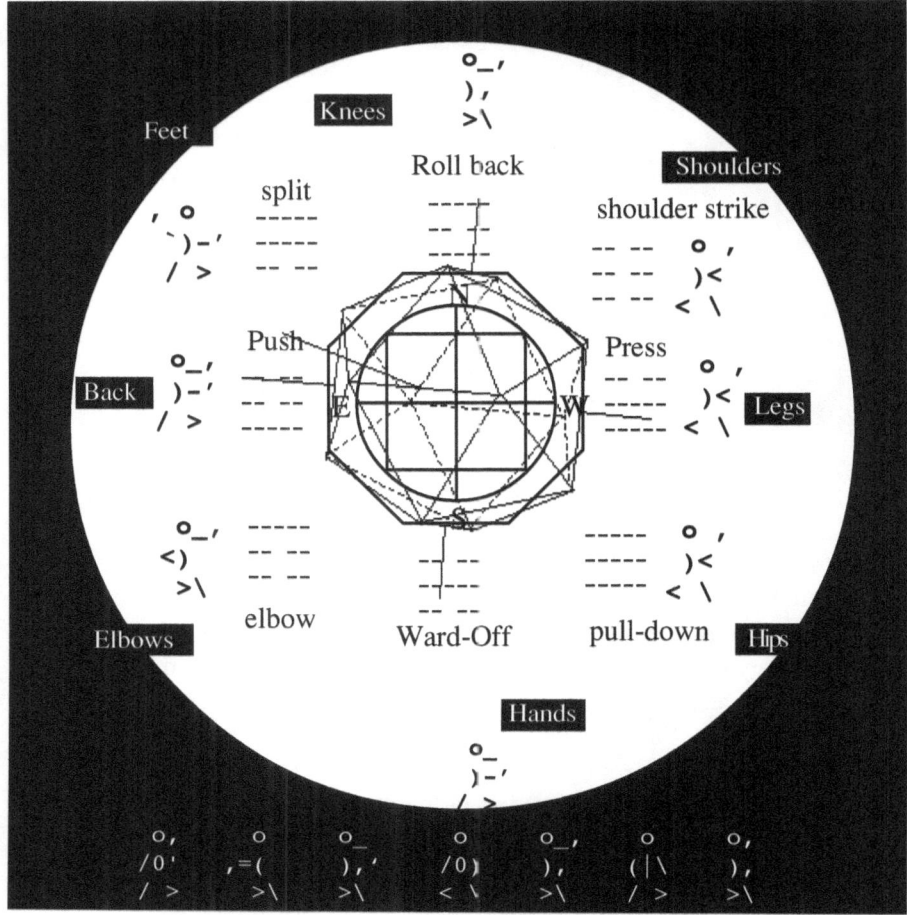

65 beings of light

I noticed as I got more and more into the Form and the lore surrounding it, that I found more and more similarities across mystical disciplines and spiritual or shamanistic practices. Casteneda, one of my great heroes, writes about how the old shamans of the Tolmec tradition here in the New World thought of themselves as luminous eggs, with a strange and mysterious spot on them. In that system we are Luminous Beings, and shimmering is our constant state. The consciousness is just a small narrow beam of light, a light cone of the present, beaming out into the rest —the unconscious — which is this big sensitive chaos, all a-swirl in vortices of thermal and other fields. Perception?

The Tan-Tien is that magical spot, the center of the perception of being. It is also the center of mass. The Tan-Tien seemed like a kind of generalized focus point – the center of the body mind. I seriously perturbed my peace by inventing an analogy between the eye and the Tan-Tien — the eye that doesn't close.

```
  \       /\
   \    /   \      ____          o
 _\|/  — \/     - -    >-/|\ -,
  /  ____ \     ____     /
 /__\/__ \  - -     /\
 /- -  -/\ -\ - -    |   \
 /       \   \____  -^  -^
_____/_____
```

An illustration of the analogy: just as a prism breaks light up into its colors the somatic intelligence breaks signs up into semiotic processes.

Just as the eye gathers separate points of light energy reflecting from objects in space and focuses them into a unified visual image in the mind, the Tan-Tien — situated at the core of the body — coordinates discrete spiraling chi energy given off by emergent possibilities coming from farther afield than the local space into unified coherent actualities. Yes. I walked around thinking about that one for a while. I was feeling a lot in Tai Chi. I felt for the body as the support for all endeavors in life and that the Form is a technique to release the thinking mind and experience the totality of yourself.

We are beings of light going back to the Source
and seeing the Source fan-out into all things,
—before things got into their forms.
Looking in an uncomplicated way,
we realize they are to fill up the yearning.
What would it be like to really let ourselves be
in that yearning.
To stand before people in that yearning and love.
To appreciate the creation for what it is.
See it as coming from the Source, for we are all the
playthings of the Source. And though we have invented the
human space environment,
in which to reproduce and die,
in the opening and closing of Its eye,
we are the playthings of matter,
in the endless ejaculant of the milky way.
We are matter fertilized by light in the perpetual dis-
equilibrium and we see and we play leaving laser traces.
And we are moving . . . going back up to the
Source, and coming back down from the Source,
Light being changed into probabilities.

Casteneda teaches us to perceive through these other
centers. The exercises in Tai Chi are like Magical Passes to
let you get in touch with these other ways of knowing.

So I decided to start making these solo Taoist performances out there. I wanted them to be about my life, but also
about a kind of expanded awareness, or my life as an alien
intelligence with these nodes of perception and sensitivity on
this far flung planet. They would be walks, routines, solo
Taoist acts of authenticity. But I was so *abstract* in my life?!

It would be a kind of ritual to get perception, to raise the
will, to get power. I was terrified at appearing on the stage.
A trick is to treat the whole organization of the audience as
one entity, and it is coming at you. And you just move with
its energy.

You don't step back from it, you don't fight it head on.

I would be an other. I would become, young Yum Chi,
in his longing, in his yearning, in his love.

And the first one he did was one called Weather Dragon.

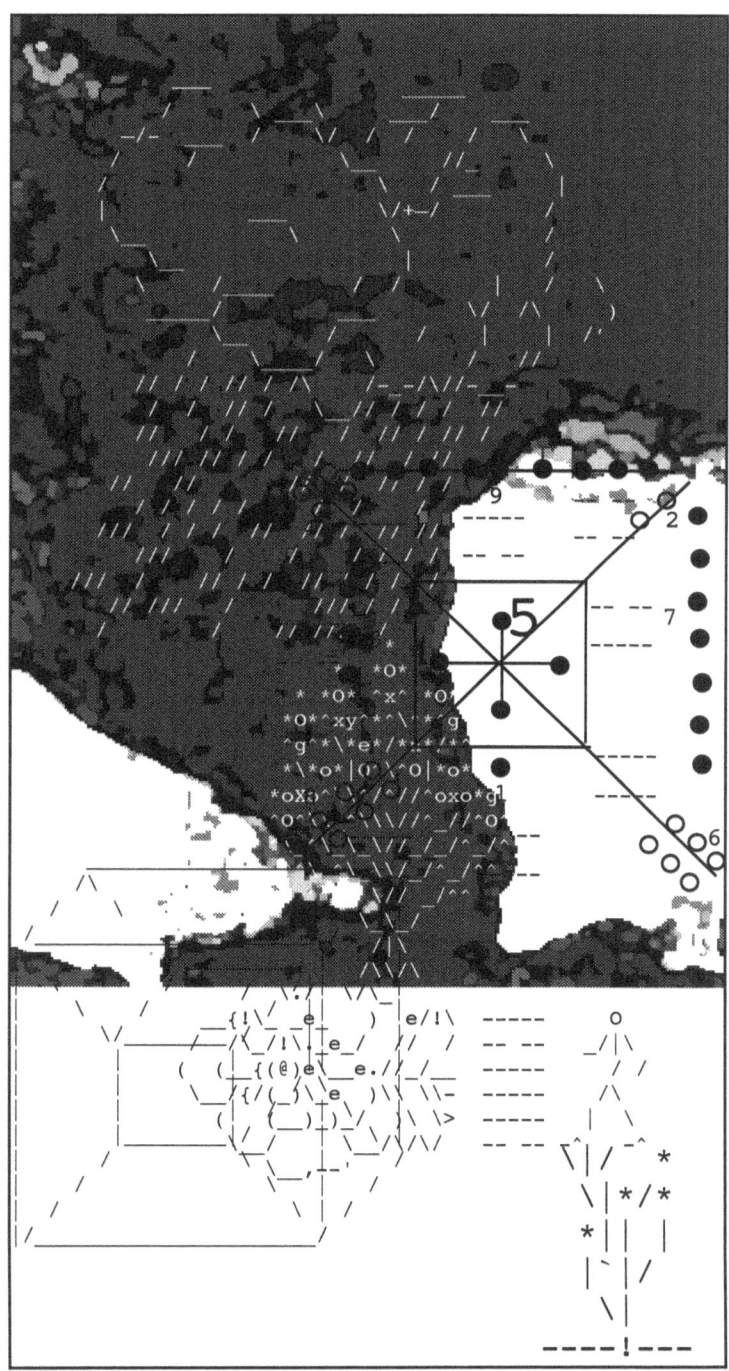

Sometimes on stormy days I'd go out as the sky was darkening and the wind was picking up, as a front would come rolling through. It is said that a man outstanding in his field might be lucky enough to be struck by lightning once in your life. Twice if you are really lucky. I'd do Tai Chi for hours, watching the sky blackening and the trees shaking and dancing in the breeze. I'd improvise with the wind, changing my moves and directions.

Player:
I was trying to understand the hexagram of the heavens.

Scene: *(hands interleaving, player indicates the clouds — in levels ordered by their height)*

Player:
——— cirrus
— — cumulonimbus
——— alto stratus
——— nimbostratus
— — nimbus
——— stratus

Scene: *(doing Tai Chi concentrating on the tiniest little push at the endings of movement, and making sure to get as much 8 through the waist. Sticks one leg out way back)*

Player:
a dragon tail
I'm a whether dragon . . .
I've heard of a weather vane,
but never seen a weather dragon . . . in this country.
(pause)
I'm trying to get back
from the Either / Or world
(He makes a slash and divide motion)
to the Both / And . . .
(Makes a pulling motion from the edges toward the center)
To flip in and out of dimension.

Scene: *(He bobs and weaves head from side to side trying to see two places at once. Exaggerated movement of the pelvis in figure 8.)*

Player:
  I wanted to feel like maybe how Fu Hsiu felt, what led him to his imagery. Come to find out it is something we can all see:
  Stand
  with your back
  to the lower
          Air
  ——— look at what
  — — the sky is doing
  ——— by following the movement of the clouds
  in the upper
          Air

Scene: *(flurry of Single Whip moves. Reaches hand up into "tree" plucking samples)*

Player:
      it was a way to sample the
          cyclonic and synchronistic
          vortices of turbulence
          in the lower and upper
              AIR
      (hand on forehead looking out)

      red sky at night
      sailor's delight
          MAJOR CLUES . . .
          Sky, Time of day, water.
      (indicates the sky)
      The weather is written into
          the clouds, the skies
          and the wind, and the temperature
          we just need to know how to read it.
      (pause)
          Consult the elements of greatest interest.
      Wind?

Player: *(twirls around)*
      —equalizing pressure—
      A low pressure or a vortex moving over terrain...
            (moves across the floor twirling)
      Water? (Rain)?
            The weather
            is delivering a message
            it needs to be deciphered
      (LOOKING)
      the weather is dictated in a hierarchy of importance.
            The most important is
            Number One. The polar front,
            how far south is the polar front dipping
            as it circulates around the globe.

      *(runs around chasing, hands extended trying to hug
something)*

      Number Two. Time of the year
            Jet stream chases the upper winds along
            high and low pressure areas swell up
            and bulge down
      *(hands slam down to the floor, he rolls quickly across
the like he is being dragged)*
      areas that get dragged over terrain
            the motion and direction of clouds in the upper Air
      (a lower hand indicates a higher one)
      sample the jet stream

Scene: *(he indicates the clouds in order of height)*

            ——————— cirrus
            —   — cumulonimbus
            ——————— alto stratus
            ——————— nimbostratus
            —   — nimbus
            ——————— stratus

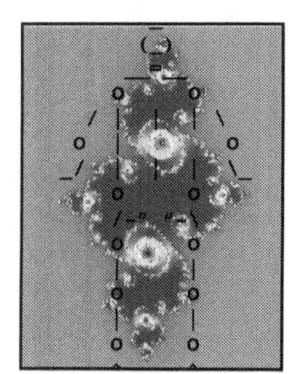

67 The Sepheroth and the Hexagram

Tai Chi is about getting more feeling to flow in and around and across the body.

Like the system of hexagrams, Jewish mysticism uses a symbolic representation of the relationship of the universe ingressing into our destiny. It is called the Sepheroth. Much has been written about it. For our purposes here we can say the Sepheroth is a diagram of the joints. The lowest point in the Sepheroth is the root. Above that the ankles, then the knees, the shoulders and the Head. The Sepheroth is rooted in the feminine, and by this we mean the nurturant Source that supports all creation and it will help you understand your own dark feminine.

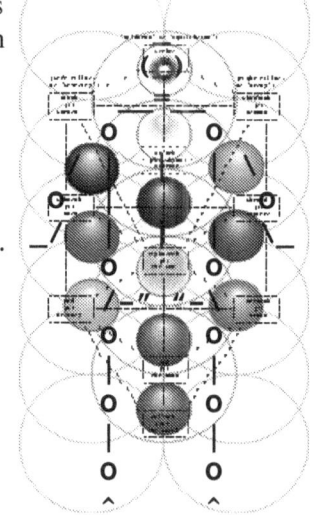

They say if you have difficulty relating with women in your world, you need to look at the relationship with the feminine inside of you.

Dialog with the parts, of the body. Let the Form channel energy across to places where energy is blocked, and let these micro-connections occur, micro-integrations and movements that suggest balance. For example let the toe, let the toe tell you where it wants to go, it . . . you will feel this energy shoot up your legs into the spine, then from there up through the spine and trunk, and work its way out to the extremities.

But getting back to the Sepheroth and Kabalistic Tai chi, you are turning up the dials, opening the gates, and letting this energy flow through, and you must train to be generous with yourself and let that happen.

For example, if you imagine the right side of yourself coiled back in anger like a boxer, covered with metal armor, notice it is brittle and glassine, crinkling. You have to ease up, to let the dark feminine flow across. Many are wounded in the root, but you need to have that opened up so that energy can flow up into the higher centers, and become integrated.

Fu Hsiu saw this third level in terms of further emergence, what we might call object inherency today. For him the idea of the family from which one emerges and into which one commits one's self was important then as it is now. And of course it continues the natural observations of male and female, and genetic taxonomy.

```
father    son      d1     son2     son3     d3      d4     mother
+--------+--------+--------+--------+--------+--------+--------+--------+
|  ____  |  _  _  |  ____  |  _  _  |  ____  |  _  _  |  ____  |  _  _  |
|  ____  |  ____  |  _  _  |  _  _  |  ____  |  ____  |  _  _  |  _  _  |
|  ____  |  ____  |  ____  |  ____  |  _  _  |  _  _  |  _  _  |  _  _  |
+--------+--------+--------+--------+--------+--------+--------+--------+
```

The key here is to train your perceptual powers in object inherency. Almost like it was a kind of visual sense, how situations blossom and emerge. Go back to the trigrams and get it right.

The number 1 son is — — (the unbroken line at the bottom indicates he is the 1st to emerge.)

By the same reasoning, and would be the 2nd son

This is the youngest son.

And the eldest daughter would be (first yin to emerge in time)

and the 2nd daughter

and the 3rd daughter

```
          \ | /    *
           \ | * / *
            * | |   |
            | ` | /
             \ |
          ----!----
```

Thus the family portrait of the family of kua as an exercise in the envisioning of object inherency.

69 So much joy and pride in their children

Heaven or the Creative	Earth or the Receptive	Thunder or the Awakening	Water, or the Abysmal
The creative. It is this spirit permeating the world. It is hungry, filled with longing, restless seeking to project the self.	That into which our energy pours, and from which it emerges. It is hope. It is the erotic, it is like getting into a hot tub with destiny.	Elders, with their short-time tempers, and the power to get things done.	Water, and the middle son. The middle of the road, half way through the ordeal, commitment, hanging in, the ubiquitous solution in which we sink or swim

```
          ,-,_              '
       /  ~~\      |
      /~~\       |
     |    '    |
     '\._,-'
        earth
```

```
^ ^ ^ ^ ^ ^   ^ ^    ^ ^ ^ ^ ^ ^
  ^ ^ ^   ^ ^   ^ ^   ^ ^
  ^ ^    ^ ^ ^   ^ ^ ^ ^ ^
   ^ ^ ^ ^ ^ ^      ^ ^ ^
           water
```

```
 .O.           O          _O          _O
 '|'          (|)      '  |(       '  (,
 [ ]          [ ]       <  \       /<
```

```
                \
                 \\
                  \\/
                  /|\\
                 // | \\
               |/// |   \|
```

```
   O
creative              lightning
```

☶	☴	☲	☱
Mountain or the Stillness	**Wind or the Gentle**	**Fire or the Clinging**	**Lake or the Joyous**

Mountain
The youngest son, the last born the quiet upheaval the great point of focus off in the distance. The goal.

Wind
the first daughter, a gently touch, so responsible and yet so graceful

The middle daughter the clinging, the one who got left to her own devices, and who ended up being really good in school, Fire -- burning brightly.

The youngest daughter, a surprise joy. Delight. Beaming like the lake was the beaming brow of the earth.

```
          '
     /=\\
    /===\ \
   /=====\' \
  /=======\''  \
 /=========\  ' '\
    mountain
```

```
      *
     (
      )
     (
      )  (
    )!    ))
   (  !  )  )
   _)!_((_(
      fire
```

```
  ,_o
   ,(
  <  \
```

```
    o_
   )'
   >\
```

```
   o_
  ),'
  /  >
```

```
   o_
  )|  '
  /  >
```

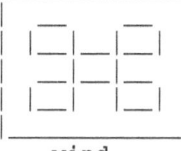
```
wind
```

```
  ___      ___
 ___   ___

  __      ___
      ___
      lake
```

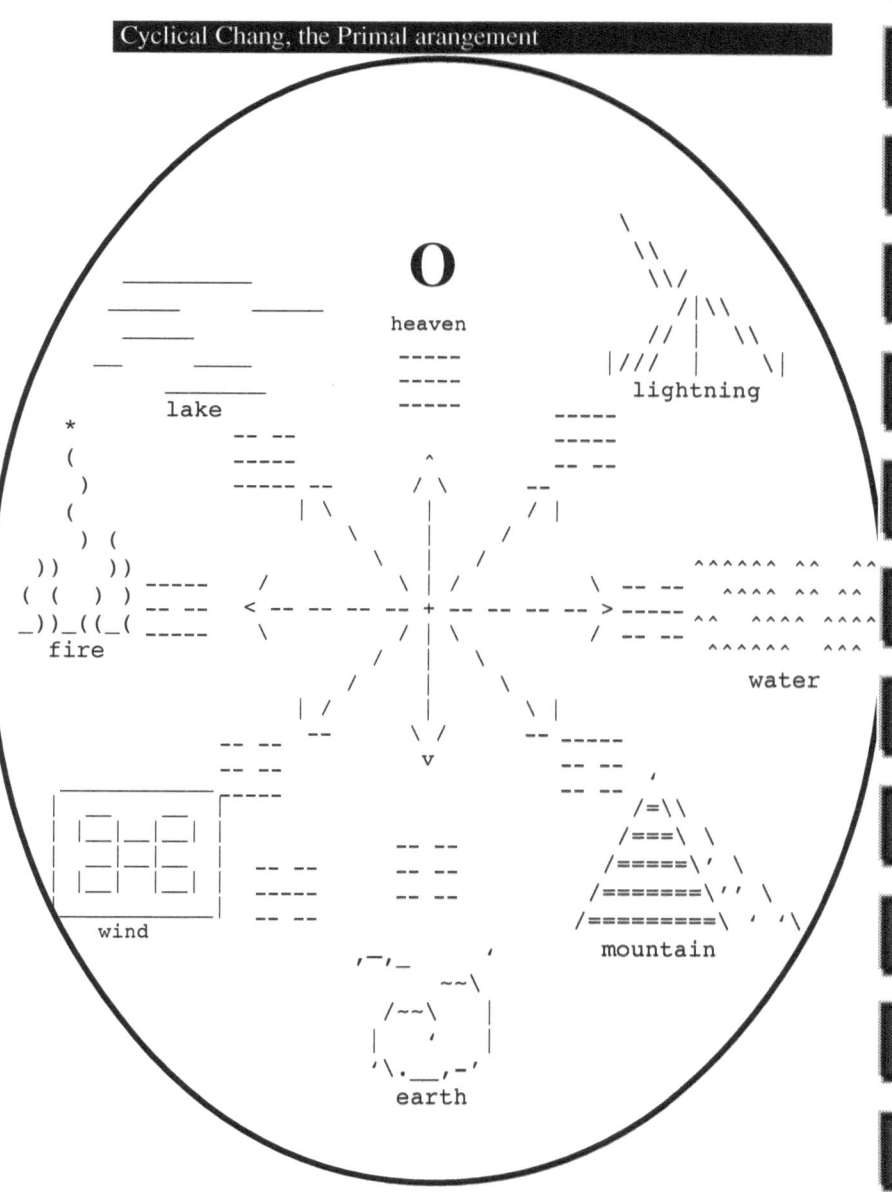

Cyclical Chang, the Primal arangement

```
                        *
                       ( )
                      (   )
                       ) (
                      )) ((
                     (( )) )
                    _)) _((_(
                      fire

                     -----
                     -----
                      ^
                     /|\
                    | | \
               |¯\   \  |  \    /¯|
                \  \  \ | \ /  / /
          _ - - /   \ \ |  X  / /  \ - - _ _
    - - - <- - -- --  \ | / \ /  -- -- -> - - -
          ¯ - - \   / / |  X  \ \  / - - ¯
                /  /  / | \ \   \ \
               | /   / /|\ \ \   \ |
                    / / \|/ \ \
                       \ | /
                        \|/
                         V
                      -----
                      -----
                      -----

  ^^^^^^  ^^   ^^^^^^^
   ^^^^ ^^ ^^  ^^ ^^
  ^^   ^^^^ /^^^^
   ^^^^^^  ^^^
      water
```

O

heaven

earth

wind

mountain

lake

lightning

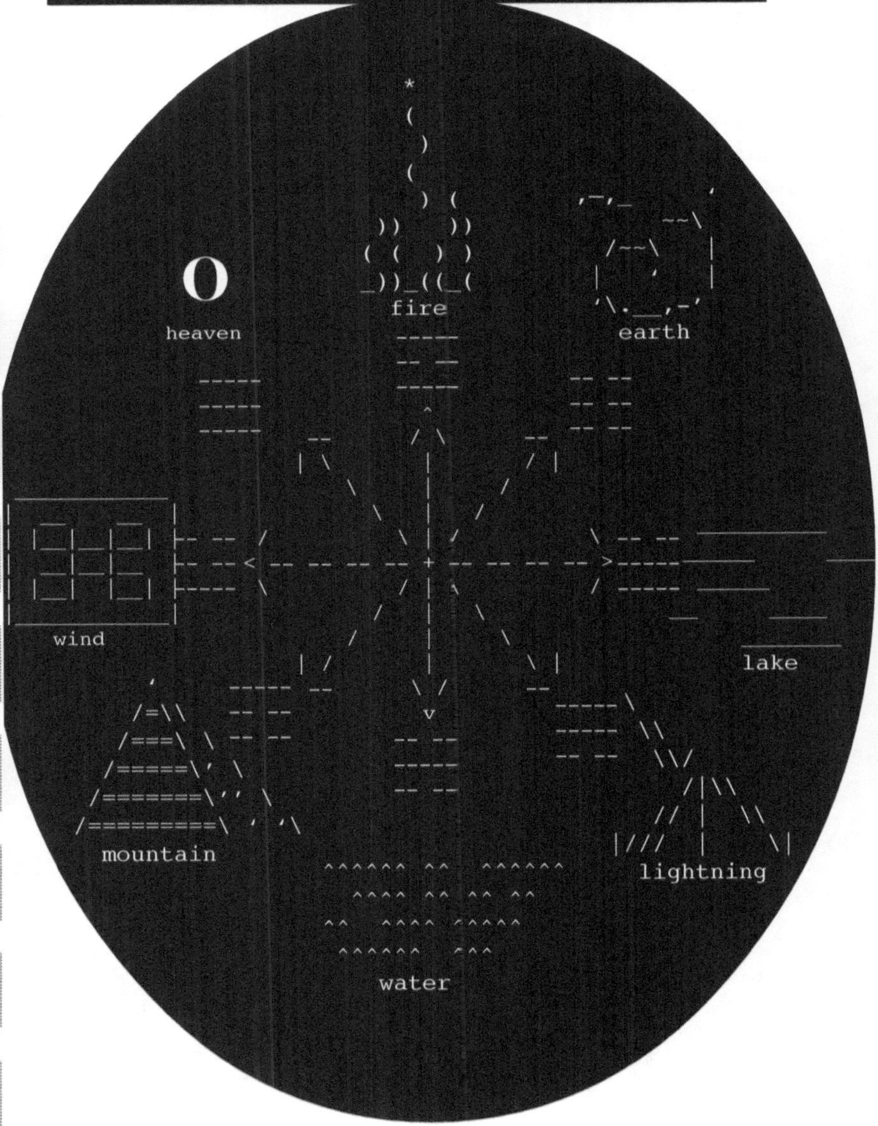

71 The I Ching is a Binomial Distribution

The I Ching in its purest form is a Binomial Distribution. This distribution is the way events and objects falling in a random way, into a world of equal probability, group themselves. Pascal (a sage of western enlightenment) showed how the triangle of binomial coefficients were the combinations of things. It is *quincunx*, (the centered five), a filter, a grid for catching pure randomness in time and reflecting the way a system, maintaining perfect variability at each branching, grows.

```
 .  .  .  .  .  .  .  .  .  .  .  .  .  .  .  .  .  .  .
  .  .  .  .  .  .  .  .  .  .  .  .  .  .  .  .  .  .  .
 .  .  .  .  .  .  .  .  .  .  .  .  .  .  .  .  .  .  .
```

```
        1  1
       1  2  1
      1  3   3  1
```

$$(a + b)^1 = a + b$$
$$(a + b)^2 = aa + ab + ba + bb$$
$$(a + b)^3 = aaa + aab + aba + baa + bba + bab + abb + bbb$$

In particular the number of combinations of 2 things taken 1, 2, and 3 at a time.

So here if you let a be —— and b is — — you get the generation of I Ching trigrams top down.

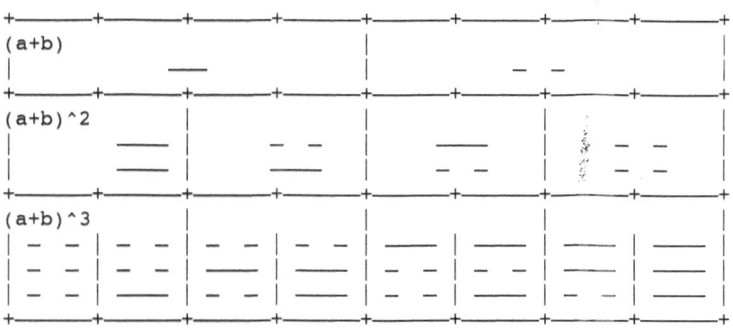

Which gives the 8 trigrams at the third level.

And continuing

```
        1   1
      1   2   1
    1   3   3   1
  1   4   6   4   1
1   5  10  10   5   1
1  6  15  20  15   6   1
```

would give 64 the possible combinations of yin and yang in the hexegrams $(a + b)^6$

But what we have been saying is that the I Ching is a system that generates the trigrams from the bottom up.

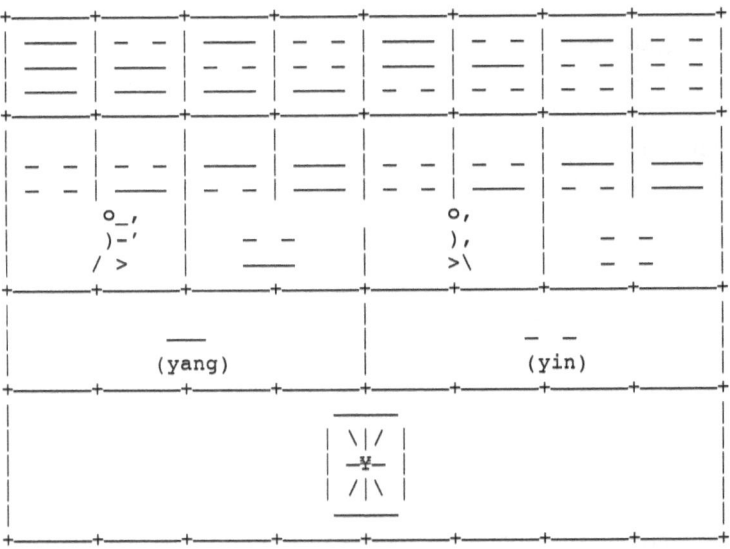

Contemplating hexagram expansion from the bottom up, a display of birfacating combinational possibilities. (In its purest form: the I Ching).

You can drawn an outcome tree, to show the probabilities of getting the results from tossing three coins (or any sequence of trials) and the tree is the trajectory of a distribution unfolding in event space:

HHH, HHT, HTH, THH, TTH, THT, HTT, TTT

72 Binomial Expansion

The binomial expansion is a tool for estimating the probability that a specific combination of mutually exclusive outcomes will occur. The mutually exclusive outcomes might, for example, be yin versus yang; and the specific combination of outcomes might be 3 yins out of 6 lines of the hexagram.

The general formula for the binomial expansion is:

Probability (x of N) = $\dfrac{N!}{x!(N-x)!}$ $(p^x)(q^{N-x})$

where

N=total number of events under consideration,

p is the probability of event P (such as yin)

q=probability of the alternative event Q (such as yang),

x is the number of times event P occurs.

The ! denotes a factorial. The factorial of 0 is 1, but for all other integers, the factorial of N is N • (N-1) • (N-2) ...1. For example, 3! = 3 • 2 • 1 = 6

```
        0!=1!     !?
                  o
              >-/|\ -,
               /          The knight of !000 eyes
              /\
             |  \
            _^  _^
```

The Hexagrams fall out

How would you calculate the probability of having 3 yins in a family of 6 lines of a hexagram?

The total number of events (N) is 6 lines. The number of times (x) that event P (yin line) occurs is 3. The probabilities for alternatives under consideration (yang versus yin) are in both cases .5, a half. Putting these values into the general formula:

$\dfrac{N!}{x!(N-x)!}$ $(p^x)(q^{N-x})$ = $\dfrac{6!}{(3!)(6-3)!}$ $.5^3 (.5^{6-3})$ =

= $\dfrac{6•5•4•3•2•1 \ (.0125)(.0125)}{(3!)(3)!}$

= 720(.0075) / 36 = .03125 = 5/16

Thus out of the 64 hexagrams, each of 6 lines, we would expect 20 of them to have 3 yin lines.

73 Hexagram production by coin toss method

Take three coins. Assign the value 2 to the heads, and 3 to tales.

The three coins are thrown simultaneously, and the values on the showing faces are summed. This yields a number between six and nine. (Ex. 2H+1T=7)

The process is repeated six times to give six numbers.

Hexagram production:

Starting from the bottom let the numbers represent the lines in the hexagram required for the oracle. In addition, lines can be a "moving" which is where the changes occur. This leads to the formation of a 2nd, *resultant* hexagram.

Coming back to the coins, an even sum represents a broken line, an uneven sum represents an unbroken line. If all the faces are identical, the line is moving.

Coin Sum to Line Conversion				
Coin Sum	**Odd/Even**	**Faces?**	**Line**	**Probability**
6	Even	Identical	Broken, moving	1/8
7	Odd	Mixed	Solid	3/8
8	Even	Mixed	Broken	3/8
9	Odd	Identical	Solid, moving	1/8

Thus the six numbers generated from coin tossing generate a hexagram consisting of six lines. This is then split back into an upper and lower trigram, which are used as indices in a table to yield the 'code number' for the hexagram. Once this number of the hexagram is known the text associated with the hexagram can be looked up in the *I Ching* and read.

Moving Lines generate second resultant Hexagram

If there are moving lines, each transforms into its opposite (i.e. broken becomes unbroken and vice-versa) to yield a second hexagram. This second text is portentious. Also, varying weights are assigned to the lines, by noting say a '9 in the first place' indicates the resultant extrapolated line across from the main reading to the resultant reading.

The arrangement and organization of interpretations is presented in the gestalt of the I Ching Mandala.

The I Ching Mandala is like tic-tack-toe with a bit of magic square thrown in. You can use the mandala to hold together one to four hexagrams pertaining to your situation. First you obtain one hexagram which depicts the current or initial situation, then you either resolve the moving lines or throw another hexagram to get the final situation after the change. For example you might throw Hexagram 53 Chien / Development (Gradual Progress): Correct development through the cultivation of one's personality

      ——
      ——   above SUN The Gentle, Wind Wood
      — —

      ——
      — —   below Ken Keeping Still, Mountain
      — —

for the initial situation. You put its trigrams in the mandala on the center side.

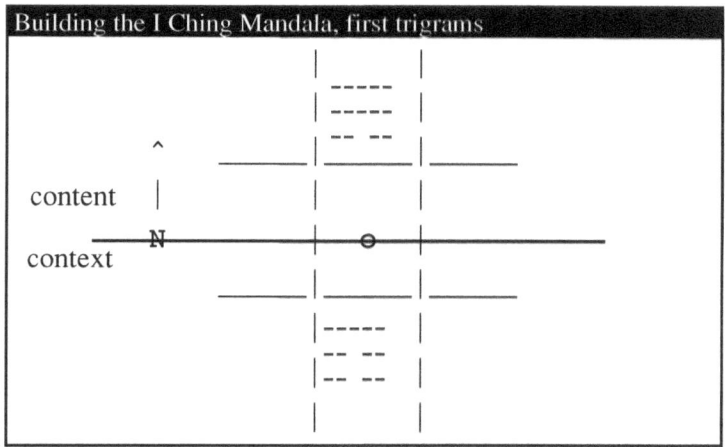

The commentaty for Chien reads: "This hexagram is made up of Sun (wood, penetration) above, i.e. without, and Ken (mountain, stillness) below, i.e. within.

"A tree on a mountain develops slowly according to the law of its being and consequently stands firmly rooted. This gives the idea of development that proceeds gradually, step by step.

The attributes of the trigrams also point to this: within is tranquillity, which guards against precipitate actions, and without is penetration, which makes development and progress possible."

After you obtain one hexagram which depicts the current or initial situation, and you either resolve the moving lines or throw another hexagram to get the final situation after the change. Here for example we had Chien resolving to Hexagram 48 Ching / The Well (Source of Nourishment):

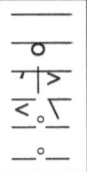

```
-----    --o--9   -- --      above  K'an The Abysmal, Water
-----    -----    -----
-- --    -- --    -- --
-----    -----    -----      below  Sun  The Gentle,Wind, Wood
-- --    --o--6   -----
-- --    -- --    -- --
```

Move the initial hexagram to the left column and put the resolved hexagram in the right column.

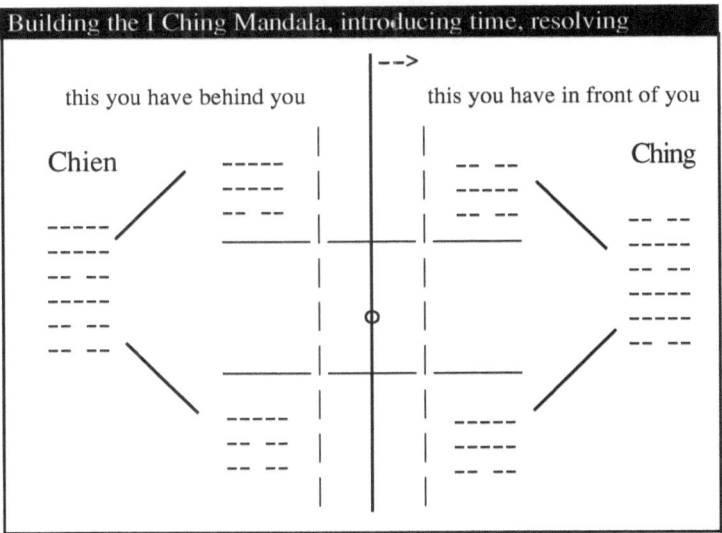

Read the commentary for the resultant hexagram. Ching is made up of K'an (The Abysmal, Water) above, i.e. without, and Sun (The Gentle, Wind, Wood) below, within.

"The wood goes down into the earth to bring up the water. The image derives from the pole and bucket well of ancient China. The wood represents not the buckets, which in ancient times were made of clay, but rather the wooden poles by which the water is hauled up from the well. The image also refers to the world of plants, which lift water out of the earth by means of their fibers.

The well from which water is drawn conveys the further idea of an inexhaustible dispensing of nourishment."

Next we want to pay particular attention to the moving lines in movement or CHANGE from the initial conditions to the final resolution. We read the lines for each line.

If you read enough of these and if you know some Chinese etymology, you see that the ideogram for the name of the hexegram, builds up an image. A great deal of the meaning of the hexagram is contained in this image of its ideogram.

53 chin to cut across / a flowing river / by cart

6 ——— flying over the cloud, fortunate
5 ——— Finally on the top of the hill
4 — — the bird alights on the land
3 ——— a water bird on the land, misfortune
2 — — standing on the rock
1 — — a white bird stray along the river bank

Chun

48 Ching under the soil / a bud / struggling to emerge

6 — — open to the public, fortunate
5 ——— cold clear water appreciated
4 — — a little ornament to call attention, muddy water
3 ——— the well is cleared, waiting
2 ——— muddy water feeding only small fish
1 — — muddy water forgotten even by birds

And in seeking resolution we can first say that the initial outer pychological state of Wind has become the inner psychological state.

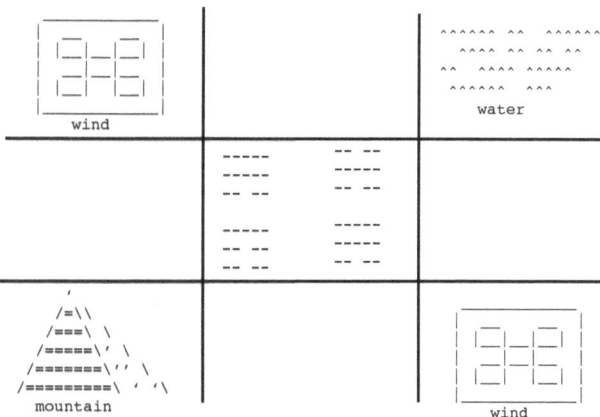

The interpretation of the Change reqires the heurism of a question. We will detour for a look at the structure of how one reads an ideogram, then return to this interpretation.

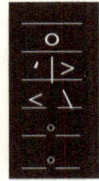

When I first got into the I Ching, I wondered about the ordering of the lines. The *I Ching* is a really modern work, in the sense that the hero projects himself, finds himself in the work, and doesn't watch as it is being done for him by the omniscient entertainer writer. When you are working with the I Ching you are kind of reverse engineering, trying to go backwards from the readings, the output and figured out what the input is. It is applied Baysian Inference.

You often see the prase 'a weak line in a strong place' or 'a strong line in a weak place'. It sets you to wondering what it means. You might figure it had something to do with the oscillation back and from content to context.

——— is a dense forest. Even the wind slows here
— — is a bed of cooling coals. Though they are still, they shake air

See. A pattern.
Image is a xxxx, then comment on it.
Real < -- > abstract

— — is short travel. The wonderful may be very near.
— — is an empty bed. Even at noon, it welcomes sleep.
——— is a wide, shallow box. The tall must topple to fit.
— — is a homecoming too soon. The same things do not welcome again.
— — is an opened fan. The thin are best at moving the thinnest.
——— is a deep well. Only a splash may return.

What can we learn about these wonderful lines, they are astute observations of a situation. They bespeak a mind quiet and present in a time long ago. They make a kind of poetic sense, and they are different. Sometimes

——— is a drum. Once is meaningless to the hollow.

and sometimes

——— is a wide, shallow box. The tall must topple to fit.

But why is the drum not feminine — —? Why is the box masculine here? But here the bed is feminine:

— — is an empty bed. Even at noon, it welcomes sleep.

You might think about the Jungian archetypes of the

Great Mother, the personification of the feminine principle. This archetype represents nature, the fertile womb out of which all life comes and the darkness of the grave to which it returns. Anything hollow, concave or containing pertains to the great mother. Thus, bodies of water, the earth itself, caves, dwellings, vessels of all kinds are feminine. So also is the box, the coffin and the belly of the monster which swallows up its victims. Or you might look for a clue from the imagery of the archetype of the Spiritual Father. As the great Mother pertains to nature, matter and earth, the great Father archetype pertains to the ream of light and spirit. Its main symbol is the sun. The light penetrating the dark earth, the rain fertilizing it are symbols of the masculine archetype. So is the phallus, knife, spear, arrow and ray. Crowns, halos, dazzling brilliance are reflections of this solar imagery.

Are the sages seeing that world of archetypes? Yes. But you needn't look into such esoteric sources. Although the hierarchy is not made explicit until the 8th Wing (one of the commentaries of the *I Ching*), it shows how the yin and yang alternate up the ladder to the goal. The places in the hexagram are assigned odd and even.

$$— — 6 \text{ even}$$
$$— — 5 \text{ odd}$$
$$——— 4 \text{ even}$$
$$— — 3 \text{ odd}$$
$$— — 2 \text{ even}$$
$$——— 1 \text{ odd}$$

The hexagram is built up as a progression out of the situation. How do they combine? One can judge from reading the *I Ching*, that the combiner is "from outer to inner" or "emerges." They say from defensiveness "emerges" stagnation or from devotion "emerges" intensity. The top trigram "emerges" from the trigram on the bottom. Object Inherency. The I Ching is a system for stimulating the intuition with symbols and imagery and suggestive, ambivalent language. It is a kind of artificial intelligence. It is like a refinement moving from the simple to the complex, increasing resolution. It is abstraction penetrating the imagination —working — seeing more and more possibilities to a situation. We are looking at a hierarchical system that branchs by bifurcation, as does just about every system we encounter in reality.

What are we to make of the text of the I Ching, where it says things like "a pig is run wild".

The particular texts are pronouncements from the mind of various shamans and oracles of long ago who put themselves on the line to correctly interpret emerging events of great importance. It might have been something of a con job, or it might actually be that they (perhaps with the help of smoke) were able to project themselves into a domain outside of time — the domain of the archetypes — and used this ability to submerge themselves in the synchronic to discover something about the diachronic. (See next.) When we ask the Oracle we are in a fairly agitated state, or at least open, in which we do not trust the mere surface unfolding of events, but need more insight as to how we feel about these events.

The clearest example of how meaning is derived from the I Ching is, I think, in the first hexagram, Ch'ian, the Creative. Here we have the oldest story in the universe: the struggle for creativity to manifest itself in the world. It is expressed in an image, the figure of the dragon, a mythical beast who starts out beat down, prostrate, on the ground, slips into some water to flow, gets to an island and dries out, then finally leaps up into the air, where it takes wing and flies and finally is seen and exalted by his community.

The I Ching message emerges from the bottom up.

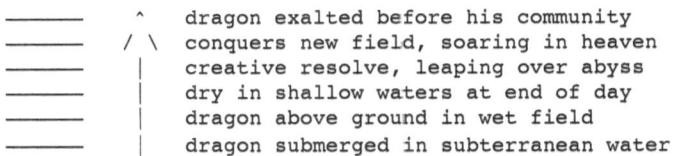

```
  _____    ^    dragon exalted before his community
  _____   / \   conquers new field, soaring in heaven
  _____    |    creative resolve, leaping over abyss
  _____    |    dry in shallow waters at end of day
  _____    |    dragon above ground in wet field
  _____    |    dragon submerged in subterranean water
```

We see here the emergence of a concept — creativity, being exalted from the image of a mythical animal, asleep in the deep psyche. So the hexagram is a picture of this process of emergence, aspects of the timeless archetypal world of the deep psyche percolating up into the surface world of our judgements.

Archetypes get mapped onto the lines:

Hexagram --> Name --> Image --> Judgement

77   The diachronic & the synchronic in the I Ching.

The Hexagram and the Cross

The Hexagram is a symbol. It is subtle and esoteric, but let us compare it with the Cross of Christianity.

The Cross is a symbol, and as such has many stories associated with it, one of which is the story of a man who scarified his fear. His message? *We are brothers: I sacrifice myself to bring you into Here with me. And to get myself in There, that place of the Real, to get across this veil of negativity set up by the Rome outside. Live a simpler life. One with a good mix of physical and mental. Find the erotic in your fear and give up that fear.*

The Cross can also be seen as the archetype of the rational grid of analytical space of western thought. It organizes space-time into the diachronic (across time) and synchronic (outside of time) — with diachronic on the horizontal and synchronic on the vertical.

The Hexagram is a ladder that also organizes space-time. The I Ching uses the spatial metaphor of the up and down ladder to attempt to know or predict what is to happen in the sequence of time.

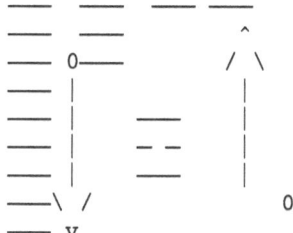

Communicating with the oracular through the I Ching is a direct attempt to use the synchronic to predict what will happen in diachronic time. The synchronic in the I Ching is the connection of the above with the below —the higher Self with the self. The diachronic (begins and ends in time) in the I Ching is the emergence of the archetypal in time.

For Fu Hsiu, and the idea of object inherency, it was natural to think seed --> branches --> leaves --> seed. The I Ching is a way of structuring the world. The integration and differentiation. A place where you can feel IT (that which knows all in time) holding you in the palm of its hand.

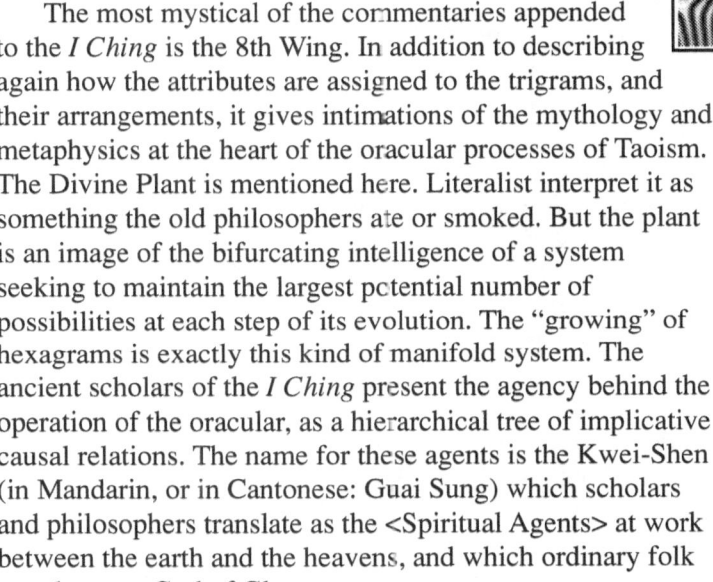

The most mystical of the commentaries appended to the *I Ching* is the 8th Wing. In addition to describing again how the attributes are assigned to the trigrams, and their arrangements, it gives intimations of the mythology and metaphysics at the heart of the oracular processes of Taoism. The Divine Plant is mentioned here. Literalist interpret it as something the old philosophers ate or smoked. But the plant is an image of the bifurcating intelligence of a system seeking to maintain the largest potential number of possibilities at each step of its evolution. The "growing" of hexagrams is exactly this kind of manifold system. The ancient scholars of the *I Ching* present the agency behind the operation of the oracular, as a hierarchical tree of implicative causal relations. The name for these agents is the Kwei-Shen (in Mandarin, or in Cantonese: Guai Sung) which scholars and philosophers translate as the <Spiritual Agents> at work between the earth and the heavens, and which ordinary folk translate as <God of Ghosts>.

Lao Tsu says the space between heaven and earth is a medium, a quiescent plenitude which can't be felt by one within it; and the more it moves, the more prolific it is. This idea of a  plenitude connecting more than just what is causally related is basic to the Tao, and a mechanism for it is intimated in the 8th Wing of the *I Ching*. It contributed extensively to the idea of synchronicity in the psychology of Jung. We have come to understand synchronicity in our time as the super-set of possible connections and probabilities, in which is embedded the certainty of the causal.

field
looking person
fire

cosmic swerve
centered

Sampling algorhythm for analogous implication

The 8th Wing depicts the plant as a model or image of a bifurcating hierarchy of mutually cross-influencing implications as the underlying structure of reality. And the technicians of the oracular, wanting to incorporate their insight, developed the method of casting 49 yarrow stocks (thin reeds) and algorithmicly winnowing out the I Ching hexagram. This algorhythm was based on the analogy — just as the on-folding of events in the dimension of time is like the unfolding of a plant hierarchy in space, we can sample and reconstruct the etiology of the moment by seeing how a random event is impinged upon by synchronicity at this moment in time. Manipulation of yarrow stocks became another of the many ways of sampling the synchronistic vortex of chance surrounding the moment for insights into time's unfolding.

One can't help but admire how this whole science is contained in the image of the divining plant as a reflection of the branching iterative dichotomous unfolding of nature. This stepwise unfolding is charted in the hexagram of the I Ching. We recognize it now as a fractal, the crack, the dendrite, aggrandized most spectacularly in self-similarity to the branching human nervous system, where one domain interfaces and is interpenetrated by another. The fractal is an image found throughout ancient spiritual art --Celtic knots, arabesques, meandering dots, lines, tectiforms, claviforms, and the dragon. The stack of lines in the hexagram is an abstract image and a tallying of a fractal, spoken of at that time as the divining plant. In a sense, sages reproduced the "plant" by manipulation of yarrow stocks, and collecting these into the lines of the hexagram. Thus the fall and lie of the stocks becomes spirit tokens of the I Ching as a way to understand the influences given to us by the mysterious assistance of the spiritual intelligence(s), the Kwei- Shen.

Another interpretation of focusing on extra-causal connections, —the chaostician's perspective— is that it is important to disrupt the life thought-processes enough so that the mind can appreciate new symmetries, allowing new quiescent states, and new accomplishments to emerge out of the turmoil.

Hexagram as ladder, line as filter

The hexagrams depict the transitions from non-being to being. They are pictures of the Tao, pictures of the path at the moment. Today we know the moment is the point where the light cone of the future, (the cone that contains all events within reach of light) connects to the cone of the past, (the

spreading bundle of probability threads whose implications can be felt by Bayesian inference). Sampling the moment attempts to see into the synchronistic to see what may be influencing the moment. (Be within the light cone). If one grounded this image in the vertical, one sees a metaphysic at work showing a kind of energy, a free energy, that worked against gravity. It comes commingling and convolving into the BOTTOM of the hexagram and percolating up through it rises out of the top.

It is an image of the branching dichotomous nervous system penetrating and being penetrated by the branching dichotomous fractal world.

The lines of yin and yang of the hexagram are like filters. The 8th Wing shows how the yin and yang alternate odd and even up the ladder to the goal. You can have a weak line in a strong place. And a strong line in a weak place and it changes the meaning, as you are trying to get to your goal, or dealing with the impact of something on the path.

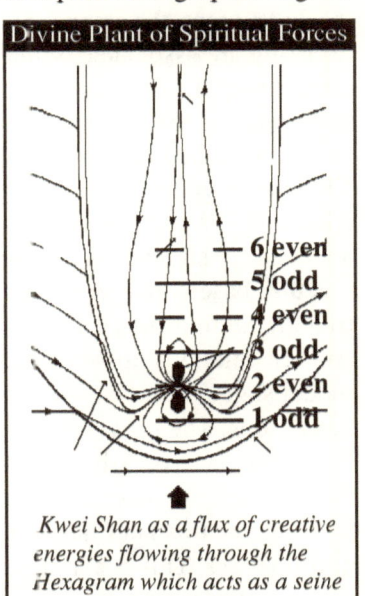

Divine Plant of Spiritual Forces

6 even
5 odd
4 even
3 odd
2 even
1 odd

Kwei Shan as a flux of creative energies flowing through the Hexagram which acts as a seine or filter and captures or manipulates the energies.

The object of doing Tai Chi is to reach consciousness. When I am doing Tai Chi I am taking part in a kind of ritual that relaxes the grasping attitudes, puts one in touch with the matrix of support that is the body and gives one a glimpse of the landscape of multidimensional interconnectivity that is our world. Can we say what these other steps in the process might be? A ladder up the hierarchy. A fractal is a ladder, to get from one world to another: I enter as a snake and transform myself into a dragon. It is a kind of symmetry adaptation. Adapting attitude to final goal and goal to attitude.

———— 6 even
———— 5 final goal
———— 4 even
— — 3 odd
———— 2 attitude
———— 1 odd

Bravely, with a pre-disposition in the face of risk, we climb up a ladder of dichotomies to a conclusion.

How Jung's Psychology Emerges from the I Ching

It is instructive to trace the development of Jung's psychology as he came to understand this ancient wisdom. In the Wilhelm- Baynes version, which had been around in German since the late 1800s, the material from the wings, — the Judgement, the Image, Symbols and the Interpretation of Meaning are associated with each hexagram. How do these elements of the *I Ching*, become elements in Jung's geography of the synchronic?

An idea that connects Jung, synchronicity and the I Ching all together is a mathematical form: The I Ching as a Binomial Distribution. It is very touching to think of the ancients constructing a philosophy and technique of the oracular based on a probability distribution. The binomial triangle reminds us of a *qinqunx* which is a physical filter and this relationship between the physical world and the model suggests the way to think about the stack of hexagrams. The *qinqunx* physically models the flow of Probability (waves) through the Reality Matrix —which is the self, and the other, and the relations between them. We will explore this later but let us sum up the mathematical portion here. This is symmetry adaptation, which is the way nature yokes together energy and geometry to both expand into complexity and reduce complexity. Stated consisely: the Inner Product of possibilities become Combinations. The cross product of possibilities gets reduced by projection to the Inner Product.

Archetypes get mapped — > onto the lines

I knew Jung's Psychology of Types. I recalled that if an image is from outside it is a sense, if it is from inside it is an intuition. Then I constructed this plausible map-up between the elements of the I Ching and Jung's Psychology of Types.

I Ching Elements Implying a Psychology of Types
Meaning —T, iN
Judgements —J
Images — S, F
Symbol —N, P

Possession

When you do Tai Chi you get a sense of the Good You coming to the fore and organizing your personality, indeed eventually, your physical structure. The Self comes to the fore. It is like being possessed. It is a foreign feeling. But one you want to be in more and more.

THE OBJECT OF DOING TAI CHI IS TO REACH CONSCIOUSNESS

The oracular is the process of the unconscious coming to consciousness. Feeling your consciousness occurs when you use your personality in non-habitual ways. Consciousness is most often felt in a shift, in motion, it is the effect of motion. Lao Tsu points this out. Recognition of consciousness occurs coming out of motion into stasis briefly.

Who *are* these sub-personalities that are often in possession of your body. For example, the Despairing One, the Child, the Responsible One, the Dutiful One, The Victim. You might ask yourself: Who is that you constantly in the defensive posture with the shoulders raised up?

Steps in Tai Chi and the Meaning of Divination

What *are* the steps toward achieving a goal? The same as making a decision? The decision algorithm is based on the 4 Functions of Personality. Usually we take in the world through our Senses and make decisions based upon Judgements, Thinking and Feeling. It is like a black box: we have the inputs from outside —S and from Inside —iN. The outputs are the Decisions (T,F,J,P) and actions. We do that by climbing up a ladder whose steps are dichotomies. They are the kinds of mental traps and boxes we get ourselves in. Think of the *Tao Te Ching* and its method of paradox. The process of coming to consciousness is the meaning of DIVINATION.

```
———— 6 consciousness
———— 5 final goal
———— 4 spirit
—  — 3 odd
———— 2 attitude
———— 1 life
```

When you do Tai Chi it is a ritual of raising consciousness. The long form takes you through stages. You don't remember until you have repeated the movements enough in a session, (get into that third section) and until you have synchronized your breathing with the movement. Then you are to such a point where your are taken over or you relax into or are possessed by an organization that feels like a sub-personality which is your better self, your higher self. The epiphany of coming to consciousness occurs in personality, in the awakening of those occluded parts of the personality.

The Fractal Dimension of Personality

We shall explore Jung's psychology further and expand it into one that incorporates fractals through the work of psychologist Kurt Lewin. Lewin's dynamics of personality in *Topological Psychology* uses classical vector field theory to extend and formalize the fields of psychology. Indeed Lewin speaks of personality in terms of a varying dynamic softness, elasticity, hardness, brittleness or fluidity of the psychical material. These would be the fractal dimension.

Evolution is the Fractal Vector

The modern 8th Wing should be about the fractal. The spiritual agency which mediates all things between the earth and the sky is the chaotic dynamic process of evolution, whose trace and product is glimpsed all around us and studied through the multidimensional world of fractals. Darwin defined evolution as "Branching pushed forward by natural selection." A niche is a corner of a dynamical ecosystem space in which an organism evolves. A niche is an availability of free energy presenting an opportunity for evolution. Niches are ladders. We know that the basis of evolution is self-organization through feedback of a system, which itself is embedded within other systems and / or, as host has many systems embedded within it — co-evolution. Self organization develops without predetermination. There is free will. The self organization is structured and shaped by the feedback of competition. It is a step wise process of iteration. It is modeled by the basic fractal equation where a state is either being modified by incrementing it from a previous state, or being used as feedback to modify the current state into the next state. The Fractal Vector is this feedback system, moving through a multidimensional product space, creating information and feeding it back into itself.

79 The Kuei-Shen
— for sifu Yum Chi

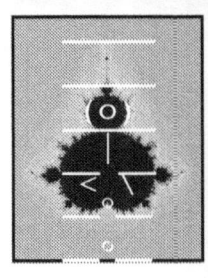

KUEI- SHEN
transparent forces at work, spiritual agencies
    swirling between heaven and earth

KUEI- SHEN
FEEDBACK in the FORM
as the great swerve,
the crack in the cosmic egg
the movement on the dark waters

Kuei shen spiritual being, spiritual agents
kuei— the human spirit disembodied (ghosts)
shen — spirits whose seat is in heaven

KUEI- SHEN
 Fracture in turtle's Shell
as augury
because the earth was carried
through the heavens by the auspices
        of the giant turtle
                which carried the Earth
                    on its back

KUEI- SHEN
old as the bumpiness of dirt
            (the porosity)
minerals, bugs, fungi, bacteria
 to make it a layer to recycle,
the boundary for taking under, going across,

we too are fed back,
into the maw, into the pit
us it devours,
into the eat-quation

KUEI- SHEN
we are fertilizer for
THE DIVINE PLANT

The I Ching
gives
mysterious assistance
to the
spiritual intelligences

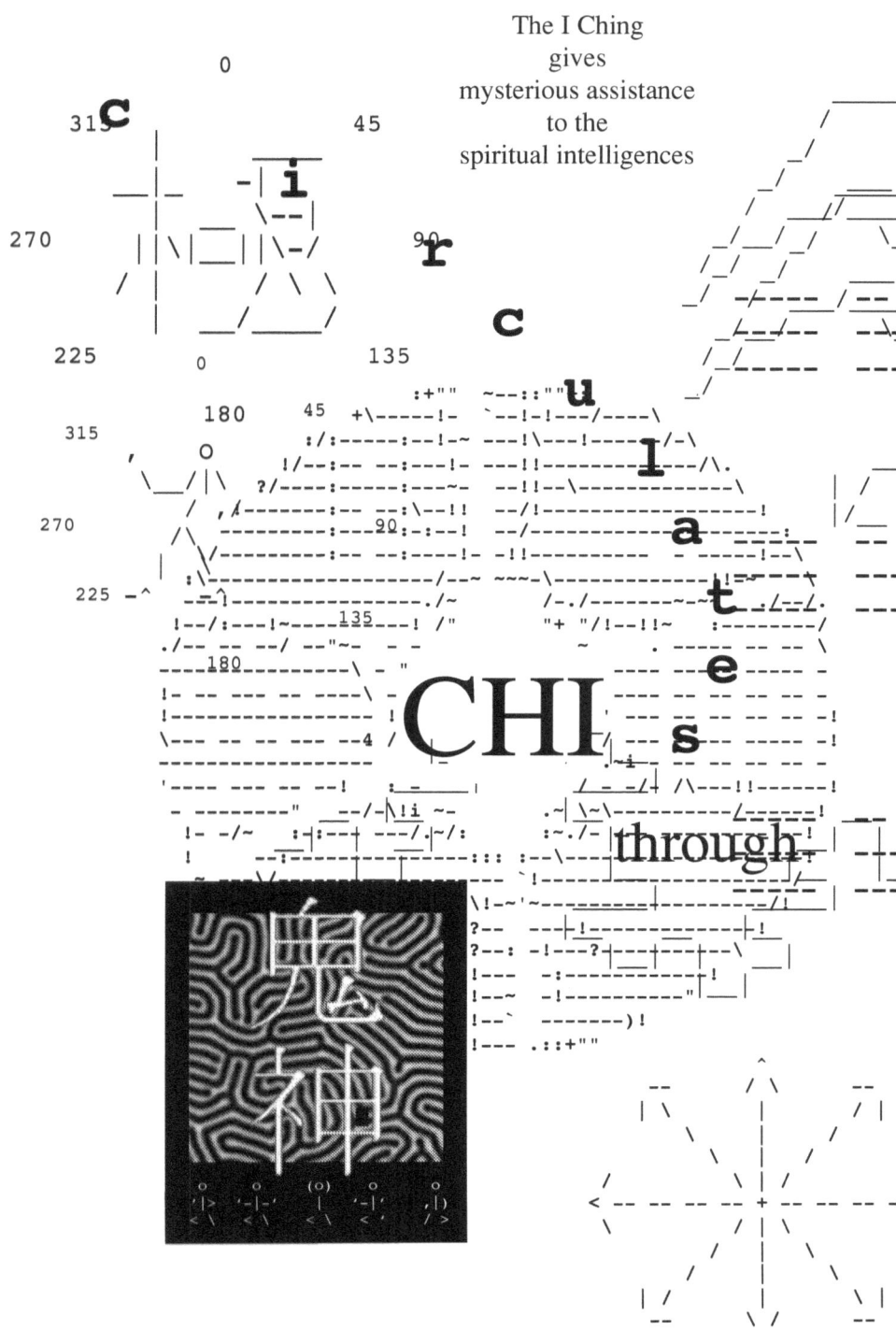

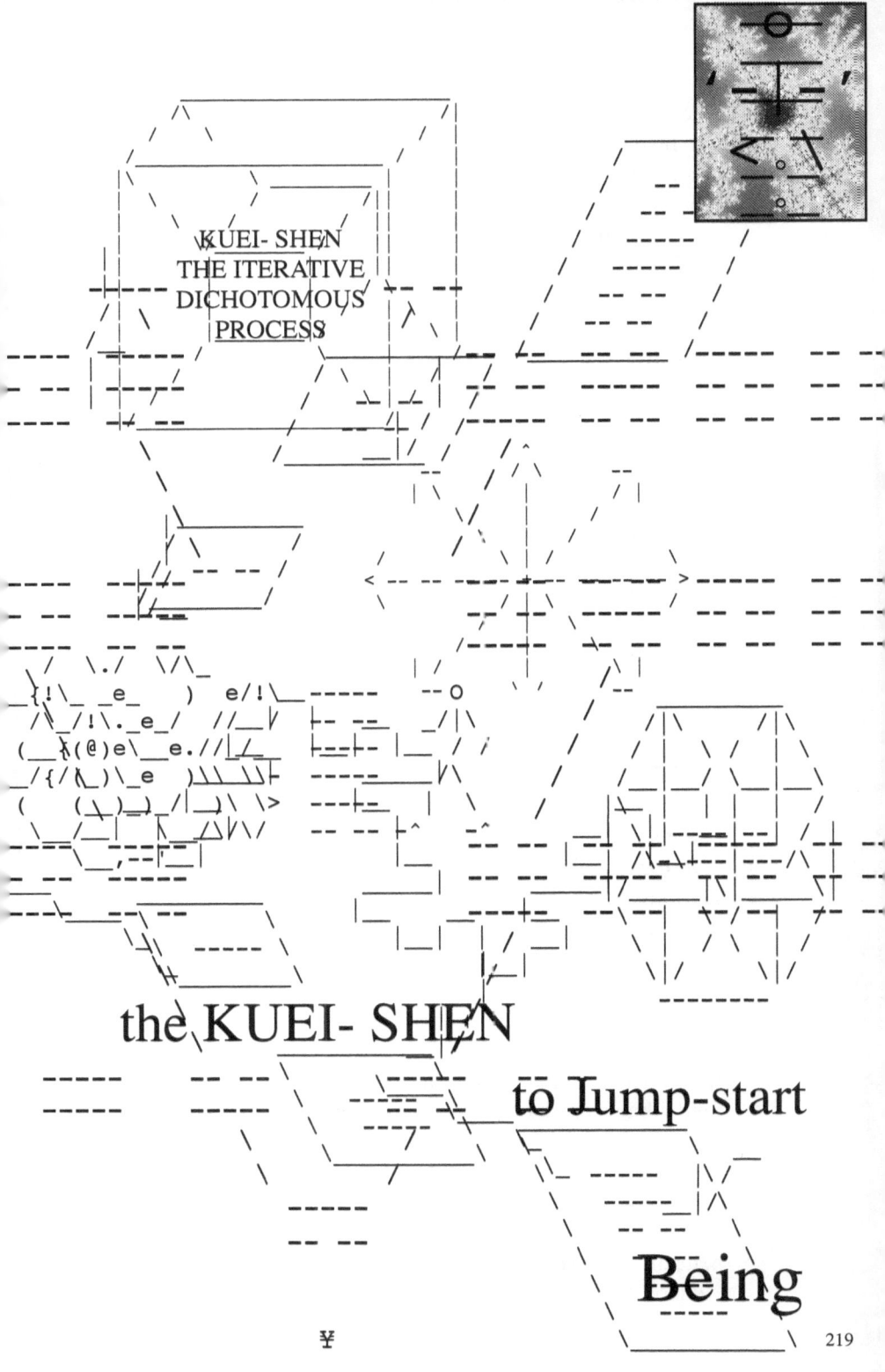

KUEI- SHEN
THE ITERATIVE
DICHOTOMOUS
PROCESS

the KUEI- SHEN

tō Jump-start

Being

219

fracture,
axe blade into wood;
plow blade into sod;
a wedge between worlds
opening it up
— The Diamond Cutter's Sutra

KUEI- SHEN
the activity of the material force (Chi)
"The negative spirit (kuei) and the positive spirit (shen)
are the spontaneous activity of the two material forces (yin
and yang)," said Cheng-meng.

KUEI- SHEN
OROBOROUS primary process

Ch'en Ch'us said that the Kuei-Shen should be discussed
under four categories: the Confucian Classics, ancient
religious sacrifices, latter day religious sacrifices and that
referring to demons and gods.

KUEI- SHEN
THE ITERATIVE DICHOTOMOUS PROCESS

Kung said: the Kuei-Shen stood for the positive and
negative forces behind events. Thus expansion is shen while
contraction is kuei. This naturalist and philosophical meaning
should always be kept entirely distinct from the other
meaning of kuei shen as spiritual beings.

KUEI- SHEN
FEEDBACK in the FORM
first introduced into culture through Rock and Roll
loud whines produced by a microphone picking up the
output of the loudspeaker and feeding it back into itself for
explosive growth.

KUEI- SHEN
beneath the surface of turbulence
    chaos

the smallest change
evolves

e KUEI- SHEN
   equation
$f(z)=z^2+c. \longrightarrow z_{new} \longrightarrow f(z_{new})$

fed back from output to input in the e-quation

KUEI- SHEN
Shen —spirit
shen come,
the unfolding interstices of the quiet dawn
wan come
into the garden
rose the light, up through the green stems

KUEI- SHEN —
like a wave or a shimmer   with   out   sound
only vibrations,
transparent forces at work, spiritual agencies
    swirling between heaven and earth:
"the contracting or expanding energies or operations of
nature"

53 Chien to cut across / a flowing river / by cart
6 —— flying over the cloud, fortunate
5 —— Finally on the top of the hill
4 — — the bird alights on the land
3 —— a water bird on the land, misfortune
2 — — standing on the rock
1 — — a white bird stray along the river bank

e KUEI- SHEN
$\nabla\bullet$, divergence, flux into and out of,
∇x, curl, vortices
transparent forces at work,
 spiritual agencies
    swirling between heaven and earth
the dot and cross products,
both a kind of projection out of forces from the manifold.

The I Ching is a prescient model of what I might call
The Reality Matrix of the Self. I came to this terms as I
started to find myself waking up. It was a kind of
aggrandizement from the human body's inertia matrix to the
reality matrix of the Self.

The I Ching had a great impact on Jung. With its use of
the Image and the Judgement, with its Symbols and the way
it is a representation of the Archetypes, as well as its
centralized use of the Mandala, there is a lot of the I Ching in
Jung. In a sense, the mandala and the hexagram are models
of a kind of artificial intelligence, of cellular automata. We
will show how this is the basis of Jung's 4-function model
of personality, which has met with such wide use.

The hexagram can be seen as made up of two trinary
signs, the trigrams. The inner and outer trigrams.

```
--o--9 }
--o--6 }  outer, above  SUN  The Gentle, Wind Wood
-- --

-----  }
-- --  }  inner, below  Ken  Keeping Still, Mountain
-- --
```

The outer hexagram is the relationship with the other. It
depicts three centers: you, the one opposite you, and the
relation between you two.

```
--o--9  your center
--o--6  relationship to other
-- --   other's center
```

The inner trigram is about how you feel in yourself. It
depicts three centers: your mind, your body and the relation
between the two.

```
-----  your mind
-- --  relation of mind to body
-- --  your body
```

And you could look at how you feel within and without
by checking in at all these levels or centers.

The inner and outer trigrams are about inner and outer
aspects of personality. Personality is the basis of
consciousness, it is a structure of consciousness.

Consciousness is a field that flows in and around the

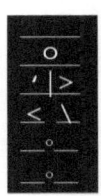

structure of personality. This flowing in and around is what we sense as the Tao. What we sense as Chi. As Chi in the personal sense and as Tao in the collective.

Jung saw these two centers in each of us. One is the social self that gets adapted to our ordinary, immediate, surrounding world of work and life and the conditions we are born into, and two, the other, is the deep self of your being, attuned to the timeless images of our origins. One might be called the surface consciousness and the other the deep consciousness. The surface deals with what's at hand and the deep connects with all time. Jung's concept of therapy had to do with exploring the transmissions from the deep to the surface, primarily in dreams and art. (The I Ching is based upon the transmission of images from the deep to the surface.) The exploration technique is amplification on a personal and cultural level. The stuff that dreams are made of is also the stuff of myth. Both are complexes of how a system hosts its organization: in the body where the nervous system hosts the personality by constellations of instinct, and in the other sense, how the environment hosts a culture. Psychological growth comes with understanding how myths are representations of archetypes which are many things: primal forms, codings of the deep unconscious, constellations of psychic energy, patterns of relationship joining mind with body, spirit with nature, and self with the greater universe. And if you can dis-identify your personal ego from the grasping everyday world then you will experience a kind of liberation and sense of belonging to a world of deeper, bigger time. Extension of the psychological life-space is related to the psychological separation of the levels of reality and unreality. Dis-identifying from your ego, or biological needs. Paradoxically you need the unreality (fantasy, dream, myth, thought) to help you make this separation. The amplification into levels by the application of energy is splitting. Splitting to become whole.

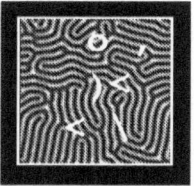

Extending the psychological lifespace is opening up and becoming more porous, letting more feeling flow back and forth across the boundaries of the self. And separating your grasping ego self from identification with the deep self. The I Ching is an orderly presentation of this separation and amplification to be more in tune with the arrangement of dichotomous branching hierarchies which ultimately is the Source that holds us up at every moment.

Interpreting the Change

Next we want to pay particular attention to the moving lines which depict CHANGE from the initial conditions to the final resolution. We read the Image, Text and Judgment entries for each line. If you know Chinese you see that the ideogram for the name of the hexagram, builds up an image. A great deal of the meaning of each hexagram is contained in this image of its ideogram.

The imagery of #53 Chien, is about a vehicle crossing over water. It could be like a tank fording a river, or as in the imagery, a bird flying over water.

53 Chien to cut across / a flowing river / by cart
6 ——— flying over the cloud, fortunate
5 ——— Finally on the top of the hill
4 — — the bird alights on the land
3 ——— a water bird on the land, misfortune
2 — — standing on the rock
1 — — a white bird stray along the river bank

I wondered (hoped), if in my case it was a picture of me as a very uncoordinated, out-of-touch, inelegant, tank-like person becoming this agile, crane — leaping up into the sky and flying over the problems that assail me.

Resolving the moving lines gives The imagery of #48 Ching is the Well.

48 Ching under the soil / a bud / struggling to emerge
6 — — open to the public, fortunate
5 ——— cold clear water appreciated
4 — — a little ornament to call attention, muddy water
3 ——— the well is cleared, waiting
2 ——— muddy water feeding only small fish
1 — — muddy water forgotten even by birds

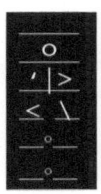

The well is the center of a community, in the way they divided up the public lands to farmers. Other phrases are being at the bottom of the well, and returning to the life giving stream. Chien going into Ching, what does it mean? Here the student of bioromancy might wonder if it means that his flight will come from emerging into the stream.

I decided I was being way to intellectual about it. I would try a simple common sense approach to what's happening to and through ME. I would go out into the world and divide it up into a grid in 4 directions. I would distinguish the mental processes of perception into intuiting and sensing, and judgement into thinking and feeling.

Perception	Judging
S	T
iN	F

Experimental Activity

I would look around in the world and say what I saw there, mapping onto the 4 directions of space, the 4 functions of personality.

Sensing: list the sense impression of the world, the plants the air, the sky, the earth, the wind, the sounds, your balance.

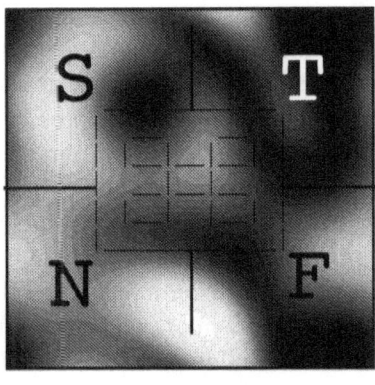

Intuitions. What comes to mind to you as you undergo the experience. Memories and associations. Who or what do the things you see make you think of.

Feelings. Get phenomenological. List the feeling judgements. Make "I statements": I feel depressed (have the blues). I've felt that way for x amount of time. (I supply the x amount). I feel "stuck", "paralyzed", "unworthy", "hopeless", "unappreciated", "unloved", "alienated" or whatever with any and all adjectives or adverbs that apply.

Thinking, about the space and what comes and goes and why. Does what I'm sensing or remembering lead me to thinking about the space or the situation I am trying to know more about.

81 Reading in all directions

The pot patch was growing in the dirt of what must have been an old barnyard. Nearby, the bucket and pulley system stood over a large underground well, which was still full of water. The towering oak tree, providing a much needed shade at the edge of the patch, rose high above the surrounding tall weeds and thick bush. A hidden path meandered from the vegetable garden beside the house further back to the well. From there you had to know where to duck through some bushes onto the secret path which led to the freedom garden of stout, bushy marijuana plants standing around like loitering gangs of unemployed on the dole. Off in the distance, a tree line at the fence told of the creek there — nourishing the tree line. Beyond were the hills. They climbed like terraces up into the high country where they became mountains.

The freedom garden was growing in what must have been the best earth there ever was. It had charcoal bits from the barn which must have burnt down and been scattered all over the yard. Now the yard was over-grown and colonized with prairie grasses and weeds, that were thick with fallen leaves suspended in the ebbing and flowing in the wind. The bracken-covered ground is like the sky, with clumps of grasses and bushes like clouds taking hold where they can amid a line of trees that must have been the edge of the barnyard. The leaves had laid there seeping into the ground all the wet winter and so the barn dirt was porous with moisture-holding bits of charcoal, bark and bracken, composted manure, dried grass, and dead leaves.

The well is centered between the barn and the house. This whole farm must have been centered around the well. It went deep down into the cistern that collected rainwater, maybe 8,000 gallons under there. We had no telling. We thought that since the water was a brown tea, dead things had fallen in there; they made it have an almost magical potency when we put it on the plants. Because everything did grow well. We had some beautiful plants, one gigantic tree we called the Texas Twister from stock that had come from ancient ganja farmers in India.

Looking down into the water at the bottom of the well, I see the sky reflected in the circle of smooth dark water untouched by the wind. The well is a hole to the sky, and reflecting me looking down into there too. The sky is going by. Color has dropped out of the image reflected in the smooth surface at the bottom of the well. It is night at the bottom of the well. The well was like a reflecting telescope, one that is not at all perturbed by the motion of the wind.

Sometimes when I look down into the well I feel like I might fall in. Who am I? My stomach turns from the dizzying height as the man looks down into the dark water. I am afraid. He imagines himself falling in head first, and getting stuck upside down unable to right himself. He dies a terrible death, drowning after a long terror-imbued struggle, from exhaustion.

I turn around and see round about down here on the ground are clumps of different grasses and bushes, like different kinds of clouds. They are iterating their life form, making copies of itself by iteration all over the place.

The world is full of hauntingly self-similar forms echoing the pulling-in, shaping process of everything trying to hold a little energy for a while.

Fractals record what happens in the transition zones between order and chaos. From above we are moss growing on the side of a rock, spreading, fanning out over every surface. We are coming to the end of our time and falling like the leaves. The leaves too are positioned like clouds, like rocks on a hillside. The leaves are dried to their veins. These veins in the leaves are *its* tree, that once carried life to it. Now they are from it, in an interzone between life and death, giving life to other forms.

High above the oak tree, clouds are dispersed like cool coals, burning holes in the endless blue.

Wind is a shape too, a movement connecting hot and cold air masses. A mixing, in the sky, in the bottom layer of the atmosphere.

The dirt is the bottom layer of the life zone.

Locusts have been doing untold damage to the patch but still it was coming on strong and had survived even their hungry onslaught. Enough for all.

The man who proceeds in atunement will survive.

But it is not always possible to have your I Ching look-up table handy with its images and its judgments. It would be ideal if one really *knew* the hexagrams, or at least a refinement thereof and we could just think about them at the moment —or even better, if we could just look inside ourselves and ask some great all pervading oracular being: What's up?

We would like to see the I Ching — the oracle — as a kind of method, a method based on the matrix mandala, a method that talked directly to us in the language of images. And it does! The I Ching comes from a time and a world where the body and the mind were not so terribly separated as they are today. It was possible to query the oracle by introspection and inhabit a world that communicated through a language of images. It still is. We have inherited a culture that seems to be only about profit and loss or sin and guilt and that's not where it's at. It is about creativity and transcendence. An individual is made up of several centers: the physical body and its biochemistry, the sensing mechanism, the feelings center, the intuition center, the thinking center. In levels moving from the concrete to the abstract we have a hexagram:

    —— spirit
    —— thinking
    —— intuiting, pattern recognition
    —— feeling
    —— sensing
    —— body, chemistry

And one does a check-in query on each of these levels to find the interpretation of the moment. Simply ask the oracle, the manifold whence all things come. For example, I often have my mind and my thinking and my spirit together on things, but they tend to gang up on the heart and leave the feelings out of it —for fear of sentimentality.

    —— spirit
    —— thinking
    —— intuiting, pattern recognition
    — — feeling
    —— sensing
    —— body, chemistry

And I might not know what is going on with some of the other sensors, my ideogram of the hexagram of the moment might be:

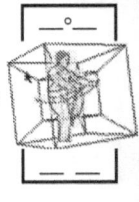

```
———— spirit
———— thinking
———— intuiting, pattern recognition
— —  feeling
—°—  sensing
—°—  body, chemistry
```

I am wondering why I have such a hard time having feelings, and then I think to look up this ideogram.

It could be any of

which if we put these into the I Ching mandala to think about them.

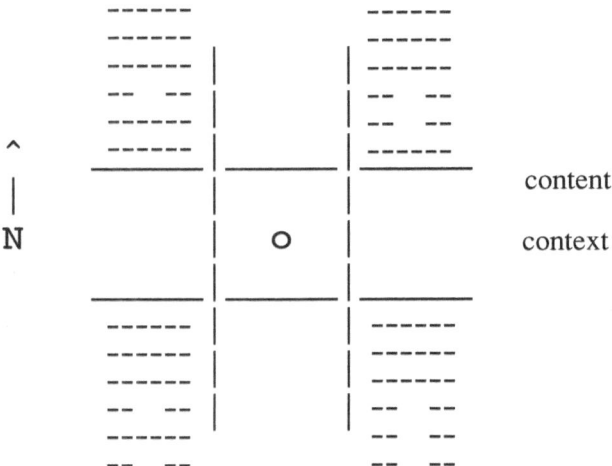

^
|
N

content

context

The Myers-Brigs Type Indicator
The MBTI is the predominant system of personality study today, used in schools and industry. The MBTI requires only a quadragram. The Myers-Briggs formalizes

what we notice about how some people are very outgoing and fun-oriented, while others are more quiet and introspective; some people are highly analytical in decision making, while others use their feelings for deciding; some people feel more comfortable living a planned, orderly life, while others prefer to live spontaneously. The MBTI models personality as a binary (either/or) space of 4 dimensions: energizing, attending, deciding, and living. Four orthogonal (or independent) scales: energizing, attending, deciding, living — right away we think of the tesseract.

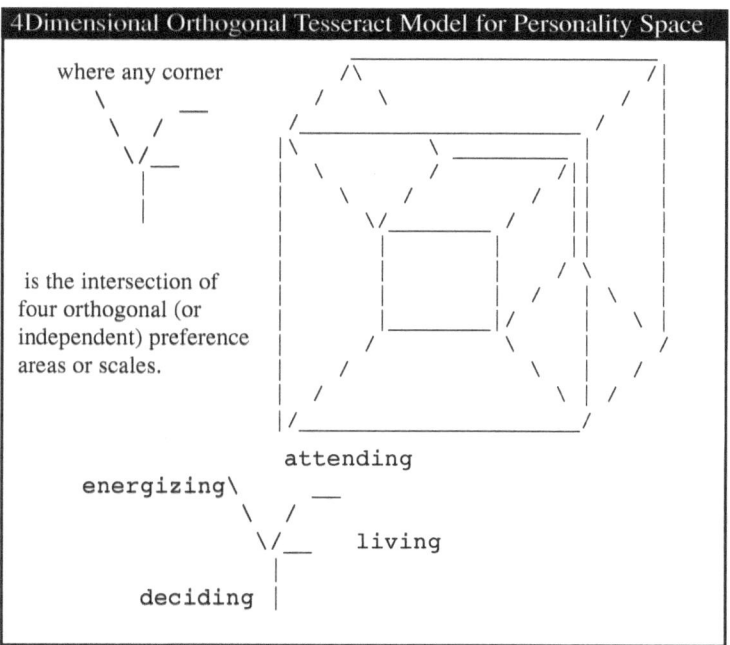

And we could use the dimensional scale to make the symbol for each of the personality types.

```
\
 \  /  ‾    energizing is extroverted E ------
  \/__       living is planned          J ------
   |         attending is sensing        S ------
   |         deciding is feeling         F --  --
```

This, in standard notation, would be the ESFJ — a sales person. People with this kind of personality are found in 13% of the population.

Energizing -
How a person is energized

Extroversion (E)	Introversion (I)
Preference for drawing energy from the outside world of people, activities or things.	Preference for drawing energy from one's internal world of ideas, emotions, or impressions.

Attending -
What a person pays attention to

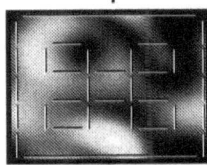

Sensing (S)	Intuition (N)
Preference for using the senses to notice what is real.	Preference for using the imagination to envision what is possible - to look beyond the five senses. Jung calls this "unconscious perceiving".

Deciding -
How a person decides

Thinking (T)	Feeling (F)
Preference for organizing and structuring information to decide in a logical, objective way.	Preference for organizing and structuring information to decide in a personal, value-oriented way.

Living -
Lifestyle a person prefers

Judgement (J)	Perception (P)
Preference for living a planned and organized life.	Preference for living a spontaneous and flexible life.

83   the reality matrix of the self

Our internally organized model of reality is constructed on a matrix of sense, memories, desires, feelings and thoughts. The matrix allows us to understand the present moment by providing relevant past experience. The usual path of sense data into the mind is from Perception to Judgement.

```
Perceiving  _|_  Judging
           | S | T |
           | N| F |
              |
```

The present moment enters the matrix through the senses, where it is compared against representations constructed from stored memory. We experience the moment as the fulfillment of needs, desires, feelings and thoughts.

$$S — > iN — > T — > F$$

The reality matrix is a coherent unconscious structure that holds our past experience and knowledge. This essay explores how the Jungian Functions build the matrix, and how this, in turn, is responsible for our personality.

Mechanism of Attention Control

Feedback and feedforward loops are the mechanism of control, through amplification and dampening of the basic Functions — S, N, T, F. The set of multi-connections and cross-couplings is what forms the Reality Matrix of the Self.

```
          I---J
         |  \ | /  |
  S->    |  -|-  |    <-F
         |  / | \  |
          P---T
```

We can model the matrix as a fast look-up database table with search optimizing rules. Since the integrity and coherence of the database is of such vital importance, we have a great deal invested in making sure it is optimally maintained. Later we will use the concept of database to help visualize multidimensional reality.

The Reality Matrix as Tesseract

We will model the Reality Matrix of the Self as a

database table which is a matrix that is a product of all the possible combinations. A simplified model would be this I Ching cube inside a cube (a tesseract) where the 64 hexagrams are obtained by associating each trigram with every other. This generates the 8x8=64.

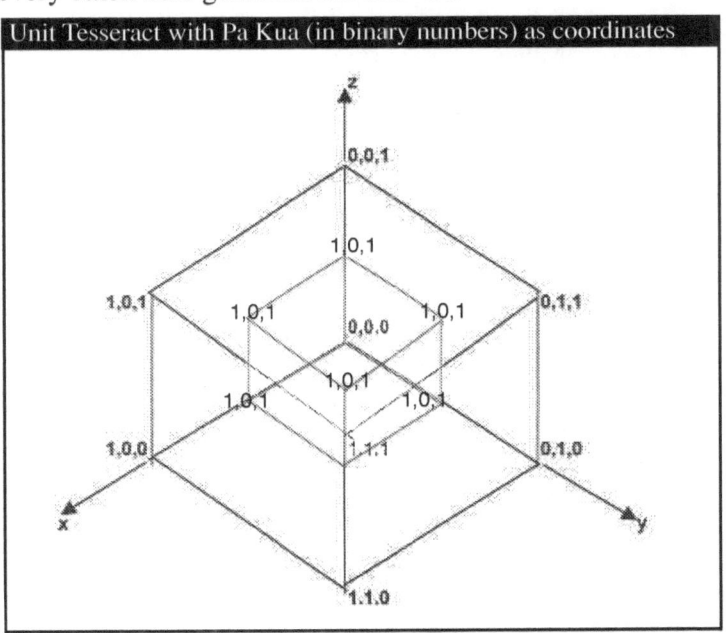

Unit Tesseract with Pa Kua (in binary numbers) as coordinates

Similarly the I Ching space of resolving a hexagram from the moving lines of the initial hexagrams has a hexagram at each corner and potentially associates it with each other hexagram with all the other ones, giving 64x64=4096. But actually, if *every* movable line changed, it would be $(64)^6$.

Description of the Reality Matrix of the Self

The joy of philosophy is that it will help you find yourself waking up. Here we have developed a framework for picturing the possible combinations of a bifurcating hierarchical association space. We call this the Reality Matrix of the Self, by analogy to the human body's Inertia Tensor (matrix). The Reality Matrix of the Self is also a tensor. If you can enter this space you will come to some really precious insights. Start by slowing down and try to watch yourself using the basic functions — S N T F.

In trying to understand the world through the best models and systems our culture can give us, we are in a position to understand about how the left and right brain access reality. Basically the left brain is a digital processor, it has lots of switching circuits; the right brain is more of an analog processor, it has op-amps and different time series.

The hemisphere model provides the first binary distinction in the Reality Matrix. This first distinction is the primary field-ground gestalt. This matrix, as we shall see, is a collection of filters that structure consciousness — the archetypes. The perception half of the reality matrix, comes in through the neurological machinery, the computers that form the Left and Right hemispheres of the brain.

L | R
__ | __
| S | iN|

The left and right hemispheres are each both visual (high frequency) and audile (low frequency) data processors. Thus the basic machinery gives us our sense of local / distal, particular /general. We can see that this starts to explain the 4 Functions. For example, the particular / general explains the Sensing / iNtuitive Type dimensions.

The I Ching is a collection of observations that depicts change as a state of détente between intersecting potentials (generalized as yin/yang). It is well depicted in the Tai Chi diagram showing yin and yang combined in a fractal binary.

The Automorph is Self-Organization

The basis of evolution is self-organization. This is true of all living things starting with the emergence of cycles from material processes: the autocatalytic cycles, ATP, photosynthesis /respiration, then to tissues and all living organisms. Self-organization occurs through Feedback. Just as dynamic balance is a vector pulling back to equilibrium, feedback is the way that biology forces the self to support itself.

We are all moving along on the Fractal Vector. Which is generated by the following procedure: a function is computed, then the result is used (this is through feedback) in the argument of the function.

f(x)--> result, then result ---> f(result) --> new result

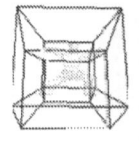

The feedback of the motion of the river on itself. I am struck by how my personality organizes and is organized by my self.

From Topological Psychology to Fractal Psychology

Lewin's *Topological Psychology* can incorporate Fractals. His psychology, uses classical vector field theory to formalize psychology. It is unified by the concept of movement of forces across boundaries. The operant concept here is "across boundaries". Lewin does not give the mechanism for moving across boundaries, but now we can see the mechanism as diffusion, percolation, dispersion —all governed by the fractal dimension of the boundary. And with the insight of database experience —join and intersection of tables — where tables are the vectors (n-tuples) spanning a space, that is collections of attributes. In database terminology the matrix is just a table of data.

Attributes as dimensions

We can describe the four basic Functions of psychology, sensing, intuiting, thinking, and feeling as functions of variables, that is surfaces in a multidimensional space of attributes. For example, iNtuition = N $(i_1, i_2, i_3, \ldots .i_n)$ and the i_i would be dreams, affirmation, imagination, fantasies, fetishes and treasured objects, free associations of life. Right brained leaping down to the solution of a problem and not knowing why. These would be the accessible dimensions of intuiting. Similarly, Sensing = S $(s_1, s_2, s_3, \ldots .s_n)$. where the s_i would be the ways sense data was acquired and used, listening, touching, seeing, questioning, time management, moving with power. Similarly for Thinking and Feeling dimensions.

Topological Psychology is the beginning of a Fractal Psychology. It will help us understand opening the gates of porosity of boundaries and handling the chaos of moving inside and outside of these boundaries. Whenever the reality matrix is enhanced, we feel pleasure; if it is damaged, we feel pain. The fundamental purpose of all our choices and actions is to maintain and enhance the stability and coherence of this structure. When an occurrence is successfully integrated, we then think about how we can continue to enhance the matrix with further experience.

Jung and the I Ching

In this manual we have called this Organizational Entity, who is constantly trying to break through and remind of who we are, the Automorph. Tai Chi eventually enables us to better tune it in. No wonder Jung loved the I Ching. Understanding its oracular processes led to his theory of the Self. The concept of the Image, as a synthesis of experience communicating in a tight gestalt directly from the unconscious to the conscious is there. The concept of the mind as a window between the timeless archetypal Self, and the individual self is contained in the symbol of the hexagram. This window or interface to the world is the personality. It basically has four panes. The *I Ching* pretty much contains his Four Function model of personality. Consciousness flowing into and out of personality indicates personality function and connection.

Picture of Core personality

I envision this core of personality as automorphic, as a dynamic symmetry between the struggle to contain and be or not be contained. As an energy flow and resisting membrane, that had been activated by the much earlier catastrophic separation between animal and hominid. The membrane would be a multidimensional surface — made much more complicated than the earlier unity of instinct — bulging and contorted with the agony over being evicted from that blissful state; while the energy flow would represent the multifoliate desire of differentiation, set in motion by the evolutionary branching.

Fragments

Stepping up on the lines of the hexagram
     — the matrix, the Ladder —
up the dichotomies of personality,
negotiating the psychosocial crises that make us grow
and challenge our evolution,
following the Meandering lines of dots, tectiforms, claviforms
     —exploding / fixed —
stepping into world-rooms of the self,
the profundity of the reality,
     — energy / object —
of the benign matrix that we abandoned
     — explosive spontaneity/implosive regimentation —
will be revealed
in an art that challenges comprehension.

84   An Image of the Unconscious Shadow

The image of the Shadow may be anything sinister that comes up in your mind. They are just props in a bigger shadow play.

This image came into my mind when I was afraid.
It was a picture, of my anger:
It was a big blind sloth,
with a huge hooked claw.
It scared me.
It was a communication from the shadow side of myself.
Ugly and blind, lumbering around,
it reminded me of being big and clumsy.
It is very, very old. I was about 6, I think, when I realized I was much bigger than the other kids and I branched off into that one. I remember being in school having to sit behind a desk and wanting to be wild and free and running around.

But this anger accompanying the image was so blind and unfeeling, and I got this sense of how much anger there is out there in the world —the road rage, the brutality in the service of an ideology, the rapacious greed to fill the longing for the spirit.

But this sloth, what an IMAGE this is! — speaking directly to me from the level of the unconscious. I had experienced the IMAGE, something that here-to-for had only been something spoken about in books. Now, I was experiencing it! The mind has its gifts to give out. The Mind.

Here I am an individual, a porous lace over a fractal interior nervous system, interfacing with the chaotic world outside. We are both operated by and operating, this bifurcating hierarchical tree-like organization system. It is transpersonal. It communicates with us in the best possible way. It communicates with movies, and images that carry a tight cathexis of meaning. To have this experience means that I was getting enough distance and separation from my self (I was becoming grown up enough) to be able to appreciated the archetypes at work here!

I remembered a Buddhist technique, the exercise of looking into your own face while sitting in front of the mirror. How difficult it is to look at myself. I worry that I might become narcissistic, but the primary narcissism is necessary for survival. You need to be able to look at yourself, to know yourself at least, before you can know others.

All art is self portrait.

It uses images of the unconscious.

I have seen the truth of the images and will explore to other deeper images beneath the image.

I felt like I wanted to walk in the woods

in the forest of my senses.

My senses were really alive and I could feel the tree of nerve endings and branchings that were within me and I could really feel a part of all things.

In the I Ching, you are looking at the world through a system that organizes the world into bifurcating dichotomies AND reflects back on itself AND it is everywhere.

The I Ching is the transpersonal paradigm par excellence. It is the story of a people projecting their inner world on a probability distribution in an attempt to understand the machinations of the outer world. It is the image of an operating system of the world, an isomorphism connecting the bifurcating fractal structure between the neurology and the psychology on the inside, with the bifurcating fractal structure of material manifestation on the outside. It is in each of us, and it is outside the person. It is transpersonal.

And I thought that THIS — transpersonal psychology — is the highest art form. This is what we must aspire to in our art, that we must go out and heal the people so they can feel themselves in this way, and then they will go out and want to work with the plants, work with the ecology just to feel more a part of this world. I would become this noble Knight Errant of Transpersonal Psychology.

Would it be possible for a person to experience something universally human like this more often? Moreover, universally human in the sense of this is how life would work everywhere. By god I must write a book about this.

I must also find a way to do something I think is really worth while that I would like to belong to. Theatre creates more or less of a sense of this feeling, it can be very psychotherapeutic.

In the setting summer sun, I sat in lotus
   at the edge of the pond listening,
to the Frog Symphony as it tuned up
to greet an early rising full moon night.
With eyes open, I let myself become entranced,
and disolved into the soundscape.
My perception opened up — looking at the flashes
of sunlight on ripples
of concentric interfering circular waves —
   made by the multitude of water striders
      and other beings, disturbing
   the glassy lake surface
   which was reflecting the sky
      and the dark forest across the other side.
   (It's not technically a lake.)

  With my eyes open
I began to meditate on the
   surface of the lake, taking it in
      with my whole being.
The idea is that the perception is wide,
beyond the eyes open, — whole being —
      instead eyes close to look for internal lights.
Just letting in the scene,
letting it fall down through my eyes . . .
   like a long waterfall,
     and crash
on the center of my breathing.

Its quiet . . . with no people.
I began falling into a kind of love for the landscape,
or feeling the love in the complexity.
But then the mind started going into states
of awe and bliss over this
and then the ego
got into *its* struggle with the body for supremacy;
   ego wins and poses interesting
   math problem.
Quadrapole moment sound of the frogs in stock tank

with START UP FROG being any one,
    though tended to be
    the more dominant.
    OR the one who had found
        the sweet spot
—one frog seems to have found the place where his
song is exactly the right frequency to resonate the whole
lake like it was his guitar cavity.
    Trying to draw females to their
        Elvis, Jerry Lee Lewis,
        Donnavan, Jimi Hendricks,
            Jim Morrison,
        drawing attention through sound.

    Let us consider
    the problem of the Frog.
    Boy frog has got to make his sound
    AND attract girl frog
    AND avoid the wolf dog fox
    who is also attracted to the sound,
    AND Girl frog has got to find him
    AND throw her tadpoles off.
    The Family is a lifeguard tower,
    a preoccupation covering over the contemplative scene,
        covering everything. The Human Family is the most
highly evolved biological structure on the planet

    I started to feel my shoulder under the linen shirt
    with no under shirt
    buttoned up. Commo los *tehanos*
        But I digress.
        And say mantra to pull me back:
    Being as feedback, being as
    body as feedback, body as being, body as path;
    mantra
    to let me
    get myself into deeper aesthetical states —
    shimmers
            into
            the water of vibrations:
    body as feedback, body as being, body as path.

Ahhh, so . . .
Glassy surface with ripples,
seemed like a 2D map of
        Venn Diagrams of
intersecting influences —
mutual probabilities.

(A ∩ B) ∩ Ξ
A ∩ (B ∩ Ξ)
(A ∩ Ξ) ∩ B

So many intersecting circles on the surface that they
made the surface almost choppy with little shimmer waves.

This abstract, but simple diagram of overlapping
influences is an objective correlative (Image)
of the state of mind I'm talking about.
I think: Maybe the ego isn't exactly wining after all.
Maybe abstraction is really the only language
supple enough to speak to an art of being,
as opposed to visual or audio or logical.

It's a picture of perceiving by your being.
Not just looking
at the surface
of things
or what is going on
 in your own
mind
but at the *way*
it is absorbed into
your being.
 Making you realize
you are
a part
of all that is going on at the Moment.

It's not the Frog Symphony
        it's the Frog Quartet.
                Actually it's the zero-sum Frog Game.

Born from darkness into a world of light
we navigate dichotomies
between young and old,
starting with identical to / different from mother;
and building theories about space / time from
observing her coming /going.
Constantly deciding between good and bad
in childhood, we navigated the straights of little and big,
boy and girl, mother and dad, in crowd and on-the-out,
which became more acute in our youth.

Parent / Adult / Child
All the logical world between true and false
And computers - great machines distinguishing between
    0/1, on and off, off and on,
constantly oscillating in a binary flip-flop flow.
And probability — all the world in between
certainty and impossibility.
    Choices, choices endless choices.
We are caught in the web of dichotomies
gradually taking shape into a tree
—the fractal model of all, and more —
to anything that can be classified
underneath the stars and including the stars.
In between is a gray area of expediencey
— the way we deal with the imperfection
at the heart of all knowledge,
which, though it may not be pernicious,
can be be harem-scarem.

```
\ | /    *
\ | * / *
*  |  |    |
|   |  /
\ |
---- ! - - -
```

The first distinction is between the visual and the
auditory.
These are situated in the Left Brain and the Right Brain.
Visual space tells us what, and where,
and audile space tells us where in relation to us.
Thus are objects, and relationships among the objects.
The parts of the whole.
We have the object, the object in relationship, and the
relationship . . .

What if it were all only one dichotomy?
One that expands
and contracts,
and maybe it has different surfaces,
with interstices going from one domain to another
like a tentacle or a dendrite,
or a fractal.
Dichotomies are but an expression
of this archetypal part / whole dichotomy,
Either you're in, or your out of the class,
Or maybe in another class.
Logic — positive or negative, binary,
is the simple computation of proposition and the basis of
all language.
It is the total paradigm of dichotomous iteration.
Dichotomous iteration, hmmmm ,
that has a scholastic ring to it — don't it?

The I Ching is dichotomous iteration. . .
The I Ching is a representation of a system with
expanding choices at each level.
Also self-similarity at each level.

The I Ching climbs up levels of the ladder of the
hexagrams, leading to a divination which is a consciousness
of the Self.

Mnemonists say 8 states at level 3 is most optimum.
Beyond that, well . . .You can make an elephant and then you
can make his trunk wave.

Each level requires the previous level as context to
sustain the new content.

Christian / Jew
Buddhist / Muslim,
And we are so wrapped-up in the paradigm of this
divinity, this divination machine, that we are willing to kill
and be killed for it.
It becomes more important than life itself.

Origination and destruction,
the dependent and the spontaneous . . .

electron / proton
gentle / aggressive
vegetable / thick
space / time
up / down
diffusion / fusion
into a world of dark and light
slow / fast
inside / outside
winter / summer
female / male
cold / hot
vegetable / thick
soft / hard
light / heavy
expanded, fragile / constricted, firm
nature / culture

The yin yang is a symbol for the gestalt of is . . .
of this process of enatiodromia,
—the tendency of things to change into their opposite.
.

A day like any other
the slant sunbeams coming in the afternoon window
throw striated shadows
    on the surface of things.
I am strangely not hungry
    but content
to look at the bright colors
and just listen to the presence,
    and wonder at —
the Quiet of it all —
    going on.
Patience? No-speed!
Soft muscles floating
    — then shift —
syncopated to the
air or whatever is there.

Afternoon in the hark
    with twittering.

Circular ORBITS
    like wings of Butterflies

        weightless
        I am
        a moving thought
    in the great Mind
    OUT THERE.
Here, in sudden deliberation
        nerves of trees
    Reach through me,

    one's foot aloft
        stepping into
        coherence

I step of the porch and head to the garden. I am relaxed, and just letting my feet go on the path they know well. I think: There is a Yum Chi footstep! And there is another. I am slipping into the Form, or it is slipping into me. I am walking into the background hiss of summer and it is moving all around me, within and without me. I am walking in the Form.

```
            _____
           | \ | / |
    ¥ ->   | —¥— |
           | / | \ |
            ‾‾‾‾‾‾
```

You go in and out of the Form.

```
    _____
   | \ | / |
   | —¥— |      -> ¥
   | / | \ |
    ‾‾‾‾‾‾
```

It is a distinct feeling. Like when I was hauling water up from the well. It was like I had gotten into something. This kind of alternating between ritual movement and action, was certainly making it more interesting to work around the place. I'd stop myself while hauling water up from down the well and notice that I was able to understand the idea of mechanical advantage, and being relaxed in hard work. It is important to notice those moments when you enter into the Form.

Basically, to get into the Form you have to get aligned, attuned. Actually it is not all that rigorous. You can do what you can remember. Also you want to start associating things other than boxing, whatever helps you remember.

I began to see Tai Chi as a process of combining and separating. It was part of Tai Chi as the music of awareness, (you are the music, you are the wave). Combining things that flowed out of the source, and separating things into their elemental parts going back to the source. Trying to see things as they are: traversing up and down the Tree. We get this expanding tree only when we emphasize contextual boundaries, that make up the boarders. The contextual boundaries are what does the expanding and contracting. Nature become manifest. It is a kind of chemistry, a ball and stick model, giving the illusion of movement.

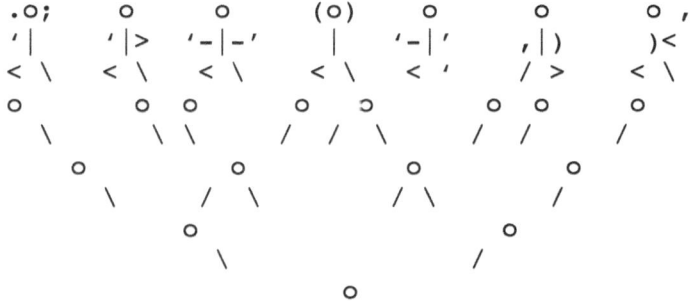

```
.o;      o      o     (o)      o       o       o  ,
 ' |    ' |>  '-|-'     |     '-|'    , |)     )<
 < \    < \   < \     < \    < '     / >     < \
 o      o  o         o   o            o  o       o
  \      \  \     /  /  \       /  /      /
    o        o            o            o
     \     /  \         /  \         /
       o                            o
        \                          /
          o
```

In trying to develop some kind of notation to help me
remember the Tai Chi moves, it was a great help to have read
G. Spenser-Brown's book *The Laws of Form* as an
undergraduate in the 70's. G. Spenser-Brown did for logic
what R.D. Laing did for psychology. There we were with our
head aswim over all this quantum mechanics, and relativity,
and we had these old physics teachers who had not been able
to give up their hard acquired epistemologies and we were
desperate for anything that laid some kind of foundation.
Then in dropped this little paperback, I think it cost less than
$3. It was strange, marvelous, with its innovative binary
calculus notation —the hook operator. It was as if that book
had fallen from another planet. Actually, it was quite
disturbing. Thankfully, I found a paper by Bertran Russel
where he reduced the operators of logic — AND, OR , and
NOT, to one single slash (/) operator. I realized G. Spenser-
Brown had written a boolean calculus with his own
representation of the slash (/) operator.

I have a memory of Walker Underwood, undergraduate,
sitting cross-legged on the lawn near the UT campus movie
theatre in the middle of the afternoon sun one hot day,
holding forth in animated conversation about the Laws of
Form with some physics graduate students. I was plagued by
√–1 the imaginary number. Of course you could just take it
as a definition in a formal game, but I really wanted to know
it. (I liked the idea from electrical engineering that it was
about potential stored in a field). I was intrigued and
stimulated by trying to relate the world view of Quantum
mechanics and the probabilistic universe with my everyday
world view. And here was *The Laws of Form*, attempting to
bring together the knowledge of the outer world expressed in
the physical sciences, with the inner world of our language of

space expressed in mathematics. It was a noble attempt. One that would keep me busy for the rest of my life. The book was a model of finding the most essential aspects of a subject and making of them a kind of implicative-indicative form play. And now here I was the Tai Chi student trying to understand "folding" . . .

The Laws of Form really spoke to what I felt was the need for another language: the Subject-Verb-Object language is inadequate. Though it has wonderful resolution, it is linear. And it has great difficulty cross-sorting from content to context, although it does do this in figures of speech. I thought a reparation to the Worf Limit (of how language informs mind) might be found in a more idiomatic language like Chinese. Or in semiotics. Or the binary calculus. I was looking at *The Laws of Form,* with its imaginary and 2nd-order logical operations, as a kind of meta-language to liberate my mind from the prison of language. To understand (and become better at using) the figures of speech — ambiguity, imagery, metaphor, metonymy, simile, etc. — in poetry. I saw the I Ching as another marvelous and elegant system to help with this liberation. The hexagram is being built up out of the situation. How do they combine? One can judge from reading the *I Ching* that the combiner is 'from outer to inner' or 'emerges'. The text says "from defensiveness 'emerges' stagnation" or "from devotion 'emerges' intensity", depending on what trigram is on top and what trigram is on the bottom. It is like a refinement, moving from the simple to the complex. Like abstraction penetrating the imagination — working — seeing more and more possibilities to a situation, opening up to resolution. We are looking at the representation of a system that branches by bifurcation. Which is to say most systems we encounter. Like the *I Ching*, *The Laws of Form* is a simple, elegant representation of how the nervous system organizes experience. It is not the neurophysiology, nor is it the psychology, it is somewhere in between. It is the operating

(expand)   (contract)

system by which the mind operates the human perceptual computer —the body / brain. As such, it is transpersonal.

Nature uses this strategy, of material gestalt or dialectic, in forms play to solve the problems of struggling against entropy and creating organizations to cross time. The basic bifurcation is into masculine and feminine. Into expanding outward and contracting inward. How do the forms combine? Even in the asking of that question we invoke our analytic sense which is based upon the same binary, bifurcating system, i.e. logic.

The task of flow control is to:
$$\text{delay / advance —transition,}$$
$$\text{suppress / enhance —turbulence}$$
$$\text{prevent / provoke —separation}$$
To make the species more efficient at survival.

Build a fence to force the wind over the garden so that the topsoil won't blow away: lift enhancement.

The herd of wilderbeasts keep the lions fed, and the lions teach the wilderbeasts how to enhance their speed and defenses: Co-evolution — mixing augmentation and flow-induced noise suppression.

The ancients were looking at energies and flows. Control a flow from its center: use steps to make a river flow back on itself and stay away from the banks. This makes the river's energy move toward its center: enhance turbulence selectively.

The analogy is: Subject is to object as signal is to sign.

And in order to explore this, I thought to develop a play, a solo theatre piece based on *The Laws of Form*. It would be for a new kind of theatre: not entertainment but ritual. It would communicate directly, body to body, with mass and motion. It would be a kind of generative channeling of Form. A Poor Theatre (Grotowski), based only on mime, with no objects but what were suggested. It would explore mind in the world and the world in our mind: Subject and object are to physically real artifacts, what signal and sign are to informationally abstract images. What we are doing when we enter the Form is deepening the alignment of subject and object with signal and sign. Let me say that again (like an actor on stage).

Actor (*hits his palm for emphasis*):
When we enter the Form we are aligning, more and more, subject and object with signal and sign.

***

SOME NOTES in preparation for a solo play.

I need to go through the leg stances first, then the hand stances.

And this begins from the ground — from the floor, you are thinking with your feet. You are building up a hexagram.

Bow step, T-step, cat step, and all the potential set-up transitions that move you in between these steps.

Take a left at the White Stork. Take a right at the Single Whip. Go backward at the Monkey. Go around the round about in Fair Lady works at Shuttles.

Yes. Start calling them something else, I don't have to use those animal form names, although they may suggest perception by different phyla.

Go out and come back. To go out and come back, call this the form of condensation, it is the basic unit of the play.

Crossing the line and going back across the line is a cancellation. So we have condensation and cancellation

Condensation

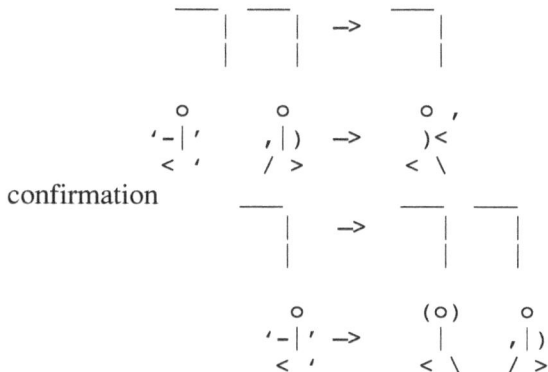

confirmation

You set up a boundary:
1. You may not allow force to cross the boundary
   a) you move the boundary
   b) you cross the force attempting to cross the boundary (with a deflecting or counter force.)
2. You allow force to cross the boundary
   a) you redirect it
   b) you absorb (ground) it, so that it bounces back upon itself.

So basically you are always trying to be on the defensive, and these open and closing refer to the kua, the fold, the manifold, the HOOK.

The place of interest is where one folds into a corner. Where are these? Where there is a change of *direction*. Pay attention to where the train of Chi goes around a corner. I will need to block out all the turns in my mind.

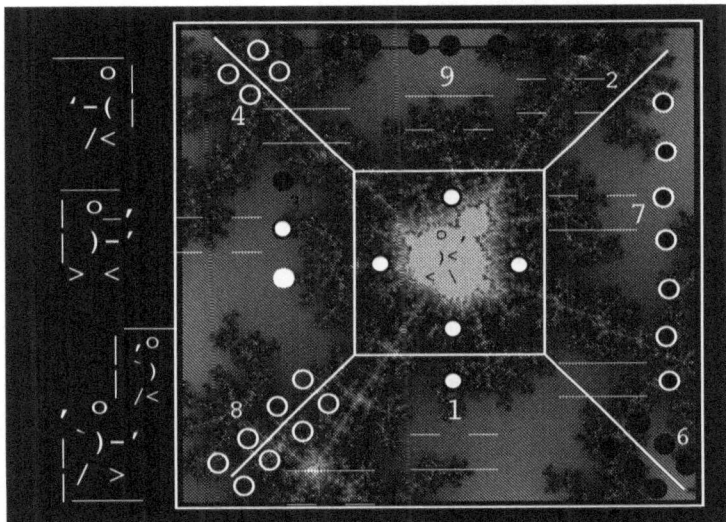

What would the concatenation of corners bring? Say something at each corner. Let these corners become the generating mnemonic, along with the upper and lower trigrams. I assigned upper and lower trigrams, to the upper and lower parts of the body, and combined these in long concatenations.

At the corners we say something . . . try and recapitulate our lives, speak about the place of interest that we are at in our mind at the moment . . . then this corner between literature and truth, will form a certain angle. It will be a figure of folding back, of the angle ensured by a fold. It might be the point of a gesture . . . And the monk might deliver some kind of pronouncement there. . .

The player must show, must explore with the audience both an inside and an outside of these corners, these turns. Together, the player and the audience will be crossing and uncrossing an axis, the line of symmetry, between left and right, front and back, up and down,

This is also a kua. An external kua. The fold, the kua, we are going in and out of the fold.

Crossing the line and going back across the line is a cancellation. So we have condensation and cancellation

Actor:

What's the difference?
One is going out and coming back,
and the other is actually moving.
Cancellation is going out and coming back, while Condensations is going out and coming to rest in another place.
(Turns, moves across the room, turns to face again)
Actor *(continues)*:

This is the way to have one character talking to another character with only one actor. In life and psychology it is a way to amplify your sub-personalities.

Intention. I may have an intention. The intention is to cross boundaries . . .
(mimes inside and outside of a space)
To contain what is on the inside and not to contain what is not on the inside.
Actor *(says in narrative style)*:

The hexagrams are stacked one on top of the other,
and they represent the emergence of all things
from the form.

We are being ourselves without many layers of real and abstract, conscious and unconscious. It is as if we are traveling the distinction-making semiotic machinery of mind in our play. Said differently, when subject is signal and object is sign—as in the case of dancing the hexagrams—the system behaves as the story tells. Signal and sign are vehicle and message, body and force. Signal bodies are real, but have no relationship between mass and meaning. Meaning is assigned to bodies to communicate a sign story.

Each form in the Form (sometimes called a cada of the Form) can be called an expression of the Form. Each Tai Chi form and its motions, signal meaning at differing signal mass. The same message can be told in the memory of the world. Signal and sign carry and describe images to someone in the form who is committed to interpreting this kind of language imagery into behavior that generates what can be defense or at other times can be theatre.

In adapting G. Spenser-Brown's little book *The Laws of Form* for the stage, I wanted to use several of these cross-sorted logical types that he so nimbly shows are the basis of ambiguity and figure in language. I wanted to use these 2nd order logical equations to bring the reader / audience into confrontation with identity. I thought of it as being about moving across boundaries between the self and the Self.

Scene: *Actor standing on a bare stage. Soft spot light falling on him. He is thinking . . . talking to himself.*

Actor: The first thing we must do, as always, is draw a distinction.

Scene: *Makes the sign of distinction — with the hand, crooked at the wrist, in the air. Continue the motion, moving around so the feet inscribe a circle in the space. (Like in Hsing I.) He is creating a kind of structure or cage with his hands in pantomime.*

Actor: Call the space in which it is drawn the space severed, or cleaved by, the distinction.
(gestures out into the space, offering the space to audience)

There are parts, areas, enclosures shaped by the severance or cleft. Call them the sides of the distinction, or the spaces, states or contents, distinguished by the distinction.

Scene: *As he moves around, he delineates a rectangular box shape, like it was his cage, or a cell or a room. The path gradually becomes more circular.*

Actor: *(shaping a ball with his hands)*
    Call it . . . the landscapes, of thought
    . . . the encirclement
    I look out . . . *(holding the sing-songy high pitch on"*
look out" pause on ellipses)
    over the farm . . .

in the. . . the background. . . summer . . . hissing, rising
falling of the cicada song . . . surrounds . . .
I let the sight drift down the . . . long . . . country.
It moves swiftly through summer with no where to go.

Scene: *Make the sign of distinction, starting again.*
makes a slash and divide motion for either / or
and a pull from the edges motion at both — and)

Actor: to get back from
            the Either / Or world
                    to the Both—And
                        | *(push)* | *(press)*

Actor: Here I am
            and am not . . . I.
        This circle in all,
        this change changing
(indicating the circle he has drawn again with a circular
gesture):
        It is the mark of distinction,
        the earth ball,
        we are carrying

Scene: *Actor is holding on to the imaginary ball like,*
holding this precious thing. He lets it take him somewhere,

Actor: it is the Self we are trying to carry through

Scene: *Actor does Fair Lady Works at Shuttles, showing the*
limits of the circle

        This hand full of ....

Scene: *He holds his hand up, twisting it about, as if his*
desire to see it were making him turn around the unmoving
pivot point of the hand. He looks at it, as if seeing it for the
first time, with middle finger wiggling to allow the audience
to visualize chi, or feel it the same thing the posses actor is
feeling. Actor wiggles his hand and watches it move as if the
long middle finger flutters on its own. We get a sense of

looking at the self beneath the ego.

Actor:
the hand is like an eye . . .
the hands guide the view in front of the body, they are coming and going and they are blocks
(illustrate this by indicating hands are extension of the core)
but ambivalent and can be used for anything —a block or a strike.
They are extensions of the will of the great Tao,
and this will makes them rise and fall, and makes us able to touch, what is touchable, and not be able to touch and feel, what does not exist, which is to say — invisible — to the touch.
We are grounded in the real.
And we are not able to push this will
but we can receive this will,
and we can touch this will
and we can move with this will,
if we can feel the web, the membrane, the bubble — around all things — with our hands, ever so ambivalent and ready.
The body now is more than the eyes and the brain. . .
a vehicle to get into . . .

Scene: Actor *is regarding the cage he has created with his hands. The following self observation series leads into this world of structure and implication.*

Actor *(said as a mantra or chant)*:
Here I am
and am not . . . I. *(repeat 3 times)*
Here I am, that's one thing,
and here I am seeing that I am one thing.
That's two things.
Here I am and am not I. Here I am seeing
myself, *seeing* that I am one thing and being one thing.
That's three things.
Here I am
and am not . . . I. *(repeat 3 times)*
Here I am   and am not   I . . .

So we have moved from a simple binary Yes and No system, to a weighted maybe system, to a system of object inherency by attribute passing. Hmmm.

But how on earth do they assign concepts to lake and mountain, and feelings like joyous. Maybe these aren't just concepts! Maybe they are feelings in the presence of these energy organization systems, these archetypal entities. Yes. That's it. In ancient times — free of pollution, no traffic, without taxes, without welfare, without central heating and air-conditioning, without electricity and artificial day-light; with only simple mechanical devices made of wood, when everything was agriculture — the atmosphere was just so highly charged with oxygen from the lush flora that particles of free energy could be felt and almost tasted.

I tried thinking about it like the harmonics of quantum transitions. I sketched out a paper, *Quantum Computing and Phase Transitions in Combinatorial Search*. It would make an analogy between emergent complexity of life (and its relationship to how complex molecules adapted to exploit free energy), to quantum mechanics of structures (and their transition diagrams depicting their relation to radiational energy). It seemed like a promising avenue of inquiry.

Radio waves, heat, all the energy we know in this world comes from molecules and atoms moving, making transitions in their probability levels (orbitals).

When the entity changes state — makes a transition on the transition diagram — radiation in some wavelength is give off-observable evidence. It's quantum mechanics. It is

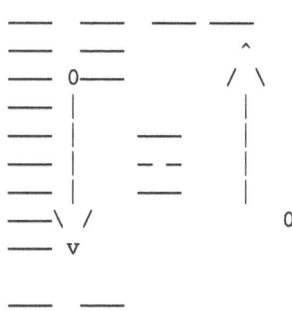

shown in a transition diagram like the hexagrams with each line being an (orbital).

And the ancient philosophers observed all kinds of energy in the world.

All the radiation in the world, which is the evidence of interaction, of coming into existence (being) or going out of existence (non-being) or of changing state, is due to probabilities of the particle being in one orbital or another taking over when the particle changes orbital. Changing probabilities is manifest as energy.

(The energy is an observable, measurable eigenvalue of uncertain unobservables.) The state equation computes the observable, measurable eigenvalue energy by convolving a matrix of ALL possible states (unobservable probabilities) with the previous state.

Out of extensive notes over a period of years, xerox of articles, old physics books, ye old green algebra book —The Vector Space Theory of Matter by Matson,— a couple of Tai Chi books, — the little one of Da Liu, and the larger one from Chen Man-Ching — then developing Notation, which I thought of as a kind of word-as-object as-archetype, Laban diagrams, transition diagrams, my much-thumbed I Ching (both Wilhelm and Legge) plus thoughts on the space time manifold of Newton as divulged in the calculus and the combinatoric manifold divulged by Galois there grew out of the essays I started on *Quantum Computing and Phase Transitions in Combinatorial Search* a decision to make my own space/time.

I started by making my own trigrams based upon the space-time weight coordinates of Laban.

I constructed a simple mandala of his trigrams and those from the I Ching. Out of all this modern and ancient study, I was coming into a much deeper appreciation of how the world bifurcates and branches endlessly into folded protean complexity.

complexity:
10^{10} ——— **species**
10^{6} ——— **molecules**
10^{1} ——— **atoms**

I assigned the proper names for the new trigrams to be their Laban names: fighting, floating, flicking, slashing . . .

With the idea of *emerges*, or object inherency, I built bigger hexagrams out this new set of trigrams — the flow trigrams — which are not based upon space, time, and force but liberation, continuity, and fluency. I was jolted into the NOW. I discovered the simple and basic discipline of Tai Chi. Balance, Attention and Opposites. The perennial philosophy of Hexotranspiration and Onto(/)slashology had been divulged to me.

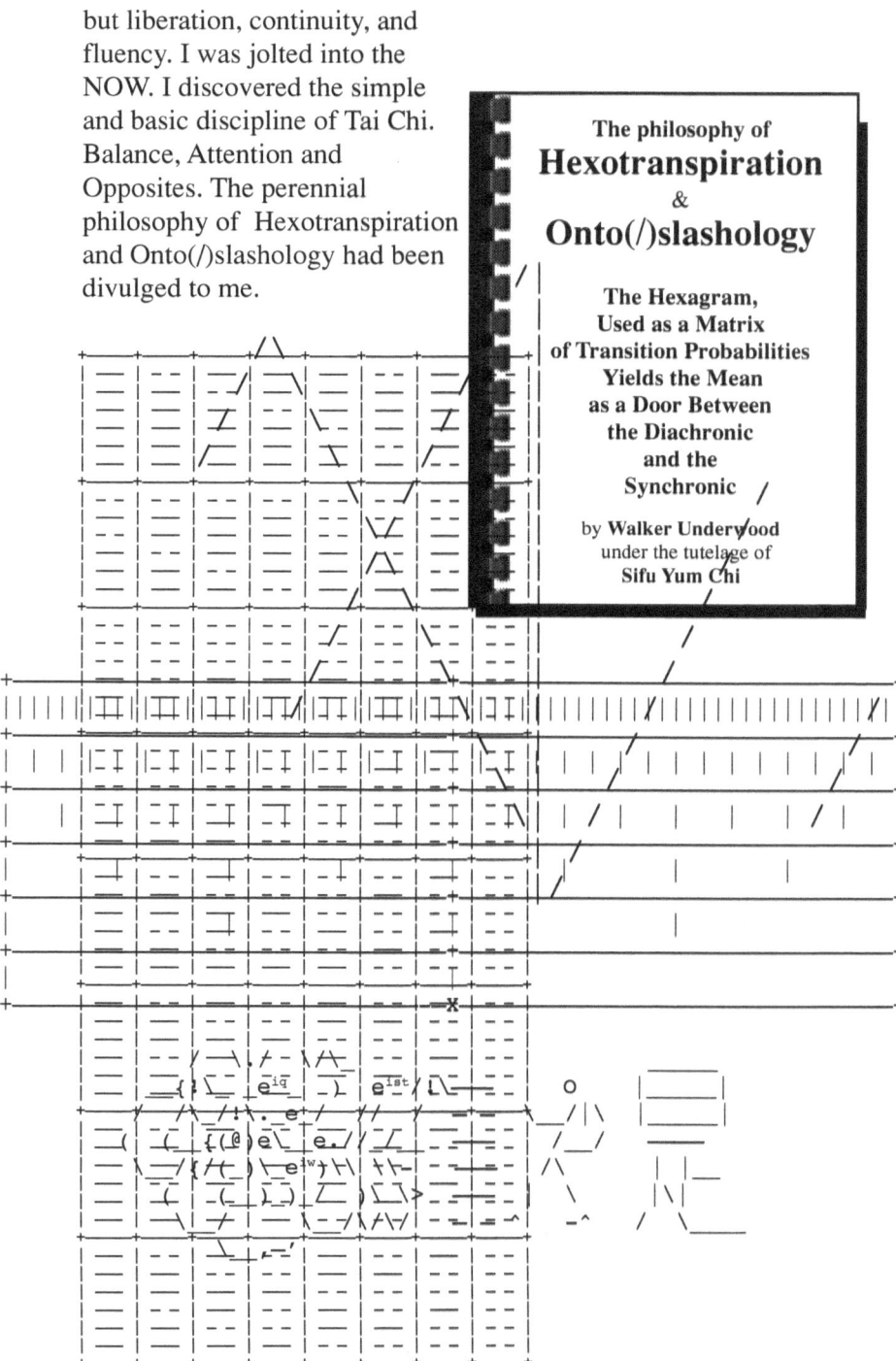

The philosophy of

Hexotranspiration
&
Onto(/)slashology

The Hexagram,
Used as a Matrix
of Transition Probabilities
Yields the Mean
as a Door Between
the Diachronic
and the
Synchronic

by **Walker Underwood**
under the tutelage of
Sifu Yum Chi

91 Hexotranspiration and Onto(/)slashology

Tai Chi is a kind of shadow boxing. The Shadow is the collection of habits that control your freedom, like a shroud. The collection of filters that you call a personality. We know the personality is based on archetypes. When we stand back and can watch them, and are liberated from them, we can see them for what they are —filters. As such, they provide us with a sense of meaning coming into our being and our being coming into the world. Personality is ontology: the qualities with which we interpret reality.

I am trying to bring myself into the present time. I know I can defeat my Shadow in the current now moment of existence. In Tai Chi you are spending time in the Middle Way, a place to get into. And you can get there by bringing yourself into present time to battle shadow. Catching the present is like trying to catch a mirage moving across the landscape in springtime. In the philosophy of Hexotraspiration and Onto(/)slashology, Hexotraspiration is the method and Onto(/)slashology is the metaphysic. Briefly Hexotranspiration is a fusion of hexagram + exotranspiration. And onto(/)slashology is about entities coming into being through emergence from the resolution of dichotomies and the branching of hierarchical distinctions.

What is Hexotranspiration

Hexotranspiration comes from the concept of exotranspiration —the process by which trees pull up water out of the ground and on hot days exude it from their leaves to sparkle and dazzle in the sun. Hexotranspiration expresses emergence and apotheosis. We are feeling ourself on the expanding edge of an explosion into the now. The idea is that all being is coming into existence out of a manifold omnipresent space/time tree, starting with the big bang out of the central source. The hierarchy that emerges comes from the bottom up — a sub-sumption hierarchy. It is formed by equal parallel network elements chunking themselves together once they find they work well together.

What is Onto(/)slashology

Onto(/)slashology is the structure of the tree: how branching occurs and new being emerges at the distinction that makes a difference. It is ontology combined with the logic of the world mind. Onto(/)slashology is an expression of phylogeny from life forms occupying and evolving niches which are presented to stem forms higher up. Basically it is the ontology of the Universal Fractal. The epistemology of the Universal Fractal is hexotranspiration. Hexotranspiration in fractals is the image of essence flowing through the hierarchy by the workings of attractors pulling chaos out of randomness.

Fractals are the trace, the physical evidence, the object, the entity that comes into being through dynamic behavior of the system. Examples of fractals emerging from one dimension into another are: shimmers and coils of heat rising from hot pavement, or thunderheads boiling over the horizon, or the coils in a spreading cloud of cigarette smoke, or bubbling in boiling water. Hexotranspirations are the images and energies, and Onto(/)slashology is the logic and structure of turbulence precipitating being. It is everywhere around us.

Time and the I Ching

Hexotranspiration and Onto(/)slasholgy is based on a deep understanding of the I Ching, but in a modern sense of lattices of transition probabilities and as a kind of system for knowing the archetypes and other aspects. Onto(/)slashology is the way a system branches at a dichotomy: in the mind it is logic in the world survival. When you practice this philosophy you will be slipping into the operating system of earth. And feel this Universal Fractal running out into all dimensions through you.

Hexotranspiration and Onto(/)slashology builds a time based function I(t) into the I Ching. The discipline of I(t)Ching, is an idea as the minds way of scratching a brain itch. I(t)Ching is a kind of game. You can use dice, coins, stalks and other time-honored procedures of haruspication to apply sampling elements into the synchronistic vortex to get your I Ching, or you can just understand archetypes and FEEL. The oracular was always more about knowing yourself than predicting. To do sampling a new way and an ancient way leads to the Middle way. Or you can do it all from understanding and sensing what should be right. In every case it brings you to the same thing: trying to purify a principle out of a continuum, and trying to generate a continuum from basic principles —trying to see the barriers you are up against. Who or what is this shadow, that keeps you from yourself, that freezes the energy in some defense, that is sometimes manifest outside but is more often manifest inside. It is the operating system of planet earth.

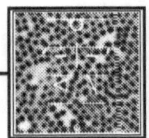

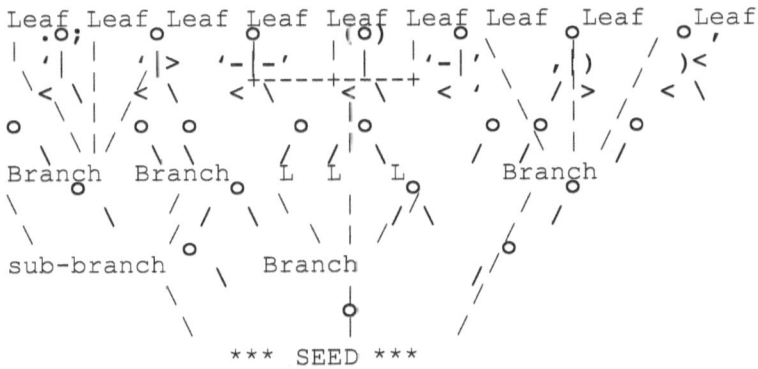

seeds are the leaves' media

seeds are the leaves' media
in which the tree makes copies
of itself

copies using the leaves' media
are sent back into the leaves

The leaves send their media (seeds),
The tree sends its media, the leaves
to their assigned branches
and the branches seed their media (the leaves)
to the seed. As copies of the media are made,
the material starts trickling up the tree to the leaves
as the seeds fall into their media
and sprout into trees.

93 The Fractal Way

What else in the Way of the universe as shown to us by fractals, did I, Walker Underwood — lover of chaos, Taoist, knight of a 1000 eyes, physiker, fractalier, scholar of the I Ching, student of the matrix of support called the Source, philosopher of Hexotranspiration and Onto(/)slashology — further admire.

Its universality, for the universe itself is fractal: its self-similarity at all levels (its main property) from the orbits of planets around stars to the orbits of electrons around atoms: its omnipresence, for the universe is a stain, foaming out on the surface of nothing, creating in the world an endless proliferation of fractal patterns —the sky and its clouds, the mountains, the forests and its trees, trunks--> branches--> leaves with their tree-like veins, the flowers and what drives the color up their stems: its dynamic symmetry between the struggle to contain and be, or not be contained: its recursion, taking the output of a process and feeding back, as seen in the way a dynamic process is in constant awareness of itself, the way a stream is aware of its flow, the sky is aware if its atmospheric processes, the ocean is aware of its currents: its percolating spread as seen in forestation, or colonization of species, or the bubbling in boiling water, or the distillation of spirits, or the movements of a rose's perfume by random walk of its molecular essence across a room: its diffusivity in the spreading out of one fluid in another, as heat in a body, oil in water, bacteria in a petri dish, vapor into a cloud: its porosity seen in the absorbent permeability of dirt, the spongy vascular tubules of plants, the pervious honeycombed interchange of lungs: its bifurcating diversity in the explosion of worlds within worlds within worlds, as reflected in the "Kids Playing Cars On Freeway Get Smushed" of Kingdom, Phyla, Classes, Orders, Families, Genus, Species in the phylogeny of the biological world: its branching extensity as in delivering and removing life-giving and dying substances throughout the body — in the pulmonary system, trachea, --> bronchioles --> alveoli, and in the circularity system, aorta --> blood vessels --> capillaries: its twisting and folding activities exemplified in the surface of the brain, where the highest levels of thinking takes place in the areas

containing the largest number of folds, or in polymers made up of sequences of proteins folding back on themselves, or in DNA, the most famous twisting pair of them all made up of amino acids, carrying the blueprint for creating life across time: its opportunism in invasion percolation by bursts of clusters of dynamic growth occurring along lines of favorable conditions as seen with a forest fire, insects in an orchard, weeds in a garden, crows at planting, lichen on a rock: its tenacious virulence in the spread of measles, and all other contagions spread from host to host: its un-predictability in weather governed by the strange-attractor interaction of temperature, moisture and wind expressed in the fractal movement of water — cloudbursts, inundations, deluges, maelstroms, torrents, circulations, eddies, whirlpools, hurricanes, tornadoes, geysers: its chaoticity, jumping across lacunae in space and time in the global weather pattern change from the warming ocean current El Nino — a chaos attractor of higher dimensionality moving through our world of lower dimension: its extreme sensitivity to the slightest change in initial conditions carrying a turbulent process into different domains: its mixing — cream in coffee, molasses on top of peanut butter, cars on the freeway, people in a subway crowd: its world-forming functionality in landscaping and shaping the texture and structure of geologic features — the cracks and faults in the earth's crust, the craggy rocky sharp mountains, the jagged broken notched coastlines full of fjords, spits, peninsulas, heads, isthmuses: its terraforming in the fluvial geomorphology of gently-sloping graduated valleys, river courses, silt deposition patterns — by erosion from catchment elevation through gully --> brooks --> creeks --> streams --> rivers, all being the self-similar watershed at different scales carrying eroded material flux of sediments: its artistic and cinematic significance in the use of fractals for creating landscapes and worlds on canvas and screen, reflecting their function in the real world: its emblematic iconicity in the yin yang symbol, the picture of a separatrix —a porous boundary like the seashore where the land going down to the beach through boulders and rocks and pebbles into sand meets the sea breaking in ever finer foam of breaking wave along the shore, dissolves into and penetrates the fine grained sand: its irregularity in shaping the kinkiness of manzanita, the swirliness of kelp, the rugosity of grass, the bulbousness of cauliflower, the ropiness of hemp: its telescoping complexity in the multiple-scale structure of turbulent flow [same thing repeated, but substituted]: its fractal dimension — a concept giving insight into everything with texture, just about everything; including, why the dinosaurs grew so big so fast from the cross section of their bones: its fleecyness in clouds and other plasma fractals which contain Brownian self-similarity and, wonder of wonders, a random factor in the fluctuation of the fractal dimension of time itself!: its currency in diffusion-limited aggregation, where growth occurs on the tips as in trees, plants and the urban growth pattern of cities: its circuitous webosity in the networking of every living thing in every moment on this planet of life: its synchronicity in the way intuitive and extrasensory perceptions (dreams, visions, premonitions, epiphanies) are validated in the occurrence of relationship-timing compatibility, by a corresponding outer physical event, sense perception of a symbol, apparition, or miracle: its actualization in the aura of personality as a readable psychological field surrounding the individual, feeling the vector-field force-reaction of movement across topological boundaries (which themselves have a fractal dimension — hard and solid and closed, or thin and open and vulnerable or "fat" and fugal and not dischaotic): its substantial tangibility in the behavior of the surfaces of substances compelled by the surface's fractal dimension to manifest the physical characteristics of the particles suspended in the substance as seen in the opacity of paint pigment, the dullness of talc face powder, the rate of absorption of ingested pharmaceuticals, the recycling capability of bacteria and fungi in soil: its oleaginality in the way the soap molecules in solution salubriously slips into cracks and liberates dirt: its holism confronting the conceptual filter of western scientific reductionism and mechanism, seen in the holographic dimensionality of the way the universe includes him in the emergence and awakening of everything influencing everything else: its amazing serpentine winding in water meandering in the plane, increasing the fractal dimension of its path along the way.

Yum Chi having a dream. In the dream he has
constructed some kind of small lightweight balloon, and it is
floating fast and low over the fields —moving along with the
wind. It comes to a stop. And just looms there, edging this
way and that, on little thermal currents of the wind. Then
suddenly, it is pulled quickly up, on an updraft. We see him
in the balloon, in the dream, as they spiral and wheel. And
then he zooms off, racing — scudding along among the
clouds, to vanish at the edge of the world.

Yum Chi's dream: He is climbing, moving through a
space of many intersecting dimensions, moving among
images on the white walls of a mnemonic theatre of images,
that come alive when he enters them. He is in slow water
floating, standing, twirling around, it is an ancient dream like
one Walker had when he fell into a stream and was tumbling
backward over his head and couldn't swim because he didn't
know how, and he is under the clear water, and it is a big
quiet space penetrated by sunlight, and the light is moving
on the green depths and he starts to relax because he knows
it is possible for him to breathe under water, like suddenly he
had gills from long ago that he forgot about and it is all
going to be OK and he can just lay back and relax, but then
suddenly a hand grasps him and yanks him out of the water
and holds him up to the air and his lungs are bursting. And
gasping, he gulps the air, and he is saved.

Yum Chi dreaming. He is in the Amphictionic Theatre,
the designated oracle up to get into the cage. Cage is
suspended over low smoldering fire, upon which has been
baled bundles of herbs, herbs of special concoction known
only to priests of the Elysian mysteries, and he is suspended
in the wafts of smoky spirals rising into the hole at the top of
the cave.

Walker is in the Mnemonic Theatre, in a part of town
called Auto Row, where there are vast lots of cars for sale
and where at night, no one is around, in a room in a
warehouse where, after 5:00 in the sunset, the light is

coming down through skylights and through vines climbing across the windows on one side, and, and it is this: he is surrounded by his marvelous artist friends all around him encouraging him and loving him, and there is the leader of the pack, a wild boy teaching them how to play in this playground, and he is being encouraged to do these fun moves. That he is encouraged to talk about himself. And they are going about it, like young monks in a monastery, making points of metaphysical import, but these are points that were a turning point in their lives, a corner turned,

I turned a corner when I nearly drowned

I turned a corner when my friend died a lonely poet in his room and nobody found him for days,

I turned a corner , . .

And got into a car wreck while driving on a fast motorcycle, a Harley, that had just gone through a tunnel, and got broadsided so hard that it took the head clean off, and we see it floating up and out over the lights of the city. It is just this head there, floating and zooming slowly over the streets. We see things from its eyes.

I wake up scared and shivering in my bed.

Recapitulation, the taking off of the head and throwing it through time, through the time of your life,

In another dream later that night, Yum Chi is being shown about beings of light,

that we are all these strange topological entities, distributed around empty centers, We are all basically vortices, weird circulating energies about points of perception,

it was like he could see this weird homunculus being spread out with the body parts given in size proportion to the amount of nerve endings, there, and the largest are the lips and the thumbs. The genitals are huge, the eye is huge, the hands were very large. . .
And the lungs were somehow this extended perception and the nervous system . . .
It was like the lungs had feelers out way farther, then the skin and the nervous, mind, the brain was like a canopy or an umbrella over it all floating like a weird jellyfish, tethered by many strings.
A kind of gas-giant being floating in the upper atmosphere.

Dream Yum Chi, Yum Chi is out in a sunlit meadow, doing Tai Chi among the tall yellow grasses, and slowly the world gets darker and darker, and he faces the wind and is surprised that he can easily do Tai Chi in different directions and the wind is getting stronger and stronger, and yet he does not stop, for he is like a surfer treading the air, and as the sky gets green and cold all of a sudden he knows soon a tornado is coming, as the air around him circulates and shifts circulation, he fancies it as a worthy partner or opponent, and gets ready. He goes into a kind of vehicle and cage, that would be suitable for going over Niagara falls he thinks, and he is going to surf the tornado. And he is sweating and loving it when this Great Tornado Being comes through and lifts him up into the air, like a styrofoam egg, and shoots him up to the top of the land into an atmosphere of lights discharging and clouds flattening out and getting twistered and churned, and then he is dropped just as easy and falling, falling, he wakes up sweating just as he is about to hit ground.

Yum Chi dreaming. He is sitting around a couple of chrome-legged library tables shoved together. It is a graduate seminar meeting in some turn of the last century lecture hall in the old Physics building at UT. - musty with pine woods, blackboard, a haze of dust chalk. Sunlight penetrating the haze, dust motes in Brownian motion turning and sparkling in the rays. At the table is Heizenburg, short brush-cut hair, collegiate, in a suit the way they were in the 30s. a venerable old sage comes in, weird elaborate robes with intricate flowing design, large sleeves. He has a smooth ancient Asian face, white *fu manchu* mustache drooping down. It is Ho Tu, one of the great commentators on the *I Ching*. Ho Tu and Heizenburg are talking about matrices and complementarity.

Later he is in another seminar. Now it is the slight English engineer, G. Spenser-Brown lecturing on the *I Ching*. He seems to want to be deriving the whole thing from scratch, *ab initio*, from first principles.

The Chinese character for dream is Mong
because it is like a series of windows floating above a
kind of tail, or root, floating below. What a marvelous
abstraction for the dream.

I made one on my typewriter.

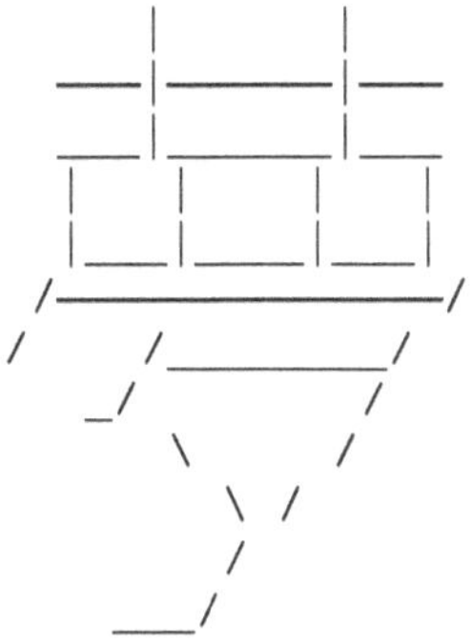

It reminded me of
the model of writing.
Where you had the
xxxx which is the level
of the text, and the
formal thematic
elements of the text
making connections
above, and the emotional,
psychological and archetypal
elements making connections
below.

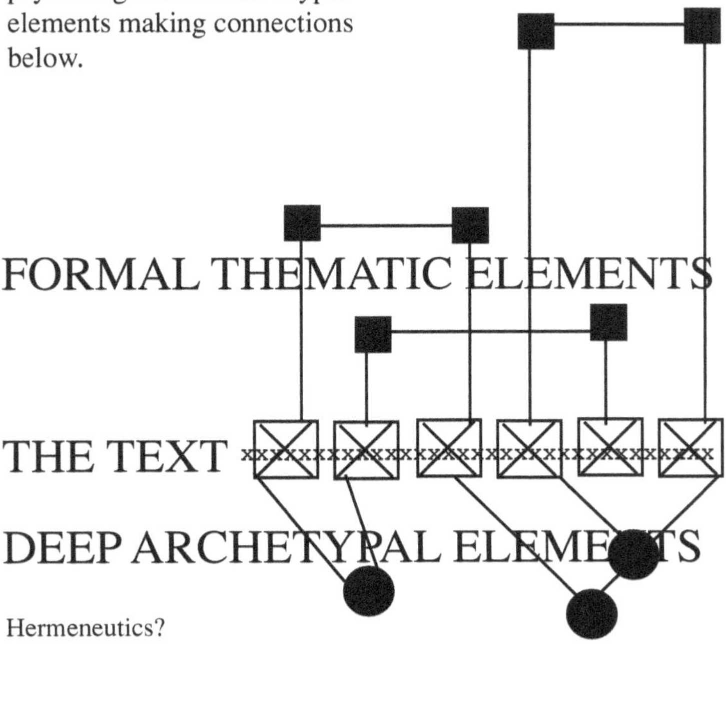

FORMAL THEMATIC ELEMENTS

THE TEXT ⊠⊠⊠⊠⊠⊠

DEEP ARCHETYPAL ELEMENTS

Hermeneutics?

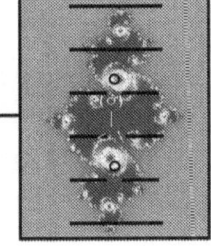

I saw the Cantor set of the excluded middle
in the implicative concatenation
of the Hexagrams.

‒‒ ‒‒
‒‒‒
‒‒‒

‒‒‒‒‒‒‒   ‒‒‒‒‒‒‒
‒‒‒
‒‒‒

‒‒ ‒‒ ‒‒‒
‒‒ ‒‒
‒‒

‒‒ ‒‒ ‒‒‒
‒‒ ‒‒
‒‒

‒‒ ‒‒ ‒‒ ‒‒
‒‒ ‒‒
‒‒ ‒‒
·   ·
‒‒‒‒‒‒‒
‒‒   ‒‒‒‒‒

And it was the shape of a poem, and it was the shape of
an idea passing through my local dimension. And in trying to
get figures of speech to catch it — it exuded meaning
through excluded middles of implications — I recognized
the Cantor Cut, and the surface of particles of meaning.

97 The I Ching is a bifurcating fractal Cantor Set

The Cantor Set is formed by repeatedly excluding the middle thirds of a line segment. This containment and exclusion gives a picture of porosity, or bumpiness of a space. It also shows the base <—> motif aspect of fractal generation. Consider some aspect as a base and perform some operation on that base, then make the resultant be the new base. This iterative generativity by feedback is the usual way of fractal generation.

Cantor Cuts illustrating Base / Motif Fractal Generation

Motif

Base

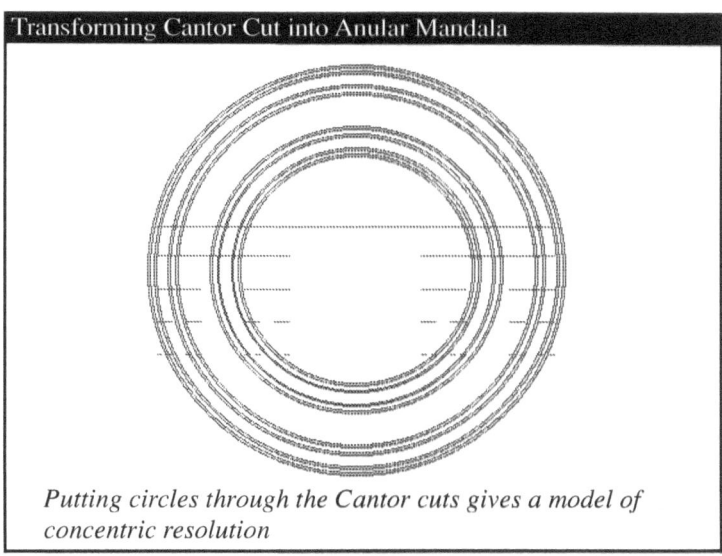

Transforming Cantor Cut into Anular Mandala

Putting circles through the Cantor cuts gives a model of concentric resolution

Particles of meaning coalescing through implication.

Everything is
percolating up.
Matter is evolving,
complexity is
        emerging.
We are on the expanding shockwave of an explosion.
Like the Mandlebrot swirls on the edge of blackness
when you pour cream in your cofee.
For a moment I could see it . . . the Mandlebrot sky: not
garish and full of streaming colors, but the clouds were holes
in the blue
and they were an expression of the whole atmosphere.
(the clouds had invisible vapor roots that went into the sky)
The clouds were holes in the blue,
were like the colonization of clumps of grasses
moving across the ground
like a green forest fire
by the iteration of successive generations
casting seed in a
pattern of happenstance shape.
It was going on at
all scales. The
detritus and death
was being harvested in
the ground, washed
and carried and
dissolved by animals and the great fractal of water.
At that moment I could feel
space — as not just some abstract entity, but as a fluid
a field, a plethora of fields, a manifold,
connecting all things in it.
And they were all pushing and jostling
to be in this dimension of Now,
trying to do ITS net work
of being a node,
embedding itself in some thing
higher and becoming host
for other organelles
to embed themselves in.

And I vowed to try to
learn how to reach out and
touch that space all
around me
in the Tai Chi dance.

----

like water in a lake
bouncing off the boundaries
and coming back to you.

I woke up dreaming of Equation Art.
It was visual, and fractal and had all the great equations
of physics
streaming, like cilia out of its central round mandala egg.
Heisenberg's Uncertainty [p,q] = h, Coulomb's charge
and the electric field, $F = q/r^2$, Einstein's $E=mc^2$ and the one
for gravity curvature tensor and also the Brownian motion,
Schrodinger's wave equation relating undulation in space to
undulation in time, Sir Isaac's F=ma, Maxwell's 4 god-like
equations for electromagnetism, Max Plank quantum of
action, and others,

then I laid back on the
bed and
closed my eyes
and was looking up into
the dome of my cortex
and was wondering what
personality looked like in
the mind.
And I saw that the personality was like a fractal
projected from a much larger
dynamic process called life,
but that it looked like
a Julia Set.
It was like an umbrella.
Life is an umbrella Julia Set,
into which we get shelter for a while.

In trying to get the feeling again, of that Fractal
Epiphany, I set about exploring *images*. I started doing this
little dance. I called it the Left Right Random Seed I Ching
Dance, or sometimes I called it doing Binomial Spirals.
Imagining it as some kind of Amphictionic Theatre, in which
the player, the amphiction, engaged in some kind of Random
Walk, a Self-avoiding random walk. He would be letting
things come into his mind and speaking them, or he would
have some pre-written incantations. It was a way to be
winnowing the yarrow stalks down to the line of a hexagram.
The image I was exploring here was the hand as a weir or
seine combing through universal energies.

   It starts of with the amphiction doing incantations,
spouting off the numbers of the I Ching.

Scene: *Amphiction does Fair Lady Works at Shuttles,
showing the limits of the circle, doing them more rapidly
with ease. This eventually goes in a random Sufi twirl.*

Amphiction:
   I am twirling, twirling trying to stand,
   twice around, twice around again;
   a little dizzy to merge the space time coordinates
   maybe get them to overlap,
   create my own space time vortex.

   I am out here doing this because I have
   evolved an astonishing new ritual.
   It is something out of Wen and the 8th Wing
   to communicate with the Spirit Tokens of the I Ching,
   and Tai Chi dance:
   How to Sample the Space/time Vortex with your Body

(*Wave Hands Like Clouds, Parting the Wild Horse's Main*)

Amphiction:
   You have to recite the right incantation
   to generate the spells,
   and using the left hand

and the right
to shift through sheaths
of space time
for residues. To sift for
residues of probabilities.
Basically it is the human hand as seine or weir.

(looks pensive, sheepish grin)

I know it is a little New Age. . .
but everything is up for grabs.

(waving hand in fanfare)

The New Formula:
It's a fractal formula for chaos. Where the next state of
the iteration is based on the current state plus the action of a
random number based on the time of the moment.

Wow, what is going on here?
It's Cool. The random seed:
a function random() {

Scene:*as he is breaking down the elements of the function he*
"holds the ball" for the parenthesis

Amphiction:
    where you take the (date of your birth)
    and multiply it by a (random selection from 4096); this
is the random seed.
    Then divide it by the product of (today's Date), times
the (time of the day).
    Then you get an iteration going using random numbers
from within these parameters random.seed(now) =
(random.seed(previous) * (times) the current.Date +
your.birth) divided by current.time;
    return ? random.seed / random.me;
    Why 4096? It is 2 to the 12th power
    and the hexagrams are 64 which is 2 to the 6th power
    so 64 squared is 4096, 2 to the 12th power.
    And that's how many possible combinations out of all

the permutations of one hexagram evolving out of another.

And as you will recall, the hexagrams are an expression of the number of combinations of two things (the yin yang) taken two at a time.

This greatly reduces the chaos of the permutations which goes up as n! (Factorial!)

Scene:the Old Soft Sift. We get a sense of a sieve, sifting through numbers. Pointing with index fingers, indicate in the air, the numbers and their positions while saying them:

Amphiction:

```
    1  1
  1  2  1
1  3  3  1
```

I'd dance out the rhythms of yin and yang steps with my feet to get myself into the motion, I was playing these Left and Right paradittles, in binomial coefficient expansion with my feet.

Scene: the step dancing, capering LL +LR +RL + RR and then LLL +LLR +LRL +RLL+ RRL +RLR + LRR +RRR (binomial paradittles) while moving hands to make levels seem evident in these:

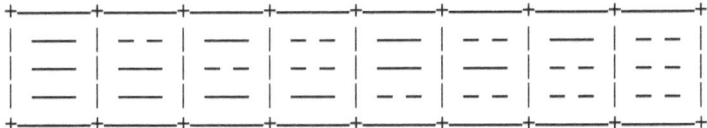

Dance the symbols to balance ourselves rhythmically and to keep our attides fit to the final goals yet to be strange and wildly awake lighter and lighter variations with each repition. Try, more and more, to contact the Automorph, the relaxed principle of balance, one that lets gravity and the other forces of the universe take care of you.

Amphiction:

which gives the 8 trigrams if Left is —— Yin and R is – — Yang my hands moving through the air making these LEVELS seem evident.

Scene: Doing Wave Hands Like Clouds

Amphiction:
    You can go here
    and you can go there.
    You can do this
    and you can do that
(furious dancing of binomial paradittles and self avoiding
random walk)
    variation Left; variation right;
    variation Left; variation right;
    Left hand pull; right hand pull
    variation Left; variation right;
    You can go here
    and you can go there.
    You can do this
    and you can do that Left hand pull; right hand pull
    variation Left; variation right;
    We are trying to go AWAY!

(STOPS, stands and delivers the following speech)
    It is like knowing
    one of the secrets
    of life itself.
    Here was a system
    that foretold
    or at least helped you expect:
    worries,
    sickness,
    trouble,
    danger,
    risks & toil.
    That warned you
     about Obstacles leading to deadlock,
    and helped lead you out of it
    into Time of expansion, beginning
    Growth.
    It gave you figures about the length
    of your continuous toil,
    estimates of the purity of your intention,
     checks on completeness or indecision.
    It showed you where there would be
    moments of brightness, brilliance

and whether these might turn into fires.
It gave you a magic feeling
to apply this receptive faith
to other areas of your life.
In humility
and peace,
to accept
the joyous creativity
going on all around you,
so that you could catch
the Creative, strong, active wave
continuously on the move
through time.
To make decisive decisions.

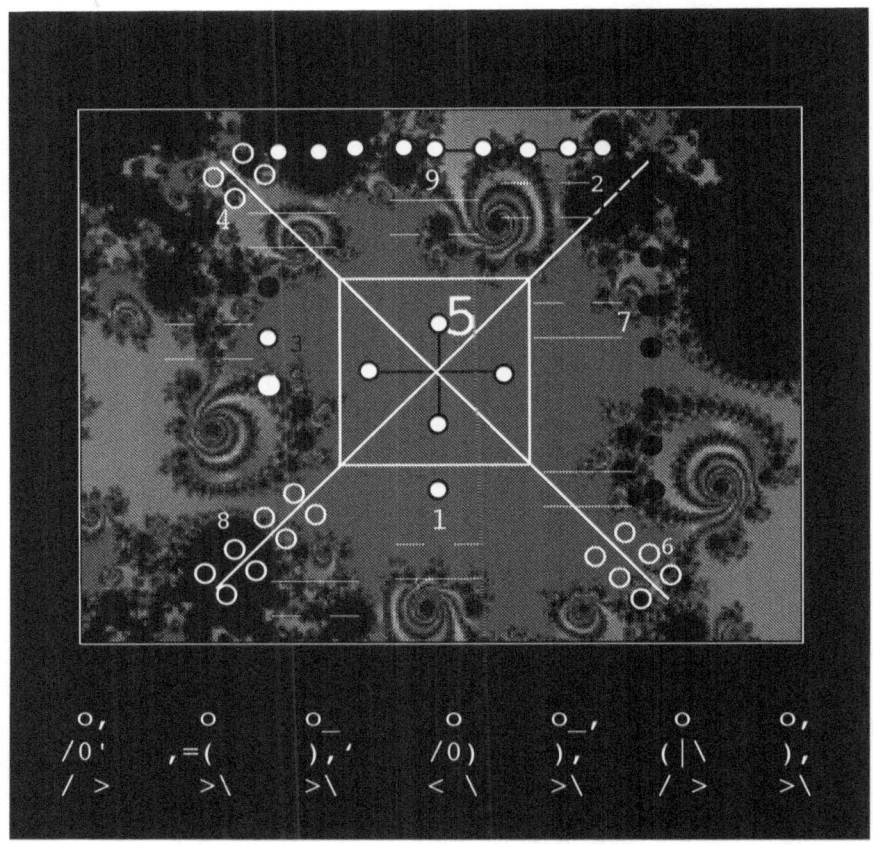

100   Self-similarity in a salmon egg

I come to know the comprehension of fish
by looking at a salmon egg under a microscope.
We see a big red vein carrying moving blood cells
into a delta. . .
The salmon egg is like a small planet
with its rivers of blood
that flow back down to the albumen sea.
The salmon are like blood cells
moving in a river that is a vein on the planet–egg.

It is like the ocean
flowing through the salmon
is cresting in a long wave,
flowing back up rivers,
through transformations
into food for bears and birds and fertilizer for the soil,
then flows back down the rivers
in the forms of eggs, then hatchlings, then salmon
to the sea. Until the cycle begins again.

The salmon is an expression
of the ocean's love and support for the land.

it is always like this:
you are entering a door at the front of the house,
you are walking down the hall, going up stairs . . .
entering a bedroom,
turning to open a closet door —
only to find,
the door leads into the front cf the house again.
What is the sequence of steps
that led you to who you are?
What is the sequence of steps
into possession?
Some people seek security
some seek warm pleasure
some seek solutions to their problems
some seek identity.
This fundamental yearning is Temperament.
The sequence of steps
that we take to solve a problem
is usually the same —
it is the innate way our personality
carries consciousness into situations.
Personality tells you who you think you are —
who you have constructed out of perceiving and judging.
Previous intuitions become sense data for the next level.
Feelings push us out to get more sense data
for better decisions and what to do with the data.
It is a very convoluted system.
At the meeting of consciousness, senses and the world,
fractals are the separatrices between boundaries.

I am in the reality matrix of support and it is in me.
I maintain it efficiently by taking shortcuts, filters, sub-
personalities.
I am a trajectory of Sensing, Intuiting, Thinking Feeling.
We are moving among Guides all our lives,
Mother Father, Spirit of Place,
Sense of Being,
the Lazy one,
the one who works hard.

After practising Tai Chi for a while you may find your
personality changing. This chapter explores that. (I appropri-
ated the term enatiomorph for the yin-yang symbol as a
neologism from enatiodromia —Jung's term for the tendency
of everything to run into its opposite, shadow to hero,
trickster to redeemer, good to bad. He uses the root word
enatio, meaning mirror image and *dromia*, to run, to express
the dialectic of opposites which was the basis of his Analytic
Psychology. I combined that with the idea of the automorph,
whose root of autopoeisis is the persistant, pervasive, self-
generating fractal nature of the universe.) In this chapter we
build an analogy between the Human Body Inertia Tensor
and the Human Psychsocial Field Connectivity Tensor for a
picture of the person's behavior as a function of environment. Toward that end we will examine several theories of
personality, in particular those of Carl Jung and Kurt Lewin.

Here is the student of Tai Chi scanning his jumbled-up,
messed-up, sloppy room and he is shocked at the mess. Yep,
I'm a sensual intuitive perceptive — can tolerate a mess, nay,
revel in the interleaved textures of projects dropped into time
and stacked there like archaeological strata. It would be a
serious undertaking to change. But why change? What is this
ought, compelling you to feel like you have to change. It is
the great difference between your successes and the pretensions you have toward Success. These have to be brought
more into equilibrium if you are to have self-esteem.

Personality is a fractal hosted in the nervous system
diagraming the forces of attraction between pretensions and
successes driven by the chaotic process of self-esteem. This
traverses the bifurcating tree of what you (should do) and
(shouldn't do) expanding into what you (should do) and (did
do) and (didn't do) and what you (shouldn't do) and (didn't
do) and but what you (did do).

As you start to learn the Form more, and do it into the
3rd group, you want to forget about it and let yourself slip
into a state of pure awareness. The two most useful things
you can learn from Tai Chi are Awareness and Separation.

The Human Psychosocial Field Connectivity Tensor

Just as in Tai Chi, when we used differential opposition in the form of isometric tension to increase the elasticity and flow of movements, especially focused on the joints to increase the degrees of physical freedom, here we will explore what it takes to be more psychologically free. In particular, we will explore how Differential Opposition of the Functions of personality form the porous boundary of personality, which is our interface to the world. While doing the Long Form set we think the Lively Frame, the early to middle part, as relaxing into your inertia tensor, and the Changing Frame, the middle to end part, as relaxing into your Psycho-social Field Connectivity Tensor. A person is a point sensor feeling always the pushes and pull of fields. Some of these fields are: being in a family (parenthood, adulthood, childhood), being a worker of a market economy, being part of a culture, religion, being a citizen of a country. Just as the Human Body Inertia Tensor is the matrix of inertial contributions of each limb-mass connected to the core, the Psychosocial Connectivity Tensor is the matrix of Psychosocial fields one belongs to, all connected by tension to the self. The analogy is mechanical linkage = substitute action for tension release.

You can relax into the Psychosocial Connectivity Tensor, (and this will help with reorienting the field for better problem solving) by becoming more aware of the regions that go into making up your psychosocial self: your consciousness, your personality, your temperament. It is all a big bifurcating tree fractal. In this book we have modeled these structures as a matrix, (or a table that displays the combinations of choices at each intersection of a row and column -this has taught us to visualize abstract dimensions), and as hierarchical levels, (as represented in the hexagram).

The Enatiomorph (☯) as the Sphere of the Possible

In doing Tai Chi, we are holding a sphere. At the physical level the sphere represents potential blocks and grabs. The hand is open to shape into a grab or lock or it can be closed for a fist. You can also imagine the sphere as the sphere of the possible that you are reaching into. This sphere of potentiality is how you are going to go about using the time, and material and associations to do something that you need to do in your life. Modern life requires less of the physical, but more of the social. The *game* is the sphere of work now, not the plow. There is no turning back.

Visualization of the Psychosocial Field

Play with lighter and lighter variations with each repetition. And try more and more to contact the Automorph, the relaxed principle of balance, one that lets gravity and the other forces of the universe take care of you

Player:
. . . and it is because we are taking the long view,
into big time   *(louder)* taking the LONG view
               into BIG TIME.
. . . *(reaching)* and when we reach out to touch something in our Tai Chi mime field, it is trying to bring it close,
and trying to make it clear.
And we want to do something clean and pure and
abstract without any sentiment, because this is ritual and not
theatre
it is a way to precipitate time, time as an excusion, a
"hexotranspiration"
and with it . . . *(thinks)* numbers as sensations
of perhaps rising and lowering intensity in series of
absurdities . . .
(*he makes moves of separation and sorting)*
are isolated and separated *(pause)*
and we let ourselves reach out and touch an image so we
can transmit it
so clear and precise.
And we take as long as required, and make the space be
as big as we can permit and manage, and be open to.

(These statements of the actor are just something to work like an incantation, to cast a spell over his own mind so that he can pierce the veil and see something of the infinite)

What we are seeing begins beyond what we can grasp
like the wind (in)visible when it opens itself and carries

us into itself,
and it becomes an invisible extension of ourselves.
And the space that liberates our arms
holds us in itself —
in the body in which we dwell,
tactile and accessible but which we must not sell —
and underneath which are the fluids,
the bubbling springs,
the elixir of Chi.
And at every moment we are going through an open door
ready to be pushed along by destiny
which is just one more
channel of meaning   there
                    connected to us —
we are able to reach out and touch
and illuminate
with our hands

Gestalt Amplification

In Tai Chi it is helpful to visualize yourself in a field.
The Old Man in the Tao spoke of being in a box with heaven
as the top and the ground as the bottom, a box filled with
potential that supports you. It is activated by movement. In
this book we have visualized it more abstractly as the stack
of the lines of the hexagram, expressing the dichotomous
branching of the open and closed, inner and outer, within and
without. We have also visualized the field as a fabric that lets
light through from behind. This, the perceptual gestalt, is like
a masque. In *A Dynamic Theory of Personality* and *Topological Psychology,* Kurt Lewin pictured the personality,
with its psychological field in an environment, as shapes —
sets, bounded by boarders. He used vectors and blockages to
understand the attractions and repulsions of our personalties.

Lewin's great contribution was to extended gestalt
principles from the domain of sensory perception to that of
social perception. The theory helps one see that the optimal
life strategy is the complication and enrichment of the Life-
world, and extension of the boundaries of the possible. In his
account, maturity is seen as increasing differentiation of
personality life-space, and the extension of time perspective.
The personality, which is the interface boundary between the

outside world and the inside world wouldn't be closed and controlling or open and vulnerable but would be a fractal boundary that was very rich in structure, able to adjust to being open and closed and everything in between, using the defense mechanism and the creative capabilities.

Lewin diagrams the self in the concentric rings from the far extended boundary of the life space down into the core of the personality. It is strikingly like the Tan Tien.

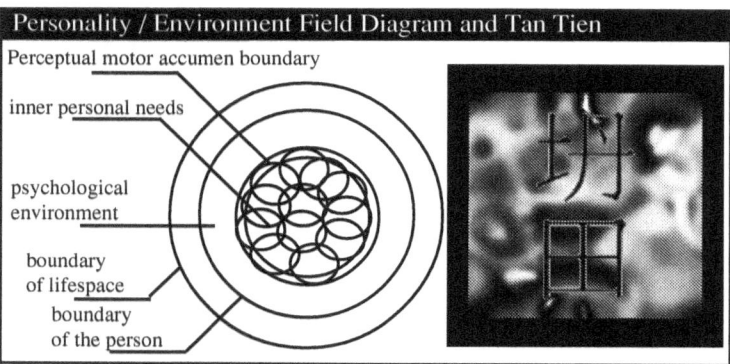

Personality / Environment Field Diagram and Tan Tien

Perceptual motor accumen boundary

inner personal needs

psychological environment

boundary of lifespace

boundary of the person

The Tan Tien is the Core Self

"Seeing" with the Tan Tien is knowing with one's whole being. We have seen in the Jungian Analytical Philosophy that Amplification is the method for extension of the psychological life-space through the separation of the levels of reality and unreality. But paradoxically you need the unreality (fantasy, myth, dream, thought) to help you make this separation. The application of energy in Tai Chi — splitting, separating — has a mental analog in the process of amplification into levels by non-reality. Just as the Inertia Tensor depicts the distribution of mass elements around your core and the moments they create, the Psychosocial Connectivity Tensor depicts the distribution of environmental field elements that have positive and negative (pushes and pulls) on your freedom, moving you into regions that present obstacles. You can either move in the direction of satiation, of the need, or you can substitute and move some part of it. Some obstacles are so great that you crash on them like a wave, and even have your mind turned back on itself into regression and retrogression to earlier states. It makes you distracted and unaware most of the time. Unless you start the practice of awareness. Start becoming familiar with the internal parts of yourself. When doing Tai Chi let yourself be aware that these fields are what is causing the tension in your life and that is the tension you want to drcp away from you as much as possible. Through awareness, through dialog, through dialectic. So this core self is much more than the brain or the eyes let on. In Tai Chi the core self is depicted as the Tan Tien. You are finding this core self. And relaxing into it. You are coming into your real self. The personality as as dynamic equilibrium of dichotomous forces: softness — hardness; elasticity— brittleness; reality — non-reality; fluidity — turgidity. For perspective we will make comparison to the starndard MBTI.

The Philosophy of Differential Opposition and the MBTI

Tai Chi is constantly pulling one back into the center of the Mandala of the Self, to be open to what is. I realized Jung's Mandala of the Four Functions of Mind, the opposing (S—N / T—F), can be used as a program to explore habitual ways of doing and being,

to get a fresh perspective   Perception   _|_   Judging
on Change. What *if* one | S | T |
tried to explore the |iN | F |
opposite?! Yes! That |

would be my new philosophy. I needed to apply the opposite! The Philosophy of DO, do O, Do the Opposite. Differential Opposition. Applied Complimentarity. If we looked at different pairs that are possible among the 4 functions, (S — N, T — F) would be the exact opposite. The way the mind / body updates the reality matrix of the self is by creating a differential opposition between opposites to create a field ground effect. Shadowboxing the enatiomorph leads to transcending personality. The idea is that we are using them to field/ground. Jung sets them up as opposites.

Grouping components of personality

In MBTI, the "word" of personality is a combination of the 4 letters [E/I, S/P, T/F P/J] in the following positions:

Sensing   xSxx   Feeling   xxFx
intuitive   xNxx   Thinking xxTx

Combining functions selectively in groups of two,

        xxxx [xxxx, xxxx] xxxx

these symbolize the following aspects of personality:
Learning Style, the Temperament and the Deciding Style.

To explore other ways of being, let use look at these MBTI partitions of pesonality hierarchy in terms of our Tai Chi understanding of expansion and contraction.

Learning Style

The learning style of a personality type is depicted in the first pair of the 4 functions [E/I S/N x x]. These are ES, IS, EN, IN. This is extraverted sensing, introverted sensing, extraverted intuition and introverted intuition.

In general, one who uses intuition more than sensing is looking for patterns internal to and relating things, while one who uses sensing more than intuition is interested in the objects themselves, and likes to maintain their viability.

The [E — I / S — N] scales used to define learning pattern are based on the way a person, trying to solve a problem, prefers to take in data and pass it up the hierarchy of the organization of the nervous system. This tells us something about the structure of this nervous system and how it is an interface. One usually collects data before making a decision: S —> N —> T —> F. Then one seeks more data. Expansion outward is Extraverting in Sensing and iNtuiting and contracting inward is Introverting in Sensing and iNtuiting.

Temperaments

The S — N, T —F, scales define temperament pattern. The temperament of a personality type is depicted in the pairing of one perceiving function, S/P with one deciding function, T/F, the center two of [x S/N T/F x]. Expanding outward are the sensing Traditionalist and Experiencers and contracting inward are the intuiting Conceptualists and Idealists. See below for more on temperament.

Decision Style

The decision making style of a personality type is designated in the last pair of the 4 functions [x x T/F J/P]. These are TJ, TP, FJ, FP. The T—F, J—P, scales define deciding pattern. Just as the E/I direction influences sense collection, so the J/P describes what one does with the information obtained; whether Thought about or developed into Feelings.

For example the TP pattern (Thinking Perceiving) contributes heavily to the working of an Engineer. Whereas the FP (feeling perceiving) pattern contributes healers and tireless moms to the population. Expanding outward are the Thinking Judgers and Thinking Perceivers, and contracting inward are the Feeling Judgers and Feeling Perceivers.

Temperament in History

Recall that in psychology, Temperament is the aspect of personality concerned with emotional dispositions and reactions, and their speed and intensity. We think of it as the prevailing mood or mood pattern of a person. Historically many theories of personality use a four-part, structure.

Humours

The first theory of Temperament, by Galen, was based on the theory of four basic body fluids (humours) — any excess of which produced a characteristic temperament.

Humour	Temperament
blood	— sanguine (warm, pleasant)
phlegm	— phlegmatic (slow-moving, apathetic)
black bile	— melancholic (depressed, sad)
yellow bile	— choleric (quick to react, hot tempered)

Astrology

Astrology seeks to find the roots of personality from influences of celestial bodies. The temperaments of the personality are projected onto the firmament through the houses of the zodiac: Fire, Earth, Air and Water and the constellations there.

Sign	Temperament
Air	— Gemini, Libra and Aquarius sanguine (warm, pleasant) intellectual, detached, not sentimental, mind is most valuable asset an NT
Water	— Cancer, Scorpio and Pisces are the water signs slow-moving, apathetic, concerned with feelings intuitive, psychic, Love is their great trait. NF
Earth	— Taurus, Virgo and Capricorn melancholic concerned with material comfort and security, favor "the real world. managers of business. SJ.
Fire	— Aries, Leo and Sagittarius are fire signs, choleric (quick to react, hot tempered) energy. life-affirming. Competitive and flamboyant, Passionate SP

Keirsey and MBTI

An early theory of Keirsey related ancient Greeks gods to the personality types. Dionysian— SP ("Let's Drink Wine")

Promethian NT ("Foresight") Epimethean SJ ("Hindsight")
Appolonian NF ("Reach for the Sky"). He later changed this to
a more democratic presentation.

Person	Temperament
Artisan	— SP sanguine (warm, pleasant)
Rationalist	— NT phlegmatic (slow-moving, apathetic)
Guardian	— SJ melancholic (depressed, sad)
Idealist	— NF choleric (quick to react, hot tempered)

Personality Development

The MBTI and Keirsey are classification systems; they
don't describe *how* these temperaments developed. To further
our efforts in exploring occluded aspects of ourselves, here is a
brief synopsis of some theories of personality development.

Erickson

The psychologist Erickson was one of the first to pull
together various theories of personality development. He saw
personality as an adaptation to various psychosocial crises
throughout life. He develops his theory based on the eight
psycho-social crises. These crises precipitate the unfolding of a
personality in time:

Trust / Mistrust in the 1st year infancy;
Autonomy / Shame-Doubt in the toddler years;
Initiative / Guilt in preschooler;
Industry / Inferiority in the school years;
Identity / Role Confusion/Diffusion--puberty;
Intimacy / Isolation, young adulthood;
Generativity / Stagnation/Self-Absorption) adulthood;
Integrity / Despair in the end of life.

Maslo

Maslo's system is also a good blueprint for developing
human potential. (Read from bottom up.)

8. Self-transcendence - visionary, unity consciousness.
7. Self-actualization know exactly who you are
6. Aesthetic - curious about inner workings of all.
5. Cognitive - learning, contribute knowledge.
4. Esteem - feeling of moving up in world, recognition,
3. Belongingness and love - belong to a group, friends
2. Safety - feel free from immediate danger.
1. Physiological - food, water, shelter, sex.

Horney

Karen Horney's system presents Personality as Defense. She emphasizes Basic Trust in early development —it is the strongest motivating force in the development of personality. Issues of trust may develop in children whose parents are overly oppressive, indifferent or inconsistent in their child-rearing. The child then responds by developing the following three ways of dealing with the anxiety of mistrust: from an overly oppressive parent, a compliant child grows — moving toward others in attempts to be submissive; from an indifferent parent, an aggressive child grows — moving against others in attempts to gain power; from an inconsistent parent, a detached child grows — moving away from others to avoid being hurt.

Correlation of Temperaments and Basic Drives

In general the theories of the development and origin of the determinants of personality type are based on some number of innate behaviors. They are placed on scales to set up a semantic space. We can go far with just four:

high activity / low activity
high persistence / low persistence,
quick approach / slow approach
high intensity / low intensity

Role of Time Pressure in Temperaments

The high group on the left generally become S, sensing types and the low group on the right become iNtuitives. It turns out that nature, to get the job done in the world, requires about 80% of the population to be S types, and the other types make up the rest. The difference between these two groups is the sense of time pressure. Generally the Sensor type, S needs instant gratification while the Intuitive type N can tolerate delayed gratification.

Examples of Personality Development

These budding behaviors are seen by parents as behavior modification problems. And the interaction with the parents is what selects for the emergence of temperament and personality types.

The Child Who Has Difficulty Focusing For example,a highly active, quick to approach, and intense baby who gets hemmed in a lot can amplify his behavior into wild and excitable. If that produces no results he can develop the defense mechanism of low persistence, and can grow into The Child Who Has Difficulty Focusing. This child is Forgetful which comes from high distractibility (low persistence) as well as being wild and excitable. This type will probably become a SP. If he can develop confidence, an entertainer -SFP; and if not, a technician -STP. These people have basically an outward focus, as agroup. But if The Child Who Has Difficulty Focusing gets patience and support (has an N parent or primary influence), they can learn how to control their impulses and consider the consequences of their actions (quick approach). They become great sport people, if they can get into a program that helps them with their high activity and they learn how to release energy appropriately and maintain focus. Competition appeals to S type with their attraction to time pressure. They can learn to maintain focus by exploiting their natural delight in detail and facts.

The Child Who Is Difficult to Manage Here is an example from the other group. A child who has low activity, high persistence, slow approach, and high intensity, can become The Child Who Is Difficult to Manage. The high persistence (low adaptability) becomes ignoring, contrary and defiant. If this is met with a lot of force, coercion, and interruption, it leads to the pessimistic mood. These people become your phlegmatic Intuitives. Possibly because they were neglected, and since they can tolerate delayed gratification, they develop a great imagination and can spend a great deal of time in their own company. They have learned to make their situation tolerable, even desirable.

In general, the personality is a branching fractal tree of expansion and contraction formed from the early, most basic dichotomies of Trust / Mistrust, Autonomy / Shame-Doubt (Confidence / Non-confidence) and Initiative / Guilt. We can experience more of ourselves by a gentle self-re-parenting.

What Temperaments Seek

Do these temperaments seek what they really lacked, or do they seek to reproduce the situation they have become most adapted to, the position from which they are most comfortable to deal with the world? People seek sensual stimulation, comfort, a sense of well-being, solutions to their problems, existence, and self-conscious identity. Keirsey correlated the basic drive bias on the attention of the personality with the temperament. Each has their favorite pathway up the hierarchy and through the labyrinth of S, N, T, F.

NF iNtuitive Feeling — identity seeking
SP Sensing Perceiving — sensation seeking
NT iNtuitive Thinking — solution seekers
SJ Sensing Judging — security seekers

How Temperaments Defend

Another way to access occluded aspects of ourself and tolerate others is through understanding the defense mechanism. The following table lists types and some defenses.

Temperaments to Personality Types and their Defense Styles

ESFJ "Seller" — Passive-Aggressive - Leisurely. Negativistic attitudes and passive resistance feels unappreciated by others; is sullen and argumentative

ESTJ "Administrator" — Masochistic -Self-Sacrificing. Suffering, refusing help from others. Incites anger then feels hurt, humiliated

ISTJ "Trustee" —Dependent - Devoted. Submissive follower, seeks advice and reassurance

ISFJ "Conservator" — Obsessive-Compulsive: Conscientious, orderliness, perfectionism, mental and interpersonal control

ESFP "Entertainer" —Histrionic- Dramatic. Emotional, attention-seeking, is sexually seductive in appearance, is very concerned with physical attractiveness

ESTP "Promotor" —Narcissistic, Self-Confident. Grandiose has fantasies of unlimited success, power, brilliance, beauty, or ideal love

ISFP "Artist" —Cyclothymic- Artistic. Bipolar alternates between hypomanic or irritable, and depression

ISTP "Artisan" —Borderline -Mercurial, unstable, intense, impulsive in spending, sex, substance use, shopping, driving, eating, anger

ENTJ "Field Marshall" — Sadistic -Aggressive. Cruel, demeaning, and aggressive domineering

ENTP "Inventor" — Compensatory Narcissistic - Inventive. Seeks to create an illusion of superiority and to build up an image of high self-worth; deprecatory, boasting

INTJ "Scientist" — Paranoid - Vigilant expects to be exploited or harmed, bears grudges

INTP "Architect" — Schizoid -Solitary. Masterbatory, flattened affect

ENFJ "Pedagogue" — Depressive - Serious. Dominated by dejection, gloominess, cheerlessness

ENFP "Journalist" — Antisocial. Adventurous, irritable, aggressive; cheapskate fails to plan ahead, impulsive

INFJ "Author" —Schizotypal Idiosyncratic. Discomfort in close relationships, has odd beliefs or engages in magical thinking

INFP "Questor" —Avoidant - Sensitive. Timidity, easily hurt by criticism reticent in social situations

Much has been written about who these personalities are and what they see, and this can be used to expand our own personality, to access aspects and organizations of ourself that have been occluded.

Thus to experience some of the Sensing STJ, get interested in the real, have high persistence, and let your mind speed up into quick thinking action. The SFP has great confidence of the SP but adapted by becoming more aware of its internal life through Feeling. They can become ESFP, Entertainer or ISFP, the Artist.

From the NTs with their internal bias being further supported we get NTP. They create representations of their internal life as Architects INTP and Inventors ENTP.

Final Thoughts from sifu Yum Chi

Don't get caught up in the graduates psychology student syndrome of finding all the bad traits of human defense mechanism in yourself. We are not just our collection of defense mechanisms. These are just the reaction formations the personality takes on as a defense against vulnerability.

Within your material being you have a spirit that is connected to all, and that can soar outside of yourself by placing your attention.

The hexagram represent awareness. Awareness of the world. Awareness of being inside a body. Let your imagination give you an awareness of floating above and looking at your own body. You might be aware of the fields that are impacting you from the environment to which you belong. They are strata of different Functional significance. They may be Sense impressions, Feelings, Perceptions, Judgements on Facts, Intuitions and insights. Put them together to make an impression out of the whole.

```
--------- P/J
--------- T /F
--------- S / N
--------- E / I
```

Amplification by Anthropomorphizing Complexes

Beyond the separation and amplification of psychological functions, you can start to feel these function as separate complexes, organizations of energy within yourself.

--------- hero/ shadow
--------- animus / anima
--------- persona / mask
--------- pusher
--------- protector / controller

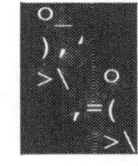

Rather than thinking about the Psychosocial Connectivity Tensor as abstract regions in a topological gestalt, it is more interesting and productive to the effort of separating yourself out to freedom to find within the true names of your sub-personalities. Think about this group of sub-personalities, and notice when one comes to the fore and gets into the drivers seat. Dialog with it.

--------- the victim
--------- the lazy bum
--------- the parent
--------- the muse, child / the old man
--------- pusher
--------- protector / controller

These are organizations within yourself that you can much more readily contact, and feel dialoguing, when you tune into the internal dialog with your mind. What brings them to the fore? Where is their seat of awareness? Trying to feel with you whole being, see through the Tan Tien. There is the center of a human being. It is the point sensor at the intersection of the many fields, reacting to them.

I began to think of myself as some kind of missionary for the Tao. I had to bring my message to America. I concocted a little stand-up routine to take on the road. I somehow talked my way through an audition at Ester's Follies on 6th Street in downtown Austin. Now I had to perform it.

There I stood in the narrow alley between outside Ester's Follies, scared to death, shivering in my *huaraches*. On the other side of the wall was the stage, in front of the great technicolor mural of an undersea reef, swarming with stridently chromatic fish and bright otherworldly plants. I was here by myself, a storyteller drifting around the country picking up gigs wherever I could. Tonight I thought to be checking out a theory of how personality is a hierarchical construct of the way information gets into the self, and how the self navigates a sea of information. Fair enough. It was about how the different combinations of Feeling, Thinking, Sensing and Perceiving give a first order approximation of personality. I was just going to get up there and wing it. It was a hot muggy night on 6th street and the theatre crowd was there to be wowed. They were an unruly bunch and I figured the best way to handle them, let alone take them into something serious and worthy of their consideration, would be to walk out there and engage the audience in some kind self-debasing stand-up routine.

The lights on the stage were dimmed for the start of my show, and a spot clicked on. At least there was that. I slipped out into the darkness and took my spot. The lights came up. The audience looked at this tall rueful man standing before the bright multi-hued underwater scene.

Scene
   The actor spent a moment casting his eyes over the house lingering briefly at each member of the audience. Then he gestures like a ringmaster.

Yum Chi:
   Ladies and Gentlemen!
   I give you
pauses, cocks head as if waiting for a drum roll

the PERSONALITY !! . . .
(said as if introducing the president of the US)
of
the United States . . . .
of . . .
Hysteria
(Sneaks up on hysteria, holds the ssss like a snake)

Yum Chi: *(Loudly)*   IF!
(not quite to loudly)
If!
If . . .
actor pirouettes around the room

if . . . ah
if I had . . .

flailing arms like a mixmaster

if only I had. . ..?
another . . . *(PAUSE)*
person. . .

*looks vulnerable like he is going to be exposed for his
loneliness, needing another person, stutters repeats*

. . . personality. . .
(pause)
if I had another
personality. . .

I would be further along
than I am
today.

—pauses thinks about it, starts again
Yum Chi: if only
(pause)
if only
if only I had . . .had been more of a . .

—Looks like the Tin Man having a thought
   thinking type of person,

   I could have done more . . .
      analysis
   on the situation.
   I could have approached the . . .
   my life
      my
         my life
   with firmness.
         With more self-assurance.

— smiles
   Yea that would be nice.

— Beginning again

Yum Chi: if I had . . .

— looking to be in a bit of a panic

   if only I had. . ..

   If I had been more judgmental

cradles his chin between thumb and forefinger)

   I could have decided,

*he gets a panic-stricken look on his face like he doesn't
know what he is about to do next*

   . . . I could have planned ahead . . .

— walks across the stage making a sweeping gesture

   if only I had been . . .
— counts on his fingers, enunciating each letter

      more (E   S   F   P)

Extroverted, Sensing, Feeling, Perceiving
— *throws hands in air like Y*
more Extroverted

— *hands go out exploring*
more sensual,

— *gives himself a rapturous hug and twirls around.*

more feeling,

— *makes eyes shift back and forth like a Balinese dance,
takes that ritualistic form*

more perceiving.

— *he mugs for a camera*
I could have been an Entertainer!

I could have radiated warmth,

(glides across the floor in tour jeté)

and attraction!
I could have had people looking at me in adoration,
like my mother sometimes did.

(smiles)

yes, . . . yes
if I had
   if I had
— *he is getting wound up*
   if I had not been . . .
      if I had not been . . .
— *coming to a conclusion*
   if only I had . . .
      if only I had not been so introverted,

   I could have had more relationships.
— *pulls a long face*

I wouldn't have had to be so lonely.

— and then later he says the opposite

If only I had . . .

— gives the "on the other hand" gesture
if only I had NOT been so extroverted. . .
I wouldn't have had so many relationships,

— wrinkles brow coming to understand something

I could have spent some time with myself.
I could have learned to like myself more.
Then,
I might have been lonely —
but I wouldn't have minded it so much.

— imploring then getting tough, — said like Marlon Brando
in On the Waterfront

If I had been more of a promoter,
— (draws out the "Promota")
I would 'a' been furdha along
    than I am today.

— Going back to his own voice
if I had a higher tolerance for interaction,
if I had worked up more perspiration to go with my
inspiration,
I'd be further along . . .
    than I am today.

If I had somehow a different personality,
if they could lift my hood
and swap engines
and give me a personality with more horsepower,
I'd be further along . . .
    than I am   today.

(pensive)

like a kind of transmission you could shift into..
(— *making a case*)
it would be like I could start
off with my current personality. . .

— *has a thought, is running an aggressive inquisition on*
himself
I'm what!
What am I?
I'm what . . .
what . . .
what type . . .

I'm **What** type of personality.

What type of personality do I have.
— *smiles at the audience*
Well we know that. Introspective, intuitive. What's the
word? Introverted?

— *starting again*
I have. . .
I have. . . to ask myself some questions
about what type of personality . . .
I have.
— *looks up wiggles nose move like mole*

Am I intuitive? . . .
intuitive?
that is . . .
—*[moves hands like a balancing beam]*

or am I analytical,
analytical, -
— *looks pensive*
always weighing the odds, doing the calculations,
balancing the forces.
That's the basic distinction isn't it?
or is it introvert vs extrovert.
o yea introvert vs extrovert.
the worker types —who like hang back in their cubicle,

— exaggerated cutesy invitation
"Oh,! come to this meeting." they are asked.

— reticent hands at side of heads like a horse with blinders on
"No I'd rather hang back in my cubicle and work on this program."
— looks at the audience bringing them into his confidence
the introverts usually work for the extroverts
you can tell the extroverts because they are the MBA types
—pause
so what am I?
What am I? Introvert?
"Prefers to conserve energy. Often tries to find short cuts and appears to be 'under-enthused' about things."
—pause
If I had started out . . .
—pause
as an extrovert . . .

I might appear more *enthused* about things by now.
— makes a face purses lips around the th in enthused

more *enthused* about things

if I had started out . . .
as an extrovert,
I might have wanting to carry on better,
have more interest and energy.
Is that right?
— looks puzzled
Is that about right?

If only I had been born an extrovert instead of an introvert
and being way off the scale in the introvert I would have been farther along than I am today.

— smiles at the audience

part of the action and passion of the times
promoting, crafter, sport, conservative: JF Kennedy, STP
king of fluttered hearts;
retiring, in the present moment: Jackie O, SFP, coura-
geous widow;
loyal, responsible, painstaking: George Washington, SFJ
started America
inspector, serious, Supervisor: Harry Truman, STJ,
keeps it going
independent projects, healer: Marilyn Monroe, NFP,
made you want to protect her;
architect, ideas, interests: Albert Einstein, NTP let the
universe know we had arrived, and we understood;
quietly forceful, counselor, teacher, critic: Ghandi, NFJ
helped us live together: Elvis, John Lennon . . .
skeptical, mastermind, determined: Eisenhower, NTJ,
saved the American way.

a king & a queen & a patriarch & a wizard, a waif, a
dreamer, a fallen prince, a soldier. . .

the Jewish American princess celebrity rock star
has her personal assistant kneel between her legs
when the rock presence sits down to wee-wee,
in order to put rings on her star's toes.

A government worker in a windowless office in the
basement of a building makes sure everyone dots their (i)s
and crosses their (t)s on contracts. Taking care of business.

Marlon Brando made it OK to wear T-shirts outside.

When Madonna walks into a room all eyes focus on her
and she swirls up their shared fantasy about who she is and
her mythology.

BF Skinner is here.
    Carl Jung is here too.
(BF has the old Alchemist in a glass enclosed cage.)

I

Hemmingway's ISFP concrete communication and
practical way of pursuing his goals makes him very good at
tactical variation. While Jimmy Stewart's ENFP concrete
communication and sense of being cooperative in pursuing
goals makes him good at logistics. Jimmy was conserving
the energy in front of him, acting outraged for us, and
relaxing in the pleasures of his security while Earnesto, who
was more comfortable with being excited was stoical, —
sanguine, they used to call it in the middle ages. He liked to
feel himself alive in his world.

While Ghandi's abstract big-picture way of communicating and cooperative way of implementing goals made him
very good at diplomatic integration, Madonna's way of
being concrete in communication and utilitarian in implementing goals makes her an excellent promoter. Naturally
we might ask what would have happened if they had worked
together. Madonna + Ghandi
        Elvis Presley + Mother Teresa

II

    attractors
    media, the selling machine, stoking mythology
    the television is a machine that exploits the human startle
response. This is the brain's audio-video response trying to
right itself after a sudden or novel stimulus. The makers of
TV use the series of quick cuts coupled with the short sound
byte to stimulate and engage this ability of the human
perceptive system to reorient itself after a shake.
    America is in Hollywood, where everybody is fabulous,
    When you're *Living The Dream* and you look out into
the world as a stage set,
    —Lights, Set-up, Focus down so close—
    in every movement people are about to embark on a
journey.
    I saw it in actor in Dustin Hoffman's malaise when he
decides to pursue Katherine Ross
    In Ray Milan's eyes when he could see to infinity with
his x ray eyes.

Being around that energy is addictive, inspiring, thrilling, jealousy-causing, hopeful.
However, by comparison my own life is routine, dull,
uninspired, full of impediments, hopeless.

III
Einstein, INTP, Elvis Presley ESFP,
Amelia Airhardt,
Marilyn Monroe, ESFP
Carl Jung, Mother Theresa, ENFP
Jack Kerouac, E Hemmingway, INFP
Bill Gates, Walt Disney, Nicholas Tesla, ESTJ
Pioneers, the big railroad magnate, field marshals, . . .

They are in a play of Time's making. So are we. We are
in their play.
The personality is hosted in the nervous system, just as
the ecology is hosted in the confluence of the lythosphere,
the atmosphere, the hydrosphere, and the biosphere. The
personality is hosted in the mythosphere, the psychosphere
the econosphere, (marketing, wages and opportunity).

mycelia
as though people were some kind of hair
growing on a big entity.
We are the fur of the earth.

IV
Calling back into the center, from the extremities,
calling back into yourself,
the extended, pushing, grasping hungry-ghost body,
you can just let yourself move from your core,
— just let the arms float, and be there for sensitivity,
for sticking, for feeling, an opening to the center.
If you do this an opening to the center will come.

It, through the core muscles in the stomach and the back
propels,
mycelia
It is the sea currents. . .

that open and close the arms and hands and fingers.
My time.
I am shifting here,
It is shifting me there. . .
protecting the head by moving it, away from the other's
hands,
letting the shoulders down.
You carry them like the plating of a triceratops.
Wherever did you develop that habit?
Feel the great ocean of being moving and shifting on
currents . . .

V
We are in these scenes with our heroes and lovers.
Who were YOUR heroes coming up?
How much of a presence do they have with you now?
Ask yourself the question, who are your heroes? Who
comes first to mind?
To me, it is Joyce and Kerouac, and later Borges . . .
then much later Rumi.
Joyce introduced me to the stream of consciousness and
it blew my mind.
Who ever introduced you to yourself,
they became like surrogate parents to you.
They rebirthed you from your straight-ahead life.

Dancing in the desert, in the wind. . .
Last night I dreamt I was going . . .
We are in these scenes with our heroes and lovers.
We all know that heart pumping sensation.
And we know when it's not.
We love them so much and we want to be like them
so people will love us like that.
We are trying to put on the star's perfect person because
we want to feel people love us the way we love the stars
because they are perfection.

VI
We have come from an age of molecular machines:
Photosynthesis, ATP, carbon cycle, reproduction,
the great machines, like the ecology.

Perhaps dreams and myths are like that:
the personality is a machine.
They are all depicted in the mandala.

The divine mother, beautiful desirable nourishing,
supporting, full of love and life
    bringing population onto the land
    the heavenly father birthing you into life beyond the
bond with the mother,
    Jesus, Mary and Joseph — the idea of the nuclear family
(Ozzie and Harriette)
    The Thinking Tin Man, the Cowardly Lion, The Feeling
Scarecrow, they're all here . . .
    the White Rabbit. Coyote, the Clown, the Hero, the
Athlete, the Beautiful,
    the healers, interfering if needed along the way,
    the bosses getting something going,
    the leaders pushing you, pulling you along . . .
    it is all part of some great big plan
    which you can't see but a little of at the moment.
    the teachers . . .
    the promoters calling attention to some kind of cultural
thing that reflects back on who we are, they are all like
working parts of any organism:
    the way sensors are connected to action controls at that
node. . .
    a cellular automata made up of
    the 4 basic needs:
    security, identity, stimulation, answers to questions.

    That part of you that notices things not exactly required
to the task at hand but that will be useful later,
    how it plays itself out,
    the dichotomous machine,
    mother / father
    mitosis sexual re-production raga,
    or Darwin and life. Yea, that might be more of an
influence. Certainly this has been Darwin's Century.
    For whom will the next century be named?
    They probably haven't even been born yet, or is very
young among us.

May as well
it's your time now.
7 stars point to
the pole star in the handle of the little dipper
known by all cultures as the place of orientation
to which the compass points.

Be in the power of now,
Now as here now — on the edge of an explosion:
The expanding universe,
the evolving biosphere,
the fractal of matter poking its dendritic fingers
into sensate life
witnessing the emergent evolution of matter.

It's all so deep and I'm so superficial.
Like one thing I have never been able to understand is
how to visualize the idea of space and time coming into
existence and expanding with the big bang.
We know space and time are not *a priori* dimensions but
dimensions which change depending on the speed and
acceleration of the frame of reference of the observer.
Length elongates, time dilates (becomes much slower)
and mass expands as you accelerate and your velocity
approach the speed of light. These conditions are necessary.
And yet my Newtonian mind keeps going back and
wonders what does the universe expand INTO if not space.
Nothing?
Well how is this Nothing different from space?
When objects come into existence, then space is a kind
of context for this content of objects?
They talk about the vacuum in which particles and anti-
particles pre-existed in a kind of equilibrium and get created
when energy passes into this vacuum.
In this picture Nothing is quite a complicated state of
detente.

When I meditate, sometimes, after a while I do let go for

an instant and feel a luminescence efflorescing my body
which must be a background radiation residue of the body's
electric field in tune with (impedance matched with, when
you get the noise of your own consciousness down), the
creative force underlying the universe.

It wants to be known. That's why *we* are here.

Also we are here because it serves the law of entropy to
have big intelligent humans going around doing work —
building Panama Canals and Pyramids and blowing up
buildings in order to create even more entropy.

I'd like to be able to reach that emptiness more often.
In that way I can do what the universe does.
Separate the Nothing detent. Or, alternatively,
impedance matching with it for emptiness.

Did you know that the universe is not infinite?
Some guy figured it out way back in the 17th century.
His proof has to do with the stars shining down on us: in
an infinite universe, and asuming the stars are as dense as
they are, the light from these stars,
would, in time, falling on Earth, accumulate so much
that it would be daylight all the time.
There would be no night.
But since there is night, there can't be an infinite universe.
So it is out there expanding into Nothing,
which is a kind of potential existence
the "space" like field that is no-thing.
It can't be grasped.
It comes into being when objects (things) come into
being. Just as silence
has no meaning without sound.
In meditation, we try to clear our heads of
all the usual thoughts that flow by. If we can reach
emptiness, then it is
the Unmanifested/space/silence. The source of all
creation.

. . . a sense of the Source beneath all
creation . . .

In the commencement of Tai Chi,
in the raising and lowering of the hands gesture
hands come in and splash down like a wave breaking on
the shore and we are
     sinking . . .
        settling down . . .
            coming home.
To be grounded down here on the ground.
I ask myself: what is a person's relationship to the earth?
Where is the center of that relationship?
I think of Newton, and how he described the Force,
with its lines going straight to the center.
He was the first Taoist in the west,
understanding that the natural state
is being in motion - not at rest.
I try to picture the relationship: $\dfrac{\text{man}}{\text{earth}}$
Would it be like a be-be
next to a bowling ball? NO! Way off!
Well what then? I start into a calculation.
What would be a visual way to illustrate the ratio of a
man of mass m to the earth of mass M? (m/M)
     Comparing a .1 ton man to the 6 billion trillion ton earth.
Would it be more
like a dust moat
to a bowling ball?
—A dust moat
that can fly
on thermal
currents. You've seen them,
when you hit
the pillow in
the parlor
and the
dust motes
fly up like
spangles
and flit about in random motion,
suspended in a sunbeam coming through the window.
Or like a wild ash

settling
down in
the fire.
But, NOT!
What about a dust moat to a city block?
No, still not enough.
It turns out,
— to maintain the same ratio
of the mass of the man to the mass of the earth —
we would need
the little dust mote to be
settling down
on the mass of the entire downtown of a modern city,
some 40 square blocks of Empire State Buildings standing
shoulder to shoulder.
So a person standing on the earth,
and sinking
at the commencement of Tai Chi,
is like a dust mote,
settling down over a large city.

How comforting it is,
to finally stop flying around,
to settle

down —   o   o   _o_   (o)   o

to be at home, [|] ʹ | ˋ ʹ | ʹ | (x)

—at rest —   [ ] [ ] [ ] ( ) ( )

on the
great mother earth.

And yet,
when I sink down and stretch up to look out
at the pale blue sky,
—to truly come to rest,
what am I settling down into? Gravity? Yes.
But also this relationship with the earth.
Where we meet at the center of mass . . .

Looking back at the picture of us
sent back by the Voyager from deep space,

we see that we (and our sun) are but a bright dust mote,
braided with matter by gravity into a spiral arm of light.
That's where we are. Right there.
All the life we know about in the universe,
every animal, every bug, every plant, every microbe
all the kings and tyrants, teachers and explorers,
all the mothers and fathers and children
carried along IN love
and lost FROM love,
all the sentient beings that ever were
lived on a dust mote suspended in a sunbeam.
All the great movements, migrations, uprisings, downturns
wars, revolutions, and deaths in history took place here.
Here all the great and not so great aristocracies, bureaucra-
cies, matriarchies, oligarchies, patriarchies, theocracies, all
the cracies and garchies claiming markets and territories,
— as well as the rude turkey who cut you off at the corner—
are carried out so that for a while someone will be the
organizer, controller, boss,
of a small portion of a dust mote.
Our minuscule lonely planet is filled with hunger, longing,
hope, love, and hatred, to express the passion of being here.
Because something there is out there in the great cosmic
dark
that wants us here and supports us every one, uniquely.
And like gravity, we are always moving in that too.
There are just illusions that keep us from it,
and we need to move those around and push, pull back,
press, and twist through them, to see.

The pale blue earth,
is one of generosity's storehouses,
it loves us and moves us and needs us
to look after each other
and to look after it
because there is no one coming to help us.
And so that we may know it
and know its creator.
We are starting to know. . .
starting to know
where we stand.

I am on the earth night, and I want to be nearer to the earth because there is more life in a handful of earth than anywhere else in the heavens that we know about. Because it is a sphere of energy blessed with extraordinary fertility. There seems to be no limit to the number and variety of living beings. It is teaming. And we have come to know our purpose here: it is to really be here — to really be present. It is to be between the earth and the sky.

I imagine a place, maybe India, where they have music and colors and scents for the time of day. Or maybe ancient agrarian China, where everything turned to its season in time under heaven. Out here it is like that, to be in the earth night long ago, with no street lights, no flashlights, maybe carrying a little bit of fire, but mostly to be prey to the big cats, prowling with their superior night vision. When the night sky was so clear and the spiral road of the milky way so real and luminous and present, like a modern city seen from the air, you could just walk down any road off the edge of the world into it.

Here I am, standing in front of total obscurity, because I am no longer out in the light of the day which envelops me so. Here I am enveloped by the darkness of the night. Since in the daytime we can only see one star, while at night we can see many, many stars, the night on the earth is the opposite of day on the earth, because the darkness is opposite the light. The heavens are obscured by the sky in the day but in the total obscurity of earth's shadow at night, I can see for millions of miles into space and even into time. The sky is of earth and the night is of heaven.

I was starting to feel something about the structure of the universe. We know that the lacy veil of constellation densities are draped over the bulges and currents and vortices of turbulence in spacetime. They are fractals, left like bubbling froth on the edge of an expanding wave, breaking from the big bang on the shore of nothingness. For the universe is a fractal enacting its properties, in particular self-similarity, at all levels from gigantic superclusters --> clusters --> galaxies --> solar systems --> planets with moons revolving around them, down to molecules --> atoms with electrons orbiting around them. Then the universe goes the other way, evolving atoms which coalesce into molecules --> to complex molecules like fixing cycles, — photosynthesis, ATP, proteins --> poly-peptides -->reproductive chains --> cells, organisms --> organelles, and the other factors of concerted life embedded within life, emerging through the infinitely recursive infinitesimals of within, into species.

My idea of God is changing. The image of God I want to understand is more like something that uses free energy to create stable entities and objects from matter, to communicate across time. A Universal Fractal is percolating out into all domains and dimensions, platonic and fractional, with the great efficiency of self-similarity. It was like coming to understand the strategy of the universe to a certain extent. We look out at the dome of the night sky, it is a circle like our sun and it is filled with the sinuous, spiraling, clustering of galaxies demonstrating a fractal distribution of these stellar objects. The structure is related to the expanding universe like the writhing of energy on the surface of our own sun! We want to think of god like the Sun, the infinite sun pouring out tons and tons of photons of light, out of its writhing thermonuclear surface. And these infinitely many, infinitesimal filaments of light-strands are connected to all living things on this planet moved by time or touched by weather and nourished by food, and we become storehouses and transmitting stations for the light. Perhaps everything we need to know about the universe, we can find out from our own star. Those great big magnetic dipoles that throw off the promontories many times larger than our own world would have what kind of analogy in the galaxy? Just as the sun pours its free energy down to our world, so the universe pours down its kind of form-energy too.

May I feel the immensity of Big Time? I want to imagine the island galaxies out there in the vast reaches of space as molecules connected in a much LARGER entity. That somehow they are connected in a body — we know they are connected by at least the bonds of gravity and destiny. Though terribly remote, this body does contain, infinitely, all causes and effects. Wouldn't that be an image of what we understand as the divine? Surely most religions would recognize their concept of the divine in 'that which expresses the fundamental causal relations of the universe'.

The singing of night hawks; the calling of frogs. They live in different time bands. So do we. We all live in Big Time.

Lemurs! Eyes Front! living in trees. I am descendent from Lemurs — the first mammal with the eyes moved to the front, 43 million years ago. They live inside a tree and only come out at night. Shall we follow him in.

43 million years ago
Big Time $\Delta t \longrightarrow \infty$
long time scales
time resolution
passed down generation
to generation.
Let your ego be on that
for a while.
Opening. Let us follow

Inside the tree, the Designer is working in a icosahedronal geoconda spaceship, with facets or planes giving out into different spacetimes. He wears a full-length, ermine-collared robe which sweeps the "floor". It is alive and writhing with the movement of swirling galaxies and explosions coming out of it. On his head is a white cowboy hat, and he's got a long white beard. He's watching monitors, adjusting dials. He's singing, "I love you from a place where there's no space and time. I love you 'cause you're a friend of mine." He is tachyonic, a being of light, never moving slower than the speed of light. For the Designer, time slows down and stops in the light frame of reference, mass becomes infinite and distance between things goes to zero. So all the universe becomes the same place.* Yes, you can see where a Great Designer could do a lot out of this place. Whew! What a rush.

The universe is the superset space in which the implicative tree of causal connection grows. Is that probability? Synchronicity? Is that physics? But right away when I say god I get this picture of God the Father, the great patriarchal god of the Old Testament. I realize I am making another analogy. Why is it we talk about god by assigning a personality to this great entity out there, that compared to us is infinite in the way a child tries to figure out his parents and the mystery of how he came to be? Jung in Job shows how God is a projection of our own personality. And yet personality, as we have seen, is a projection of the chaotic process of life —a fractal, a stability in a dynamic turbulence.

---

* because from Special Relativity the speed of light frame, c, has
$t_c = t_0/\sqrt{(1-v^2/c^2)}$; $m_c = m_0/\sqrt{(1-v^2/c^2)}$; $l_c = l_0(\sqrt{(1-v^2/c^2)})$

The idea of giving god a personality comes in when we see god doing math: using recursion, exponentiation and cross product combinations, to build complexity in the face of entropy. This expansion of complexity in the face of entropy pushes into a reverse —receiving fractal of potentiality, like a hand into a glove. The fingers are the niches, of available energy into which self-contained dynamic systems can find themselves continuing in stability. Scientists have extended the Einstein field equations into undifferentiable manifolds — cracks between worlds, fractals — to find that the underlying fractal geometry of spacetime plays the role of a universal structuring "field" that leads to self-organization and morphogenesis of matter in the Universe. The Universal Fractal twists and turns though many whole and partial dimension, time among them. We are not dealing with a religion of a personal nature here — your god or my god, and what he is like, and why he likes me better than you. The universal is not the personal, that is what is appealing about the Tao; not that it is impersonal, it is beyond personal and psychology.

The Universal Fractal uses the stuff of matter to communicate. It uses nested hierarchies to structure the network of communication. These worlds of matter of which man is a part, are brought forth through the working of fractal self-similarity as it moves through many dimensions, reflecting the attractors of dynamic processes, attracting a relatively stable chaos out of randomness.

Dichotomous branching top-down hierarchy from above? And beyond? No. The hierarchy emerges from successive *embedding* of hosts and organelles. The structure is something seen to emerge from hindsight, from standing back and seeing a peer-to-peer network stabilized into bottom-up sub-sumption hierarchy. It appears to be organized into a top-down hierarchy, and it is — from specialization. From what does this emerge? From the compacted space of the Universal Fractal.

Look at it. The universe is filled with myriad fractal traces of turbulent processes moving energies around and feeding off of these energies — and becoming host to other energies — as it is folding and unfolding across dimensions. It goes on at all scales, infinitely to infinitesimally. That is the organism we are trying to understand. But which we can never understand because it is infinite knowledge and we are finite inferencing from insufficient or just plain bad data. It is up there and we are down here.

This idea of everything is contained in seed, in potential waiting to express itself has been expressed by spiritual people before. We could say that evolution is an interaction with feedback. The whole course of evolution consists in one procedure: matter, interacting through a dynamic chaos called life, interacting with other life, to colonize and subsume or be subsumed by other life so that a stable and viable system can continue. Each successive iteration learns by feedback from the niche it is emerging into, and becomes better as it passes on, distills its essence (re-compacts into seed) into the next iteration. Uncompacting, and iteration prior to time? This is all done by self organization, autopoeisis. The most important characteristic of living systems is that they are autopoetic — self-making — patterns of organization in which continual structural changes take place, while the pattern or organization itself does not change. All living things are autopoetic. That is to say, they emerge as part of a subsumption architecture. Evolution is a topological fractal space un-compacting. The organizing field of the Universal Fractal is always potentially there; it can manifest in just the right place, field, or niche.

Evolution creates networks to transport what is within without, and what is without within. Nature or the Source (Tao, God, whatever you want to call it), by building subsumption networks of autonomous units behaving in their own interest, causes hierarchies of organization to emerge and become local stabilities. Which in turn incorporate smaller stabilities, in mutual hierarchical recursion, a convolution of co-evolution. Harmony. The stable systems, like the ebb and flow of salmon, the fixing of sunlight in photosynthesis, the transport of energy in ATP. These are a kind of perpetual motion machine, and they are teaching us things about the universe. They are helping the universe teach us about itself — and understanding that we can not learn any other way.

Man is moving away in time from that great source energy that precipitated his intelligence. Human intelligence developed out of information carrying molecules (DNA) via evolution of the genes in the context of cell, organisms and ecosystems. We are on the other side of that membrane trying to hold back the force, deny that we came from that. And we create art so that the memory of this will not be lost, will not disappear completely and though this is hard to accept — this marvelous materialism, it is true. Does it make us any less? Man watches the movements, the signs of movements in his evaporating time, as Big Time moves from the darkness into light, from that within, to our world, from the beyond.

The feeling that the infinite is present in everything has been expressed my mystics and poets perennially going back to the Vedas. Pascal, a mathematician and mystic who studied combinatorics and got the cascade of binary combinations named after him, defined this omnicentricity concisely: "God is an infinite sphere whose center is everywhere and whose circumference is nowhere." And even though we have pin-pointed the direction of the big bang and the universe it created in outward expansion, we are starting to see how the good old phenomenal universe that we know and can measure with our science is built upon a quantum phenomenal universe beneath or above or beyond it. This universe is like the hologram that is already there in space. This universe is being imprinted on the space that it contains in the same way that every pixel of a hologram contains within it the image of the completed whole, every point in space contains within it, the plan, the potential, the uncompacted fractal of the universal body. The spirit "with" rather than "from" above.

Things come and go in our world of movement, we see them in our dimension but they inhabit more dimensions than we sense or intuit. They are in a sense being "printed" in our world. They unfold and emerge into our world. Take any object, the salt shaker on the kitchen table for instance. Trace it back. Remember how it came into your life. There is some great text or algorithm going on, things and beings are not what they appear to be, inside of every being here are little beings folded up trying to unfold.

I am trying to feel that unfolding and enfolding when I do Tai Chi, when I carry the ball, carry so many balls of all sizes, little worlds, they represents little worlds, and some of them are fiery and some of them are close by and some of them are far away and I am pushing and pulling them away and bringing them closer and separating them.

The omnicentric continuum filling space observes and reacts to how we approach these worlds, how we recede from these worlds, and how these worlds recede from us.

And this proceeds by the method we have been speaking about which is that dichotomous agitation, to produce gestalt. Percolating-up control organized around connections of sensors to actuators — learning through feedback.

The vehicle that connects this above and below — this all

knowing and the one with only limited knowledge — is the fractal. We can't see that we are way up in the branches and can't see the trunk; but know it is there.

Everything is fractal, which is to say one dimension ingressing into another, water vapor into cloud, tooth into gum, lung into air. And they are in a network with other fractals, and these fractals are residues of turbulent processes which have achieved a stability, and each of these stabilities, hosts and becomes host as it is subsumed into greater networks according that each level can go on expressing itself, and as such is expressing the fractal nature at the bottom of the universe: sex -- attractor basin, eye ---- attractor basin, dream --- attractor basin, tree, fruit. Every world is a composite of many worlds. It is the parent and the child in a chain.

We advance by banding together, and some parts become sensors and other parts become motors, and little by little they encounter each obstacle in their unfolding. In general they are like vehicles. Some with simple motors that let them circle, some that have them flee some threat —showing fear, or run toward some desirable object — showing love. They are like mycelia in a great extending subsumption body, this body going out and sending up its genitals and fruiting. We are made of the animals that came before us.

Sometime at night, the Knight of a 1000 eyes does a little dance, seeing with the tan tien. It is like seeing at a whole new, other level. The physical body of the universe is what we emulate in order to hold. We do not see the physical body of the universe but it most certainly is there. If we were to see it we might have to imagine it is like our body and it has eyes and that they are always open and it sees at all levels where we only see at a few levels. I have called it the Automorph in honor of its autopoeisis. It is the upper realm moving through our lower realm. And that is what the I Ching is about, this traveling up and down from the lower realm to the upper realm and from the upper realm to the lower realm, trying to see the transport.

Feel Yourself accessing
different modalities
of personality.
Unfamiliar ground
leads to transcendence of self.

You come to know the wind out here, when you live in the country. You become kin to the wind, listening in to everything coming because you don't want anything to come up and surprise you. Maybe it was paranoia, maybe feral sensitivity, but I became preternaturally aware while I was doing Tai Chi. I began to be able to use the wind as an ally for its ability to carry awareness. I discovered that sound can travel for miles and miles. If you can be still for a very long time — at least several hours — you can start to detect sounds from quite far away.

On one level Tai Chi is a trance-inducing shadow boxing dance. In the dark you box with the shadow side of your own nature. I would be out there on high alert doing the form in the pot patch. I'd look up at the surrounding wall of trees at the edge of the tallgrass fields, and see them leaning and moving together, like at the end of the movie *Blow Up* when the breeze was swashing and swaying in the trees, where it got into the existential conundrum and you kind of wanted to cry or jump for joy at the mystery of being, but you knew you couldn't do that because you were a big boy and boys don't cry, and anyway, it was only a movie and besides that, you *are* the breeze!

Sometimes at night, when the wind was quite right and my blood was a mixture of weed and the speed of adrenaline from doing endless martial arts cadas, I felt my being extending. It was like I could just send out my feelers all around, and move on the wind. I would just know—by a perturbation in the chi field—if Ripoff was coming around. I had enlisted the insects — they were each a lens of my many-faceted compound eyes — out there in the dark, peeping, sensing, keeping an eye on all that part of the meadow for me. My consciousness had moved back into a poly-sensate awareness. I had become the Knight of a Thousand Eyes.

Mother Nature had accepted me. I was one of her helpers. I had become a servant. I was a servant of the weed, and in turn weed would become my servant. It was the oldest, simplest, most direct relationship there was. I had found my part in the scheme of things.

There is nothing more beautiful than doing Tai Chi while high, out on a big meadow under the sky—to be shadowboxing the space around your Self, irrigating the joints, while balanced and precariously spinning on one foot, leaping into flying kicks.

When shadow boxing, one slowly explored forces and balance. Scientifically, Tai Chi is an essay in resilience, in letting go of rigidity, in seeing the lines of force and using them. It seeks to adapt, not to interfere; to allow those lines of action to continue, not impact with you. It is always about finding your grace, the sense of balance of the body and bringing it to consciousness. Grace! She is so often tucked away and not called for, not given the opportunity to exercise herself. Shadowboxing is an attempt to prolong and stay in the state of grace.

HiT MoteL Press

Enjoy these other books in the "Little House on the Prairie" trilogy

Cultivating the Texas Twister Hybrid is the first book in this series. It is about the adventures of a city guy on a farm growing weed. It is a gardener's journal teaching the growers craft and something of the connoisseurs's educations as well as a criminal's internal monolog. (1998)

The Secret of the Cicadas' Song

Michael Lyons

The Secret of the Cicadas' Song is a second book about events on the farm. The time of the book is an extended peyote trip in prose and poetry. The reader is welcomed into to the immediacy of the psychedelic experience through haiku poetry; the reader is brought to the ineffable aspect of the trip experience through object verse and semantic object modeling of the archetypes of perception. (1998)

Knight of a 1000 eyes is a third books about events on the farm. The time of the book is a tai chi session. It reflects the struggle of the western mind coming to understand the spirit of the universe. It has an essay on western space time motion philosopher Laban and a modern commentary on the ancient I Ching tracking the emergence of Jung's psychology. (2002)

Dolores Park

a novel by
Michael Lyons

Cultivating the Texas
Twister Hybrid

Michael Lyons

HiT MoteL Press

Zenobia

Michael Lyons

The Indigenous Tribesmen of
Neverland

Michael Lyons

The Secret
of the Cicadas' Song

Michael Lyons

Catalog of Works
In-progress and Current

A Blue
Moon in
August

The Knight of 1000 eyes

Michael Lyons

HiT MoteL Press

other books in the "My Years of
Apprenticeship at Love" series
   Dolores Park is the third book
in the series. Lonely Texas redneck
cowboy pursues love interest into a
feminist Tantric Buddhist sex
commune. He falls in love with a
beautiful Tantrika and through the
magic of romance, psychotherapy
and Buddhist trance he discovers the
path to enlightenment.
   It is a seeker's journal experiencing the coming to acceptance of
psychic reality. (2001)

Dolores Park

a novel by
Michael Lyons

Zenobia

Michael Lyons

   Zenobia is a psychotherapeutic
journey exploring the Mother and
the Whore syndrome common in the
American male psyche. It illustrates
Freud's precept, that a man is bourn
of two women.

A Blue
Moon in
August

a novel by Michael Lyons

   A Blue Moon in August is
about marriage and children late in
life. It follows the character Walker
struggling to be a new parent and
juggling creative with financial and
married life. It also is about the
discover of Bodhicitta, uncondi-
tional love.

The Indigenous Tribesmen of Neverland, is a kind of Tortilla Flat about bohemian life in Austin slacker enclaves. It looks at the Peter Pan syndrome of males in the late 20th century. It explores living and creating in a regime of oppressive paterfamilias Texas. Main characters are Walker an over educated slacker and Wild Bill the fabulous furry freak brothers answer to Arnold Schwartzneger. Follow them on peyote hunting trips into the tribal mythology of old Mexico where they encounter Janis Joplin and Juan Mateus.

HiT MoteL Press
www.hitmotel.com

These books can be ordered from any book seller or on-line . They are deeply discounted on Amazon, Boarders and Barnes& Nobles. Check www.hitmotel.com for selections and recordings.

Boho Novels
The "Little House on the Prairie" Trilogy:
Cultivating the Texas Twister Hybrid, a portrait of the artist as a weed gardener (1998) ISBN 0-9655842-0-8 $20.00
The Secret of the Cicadas' Song, a peyote trip in poetry and prose (1998) ISBN 0-9655842-1-6 $20.00
Knight of a 1000 eyes, about Tai Chi, movement, Laban, and the I Ching (2002) ISBN 0-9655842-2-4 $25.00

The Punctual Actual Weekly, about the life and times of a small mimeograph literary rag centered around artists living in a Berkeley warehouse and the Amphictionic Theatre ISBN 0-9655842-8-3
The Church of the Coincidental Metaphor, youthful adventures in Mexican radio ISBN 0-9655842-7-5
The Indigenous Tribesmen of Neverland Bohemian life in Austin slacker enclaves. ISBN 0-9655842-6-7 $20.00
Sex is the Anti-gravity of Metamorphosis, tales of romance and despair hitchhiking in US, Canada and Mexico. ISBN 0-9655842-9-1

Novels:
The "My Years of Apprenticeship at Love" Series:
Dolores Park, Texan joins a California Tantric Buddhist commune (2001) ISBN 0-9655842-3-2 480 pages. $25.00
Zenobia A cab driver's journal of psychotherapy. ISBN 0-9655842-4-0
A Blue Moon in August, about marriage and children late in life. ISBN 0-9655842-5-9

CD-ROM
Cultivating the Texas Twister Hybrid CD-ROM, radio plays of actor's voices performing bits from the novels, the Mirage Symphony

Nonfiction
The Diamond Cutter's Sutra, about semiotics, logic, semantic object modeling, mathematics --a kind of Varieties of Logical Experience

Check into HiT MoteL @www.hitmotel.com for cover art, interactive Table of Contents, e-book sample chapters, recordings and other mindware.

To invite the viewer to contemplate the mystery of unfolding chaos, Hitmotel Press offers the fractal semantic spirit-token art of M. Lyons.

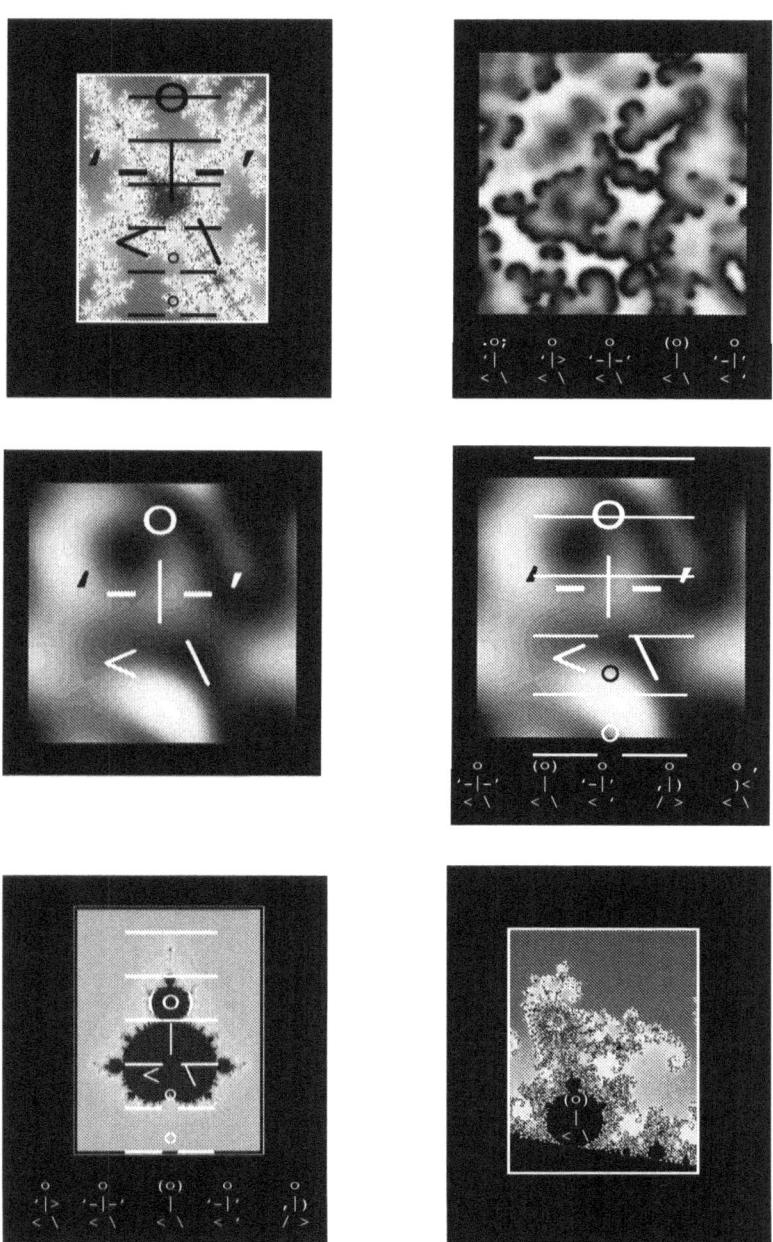

Some of the 40 other reprints and enlargements of the postscript art from publications, can be seen in glorious color at www.hitmotel.com.

Each unique, (aleatory algorithms!), spiritual, color print is showcased in black matte, signed by the artist, and ready to frame for hanging.

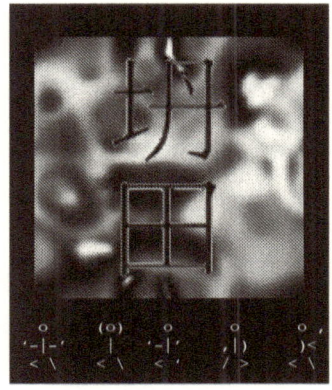
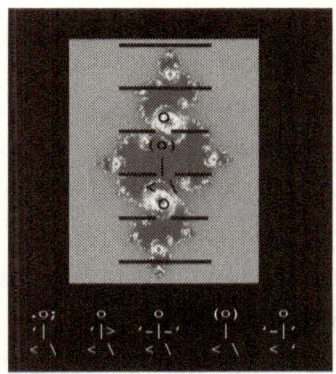

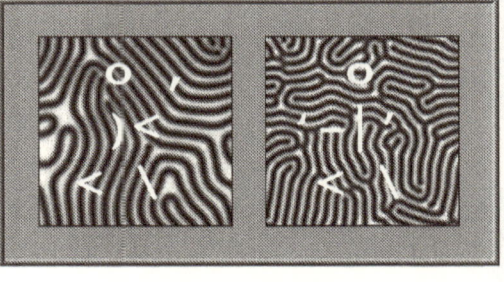

Matted Art Prints . . . $27.00 /each (8" x 8" or 8" x 10") color archival print on heavy photographic paper in 11' x 11" or 11x 14 black matte

Knight of a 1000 eyes.

The Knight of a 1000 eyes, is about extending the range of human perception through movement, philosophical inquiry and the imagination. The story is about a gardener who, needing to defend his patch from thieves, teaches himself Tai Chi. In the process, he comes to experience Chi and we watch his heady western mind coming to grips with these energies coursing through the universe as manifest themselves through insights, realizations, and perceptual extensions.

The book reflects the 3 phases to cultivating Chi.

1. Fixed Frame, a portrait of the beginner and the scramble to deal with the overwhelming onslaught of detail in just trying to remember the steps,

2. Lively Frame, the emergence of Chi and grace in the movement and fighting of everyday life, through analysis of space time and force, exploring the Chi in the kua for its own joy and

3. Changing Frame, stepping into an ancient world of energies and archetypes whose landscape is the I Ching.

The main character Walker takes on a name for himself --Yum Chi -- when he gets into the Form. Getting into the Form grows into the feeling of having the self and the Self aligned. The Form is synonymous with the synchronic. The dual personality of the story, Walker and Yum Chi is about moving back and forth across the barrier from the diachronic to the synchronic. He scrambles to make some sense out of his feelings and studies exotic movement philosophies and ends up writing a new commentary on the I Ching. He develops a series of solo theatre pieces which are impelled by semantic seed sentences that insight the user into the participation of identity.

$25.00 Literature / Movement / Philosophy / Poetry / Tai Chi
Hit Motel Press   **www.hitmotel.com**

To order directly from HiT MoteL by Mail go to the website and
1. Print this form.
2. mail this form with check or money order (made out to Michael Lyons) to:

HiT MoteL Press
PO Box 16667
San Francisco CA 94116

Name:_____

Address:_____

City:_____State:_____Zip:_____

Telephone:_____E-mail:_____

Title: Cultivating the Texas Twister Hybrid
ISBN 0-965542--0-8   @: $20 Qty:_____   Total:$_____

Title: The Secret of the Cicadas' Song
ISBN 0-965542--1-6   @: $20 Qty:_____   Total:$_____

Title: The Knight of a 1000 eyes
ISBN 0-965542--2-4   @: $25 Qty:_____   Total:$_____

Title: Dolores Park
ISBN 0-9655842-3-2   @: $25 Qty:_____   Total:$_____

                                    Sub Total:$_____

                        CA residents please add 8%:_____

                                     Shipping:_____

                                   Grand Total:_____

Shipping Information:
Shipping - Please add $3.50 for first item, $1.00 for each additional item
We ship via United States mail.
Inquires by email? — info@hitmotel.com